Praise for Brianna Labuskes

"Masterfully woven and intricately rendered, *The Lost Book of Bonn* is a poignant tale of courage and sacrifice in the face of great evil. Brianna Labuskes gives us a fascinating glimpse into the Edelweiss Pirates and those in Germany who were brave enough to take a stand against the Nazis. Both enlightening and heartrending, this book is impossible to put down!"

—Sara Ackerman, *USA Today*
; author of *The Codebreaker's Secret*

"As Labuskes weaves perspectives together, she not only highlights the pain of censorship, suppression, and dehumanization but also issues a stark reminder that history repeats itself. At the same time, she plants seeds of hope in her characters' refusal to let the stories that should bring us together be silenced."

—*Booklist* (starred review) on
The Librarian of Burned Books

"I've always believed that the most memorable historical novels are those that by shining a light on the past show us a better way forward into the future. Brianna Labuskes's masterful debut is one such novel. Alternating between time periods, and armed with three richly drawn characters, Labuskes unfurls a story of censorship and fear in 1930s Germany and of hope and grit in 1944 New York. A propulsive, immersive, expertly crafted debut that reminds us of the perils of censorship, the power of books, and the duty we all have to stand up for the freedoms we hold dear."

—Kristin Harmel, *New York Times*
bestselling author, on *The Librarian of Burned Books*

"Each of the main characters is clearly drawn and sympathetic, the plot kept me awake turning pages far into the night, and the well-earned resolution was poignant and emotional. The depiction of lesbian romance felt authentic and respectful. This novel is a timely reminder that the burning or banning of books is the first step in an escalating war on freedom of thought and expression that can have devastating consequences. The women in this novel develop the strength to overcome fear, doubt, and trepidation to resist censorship and hate each in her own way. . . . An entertaining and riveting read."

—Kim van Alkemade, *New York Times*
bestselling author, on *The Librarian of Burned Books*

"In her excellent debut novel, Brianna Labuskes writes lovingly of the power of books, libraries, and friendship to sustain us in difficult times, while also offering a stark, unmistakably relevant warning about the dangers of censorship. Fans of historical fiction featuring courageous women will savor *The Librarian of Burned Books*."

—Jennifer Chiaverini, author of *Resistance Women*

"Terrific research buttresses strong writing that will keep readers riveted." —*Library Journal* on *The Librarian of Burned Books*

"Inspired by the fascinating real story of a little-known World War II–era group of librarians, authors, publishers, and booksellers who united to fight fascism with literature, *The Librarian of Burned Books* is a thoroughly engrossing page-turner that proves how powerful words and ideas can be, no matter the era. Filled with intrigue and secrets, this timely novel follows three women from Berlin to Paris to New York City to right past wrongs using books as their weapon of choice."

—Elise Hooper, author of *Angels of the Pacific*,
on *The Librarian of Burned Books*

THE

LOST BOOK

of BONN

Also by Brianna Labuskes

THE
LOST BOOK
of BONN

A NOVEL

BRIANNA LABUSKES

WILLIAM MORROW
An Imprint of HarperCollins*Publishers*

This book is a work of fiction. References to real people, events, establishments, organizations, or locales are intended only to provide a sense of authenticity, and are used fictitiously. All other characters, and all incidents and dialogue, are drawn from the author's imagination and are not to be construed as real.

THE LOST BOOK OF BONN. Copyright © 2024 by Brianna Labuskes. All rights reserved. Printed in the United States of America. No part of this book may be used or reproduced in any manner whatsoever without written permission except in the case of brief quotations embodied in critical articles and reviews. For information, address HarperCollins Publishers, 195 Broadway, New York, NY 10007.

HarperCollins books may be purchased for educational, business, or sales promotional use. For information, please email the Special Markets Department at SPsales@harpercollins.com.

FIRST EDITION

Designed by Diahann Sturge-Campbell

Stack of books image © Rose Carson/Shutterstock

Library of Congress Cataloging-in-Publication Data has been applied for.

ISBN 978-0-06-325928-7

24 25 26 27 28 LBC 5 4 3 2 1

To the Pirates, the women of Rose Street, and anyone
who has protested injustice in this world

Chapter 1
EMMY

Emmy Clarke was a librarian not a soldier.

She met her eyes in the cracked mirror hanging in the Frankfurt train station WC and told herself that again. She was a librarian.

The United States Army uniform Emmy wore mocked that assertion.

It was a costume, though. A powerful one that offered Emmy protection as she traveled through postwar Germany, but a costume nonetheless.

Mr. Luther Harris Evans, the director of the Library of Congress, had told her that all the trappings—including an army title she certainly hadn't earned—were a precaution. She wouldn't be in a single moment of danger if she accepted the two-month assignment abroad.

Had Director Evans known her well, he would have realized she didn't care about the potential danger.

She just didn't want to see herself in the uniform that her husband had died in.

Emmy touched the tie at her neck, and remembered how she'd tightened Joseph's four-in-hand knot the morning he'd shipped out, like she had a thousand times since they'd been married.

The pain of the loss had dulled, as everyone had said it would, but being in Germany was bringing it all back. And this was only the first day of her new assignment.

"A faint heart never filled a spade flush," Emmy whispered to herself, a saying her mother had picked up in the Montana logging towns they traveled through, poker a religion more than a pastime out there. The phrase was a bit of card sharp nonsense, but it always reminded her of what she had already been through in her life and survived.

She could do this, too.

Emmy gave her reflection a firm nod, and then bent to retrieve her bag.

Stragglers were still disembarking from the train when she stepped back out onto the platform, but the crowd was thinning. She was thankful for that. There were too many people in U.S. Army uniforms and she needed to find a specific one.

Major Wesley Arnold.

The major was a member of the Monuments, Fine Arts, and Archives unit, the group that had been irreverently dubbed Monuments Men. Emmy had always loved the idea of them—scuttling about Europe, protecting artistic and architectural masterpieces from bombs, Allies and Axis alike. Safeguarding humanity's cultural inheritance.

No one on the platform looked like an academic who also punched Nazis in the name of defending art, so she kept walking, hoping he would find her first.

When she got to the lobby, Emmy was immediately surrounded by a group of young children, their thin little bodies pressing into her legs, their hands reaching up, palms and fingernails crusted with dirt. She wasn't fluent in German but knew enough to realize they were begging for food.

After several days of traveling by train through the country, she had been prepared for this onslaught. Starving children gathered at spots along the railroad all the way from the port to Frankfurt, calling out to passengers for cigarettes and candy and sandwiches. Never for money, that wouldn't do them any good.

"Bitte, bitte, bitte," they cried in unison.

Please. Please. Please.

Emmy resented them. She hated them, even.

Because they made her care, and Emmy didn't want to feel any kind of complex emotion for Germans—children or not. Her chest went tight as she pictured that moment of fixing Joseph's tie once more. His smile, the dark curl that fell over his forehead.

Don't you forget me, he'd said. A tease, a joke. But there had been a serious thread that ran through those words. They both knew his likely fate.

"Bitte, bitte, bitte."

A sharp whistle cut through the pleas, and Emmy looked up into the eyes of a man holding a placard with her name scrawled across it.

The begging children didn't scatter, just shifted their attention, and the man held out a package to the youngest one in the bunch with a single command: "Share."

They seemed to collectively decide they had gotten all that they would and scampered off after the rest of the passengers. The man watched them go and Emmy watched the man.

He was of medium height and medium build with a medium-brown hair color that matched medium-brown eyes. Silver threaded through the strands at his temples, suggesting he was at least in his midthirties. A constellation of freckles sat at the corner of his mouth, which was the only objectively interesting thing about his face.

But there was a magnetism about him that was hard to look away from.

Maybe it was her travel-induced delirium, but she had to admit that he did, in fact, look exactly like an academic who also punched Nazis in the name of defending art. That impression might have to do with the spiderweb of freshly scarred skin that peeked out from his collar. Or the way he leaned much of his weight on his cane. He had seen action.

When Emmy met his eyes, they were hard, but there was a slant to his lips as if he found her scrutiny amusing.

She flushed and looked down, caught out. What assumptions was he now making about her? Emmy had never given much thought to her looks. She was unremarkable but not unattractive, with a face that most people forgot a few minutes after meeting her. Throughout her life, she'd received the advice to skip dessert plenty of times. The one feature that garnered any attention—her thick, glossy black hair—was currently dull from travel, tucked back in a low chignon.

For a silly moment, she wished she'd applied lipstick in the WC.

"I'm Mrs. Clarke," she said after realizing they had been standing in a strange, weighted silence for too long.

His half smile became a full one that still didn't meet his eyes. Her own flicked down to his scars again, and she wondered if the flint in his personality was innate or forged through war.

"Major Wesley Arnold," he said, his voice a lovely rumble, his accent American but hard to place beyond that. "At your service."

He reached out a hand for her bag and she fought the urge to refuse his help because of his cane. If he'd offered, he could handle it.

"I hope your trip was uneventful," he said, stilted in that way of people who weren't natural conversationalists. She followed him into the street where an open-air jeep was waiting under guard by a young private.

"Quite." Emmy eyed the step up into the vehicle. There was no way she was going to climb in there in a graceful manner with this impractical skirt tight around her knees. How the army thought this was a suitable uniform, she would never know. Women working for the war efforts should have been supplied with trousers.

Before she could even make an attempt, Major Wesley Arnold's hands cupped her waist. He boosted her into the passenger seat with an ease that suggested a hidden strength not obvious to the casual eye.

Emmy blinked, thrown once again. He'd handled the whole affair with an efficiency she found intensely refreshing. She had needed to get into the jeep, and so he had made it happen.

Major Arnold slid behind the wheel and stowed his cane, all with well-practiced movements. Maybe the injury wasn't quite as new as she'd thought.

"Thank you," she murmured. He paused with the key in the ignition as if her response surprised him. Perhaps he'd been expecting a reprimand for how his thumbs had pressed into the soft flesh of her hips.

They drove for a while in silence, and maybe in some other circumstance it would have been uncomfortable. But mostly, she was too exhausted to feel anything but gratitude that someone had taken over the logistics of getting her to where she needed to go.

Emmy wasn't sure she could have made idle chitchat, anyway. They were driving through destruction that was so complete and devastating she couldn't look away from it—the buildings that were no longer buildings; the skinny dogs that, judging from the state of the few people she saw out, would likely become food themselves; the air that was thick with dust and the stench of human suffering. Sour rot, copper blood, disease.

Why was she here again?

She hated that she was here.

Joseph hadn't died in this country, but he had died *because* of this country.

Emmy had been more than happy toiling away in the acquisitions department of the Library of Congress. It was a prestigious position for someone as young as she, and it let her get lost in books. Grief, she'd found, had a way of receding when she was reading. Her work in acquisitions often had more to do with examining the book itself than consuming the story, but she'd never been good at ignoring the words that beckoned her into another world, into another time period, into a place where her husband hadn't died along with millions of other young men.

Then Director Evans had called her into his office. The Library of Congress needed a volunteer to head to Offenbach am Main where the government had set up an archival depot that held the millions of books the Nazis had plundered from occupied nations. They were to sort through all that loot for anything that could be deemed "enemy literature" in an effort to learn more about why and how all this had happened.

One of the original members of the mission had become ill and had to bow out, and Emmy would serve as a placeholder until they could get someone in longer term.

Everything in her had balked at the request. How could she go to Germany and be anything but the cruelest version of herself?

But she'd never been able to say no to books.

So instead of walking to work on a crisp spring morning back in Washington, she was being driven through a bombed-out Frankfurt by a man with scars and darkness in his expression in the very country she'd sworn never to step foot in for her entire life.

More children ran behind their jeep, their bones pressing too tight against their skin, their lips dry and cracked, their feet bare. Emmy wanted Major Arnold to drive faster, but even when they left the children behind there was little relief to be found. On the sidewalk, a pair of shoes stuck out from a dirty blanket, the lump underneath too still to be anything but a corpse.

"Should we stop?" Emmy dared ask, even though she wanted nothing more than to pretend she hadn't seen it.

But Major Arnold shook his head. "I'll send someone out. It's . . . not uncommon."

Three weeks ago, before Director Evans had given her this assignment, Emmy would have said she would be perfectly happy to consign each and every single German to hell. Yet here they were in hell, and Emmy couldn't find any satisfaction in the suffering that she saw.

As they crossed the bridge toward Offenbach am Main, a town that sat over the river from Frankfurt, she felt Major Arnold's eyes on her. When she looked, though, he was back to watching the road.

The potholes that came not only from bombs but from neglect and budgetary prioritization required careful navigation.

"Your first time in Germany?" he asked, his voice neutral.

"First time out of America," she admitted. And then, her defenses lowered, "I don't know what I expected."

"Some people think the Germans deserve all this," Major Arnold said.

She thought about all she'd seen since arriving in Germany. Her train had passed through whole towns that had been leveled to the ground. That rubble represented more than stone and mortar.

She thought about Joseph's last letter, which she carried around in the breast pocket of her army-issued jacket. The paper was yellow at the edges, tearstained now. He'd written the message the night before the Normandy invasion, the night before he'd died alone on a beach, if he'd even made it that far.

"I'm not an expert," Emmy said slowly. "But I don't think this is what justice looks like."

That earned her an approving glance from the major. They fell silent once more and Emmy was glad for it. She had no desire to bare her soul to this stranger. Instead, she twisted the wedding ring she still wore and tried not to think about anything at all.

Major Arnold finally pulled to a stop in front of an ugly, giant warehouse. During the war it had been used to make chemicals and pharmaceuticals for purposes she had been afraid to ask about.

Now it was the army's Offenbach Archival Depot. Emmy had been half hoping that the major would drop her off at her cottage for today, but now that they were at the collection point she couldn't ignore the thrill of excitement that coursed through her.

She trailed behind Major Arnold, studiously not looking at the fit of his uniform. When he opened the door to the depot, the intoxicating, earthy scent of books crashed into her, not a ripple but a tidal wave. Glue and paper, bindings and ink. Time.

Inside, there were millions of books that had been stolen by the

Nazis. They came from all over Europe—from research libraries and private collections and universities and government agencies. There would be ones that were encrusted with jewels whose pages were adorned with gold; there would be slim, cheap throwaway paperbacks that came from someone's bedside table; there would be priceless documents that held information on civilizations that would be forgotten had the volumes not been salvaged.

They had been found by men like Major Arnold in castles and wine cellars, in homes and apartment buildings, in schools and hidden behind wallpaper. They had been found in that horrific institute across the river that had been set up by the high-ranking Nazi Alfred Rosenberg, with the sole purpose of studying the Jewish culture.

Since she had been tasked with this assignment, Emmy had been focused on how hard it would be to go to Germany. How much it would be a constant reminder of everything she'd lost.

She should have known better, though.

What better way to soothe the broken parts of her than to be part of the effort that was helping all of these books find their way home?

Chapter 2
ANNELISE

Annelise Fischer pulled her modest dress over her head the minute she passed the tree line. She dropped it on the ground and spread her arms to the sky above, clad only in her underthings.

Despite the woods' thick canopy, the sun cut patterns through the leaves, kissing her cheeks, her chest, her arms. She lived for this moment, for this freedom.

The air was cooler in here, the sounds of nature waking back up as they always did once the creatures of the forest became accustomed to her presence. She wanted to take her leather sandals off as well and press the souls of her feet into the soil, to feel the earth beneath her.

A low whistle brought her back to herself.

"Better be careful," Marta Schmidt said, tapping Annelise on the rump in greeting. "There be wolves in these woods."

Annelise flashed a smile that she knew bent toward predatory. "Wolves should be scared of me."

"You are positively terrifying," Marta teased, as Annelise rummaged through her rucksack. She shimmied into a pleated skirt that hit just below her knees, and then pulled on the bright turquoise blouse she'd bought at the market the past weekend.

Annelise tied a daffodil-colored scarf around her neck and then yanked her socks up to her knees. Marta watched it all with the patient eye of someone who'd just finished her own adjustments.

Some of the Edelweiss Pirates wore their flashier outfits out around town. But, so far, Annelise's parents hadn't made a fuss about where she was spending her time after school and on weekends. She wanted to keep it that way, so she played the part of a good German girl when there was a chance her neighbors would see and report back on her outfits.

As her final touch, Annelise secured the edelweiss pin to the corner of her scarf. The flower was the symbol that bound them all together. Once upon a time, it had represented groups of young people who had devoted themselves to outdoor pursuits—to hiking, to camping, to skiing, to frolicking in the woods. Those had been simpler days.

Now the symbol had weight. They were the Edelweiss Pirates, the youth who wouldn't conform, who wouldn't join the Hitlerjugend, who would wear what they wanted, say what they wanted, act how they wanted. And in doing so, the Pirates had become more than a flower—they had become a thorn in the side of the Nazis at a time when it seemed most of their fellow countrymen were begging to lick the boots of the Führer.

"Are you finally sleeping in Stefan's tent tonight?" Annelise asked Marta, as they started deeper into the woods. The hiking trails that wound up the Seven Mountains outside Bonn were plentiful and well-marked, though they were used with less frequency than they had been in Annelise's parents' generation. Now the adults were too busy working in the factories and the young people were too busy with the Hitlerjugend.

That did mean more often than not the Pirates had the woods to themselves. Most of the boys in the group had dropped out of school a few years back, so they came here ahead of the girls who still went to classes and set up camp at the top of Lohrberg Mountain. They always brought extra tents. Annelise and Marta often shared one, but Stefan had been chasing after her friend for a few weeks now, and Annelise had a feeling Marta was ready to be caught.

"That depends on what present he brought me today," Marta said, nose in the air as if they didn't both know it was a foregone conclusion.

"He'll have written you a song."

Stefan was one of the more proficient guitar players in their little group, though a lack of skill rarely stopped any of their boys from strumming along or showing off.

"Then maybe I'll leave you in the tent by yourself." She shot Annelise a sly smile. "But only if the song is good."

An acrid jealousy crept in behind Annelise's amusement. It wasn't that she wanted either Stefan or Marta, nor did she worry she would lose Marta's friendship and attention.

No, Annelise was jealous because she desperately wanted that feeling. She wanted to *want* someone.

Marta made the flirtations look fun. She'd *shared her tent* with a few of the boys, broken a few other hearts, and laughed her way through it all with such charm that no one resented her after all the dust settled.

Annelise wished she could love so easily.

The boys in their group had never appealed to her beyond friendship. She adored them, but they were silly and sweet and she'd seen their pale rear ends on the days they swam in the cool mountain lakes. She hadn't been impressed.

Beyond the Pirates, though, there were only the boys who had gleefully donned the Hitlerjugend uniform, and she didn't think she'd ever be able to flirt with, let alone kiss, someone who supported that lunatic.

While she didn't naturally draw attention like Marta, who was all plush curves and big grins and luscious red curls, Annelise could admit to her own subtle kind of beauty. Her wheaten hair was thick and long, her legs trim from weekly hikes, her face pretty enough. Had a boy struck her fancy, she didn't think she'd have trouble getting him to share her tent.

That hadn't happened yet. Maybe it never would.

Marta's fingers wrapped around Annelise's wrist, drawing her to a stop. They were only about halfway to the summit and Annelise tensed when she noticed Marta's expression.

"You have a little shadow," Marta whispered, her lips brushing Annelise's ear.

As casually as she could, Annelise glanced over her shoulder and caught the flutter of the Bund Deutscher Mädel uniform. Everything in her relaxed and she rolled her eyes.

"Christina, out," Annelise demanded. "Now."

For a moment nothing happened, then her sister slunk from behind a tree, her shoulders rounded, her mouth set in a petulant pout.

"You're not supposed to be out here," Christina said, ever the prim and proper BDM girl. At fifteen, Christina was a little more than a year younger than Annelise, but sometimes Annelise wondered if one of them was a changeling. They were so different. Not in looks—they could be twins and had been told so many times—but in temperament.

Her little rule-follower of a sister knew nothing of freedom, of *wanting*. Christina liked being told what to do, liked wearing that ridiculous uniform and spending all her free time learning how to be a good German wife and mother for the Fatherland. She'd been a tattler and an apple-polisher as a child and it seemed she'd never grown out of the impulse.

"Yet here *you* are," Annelise countered, irritated. Christina was always following her, trying to catch her in some kind of trouble.

"Trying to save you," Christina said, cheeks flushed in what Annelise knew was righteous indignation. "From ruining our family."

Annelise considered arguing, but they'd had this discussion so many times over the past year, she could practically run the lines playing both of their parts. It would end with bitterness from Christina—who did genuinely believe she was doing what was best for Annelise—and exasperated annoyance from Annelise. None of it was worth the wasted breath.

"Come on," Annelise said, and then started up the trail once more.

"You're sure this is wise?" Marta asked beneath her breath. Christina hadn't fallen in behind them yet, but Annelise knew it wouldn't be long before her little shadow caught up.

"No," Annelise said, with a grin. "But when does anything we do count as wise?"

They both ignored Christina as she finally joined them, and continued to gossip their way to the top of the mountain.

For all that Christina liked to prattle on about how important sports and athletics were to the BDM, she was huffing far more than either Annelise or Marta by the end.

Annelise handed over her flask of water. Just because she was frustrated with Christina didn't mean she wanted her to suffer.

Christina took it without thanks. But that was her sister—so used to Annelise's care that she would only notice it if it was gone.

Marta and Annelise soaked in the view as Christina tried to subtly catch her breath. The thick Rhine wound its way through the farmlands that surrounded Bonn, the hills in the distance matching their own high point, the bluebird sky dotted with puffy clouds. They could have been standing in a painting for how perfect the day was.

Being up here, so far away from the struggle of her daily life, made Annelise almost forget everything that was going on down below. The politics, the hardship, her parents' dead-eyed stares.

The way that all of the Pirates faced backlash for refusing to fall in line with Hitler.

Annelise had to watch as her friends were denied good positions at warehouses, had to put up with being shunned by all their neighbors and given poor marks by teachers. But worse, in the past few months, the bullies in the Hitlerjugend—or the HJ as everyone called them—had begun violently targeting the Pirates. There had been several all-out brawls in the street that had resulted in more than a few broken bones and black eyes for the Pirates. And it was only going to continue to escalate.

But if resistance had been easy, it wouldn't have been resistance.

Annelise had always believed that the traits that had caused the Pirates to seek belonging in outdoors groups were the same that led them to identify the brutality in the Nazis' worldview while everyone else bought into the propaganda. The Edelweiss Pirates, by nature, sought peace, sought equanimity, sought love and freedom and self-expression. They had never been the type to conform to what was expected—rather they ran through the trees, they climbed impossible mountains, they breathed in air that hadn't been tainted by warehouse smoke or by hatred.

They were pirates, which meant they could never be serfs.

Marta whooped and Annelise turned to see the smoke rising just off the summit.

Annelise looped an arm around Christina's neck as they followed a skipping Marta at a slightly slower pace.

"Aren't you missing your precious BDM practice right now?" Annelise asked, hating the part of herself that made her poke and prod. "Or is this a spy-in-training assignment?"

Christina wasn't cruel like some of the Hitlerjugend, but she loved handbooks and guidelines and being told what to do. If one of the women who ran the BDM asked her to find out what the Pirates got up to in these mountains, Annelise wasn't sure Christina wouldn't give a detailed list of how to identify everyone involved. She was a teacher's pet in a new world where they reigned supreme.

"I said I have the same illness as you've mysteriously had for the past six months."

Annelise had been putting off the quite persistent local BDM office with the excuse that she didn't want to infect the rest of the girls.

"You lied?" Annelise asked, eyes comically wide in shock that was only half exaggerated. Christina was typically so earnest, Annelise had a hard time picturing her sister delivering even the smallest fib.

Christina took a fortifying breath. "It was for the greater good."

Of course, that's all Christina cared about. She had bought into all that Nazi propaganda that made all the girls like Christina think themselves more important than they would ever be. "I am terrified to ask what you believe is the 'greater good' here."

"Making sure our family is in good standing with the NSDAP," Christina said, as if it were the most obvious thing in the world.

Perhaps it was petty of Annelise, but she couldn't help but add, "You mean the Nazis."

That earned her a glare and a hard pinch to the soft side of her arm. "You think you're so clever, but it's comments such as that that will doom us."

Hitler wasn't particularly fond of *Nazi*, which had roots in a name synonymous with backward peasants. It was a sore point for the party that it had taken off so.

Annelise smirked and pinched her sister back.

Up ahead, the Edelweiss Pirates' camp came into view. Marta launched herself into the arms of the tall boy with bronzed curls and a guitar strung around his back. Christina made some offended sound—boys and girls were kept strictly separate in the HJ and the BDM.

"You won't tell anyone about this?" Annelise checked one more time, dropping the pretense of teasing. She had no desire to endanger her friends simply because she'd naively trusted her sister. As much as Christina toed the line, Annelise didn't think she would do anything that would actually endanger Annelise.

Christina sniffed as if she found the question preposterous. "I don't want myself associated with these hooligans."

"Well, when you put it that way, I'm convinced," Annelise said, dry but honest. If she could count on anything it was that Christina wouldn't want to get in trouble herself.

The fire was already going, logs set up around it to create a gathering space. The tents had also been constructed, a mishmash of painted canvas and sticks.

Annelise always took the one with the three pines on the flap. She threw her rucksack inside without even checking to see if it was taken, and then found Walter Schubert in the small crowd. She kissed his cheek in thanks because he'd set up the tent without any expectation of sharing it with her.

That's how the Pirates were. They looked after each other.

"Who brought the Nazi?" one of the boys called, clearly having come back from relieving himself.

"Shove off, Hans," Annelise snapped, wrapping a protective arm around Christina's waist. Only she could be mean to Christina, that's how sibling relations worked. "She's my sister."

Muffled grumbling followed the introduction, but no one really put up a fight. Annelise was far from the leader of the group, but she was well-liked and had been around long enough to have earned some goodwill. If she vouched for someone, most of the Pirates would go along with it.

Meanwhile, Christina looked like she wanted to take a running leap off the nearby cliffs to escape the scrutiny, so Annelise squeezed her hip in a comforting gesture while wishing she'd brought an extra set of clothes for her to change into.

There was nothing to be done about Christina, though. Annelise's school clothes were sweat-damp and unpleasant, and even if she had brought something that would help her sister fit in with the group, Christina would have refused. She wore her BDM skirt and jacket with pride. Annelise directed Christina onto one of the logs beside Walter, who would treat her the gentlest, and then grabbed a package of warmed nuts that had been resting against the fire. She poured most of them out into Christina's waiting palm.

Marta sat herself in Stefan's lap, which prompted Hans to grab for the guitar. The strap was completely decorated in pins, but at the top was the edelweiss flower. Annelise fiddled with her own as Hans strummed the opening bars of one of their favorite songs.

The three hitchhikers met, who'd traveled around the world.
Let's all hitchhike together.

An ache filled the hollow spaces in her body—that *wanting* of something she couldn't quite name. To be somewhere else, to be someone else, she didn't really know. But life had to be more than working in factories and producing infants for the Fatherland and passing simple day after simple day in this tiny town.

The Pirates sang, handed the guitars around, doled out the liquor one of the boys had smuggled from his house in a flask. Some kissed, some danced, they all laughed and talked and felt at home for once.

The closest they came to discussing the HJ or the Nazis was when they were performing skits for each other.

In one of them Stefan and Marta pretended to be two members of the HJ. The Pirates around the campfire booed and hollered when they announced who they were and then dissolved into a fit of giggles when the two buffooned their way into setting up a one-man tent. They argued who would take it and settled on Marta inside, with Stefan sleeping outside. A "family of bears" wandered by and began "attacking" Stefan. They ran away when Marta stuck her head out of the tent. Stefan begged to switch places, but Marta refused. When they went back to sleep, the bears returned and batted Stefan around again.

A couple Pirates called encouragement to the bears as they once again ran off when Marta "woke up." Stefan pleaded to be given the tent, and Marta reluctantly agreed.

When the bears came back the third time, the head one said, "We've given this Nazi a hard enough time, let's go for the one in the tent."

Even Christina couldn't hide her laughter at the punch line, despite the angry flush Annelise had spotted riding along her cheek-bones.

Apart from the silly skit, though, the Pirates stayed away from controversial topics. It was rare they delved into politics anyway. Some of them really had simply joined because it was an outdoors group, some because they didn't like being told what to wear and how to act. Many of them simply didn't like the HJ. Despite the fact the very existence of the group had become an annoyance to the Nazis in town, the boys didn't often get philosophical about the NSDAP's policies. Regardless, with Christina there, that kind of discussion was off-limits.

When Annelise and Christina crawled into their tent long after the sun had set, smelling of smoke and gin and laughter, Annelise gathered her sister in her arms and placed a sloppy kiss on her forehead.

She and her sister used to be so close as children. Their brother, Anders, was older and commanded all their parents' limited attention, so it had been up to the girls to entertain themselves. Ever since Christina joined the BDM two years ago, though, most of their conversations had devolved into petty fights.

Annelise could admit more often than not she dismissed Christina as silly, not worthy of a debate. But how could she spend the night with the Pirates and not see what Annelise loved about them? They didn't judge anyone—more than a few harmless chirps—nor did they hate or belittle those with less power or social status. They were creating a community so much stronger than the BDM because they actually cared for each other and loved the things the group valued.

"You could be a Pirate, Christina," Annelise whispered, almost nervous.

"Never. They're nothing but riffraff who will get you killed one day," Christina said.

A door shut in her face. Annelise wasn't quite sure why she kept trying, except that hope was a stubborn weed, hard to kill.

Christina could be extraordinarily kind and clever and caring. She always tucked an extra apple into their father's lunch box on market days, filled hot water bottles for their mother's aching back. She stood up for the odd children who were targeted by older classmates, and nursed sick birds back to health. Christina wasn't a saint, but at heart, she was a loving, fair person.

Everyone had flaws and weaknesses, but Christina's seemed amplified beneath their current troubles. Perhaps everyone's did.

Annelise finally put into words the one thing she wanted most from Christina and the one thing she was losing hope of seeing from her sister.

"Oh darling," she whispered. "My greatest wish is for you to realize that sometimes choosing the right thing is more important than whether or not you'll get hurt doing it."

Chapter 3
CHRISTINA

February 27, 1943
Berlin

The massive roundup of the last Jews in Berlin—meant as an early birthday present to the Führer—started before dawn on the second-to-last day of February.

The city would be Judenfrei by the end of April.

Christina Fischer had been waiting for the Gestapo to act ever since Joseph Goebbels's speech a little more than a week ago. No one talked about how he'd slipped in the beginning, how he'd almost said *exterminated* when talking about his plans of total war.

She had heard it, though.

A sharp left took her through a shortcut that had been made possible by RAF bombings. What had once been a boutique featuring the latest styles from Paris was now nothing but a new path to work. It made Christina's trek easier, so she couldn't say she minded.

Coldhearted. She'd heard the pejorative many times in her life, from men at school, from girls who'd wanted to be friends. Her current colleagues at the Abwehr were too professional to say it to her face, but she had no doubt it was muttered behind her back.

It wasn't that her heart was cold, though. Instead, it was shattered, never to be repaired.

Christina pulled her coat tighter and burrowed deeper into her scarf—the weather was cruel today. Her cheeks were already chafed from the wind, her ears frozen to the touch. A storm was coming.

Four covered trucks roared by, their wheels kicking up icy slush in their wake. Globs of dirt and snow and something she didn't want to think about landed on her boots, on the hem of her coat. She lifted her eyes from the sidewalk to glare, but then tripped to a stop when she got a glimpse into the backs of the trucks.

People. A mass of bodies, shoulder to shoulder, bellies and thighs pressed together as if they didn't deserve the dignity of personal space.

Christina shook her head and began walking once more. There was nothing she could do for them.

She quickened her pace, cutting through the Tiergarten. When she'd first come to Berlin, the park had reminded her so much of the Seven Mountains and of Annelise that she'd nearly wept at the sight of it.

Now it had been completely stripped bare of its trees—the wood too valuable over the long, starvation winter to be left standing. Once gorgeous and thriving and now empty and desolate, barely a ghost.

Christina no longer lingered in the park.

The concrete building that housed the Abwehr took up the entire corner of Bendlerstrasse. Christina didn't bother to take her coat off as she entered. They hadn't been able to properly heat the place in months despite the fact it was the home of the intelligence-gathering arm of the Wehrmacht. Christina wasn't sure how anyone believed the Nazi propaganda that they were winning the war.

Would the recent, horrific defeat in Stalingrad change any minds? Would everyday, average Germans even be given enough information to realize how crippling the loss was?

She doubted it. But she was a cynic.

By the time she reached her desk, she was dreaming of the one cup of coffee she was allowed. It tasted of disappointment and a tiny bit of sewage, but it did wonders to warm a body up. Then she caught sight of the metal inbox on her desk. It was only seven forty-five on a Saturday morning and already it was full.

Christina sunk into her chair. Officially, she was a low-level secretary for the postal bureau of the Abwehr's counterespionage unit. She was responsible for handling any letters or intercepted communiqués that were deemed suspicious. Of course, she wasn't in charge of reading them herself, but she was supposed to sort them and get them to the right code breaker or scientist.

The work wasn't taxing, and had it been her only job Christina might have been driven mad by the mind-numbing simplicity. But she kept herself engaged in other ways.

The quick click of heels against hardwood had her glancing up.

"Good morning, bunny," Johanna Ritter said, perching on the corner of Christina's desk. She was too bright and bubbly, always, but especially on this cold February morning when Jewish men, women, and children across the city were being shoved into the backs of trucks and carted off to God knew where.

Usually when dealing with Johanna it helped to remember that she was likely one of the many Abwehr employees loyal to Admiral Wihelm Canaris, the head of the agency, rather than to the Führer. The Abwehr was riddled with Canaris supporters who—like the man they followed—blamed Hitler for ruining Germany. They wanted to take down the Third Reich almost as much as the Allies did.

She wasn't sure how many double agents Admiral Canaris had on his side within the agency, but it was not insignificant. On the other hand, there were just enough fanatically loyal Nazis here to keep it afloat for now.

Canaris's strategy of threading the needle between keeping the Nazis happy and undermining them enough to hurt their war efforts was a high-stakes game, and, if she was being honest, it didn't make life easy for her. Working as a double agent in an agency whose rivals rightly suspected it was full of double agents was precarious at best. If she made it through this war, it would be a miracle.

Sometimes she couldn't believe everyone who worked for the organization hadn't all been summarily taken out and shot just to clean up the reputation of the agency, but they were more often than not labeled as simply incompetent instead of traitorous.

It helped that Canaris's British contacts had assassinated Reinhard

Heydrich—Canaris's rival in the SD and one of the Abwehr's fiercest critics—when he'd started investigating the agency too closely.

At least those were the whispers in Christina's circle of acquaintances.

Christina wasn't a Canaris loyalist—she was loyal only to herself—but she considered them allies.

"Can I help you?" Christina's voice came out terse, but Johanna had dealt with far worse from her fair share of angry Wehrmacht officers.

"I had the most interesting night," Johanna said, inspecting her nails. "Dinner at Horcher."

Christina tensed at the mention of Hermann Göring's favorite restaurant. It was where Nazis took women they wanted to impress—and when they wanted to impress women, young Nazis tended to brag about privileged information they had.

For ladies in the business of double-crossing the Nazis, accepting dinner invitations to places like Horcher was one of the best ways to get secrets, if pillow talk itself wasn't an option.

"Such an eager young buck, I won't be seeing him again," Johanna continued casually. "He did say the most curious thing, though."

Christina bit the inside of her lip, wishing they didn't have to go through this pony show. But she understood the necessity of it. Anyone watching them would think they were nothing but two gossiping secretaries, maybe wasting time but not worth much notice otherwise. "Did he?"

"Mm-hmm." Johanna finally dropped her hand, and met Christina's eyes. "He passed on dessert because he had an early morning assignment."

"Yes, I noticed the trucks while coming in to work," Christina said, on the edge of annoyed now. Most people in the Abwehr, if not most people in Berlin, knew that a roundup had started that morning.

By the end of the day, more than twelve thousand Jewish Berliners would likely be detained by the Reich Security Main Office. The Gestapo had been tight-lipped about the assignment—they never liked sharing anything with the Abwehr.

But a few days ago, the Gestapo had started informing factory employers that their Jewish workers would be gone. Word got out.

"Right, this young buck had a particular assignment, though," Johanna continued, her voice prodding, like she wanted Christina to understand without having to say it explicitly.

Why would she assume Christina would be able to follow her? Christina wasn't working on anything to do with the roundup—either for her legitimate position or the one that could get her killed.

No, it would have to be something personal. But she didn't have a personal life. Except, of course, for . . .

She stilled, her breath catching in her throat.

Eitan.

But that didn't make any sense. She hadn't thought he would be in danger, because he wasn't supposed to be in danger.

Christina didn't want to ask. She forced the question out through numb lips anyway.

"Not intermarried Jews?" Christina said. "Surely."

They were supposed to be a protected category. At some point, someone high up in the government had decided that to keep the peace with the families of tens of thousands of intermarried couples in the country, intermarried Jewish citizens would be safe from deportation. The Reich needed laborers, after all. They could work in factories to aid the war effort.

They were supposed to be exempt.

Johanna didn't answer, simply leaned over and scooped the pile of messages out of Christina's inbox. "I'll take care of these; it seems like you may have a few telephone calls to make."

Then she was gone.

Christina ignored another colleague's greeting as she headed for the exit, past the guard, onto the street. She ducked down an alleyway three blocks over, and entered the back of a bakery without knocking. The owners would be busy in the front. It was Saturday, and despite the fleets of Gestapo out and about, wives still needed to get their bread.

A telephone hung on the wall in the small office tucked at the back of the building, and Christina picked it up to dial a number she'd memorized the first time she'd been given it four years ago.

The line engaged, but the person didn't speak.

"Intermarried Jewish men, where are they being taken?" she asked and then hung up.

Christina paced the small space of the office as she waited, rubbing feeling back into her fingers.

Eitan. He was supposed to be safe.

If he died—

She cut off the thought. Now was not the time for panic. Now was the time for rational, unemotional plans.

The Nazis always kept their detainees for two days. It had only been two hours at most since he would have been picked up at his factory job.

All was not lost.

It took ten minutes for the phone to finally ring. She pressed the receiver to her ear. It would be quick, an address, and then the person would hang up.

Christina held her breath as the static crackled over the line. And then came the answer she needed.

"Rose Street."

Chapter 4
EMMY

E mmy had been working in libraries since as long as she could walk.

Her mother had helped create a beloved boxcar library that traveled between lumberjack camps in western Montana, bringing books to the workers. Emmy had spent her childhood with train tracks beneath her feet and any novel she wanted at the ready.

When she'd been older, she'd worked in her college's library and then at the Boston Public Library before finally landing her dream position with the Library of Congress.

Emmy had thought she'd seen every kind of library there was, and yet she could never have prepared herself for the sheer magnitude of the Offenbach Archival Depot.

There were rows and rows of crates packed full with books as far as she could see, librarians and local workers and army men bustling around, unloading and loading, taking photographs, scribbling in ledgers. Telephones rang in the distance, and voices lifted and blended, becoming an indistinct hum that matched the buzz of energy running through everyone. Connecting everyone.

And this was only the first of five floors.

"I'll give you the tour," Major Arnold said after a moment of letting her gawk. They'd already made it through security, which had been surprisingly tight. The man in charge of the front desk had informed her she would be searched every day to make sure she wasn't sneaking out any treasures to sell on the black market, a suggestion that had seemed absurd until she realized it had probably happened enough times they'd had to institute these measures.

"Are you a librarian, Major Arnold?" Emmy asked as she fell into step beside him. She couldn't deny she was curious about this man, even in her tired state.

"Historian."

"Oh, should I be calling you Doctor?"

That got her his half-slant smile. "I suppose it's there in my titles. But no. You should call me Wesley, if you like."

"Oh." She hesitated though she didn't know why. Being raised in the American West had given her a laissez-faire attitude toward propriety, but calling this quiet, stoic man Wesley didn't seem right for some reason. Maybe because it felt like an intimacy she hadn't yet earned.

"Or Major Arnold will do just fine," he said, reading her silence for what it was. He said it in the same manner that he'd boosted her into the jeep—efficient and without any messy emotion.

"How does all this work?" Emmy asked to cover her own awkwardness. "There must be some sort of system in place to handle so many books."

"Some have been straightforward," he said, as he nudged her out of the way of a boy with what looked like an ancient Tanakh. "There were full collections of books sitting in various dungeons around the country, in boxes, labeled with their origin. One thing no one can fault the Germans for is their recordkeeping."

Those would have been from the big research libraries, the universities, and the world-renowned personal collections, she knew from her briefing on this place. "And those will be shipped back to where they came from?"

"Yes. The goal of the United States Army is to return any plundered property to its rightful owner," he said, as if reading off a placard.

"But?"

"Our hands are tied when it comes to international law. We can only return the looted material to the country and then their government is required to redistribute it," he said, the starchiness gone from his voice. "And for the individual collections . . . well. For many of these books, there's no one to return them to."

There were hundreds of thousands of books she could see, and millions more that were stored in the warehouse. Like the rubble in Frankfurt, this wasn't simply stone and mortar or paper and glue. Each of these books represented victims of the Third Reich. Black crept in at the sides of her vision and she threw a hand out to stop herself from swaying into the closest stack.

Major Arnold's palm cupped her elbow, steadying her. She shook her head, stepped away, and forced out a laugh that sounded hollow and empty even to her own ears. "All that travel."

It was a weak excuse, but he let her get away with it, gesturing them forward.

"We have a conveyor belt–type organization in place," Major Arnold continued, as if the moment hadn't occurred at all. She appreciated the kindness. "Our director is—"

"Mr. Seymour Pomrenze," Emmy said, and then shot him a half-apologetic, half-embarrassed look. "He works at the National Archives in Washington. I'm a fan of his."

"He'll be pleased to hear that. Pomrenze was brought on by Leslie Poste, a librarian"—he tipped his head toward her—"who was the brainchild behind this depot. He's spent the past year or so criss-crossing Europe trying to find hidden caches of books."

"How thrilling." She liked the image of Poste, a dashing librarian, in an open jeep, braving the chaos of postwar Europe in a wild hunt for plundered books.

"He's a Monuments Man," Major Arnold said, as agreement, as explanation, she didn't know. But she was starting to have an even greater appreciation for the unit—and she had already admired them. "Pomrenze took over the day-to-day operations of this depot from Poste, and hired a local team of librarians, archivists, and general laborers. The first step of the sorting process is dividing the books between identifiable and unidentifiable."

"Ones that have markings in them, I suppose," Emmy guessed. "Ex libris, bookplates, stamps on the title pages, things of that nature?"

She'd had her own stamp made long ago—an investment that had seemed indulgent, but every time she ran her fingers over the embossed design with her name on the title page of her most beloved books, she got a tiny thrill.

"Yes, the ex libris are the most helpful besides the labels on the boxes," he said. "The books that have any identifiable marks get photographed and then sent to experts not unlike yourself to help determine if there's a chance the owner can be found."

Her eyes tracked the sea of crates and piles of haphazard books holding on to their place in the stacks with a wish and a prayer. The organizational challenge seemed incredibly daunting. "And the others?"

"For our side to plunder," he said, sending her a look she couldn't interpret, until his words caught up with her. There was a definite edge to his voice that hadn't been there before. Did he consider her a looter? No better than the Nazis?

"Pardon?"

"We've had . . . interest in these books from a variety of places that have no right trying to claim them," the major said, his expression tight. "For that reason, we have strict rules in place. You'll only be allowed to work on books, documents, and film reel that originated in Germany or was created or owned by Nazi Party leaders."

"Yes," Emmy said, not sure if he expected an argument. "That's what I was told by Director Evans."

That was a crucial part of the agreement between the Library of Congress and the Monuments Men in charge of the depot. Everyone was being extraordinarily careful about what the United States government was allowed to acquire.

She'd been told the Library of Congress had a particular interest in books that came from Rosenberg's Institute for Research on the Jewish Question, but anything related to Nazi strategy or propaganda was fair game to acquire.

"Why are you angry?" Emmy asked, too tired to swallow the question.

"You think I'm angry?"

He wasn't now; in fact, he wore that amused half-slant smile again. But he had been before.

"We only wish to take home enemy literature," she explained, though she had the feeling she was repeating herself. Or perhaps defending herself in a fight she had never intended to enter. She was not at her sharpest at the moment.

"Apologies, Mrs. Clarke, I did not mean to offend," he said, sounding tired all of a sudden. "Only, I've witnessed large American libraries sending delegations over to Europe for the sole purpose of scooping up books that no longer have owners. I've grown wary of the 'acquisitions' process I suppose."

"The spoils of war." Emmy certainly understood the impulse to grab at all of this with both hands. The amount of knowledge in this room, let alone all of Europe, was staggering, irresistible. And for the past half decade, an international literature vacuum had been created by the Nazis.

But then she thought again of what each of these books meant. They had been someone's property once upon a time.

"There were entire towns being used to store books," Major Arnold said. They had reached the end of one of the rows.

"I'm sorry?" Emmy asked, the words not quite making sense.

"I went with Poste, looking for loot," Major Arnold said patiently. "We came across entire towns where every building was used for storing books."

She met his eyes, the implication sinking in.

"Where had all the people gone?"

He didn't answer. He didn't need to.

AT THE END of their tour, Major Arnold set Emmy down at a workbench and promised to return shortly to take her to the cottage she was sharing with an American woman named Lucy.

Emmy was so exhausted all her thoughts became scattered upon trying to hold on to them. To keep herself awake, she reached for a carton of books sitting on top of a stack of boxes. They weren't expensive or beautiful like some of the volumes Emmy had already seen. Instead, they looked tattered and beloved.

In Emmy's position with the Library of Congress, she more often found herself working with a rare first edition than normal, everyday books, but the latter were the ones she'd always cherished the most.

One of her favorite things in the world was to be let into someone's home, to see the creased bindings, to figure out which pages they'd dog-eared. To see if they neatly arranged their shelves by topic or if they preferred the anarchy of random stacks. Most of her Saturday afternoons were spent wandering in and out of secondhand bookstores in Georgetown and behind Capitol Hill. Emmy especially loved when she found notations in the margins. They always felt like dear conversations with strangers she would never meet.

The book she grabbed from the carton had clearly been read time and again.

It was a slim volume. Poetry, Emmy realized. A collection by Rainer Maria Rilke.

Emmy glanced around. The workers nearby weren't paying any attention to her, and Major Arnold had been pulled into a conversation with a jovial-looking man a few tables away.

She flipped it open to the title page—at the top right corner, there was a stamp, a flower with pointy petals. At the bottom left corner was a penciled letter *J*, which, according to her briefing packet, meant this book had been owned by a private Jewish citizen. Across the bottom was the name of a bookshop with an address in Bonn, Germany.

The part that caught her attention was the inscription, in what looked like the hurried hand of a young man.

My dearest Annelise, my brave Edelweiss Pirate,

*"We need, in love, to practice only this: letting each
other go. For holding on comes easily; we do not need to
learn it."*

*Forever yours,
Eitan*

Emmy blinked against a rush of emotion.

She had cried the day she'd received the telegram about Joseph, and then hadn't let herself weep even once since then. Grief became intoxicating in its own way. She knew that all too well, and so she'd fought it with every ounce of her being. The waves had tried to drown her, but she'd sworn long ago that she would never give in to them.

So she'd swum on, her head above the water.

Now, though, a simple Rilke quote tugged her down, threatening to pull her under. Of course, it wasn't just the dedication. She'd been hanging on by a thread for a while now. With all she'd experienced since leaving Washington—the international travel, the horrific sight of a war-ruined country, the physical ghosts of a slaughtered people—she was thankful not to be curled on the floor sobbing.

She read the little note again. How could she have so many questions about such a short message? But she found herself wondering who Annelise and Eitan were, what an Edelweiss Pirate was, and why Eitan had believed he had to let Annelise go.

Movement to her left caught her attention. Major Arnold. He was still talking to the jovial man, but gesturing in her direction.

Emmy didn't know what possessed her, but all she could think was that security might not frisk her today, not when she'd been with Major Arnold almost the whole time.

It was now or never.

She silently begged for forgiveness even as she stood with her back to Major Arnold.

In one quick move, she slipped the thin Rilke collection into her jacket, and then, as smoothly as she could manage, turned to greet the major, Eitan and Annelise nestled snuggly and safely against her rib cage.

Against her pounding heart.

Chapter 5

ANNELISE

Fall 1937

The paint can's handle dug into the soft flesh of Annelise's palms, the edges of the tin tacky from recent use.

Annelise shifted the weight in her arms as she followed Stefan and Marta through the dark but familiar streets. The Pirates had split up into small groups for the night's mission because they hadn't wanted to draw any extra attention to themselves.

The HJ building shined like a beacon against the dark sky where it stood right off the main square in a place of prominence in their town.

Hot, white anger pulsed in time with her heart at the sight of it.

She couldn't afford to be emotional. Not tonight. This was the most dangerous mission the Pirates had attempted since Annelise had joined the group. If they were caught, the consequences would be far more serious than a simple slap on the wrist.

Most of the other Pirates were going around town filling the HJ's gasoline tanks with sugar.

Annelise had quickly volunteered for the more dangerous job. She was one of the handful of Pirates who not only disliked the HJ for their pretentious attitudes and violent nature, but also hated the youth organization for the ways it was corrupting the minds of people who used to be her friends, her neighbors.

Her loved ones.

There would be no explaining away the cans of paint she was hauling if she were caught.

But she and Marta and Stefan had grown up on the street, they were riffraff with parents who were too overworked in the factories to care about anything other than feeding and clothing their children.

They knew how to move in the dark.

It took ten minutes to get to the HJ headquarters and another minute or two to crack open the cans of paint.

Marta leaned against the wall, making sure to be obvious in her attempts to ignore Stefan.

"You had a falling-out?" Annelise asked quietly as she went to work on the stem of the edelweiss flower. Stefan was painting the words *Down with Hitler*.

The message wasn't grandiose or even clever, but that wasn't the point. The Nazis were quickly amassing power, which they'd accomplished partly through their campaign of terror. That fear had settled over Bonn, had slipped into the nooks, the cracks, the dank cellars and dusty parlors and into the hearts of its citizens. People were afraid to even talk about the HJ, which was made up of *boys*. Not men. Boys.

Any sign of rebellion, no matter how small, was amplified because of how hard it had become to even say no to them.

"He doesn't appreciate fine wares," Marta said, with a flick of her wrist toward her own body.

"Who's next, then?" Annelise asked.

"I think we should focus on you," Marta said, her smile widening. "Who do you fancy? You never tell me."

"Out of these boys?" Annelise asked, eyebrows raised. "Please."

"They can be a fun way to pass the time."

"I don't want to pass the time," Annelise said honestly. "Not that there's anything wrong with doing so. But I want . . ."

"An all-consuming love," Marta drawled, clearly exasperated.

"You make that sound like a foolish wish."

"Not foolish," Marta corrected. "Naive, maybe. Optimistic. Most boys are just boys. Their lives are very simple. They like rocks and blue jokes and fuc—"

"Bad," Annelise cut in, though she was laughing. The Pirates were less squeamish about sex than the general populace, but that didn't mean they should be vulgar. In her distraction, the brush dripped paint on her boot. "I think we're in a particular moment in time. Where everything is about to feel very big and scary and important. And when things are very big and very scary and very important, there are two ways to approach love."

"Grab at it with both hands," Marta said, gesturing to herself.

"Or hold out for something equally as big and scary and important," Annelise said, hoping she didn't sound judgmental. She wasn't. She understood the desire to find pleasure where you could right now when everything was terrible and seemed like it was only getting worse. What good was *yearning* when the future couldn't be guaranteed beyond the next season?

But in the past few months, Annelise had started to see the bigger picture. She read the newspapers front to back when her father finished with them, she listened to the chatter in the shops, she paid attention to what Christina parroted at home from her BDM practices.

Every part of Annelise wanted things to be as simple as they used to be. She wanted the adults to take care of things, to oust Hitler and maybe even help make her parents' lives a little easier. But the men in power were doing nothing. Her friends, her brother, they would be the ones to pay for this inaction if Hitler got the war he was so clearly courting.

A warning whistle shattered the still night air, interrupting her thoughts.

Annelise and Marta met each other's eyes, and they both cursed.

The HJ patrol was swinging back to headquarters early.

"Go with Stefan," Annelise said. Whatever had happened between the two, the boy would still do everything he could to protect Marta. The Pirates looked after each other.

Marta squeezed Annelise's arms. "Will you be all right?"

"Always," Annelise promised with fake sincerity.

Boots on pavement, shadows sliding closer to them.

They ran, their paint cans and brushes forgotten, chased by a shrill command for them to halt.

When the Pirates had started fighting back against the HJ, they'd come up with a few simple rules. The first was that, if caught, no one had ever heard of the group. The second was that if they were interrupted, they would take off in as many different directions as possible. The HJ patrols couldn't go after all of them. Or, if they tried, their numbers would be severely diminished.

When Marta and Stefan went left at the far end of the alley, Annelise went right. Like with Christina, the Pirates easily outpaced the HJ boys, their hiking in the Seven Mountains paying off.

The night wrapped itself around Annelise, urging her on. She laughed into the wind, glancing back to see that her closest pursuer was a block away and fading fast.

She was free. She was fine.

Then she slammed into an unmoving force.

Annelise would have gone sprawling to the ground had she not perfected her balance on the cliffs high above the city. Still, her arms pinwheeled, her heels skittering against cobblestone.

Felix Hoffmann stood there, calm and unruffled, hands clasped loosely behind his back as he watched her with narrowed eyes.

Of course, it had to be Felix. The boy had been a childhood friend and used to run wild in their house as if it were his own. But his personality had curdled when he'd entered the HJ a few years ago and it had only gotten worse when he had been promoted to a leadership role a handful of months earlier.

Christina fancied herself in love with him, but he only had eyes for Annelise. It proved her theory about his rotten soul since she and her sister were so similar in looks. He only wanted Annelise because she was the Fischer who had rejected him.

Annelise met his eyes now, her chin tipped up. He was tall and broad, a farmer's son whose skin was burnished gold from actual work in the field. His eyes were green as the pines in the Seven Mountains, his jaw firm and resolute. Annelise understood Christina's shallow infatuation. Felix was considered the biggest catch by the girls in the BDM. All Annelise could see was his sneer though, the disdain he wore as if it were a well-tailored coat.

Sometimes, she remembered the boy he had been—perhaps a little supercilious at times, but mostly charming, mischievous, and caring.

Whatever good had been in Felix had been burned to ash by the HJ, though. The mean, petty part of his personality had flourished beneath Nazi rule, and she could see how much he would fit in with the blackshirts, who did the dirtiest work of the dirtiest party.

"I've caught myself a little mouse, it seems," he said now. "You're going to try to run, and it will be pointless."

Annelise trembled at the threat in his voice.

"Surely you don't want me to turn you in to the authorities," Felix continued. "But what will you do for me if I don't? Hmm." He tapped his chin. "I've been thinking too small, I believe. Why ask for dinner when there are so many more interesting things on the menu."

It was time to run. She didn't wait for the right moment, didn't calculate the best path to take. Annelise simply took off.

His hand caught her hair, yanked her back. Needle-sharp pain lanced through her scalp and she had to swallow a yelp.

Felix pulled her close, wrapping an arm around her heaving chest, below her breasts. He licked a fat stripe up her neck, marking her as his, the hot saliva going cold in the night air. Annelise gagged, panic creeping in.

This wasn't a game, she realized. Felix had a lifetime of getting what he wanted. And he was going to take the only thing he had been denied.

She opened her mouth to scream, but Felix anticipated the move and clapped a hand over her face. Fighting every instinct she had, Annelise went limp, letting him bear her weight.

This time he was taken by surprise.

Felix fumbled, struggling to keep her upright against him. Annelise brought her elbow up and back, the snap and crack of bone confirming she'd made contact with his nose.

He flung her to the cobblestones, blood pooling in his palm. Annelise tried to find her feet, but her legs had gone shaky and useless.

She scrambled back as Felix's attention once again narrowed in on her. He advanced. No longer was she simply prey, she was prey that had fought back. Even more tantalizing for predators like him.

His eyes flicked to something behind her.

Then there were hands on her again, lifting her off the ground.

Fear coursed through her body. If there were two of them, she wouldn't stand a chance. But the grip wasn't demanding like Felix's had been. Once she was steady, the newcomer released her.

He watched Felix warily, then he nudged her shoulder in the slightest warning.

"Run," he said, and threw a handful of dust directly into Felix's face.

Annelise didn't need to be told twice.

The boy followed her down an alley, down the next street, through the park along the riverbank. Time blurred and so did distance. She wasn't sure how long or how far it was that they slowed from an all-out race to something like a cautious trot.

The night no longer felt welcoming, but menacing, full of shadows and lurking enemies. Annelise wanted to be home, in her bed, cuddled up behind Christina. Safe and warm.

With only that thought keeping her sane, she started toward her house.

But then she stopped, turned.

The boy—man? Boy, she decided—was watching her. Her breath caught as she finally looked at him, really looked at him without terror flowing through her veins.

He had tight, glossy brown curls that fell over his forehead, dark eyes and high cheekbones, a generous mouth contrasted by a sharp jaw. He was gangly in that way of boys who were on the cusp of manhood, but she could see the lines of him, where he would grow into his frame.

The moonlight loved him, caressed him.

He was beautiful. There was no other word for it.

"What's your name?" Annelise asked, nearly, but not quite struck dumb at the sight of him.

"Eitan," the boy said. "Eitan Basch."

Chapter 6
CHRISTINA

February 27, 1943

Rose Street was little more than a crooked lane in a historic Jewish district north of the Spree.

As soon as Christina turned onto the street, it became obvious where the intermarried detainees were being held. The Jewish community center was surrounded by Nazis—wearing both SS black and the city's police uniforms.

A truck that looked exactly like those she'd seen that morning had been parked at an angle, its back to the door, so that the guards could shuffle the men inside efficiently.

Christina rushed forward for a glimpse of the detainees' faces, searching, without much hope, for Eitan. Instead, she saw bloody noses, black eyes, tears streaking down the cheeks of the handful of children piled in along with the men.

They would be the sons and daughters of the intermarried couples.

One of the men fell to his knees in front of the officers, hands clasped, begging.

"Take me, but let my daughter go," he cried. His girl hovered at his shoulder, big, wet eyes on the Nazi in front of them, who did nothing but sneer.

"I think I'll take both of you," he said, and brought the butt of his rifle down on the Jewish man's face.

The man crumpled to the ground and the daughter screamed before throwing her body on top of her father's.

Both were hauled away, the man unconscious, the daughter sobbing.

The rest of the detainees averted their gazes. This was life.

Christina backtracked toward the far end of the line of police guarding the community center. After digging her military identification out of her inside coat pocket, Christina went straight up to the youngest-looking guard. "I'm with the Abwehr. I need to know if Eitan Basch is one of the men who has been detained."

The guard's eyes flicked down to her papers. "You need direct orders to be admitted."

Christina bit back a curse. It had been a long shot. The Reich Security Main Office—the agency in charge of the Gestapo and the other law enforcement departments—despised the Abwehr.

"I want a list of your prisoners," Christina demanded, using her most supercilious voice.

"They're not prisoners, Fräulein," the young man said. There were far fewer defectors in the city's police force than the Abwehr, and almost none in the Gestapo, at least from what she could tell. "They're workers reporting for registration."

Christina bit back a grunt of frustration. That would bring scrutiny, and nothing good ever came from scrutiny by the RSHA. Instead, Christina offered a tight smile and quickly turned, though she was careful not to run and draw more attention.

She headed toward the far end of the street and ducked into a café a few storefronts down from the Jewish community center.

There was a seat by the window that offered a view of the detainees, of the police, of the swarming Nazis.

"All morning, the trucks have been rolling in," the woman at the counter called over.

"Coffee," Christina ordered, knowing it was ersatz and not caring. "Have you heard anything about what's going on?"

"Two members of the Tall Guys Club were in here earlier," the woman said, using the well-known nickname for the SS Leibstandarte, an elite Gestapo unit that required their members to be at least six feet tall and blond.

It was the kind of signal Christina always listened for. Had the woman called them by the official name, Christina would have

known which side she was on. It was a shibboleth of sorts. Not obvious enough to get the Gestapo's back up, but clear to anyone paying
attention.

"They didn't talk at all, though," the woman continued. She was
tall and thick, a robust Frau with a dark mustache, serious eyes, and
jowls despite the hard winter. "The men coming off the trucks . . .
they didn't seem too bad."

Christina nodded her thanks as she pictured the man who had
been struck in the face with the butt of a gun. Under Hitler and the
RSHA, *didn't seem too bad* was a low bar.

She tried not to think about the state Eitan would be in.

Was he in there?

He was supposed to be safe.

Christina made a frustrated sound, annoyed with herself. It had
obviously been naive to think being married to a German woman
would be enough protection when Hitler's ultimate goal was to have
Berlin be Judenfrei.

She glanced across the street as the truck pulled away. Off to
round up more human cargo. SS agents scurried like ants in and out
of the building as two Gestapo agents shared a cigarette by the human barricades formed by local police.

Workers reporting for registration. That almost sounded believable,
but so did all of the Nazis' pretty euphemisms. Had Christina been
a regular citizen she might have even bought it—mostly because the
neutered stories were easier to accept than reality.

There was always some grain of truth in the lies. The Jewish
men had likely been told to report to the Bureau of Labor and then
been shipped over to the Rose Street building, which had clearly
been turned into a holding facility.

She had to find a way in; waiting an entire day to see if Eitan
returned home from his factory job was not acceptable. Christina
needed to know if he was in there now.

Because she knew he was. Of course he was.

There was no point in wondering.

In hoping.

As Christina drank her fake coffee and tried to formulate a plan through all the panicked static in her mind, she watched a petite woman approach one of the guards. The two chatted for a minute, and then the guard went inside the building. The woman paced in short, jerky passes until the guard came out and handed her something Christina couldn't see.

Christina took off after the woman immediately. "Excuse me."

The woman whirled, clearly as on edge as Christina, if not more so, her face drained of color despite the cold. She swayed as she stared at Christina, clutching to her chest whatever the guard had handed over.

"My husband is in there," Christina said. "May I ask, what did the guard give you?"

"I told him I need the key to our house and only my husband had it." The woman held out a shaky hand. Sure enough, a gold key rested in the dip of her palm. "I wanted to know if he was there. The rumors going around . . . Well, I couldn't believe them. I thought he was . . ."

Safe. That damn truism again.

"That was brilliant," Christina breathed out, already thinking ahead. She couldn't pull the same stunt, but there were variations on a theme. "Thank you."

"I—" the woman started and then shook her head, a sob cutting off whatever else she was going to say. The tears spilled over onto gaunt cheeks. She was Aryan and so she was far luckier than so many others, but her life must have been hell for the past few years. Intermarried couples lived off severely reduced rations, and it would have been hard for either one of them to find a job. On top of the economic hardships, the societal pressure would have been brutal to bear. Families had disowned their daughters, friends had disavowed their loved ones, matrons went around warning every other resident in apartment buildings that there was an intermarried couple living there and that they should be shunned.

Hitler had made it incredibly easy for Aryan women to divorce their Jewish husbands. And yet, despite the overwhelming pressure to do so, this woman had not.

"I hope your husband is not in there," the woman finished, and then scurried off without waiting for a response.

When Christina returned to the Jewish Center, she had her scarf wrapped around her hair and the collar of her coat turned up. She didn't think anyone guarding the doors would remember her, but she didn't want to take the chance.

In the time she'd been gone, a handful of women had gathered as close as the police would let them to the doors of the building. One woman clutched at a young officer's gloved hands, another was speaking so quickly, so urgently her words blended into nonsense. All of them were looking for information on their husbands.

Slipping in on the edge of the small crowd, Christina called out to the closest guard.

"I need my food ration card," she told him. "My husband has it. Eitan Basch. Please, my children . . ."

The women around her who had heard her request were quick— they shouted names and pleas to match Christina's. The guard rolled his eyes, but then gave a curt nod and disappeared into the Jewish Center. Christina didn't react, but she was shocked that the ploy had worked. If they got their confirmations, they all owed the woman with the key a debt of gratitude.

Twenty minutes passed before the guard returned. He handed Christina and two other women ration cards and then tsked the rest of the group away.

Christina didn't notice, though. All she could do was stare down at the incontrovertible proof that she had failed to keep the one promise she had ever made to Annelise.

AT FIRST THERE were only a handful of women. They had stayed even after they'd received confirmation that their husbands were in the building.

But then more came. And more after that.

By the time evening was creeping in over the skyline, there were at least fifty women crammed into the narrow street.

It made Christina nervous.

This was officially a gathering, and Nazis didn't tolerate gatherings. Even ones that weren't political demonstrations. They were swiftly and oftentimes violently shut down. Men had received death sentences for crowds that were less rowdy than the one Christina was currently standing in.

She wrapped her arms around herself, rocking back on her heels to keep warm. The temperatures were plummeting as the sun slipped away. How many of these women would last through the night?

Was that the plan? To all freeze to death? What good would that do for the men inside?

Christina was exhausted already. She'd been pacing, loitering, scheming since that morning and she hadn't arrived at any actual answers.

All she could think about was Eitan, his sweet face, those beautiful curls that fell over his forehead, his easy smile.

And, of course, Annelise.

Always, Annelise.

What would her sister do in this situation?

Christina glanced around at the women and knew the answer immediately. Annelise would organize them into an actual protest.

Most of the women seemed intent on simply getting information. Perhaps that was why the Nazis hadn't acted yet. There was no undercurrent of dissent, no tension about to snap taut with the wrong word. The wives had bundles of cheese and bread and toiletry kits; in return they were asking for ration cards and house keys and medication information, anything the women could dream up to get the

Nazis to confirm what they didn't want to confirm—that they were holding Jews who had previously been cleared as privileged.

A few adventurous women climbed onto balconies and ledges on the neighboring buildings, but the Nazis quickly realized what was going on and boarded up the windows so no one could see in. Or out.

"They're packed in shoulder to shoulder," one of the women reported when she returned to ground level. "No room to even sit."

An engine roared at the mouth of the street, cutting off any other details, an open-air 4x4 headed toward the crowd with no signs of slowing down. The women were forced to scatter into the alleyway and onto the far sidewalk to avoid being run down.

The men who got out of the vehicle were obviously part of the Tall Guys Club, the last rays of the sun catching on their golden blond hair as they towered above even the most imposing Gestapo agents. They swaggered into the building with a confidence that made Christina sick.

They didn't once look at the women, nor acknowledge the questions hurled in their direction as they disappeared into the community center.

"Pigs," the woman beside Christina said before spitting on the ground.

Christina reined in the instinctive desire to distance herself from the woman, an urge cultivated and nurtured by BDM leaders who had zeroed in on her as a teacher's pet from the start. Their favorite type of girl.

She had never—and would never—think of herself as courageous. She had written off the possibility of that kind of steel spine back in Bonn five years ago. But at some point, with her work smuggling information to the Allies, she'd started to believe that maybe she could be something close to it.

And still she had to fight not to bow and scrape to these men, not to duck her head and passively agree to all their demands.

Outright rebellion was not a part of who she was.

Christina excelled at subterfuge, not confrontation.

But she knew she couldn't leave. Not when Eitan was inside. It seemed plenty of other women had the same thought.

Even as the day deepened into night, more women poured into the narrow street. They didn't group together, not really. Instead, they huddled either in pairs or by themselves, all eyes focused on the building. Their postures warned off anyone interested in talking to them.

The gathering still wasn't a protest.

Yet.

Christina had a feeling their lives hung in the balance of that *yet*.

Chapter 7
EMMY

Even in the best of times, someone would be hard-pressed to find Offenbach am Main charming. It was clearly an industrial hub, warehouses crammed shoulder to shoulder, the sky heavy with soot.

Eventually the factories faded into small cottages, neatly packed into a compact neighborhood right off the river.

"Do you know how to ride a bicycle?" Major Arnold asked Emmy as they turned down one of the streets. This day had been so interminably long that she couldn't remember how many hours she'd been awake.

Emmy stared at the major blankly, already having forgotten his question. All she could think about was if the outline of Eitan's book was visible through her jacket.

"A bicycle," the major repeated, with that half-slant smile of his.

"Yes," Emmy managed, grateful a guilt-induced confession hadn't been what spilled out.

"Miss Cotler will you show you where to go tomorrow, then," he said. "She knows the way to the depot."

Lucy Cotler, her tired brain supplied. The roommate.

The jeep pulled to a stop in front of a house with a white stucco body and a bright orange roof. A fence enclosed a postage-stamp lawn, and two sunny yellow bicycles leaned against the front wall.

When the major shook her hand good night at the door, his thick calluses scratched against her palm.

"Mrs. Clarke, please let me know if ever you have need of anything."

"Thank you." The afternoon had given way to twilight, and there was a quiet coolness in the air that had her shivering, wanting to press in closer to his warmth.

It took a moment to realize they were still holding hands, not shaking them any longer, just . . . lingering.

Emmy yanked her own away, nervously tucking a few loose strands of hair back behind her ear to hide her face from him.

The door swung open.

"Was wondering if you were ever going to make it inside, or if you had decided to set up camp on the stoop," a woman said, a laugh in her voice. She was tall and slim, with dark, curly hair and golden eyes. A generous smile revealed two big bunny teeth and a dimple in the corner of her left cheek. Her bright green trousers were silky and flowed around long legs, cinching in tight at an impossibly narrow waist; her white blouse draped loosely enough to reveal deep collarbones.

The woman placed a hand on her hip, cocked it out to the side, as if enjoying the scrutiny. "Miss Lucy Cotler, at your service. And if we're to be sharing a water closet, you might as well get used to calling me Lucy."

"Mrs. Joseph Clarke," Emmy murmured. Then she shook her head. "Emmy."

"Divine," Lucy said, reaching out for Emmy's bag before pulling her inside. She sent a wink toward Major Arnold, who seemed used to the sight of the movie-star beauty. "I'll take it from here, Major."

Major Arnold gave a shallow bow, his eyes meeting Emmy's. "Good night, Mrs. Clarke."

"I think he would almost be handsome if he smiled," Lucy mused absently as she closed the door. Emmy fought the urge to defend him as handsome already. He wasn't, objectively. She knew that. And saying anything else would draw Lucy's attention to the fact that she'd noticed. Lucy wasn't waiting for a response anyway. "But he's *so* stuffy. All buttoned-up and prim."

Emmy couldn't help herself this time. "He's a historian."

"Hmm," Lucy agreed, her eyes narrowing on Emmy. It made her want to fidget and fix herself up. She hated that she was meeting so many people fresh off travel. "Buttoned-up and prim can work, I suppose. It's fun to muss those ones up."

Emmy blushed, and Lucy laughed, though not unkindly.

"Oh, I'm simply teasing. You'll get used to me, I promise," Lucy said. "Now, let me show you around our luxurious villa."

This was not one of those homes that magically looked larger on the inside. They had a tiny sitting room, a basic galley kitchen, and one bedroom.

"You'll want to watch your elbows when you're doing your hair," Lucy said when they were in the bathroom, and Emmy could see what she meant. The walls were so tight that Emmy wondered if she would be able to turn sideways without her hips pressing against both the sink and the towel rack. "I got too many bruises learning that lesson."

The bedroom had two narrow mattresses, though they both had a side table and got a set of drawers of their own.

"Since you're a married lady I don't suppose I need to come up with a sock on the door system for you," Lucy said, winking.

Emmy twisted her wedding band. This was the reason she'd considered leaving it back in Washington. "My husband died. At Normandy."

It hadn't gotten easier to say with practice or time. The words still cut along the inside of her mouth, jagged and painful.

"Oh, lovey," Lucy murmured, some of the humor dropping out of her expression. She cupped Emmy's cheek in an overly familiar—though comforting—gesture. Emmy was afraid of the platitudes, the *thank-you*s even. She'd gotten plenty of those in the past two years. "Our little nation of widows."

The sentiment seemed harsh, but Emmy found she preferred feeling a tad offended to being weepy, so she nodded.

"I've saved the best for last because I like to test the girls' mettle first," Lucy said, the heavy topic already in the rearview mirror. That's how they'd all survived the past half decade. Tenacity and resilience had been thrust upon all of them, whether they liked it or not. "If you can't take this house at its worst, you don't deserve it at its best."

"I can take it at its worst" was all Emmy could think to say.

"Good girl," Lucy praised, and then took Emmy's shoulder, directing her down the hallway toward the back door.

When they stepped out onto the lawn behind the cottage, Emmy gasped. She hadn't realized they were right on the river.

Or, not quite, but close enough. Their yard sloped down gently to a walking path, which gave way to the riverbanks. In the fading light, the water of the Main was an inky dark mirror, the spring sky a royal blue that deepened into velvet when Emmy lifted her face toward the stars.

"You should see it at sunset," Lucy said. "Stay here."

Emmy didn't even think about arguing. Her bones ached, her soul ached. She wasn't sure she could move if she wanted to.

She was in Germany.

It still didn't feel quite real to her. For years, this was enemy territory, and now she, little Emmy Clarke of Helena, Montana, was standing on the banks of a river deep in the land of monsters.

"Here," Lucy said, nudging Emmy's shoulder. The next thing Emmy knew her arms were full of a blanket, and Lucy was arranging two of their kitchen chairs on a little patch of level earth. She disappeared into the house once more, and Emmy took that as her permission to sit. She wrapped the blanket around her shoulders, and only when she sunk into its warmth did she realize how cold she'd been.

"It's the good stuff," Lucy crooned, waving a bottle of something amber in the air. She slid into the free chair, a second blanket artfully draped around her shoulders, effortlessly graceful. She spilled a swallow of the liquor into her mouth and then grinned at Emmy, holding the bottle out to her. "Welcome to Germany, lovey."

Emmy took a fairly generous gulp, which seemed to delight Lucy.

"You're already coming out ahead of my last roommate," she said, taking the scotch back. "I thought she would be fun. She was from California, after all. I've only ever heard good things about people from California."

"You've never been?"

"New York City, born and raised and settled," Lucy said. "I've been to Vilnius, Lithuania, but never to Los Angeles."

"How long have you been here?" Emmy asked, accepting the bottle once more. She took a moderate sip this time. She wasn't sure when she'd eaten last and she guessed that if she got even a little bit tipsy she'd end up sprawled on the kitchen floor at the end of the night. That wouldn't be quite the first impression she wanted to make.

"Only about two and a half months now," Lucy said. "Since Mr. Poste set up the depot. But I've had a handful of roommates. Some girls are here only for a week or so to observe the work at the depot."

"And what do you do there?" Emmy asked.

"Me? I'm here collecting books for refugee camps," Lucy said. "You've heard of those?"

"Of course." There were millions of displaced Jewish people all over Europe. Emmy thought about those towns Major Arnold had talked about. It wasn't as if any surviving former residents could return to empty buildings and the ghosts of everyone they once knew.

"I sort through those personal collections that no longer have owners," Lucy said, her voice light, but Emmy sensed the deep sorrow that lurked in the spaces between words. "At least they're going somewhere good. I particularly like when we can find Jewish books for the children. I unearthed a well-loved volume of Jewish fairy tales the other day that I'm certain some of the children in the camp will like."

Emmy pictured the rows of crates she'd seen that afternoon. The depot was five floors, and according to Major Arnold there were still plenty of books out there in the wild to bring in and sort through.

All of them stolen in some way or another.

"I like to focus on the positives," Lucy said, shooting Emmy a self-aware look. "Otherwise, I'd be drinking one of these a day." She held up the bottle, and then stared down at the river. "I was in Vilnius right before . . . well, before. At the YIVO institute, as a part of my master's program. Have you heard of it?"

Emmy shook her head, now even more intimidated by this woman. Brains and beauty.

"It's an institute that was created to celebrate Yiddish culture," Lucy said. "I almost wish the Nazis had simply razed it to the ground. But they took all the research instead and studied everything to better figure out how to control and kill us." Lucy laughed, but there was no humor in it, and Emmy wondered how fragile her charming, happy-go-lucky veneer really was. Likely paper-thin.

Ever since the war ended, people forced smiles and laughter and cheer as if they all hadn't just lived through the past five years. This normalcy was what all that sacrifice had been for, right? The other side.

But winning a war came with a price, and Emmy wasn't sure any of them had emerged unscathed. *Our little nation of widows.* It sounded sharper in her memory now than it had only a half hour ago.

She couldn't imagine all the ways she'd bleed if she worked for one of the camps Lucy was talking about. It was hard seeing the books, and knowing what they represented. Seeing the people . . . the ones who had survived, Emmy wasn't sure she was strong enough for that.

"It's lovely that you're bringing them books," Emmy finally said.

"The librarians always understand the importance of books," Lucy said, with a jaunty salute of the bottle. "Life is more than food and water."

"And scotch," Emmy said, taking the liquor once more. "But it certainly doesn't hurt."

Chapter 8
CHRISTINA

February 28, 1943

The white puff of Christina's breath dissolved in the early dawn light.

It was Sunday morning. She had made it through the night.

Some of the women had left, likely to go care for children, or to stomp feeling back into their feet. But the spaces their absences had created had been filled almost immediately.

At first Christina had paced to stay warm, but then she realized the group offered more heat than she could generate on her own.

Most of the women had seemed to come to the same conclusion. They glanced at each other warily but then inched closer until they were pressed to their neighbors, holding each other up, keeping each other awake and alive.

Christina could tell none of them felt comfortable relying on strangers. That vulnerability had been trained out of them, ruthlessly and efficiently. But another instinct had flourished in that darkness—the instinct for survival.

If they had to huddle for warmth, they would, if they liked it or not.

This still wasn't a protest. None of them were raising their fists in the air, there was no edge of violence to the crowd, only confusion and determination. They couldn't leave because their husbands were in that building.

The Nazis had become more agitated as the hours passed, though.

They'd ordered the women to disperse several times.

The wives knew that if they did so, if they left, they'd never see their husbands again. Right now, they were clinging to the idea that as long as they were here, as long as they were asking questions, their husbands' fates might not be sealed.

Why any of them believed that, Christina wasn't sure. But she hadn't left either, so she was as foolish as the rest of them.

"Perhaps it truly is just a registration effort," the woman beside Christina said beneath her breath. It was the lie they were all telling themselves.

"Perhaps," Christina agreed anyway, because she also wanted to believe it. The woman flinched as if she had forgotten she wasn't alone, and then she hurried away.

The anxiety in her expression struck Christina. While Christina gambled with her life daily in her work to thwart the Nazi regime, there was some safety in being seen as Aryan, as working for the Nazis. Her life was shrouded in danger, but it was a different kind. She didn't go about her day thinking she would be spit on or, worse, whipped because she looked at a Nazi wrong.

These women, though, had been living with constant fear for years. That changed a person.

Christina fought the urge to chase after the woman, to reassure her, because of course following a fleeing person was exactly the opposite of the message she wanted to send.

Her attention was soon pulled away, anyway, by a collective gasp that rose from the front of the crowd.

She went up on her tiptoes so she was tall enough to see what had caused the reaction.

Machine guns.

The Gestapo were setting them up behind the chain of twenty or so policemen who stood guard as some kind of human barricade.

Christina didn't gasp, but she wanted to curse. This had only been a matter of time. Quite frankly, she was surprised the Nazis had taken this long to resort to threats of violence and death.

Her eyes strayed to the end of the street.

She could walk away. There was no reason to be here any longer now that she had confirmed Eitan was inside.

He would be deported along with the rest of the men.

What she should concentrate on now was using her contacts to make sure Eitan had the best chance possible of making it out of the camps.

But her feet wouldn't move. Even as her hands trembled and her heart raced and her body yearned to be anywhere but where she was, her feet wouldn't move.

The woman beside her shifted back, but then stopped, her shoulders rounding forward as if she were connected to the community center with a string.

A tall Nazi who had been lurking behind the row of policemen stepped forward. He wore the civilian clothes of the Gestapo and had the hard eyes that always proved her guess correct. The Gestapo weren't quite as omnipresent as some people thought, but their reputation for cruelty, brutality, and ruthlessness was well-earned. She doubted any of them would care much if the streets ran red with the blood of all these women.

"Disperse or we shall shoot." His command carried easily, no one needed the directive repeated.

Silence fell over the crowd.

Again, Christina's eyes darted toward the end of the street. They should run. They should run now.

Annelise wouldn't have run.

Christina wasn't Annelise, but, still, her feet would not budge.

"Disperse," the Nazi barked once more, his face an ugly, violent red. They were so used to obedience, they couldn't handle being ignored without immediately accelerating toward rage. "We will shoot. You have been warned."

A terrified energy crackled through the wives. These women weren't freedom fighters or resistance members or even Annelise's Edelweiss Pirates. They hadn't signed up to be brave. This was just loved ones at a loss for anything else to do.

None of them came prepared to face down machine guns.

She closed her eyes, willing herself to *move*.

But the bullets didn't come. And then they still didn't come.

Christina's focus narrowed in on the Nazi in charge.

He looked like he wanted to take his horsewhip indiscriminately to the crowd, to tear the clothes and then the skin off the backs of these women who weren't listening to him.

He didn't, though.

He hadn't moved, like they hadn't moved.

The panic started to recede, and in the quiet it left behind, Christina was actually able to think.

She looked around, taking stock.

The community center was ideally placed for the Nazis—around the corner from the office of the Gestapo's Jewish desk. There were twenty policemen standing in front of the doors, all of them fully outfitted with weapons. If the Gestapo actually wanted to put a stop to this, they could do so without gunning down hundreds of Aryan women in the streets.

Which meant . . . they were bluffing.

The tight knot in her chest that had made breathing nearly painful relaxed.

"Disperse," the tall Nazi yelled again, but the other women seemed to be coming to the same realization as Christina had.

If they hadn't run from potential bullets, they weren't going to from hollow threats.

This gathering still wasn't a protest . . . but maybe it should be.

What would Annelise do?

Why not use this moment to demand what they wanted? When they had the Nazis bluffing when the Nazis never bluffed.

Her mind raced ahead of her so that she was barely able to keep up with it.

If this was to be a protest, the message would need to be simple and straightforward, and not too political. This couldn't turn into an anti-Nazi protest. Christina didn't want them to enrage the Gestapo, she just wanted what they all wanted.

For the men to be freed.

The woman next to Christina slipped her wedding ring off, cradled it in her palm, and began to pray.

A wife who wanted to see her husband again.

Simple. Straightforward. Not too political.

This was what united all of them and was protecting them from the bullets. The Nazis had been preaching for years that the very best women—the very best of the Fatherland—were Aryan wives. Their own propaganda had created a wall that would shield the women in the street.

She nearly laughed at the poetic justice of it all. But then the nerves caught up to her grand ideas, and for a heartbeat she worried she'd be sick right there on the cobblestones.

She closed her eyes, concentrated on the press of her shoulders against the women on either side of her. They had barely talked, they had barely even acknowledged each other.

But they were in this together. That was the only way they'd win.

Christina pictured Annelise on a summer night in her beloved Seven Mountains.

My greatest wish is for you to realize that sometimes choosing the right thing is more important than whether or not you'll get hurt doing it.

Christina tipped her head back and yelled, "Give us back our husbands."

Not everyone heard, but the women directly around her dropped silent. Some even took half steps away from her so as not to be associated with the troublemaker.

Christina inhaled to fill her lungs. "Give us back our husbands."

The demand rippled over the crowd until it reached the line of Nazis. They shuffled, unsure, as they glanced back at their leader. Christina wasn't entirely certain, but she could almost swear the man's eyes landed on her.

She was just one of many, though. That was their power.

If they could only realize it.

"Give us back our husbands," she cried again, expecting to be the lone person calling out.

But her voice was amplified by a woman a few people over. She gave Christina a tiny, rueful smile, as if to say, *Might as well try*.

The next time they yelled, more joined in. And then more. And then more, until all the women of Rose Street spoke with one voice.

"Give us back our husbands."

Chapter 9
EMMY

April 1946

Emmy tilted her face to the sky as she rode behind Lucy toward the Offenbach Archival Depot. The brisk April wind kissed life back into her cheeks following her night of imbibing.

On this side of the river, the destruction had a different tint to it. In Frankfurt, it was obvious how beautiful the buildings had once been, their facades crafted long before Hitler had even been born. Their collapse was a blow to a culture that had nothing to do with this war.

The warehouses in Offenbach hadn't avoided the raids—likely they had been heavily targeted—but it didn't hurt to see the ruins. There was no history lost here, no heart. These were the carcasses of corporations that fed and fueled the Nazis with motorcars and chemicals and weapons.

"I'm on the top floor, lovey," Lucy said as she stowed her bicycle. "A few days back, we found a cache of documents from the YIVO institute—Yiddish folklore songs, if you can believe our luck—and they need my help authenticating them."

The depot already buzzed with workers sorting through the crates of books and documents, a handful of them photographing ex libris, others packing up boxes that would be shipped out on the next truck. Lucy called out greetings as she headed toward the stairs. She was that type who knew everyone, and whom everyone loved.

Emmy let herself take it all in for a moment. Yesterday, she'd felt the weight of the ghosts this room represented, but now she let herself feel the wonder.

They had won. Hitler had lost.

In the States, that hadn't always felt real, because the war had been so far away. She hadn't had to weave through falling bombs and hide in dank shelters like those who lived in London or Africa or even Frankfurt had had to. The darkness had swallowed up her life, of course, but it had come in the form of a sterile telegram.

Here was tangible proof, though.

Here were Hitler's spoils, and they were being returned to their owners.

Her supervisor Mr. Dernbach turned out to be a portly man with a large handlebar mustache and ink stains on his hands. He had worked closely with the man she was replacing—the man who had fallen ill and was the sole reason she was here, pinch-hitting on an assignment she'd never expected to be given.

"Apologies, Mrs. Clarke, apologies," he said, futilely wiping his fingers on a snow-white handkerchief. Now neither his hands nor his hankie was clean.

"A hazard of the profession," Emmy said, offering up a wry smile.

"Right you are, right you are," he said, before directing her to a workbench. "Now, the Monuments Men get a little prickly about keeping us away from their restitution efforts."

Emmy remembered the flash of anger in Major Arnold's expression, the reason for it. The "prickliness" seemed well-earned.

"Your job will be sorting through the cartons we've hauled over here from that Rosenberg fellow's odious institute. All of those books will be marked with a sticker," he said, pointing out an example of one on a book close to them. The label was white, with two sets of letters Emmy assumed had worked like a Dewey decimal system.

Emmy had done a quick study of the institute in the few days she'd had before being sent overseas. Apparently at the opening, Rosenberg had boasted that it was "now the largest library in the world devoted to Judaism," because of how many research institutes, personal collections, and other books he'd stolen from conquered nations.

"You shouldn't encounter too many books that you shouldn't

be working on. We've already separated out most of the personal collections—especially the valuable ones," Mr. Dernbach said, a particular gleam coming into his eyes, one she recognized from the mirror anytime she discovered an incredible, rare book to acquire. "Yesterday I found a first edition Proust with a dedication from the author himself."

Thanks to art, instead of seeing a single world, our own, we see that world multiply itself..." Emmy thought absently. Her favorite Proust quote.

"What happens to those books when you find them?" Emmy asked.

"Well, that one was stolen as part of Louise Weiss's collection," he said, and then seemed to notice her blank look. "She is a French Jewish woman of some renown, I think it would be safe to say. A champion of women's rights."

He went pink at that. Clearing his throat, he continued. "Her library in Paris was raided in the summer of 1940 along with the collections of many other Parisian Jews. She made it through the war, so we'll be able to return her property to her."

The knot in Emmy's chest released at that knowledge. Her own personal library was small and unimpressive in comparison, and still she would be heartbroken to have it taken from her. Not only taken from her, but *plundered* by the enemy.

"They had a field day in Paris, those bastards," Mr. Dernbach said, seeming lost in his own thoughts now. "More than seven hundred and twenty libraries were raided that summer. Nearly two million books."

The scope of that was nearly unimaginable. She knew the Nazis had looted the museums for priceless artwork, but for some reason, before this mission, she'd never thought they would care about books beyond burning them.

"Well, you'll certainly find some of those in these crates," Mr.

Dernbach said, refocusing on her. "They also swept through Jewish apartments in the city, packing up any books they found along the way."

"But those aren't for us, correct?" Emmy checked.

"No, indeed not," Mr. Dernbach said. "It's inevitable that there will be some crossover. There are just too many books coming from too many places to keep it strictly separate. But if you find anything that belonged to a private Jewish citizen, you should immediately send it over to Poste's local team to process it."

Emmy's cheeks flushed at the thought of the Rilke, now safely tucked away in the cottage. But the fact that she might actually be able to find someone connected to the book, when it would be likely simply sent to a refugee camp otherwise, stayed any guilty confession.

So Emmy simply nodded and let herself be directed to a workstation. At first, the documents and books she worked through met her expectations—official documents, journals, and philosophical writing, along with books clearly used by the Nazi ideologues. But it didn't take long to stumble onto a cache of books that were clearly personal and well-used.

She knew most of them would have to be sent over to Poste's local team, but she let herself flip through them for messages like the one she'd found in the Rilke the day before.

An hour later, she was deep into a copy of Kafka's *The Trial*, the notes in the margins as entertaining as the book itself. She wasn't an expert on handwriting, but she imagined they were done by a girl of maybe fifteen or sixteen.

Next to the classic quote "It's only because of their stupidity that they're able to be so sure of themselves," the girl had scribbled, *Boys!* and then *Nazis!*

Next came a message beside the line: *The books we need are of the kind that act upon us like a misfortune, that makes us suffer like the death of someone we love more than ourselves, that makes us feel as though we were on the verge of suicide, lost in a forest remote from all human habitation.*

What we need, sir, is less of whatever this is. It's too early in the day for such dramatic talk.

Emmy bit her lip against a smile.

The title page had the same *J* as Eitan's book. Scrawled across the top was a message:

Property of Sarah Anne. Do not touch. (That means you, Clara.)

"Mr. Dernbach," Emmy said, half turning on the bench to show the man the book. "This has markings. Will they be able to identify the owner?"

He gave it a cursory glance. "No last name, no country of origin. No way to tell, my dear." He squinted to see the title. "Ah, that's exactly the kind of book you needn't waste time on. You'll learn to identify those personal collections quickly and send them to the Monuments team."

"Of course," Emmy murmured. As she located the correct crate, she imagined two sisters. With the way the warning had been written, Sarah Anne had likely been the older one, Clara the younger. Probably, Sarah Anne had been irritated more often than not with Clara, but Emmy had always envied that kind of relationship.

Emmy rested her fingertip against the *J* marked on the spine.

She had known from her quick research that some of the Rosenberg Institute books were the ones Jewish Germans had to sell to escape from the country back in the thirties. Just because this came from that terrible place didn't necessarily mean that Sarah Anne had been deported to a labor camp.

Perhaps they were both alive, Sarah Anne and Clara.

As gently as if she were handling precious memories, Emmy straightened the haphazard pile of books.

Even if it could never be returned to Sarah Anne, it did help imagining a young refugee receiving the novel, giggling over the notes and finding comfort in them.

Still, lunchtime couldn't come soon enough. When it did, Emmy all but ran from the concrete warehouse, desperate for some space from all those ghosts.

The sun was out, but the breeze off the river chilled the air into something bracing and pleasant after the oppressive mustiness of the depot.

"First day is harder than you would think."

Emmy spun to see Major Arnold leaning against the wall, his weight completely off his bad leg. Like her, he wore a crisply ironed army uniform, the tie tight against his throat, the scars once again peeking out near the collar. *Prim and buttoned-up,* she heard in Lucy's voice, but Major Arnold simply looked well turned out to her.

He held out the pack of cigarettes in his hand. Emmy didn't usually smoke—they'd made Joseph's chest go tight—but she let herself be tempted right now, everything shaky and too brittle.

She leaned in so he could light the cigarette and it was only when she could feel his breath on her cheek that she realized how close it had brought her to him. Once the tip caught, she stepped away as calmly as she could, taking up the space next to him on his good side, her eyes on the river.

"I thought it would be different," she said, an echo of their conversation from the day before as they'd driven through Frankfurt. "I thought I would be able to help shepherd the books home, but that won't be possible, will it?"

"The ones from Rosenberg's institute are some of the most disheartening," the major said. "You're not seeing the victories."

"What do you mean?"

"Rosenberg's catalog, those aren't the easy ones," he said. "If you stumble on a novel owned by a person and not a Nazi, it's unlikely the person made it through the war. But we have other books here. We have wins that are both big and small. In the past month or so, we've shipped out nearly two million pieces of documents or research or novels, all of them making their way back to their country of origin."

"I don't remember you being this optimistic yesterday."

He barked out a startled laugh, and she found that she liked what it did to his face, softening it in places, adding lines in others, the mountains and valleys of his expression deeply carved.

He'd be almost handsome if he smiled.

"I don't believe I've ever been accused of being an optimist," he said.

"You see it as an accusation?" she asked after taking a long drag on the cigarette. It made her jittery but in a way that she could handle. Not like seeing those girls' names had.

"No." He crooked a finger at her to get her to lean in, then whispered, "I *am* an optimist."

Emmy laughed, and once again put space between them. She hadn't been this aware of someone else's body since Joseph and she didn't like what that meant.

"It seems as if it would be hard to be a historian and not be an optimist."

"You think humans bend toward good?" he asked, easily following her line of thinking. "Despite how much we try to hurt each other?"

"I think everything that is burnt down is rebuilt," she said, even though they were standing in the aftermath of hell at the moment. She had to hold on to hope that was true. "We persevere. It's what we do."

"It would be nice if we had to persevere a little less," he said, with the dark dryness of someone who'd studied too many tragedies.

"Are you the devil's advocate, Major Arnold?" Emmy asked, with what she hoped was the right amount of teasing in her tone. "You seem to be arguing against your own self-proclaimed nature."

"'We are all in the gutter but some of us are looking at the stars,'" Major Arnold quoted with a sly smirk that seemed out of character.

Emmy returned it. "I wouldn't have pegged you as an Oscar Wilde aficionado."

"Don't judge a book," Major Arnold chastised.

"Touché." Their eyes locked, held, until Emmy took a breath and pushed off the wall.

"Thank you." She realized she had said that to him more in the past two days than anything else. "For the distraction."

"I am, if nothing else, a good distraction."

On the way home, Emmy asked Lucy, "Do you know Major Arnold well?"

Lucy glanced at her sharply enough that her bike wobbled. "He's Mr. Poste's left-hand man, so he must be smart and competent. They travel all over together, through places that might as well still be war zones, which means he's braver than your average paper pusher."

"Do you know where he was injured?" Emmy hadn't meant to ask, but she couldn't regret doing so, either.

"The rumor is that he was in Italy trying to rescue some Medici manuscripts. There was a land mine, I believe," Lucy said, as they pulled up to their cottage and dismounted. "But you know how rumors are. He's certainly never said anything about them."

"Did the manuscripts survive?" Emmy asked.

Lucy tipped her head back, laughing. "Only a librarian."

Chapter 10
ANNELISE

Winter 1937

For the Pirates, a big December snowfall meant skiing trips to Rehberg. Most of the boys weren't in school and the ones who were didn't mind skipping it. These days it was all Nazi indoctrination anyway.

"The foreman at the Ford factory in Cologne said he won't give me a chance if I don't join up with the HJ," Hans complained. He was sprawled by the window of their tight train car on the way back to Bonn. Annelise kept trying to ignore him, but every time she looked away he kicked out his foot to get her attention.

"Then find another job," Annelise snapped, watching the passing landscape. The snow out in the fields remained untouched and she pictured running through it, dropping to the ground to make shapes with her arms and legs. They had spent three days in the mountains and still she craved the fresh air. More, always.

"As if that's so easy to do," Hans said, but he was mostly drowned out by Stefan and Marta next to him. In their fickle relationship, they were hot again, Marta's legs draped over Stefan's thighs as they crooned one of the German folk songs the Pirates had co-opted as their own. The original was drenched in the Nazis' idea of patriotism, but the Pirates' version was rather risqué.

"Keep it down," Hans hissed. "You want to get us searched?"

Stefan rolled his eyes, but Hans might as well have summoned the guards himself.

The door of their train car slid open, and three uniformed men loomed over them. Annelise caught sight of Felix Hoffmann lingering in the hallway and she burrowed deeper into her scarf. She had managed to avoid any interactions with the man since he'd attacked her two months earlier and she had no interest in changing that now.

The officer who was clearly in charge eyed them all carefully. By now, the Nazis were well aware the Pirates existed and she knew there would have been dispatches from Berlin on how to identify them. They likely emphasized the colorful nature of their clothes, the scarfs and pins, the leather boots and shorts in the summer, the long, untidy hair and general "scruffiness" of the boys. She wondered if the reports mentioned the pocketknives most of them carried tucked into shoes or waistbands.

It helped now that it was winter, so they were bundled in coats. But at least two of the boys wore their skull rings, all of them had long hair, and the very fact that this was a mixed-sex group would give them away if the other things hadn't.

"We heard you singing bündische songs all the way down the car," the man snapped.

"They were songs to praise the Party," Marta said, confident and unruffled. "Sir, surely you can't fault us for that."

The man's eyes narrowed, taking them all in once more. There was nothing illegal about what they were doing, but when had that ever stopped the Nazis?

"Sing it," he said, his hand resting on the whip holstered to his leg. Annelise shivered, imagining the crack of leather against bare flesh. "We would like to hear it."

Some of the Pirates shifted, throwing each other uncomfortable glances. None of them had sung the original song in years and the Nazis wouldn't appreciate the altered lyrics.

Annelise didn't want to stand out, didn't want the Nazis to remember her face. Didn't want Felix Hoffmann's stare on her.

But she didn't want her friends to be arrested, either.

She closed her eyes, pictured Christina getting ready in front of the mirror three mornings ago, singing under her breath.

We are the army of the swastika
Raise the red flags,
Paving the way to freedom.
We want German work.
Paving the way to freedom.

The others joined in and they made it through the entire song, Stefan strumming on his guitar. There were only a few hiccups, ones that could be written off as youth instead of rebellion.

Annelise didn't dare look at the Nazis as the Pirates' voices trailed off. Nor did she look at any of her friends. She felt dirty.

"No more singing," the officer decreed before turning on his heel. The other men trailed after him obediently.

"I told you," Hans said, and Stefan kicked him in the shin.

Hans pouted in the corner the rest of the way back, and the other Pirates were equally quiet. A year ago, they would have laughed and teased each other over the close call. That had been a different time, a different atmosphere. They couldn't laugh the encounters away any longer. Each of them had watched a Nazi whip the skin off the back of someone in the street for a minor offense. They'd all heard the dark rumors about detention camps and the Gestapo's EL-DE Haus in Cologne where they tortured information out of their detainees.

Their goodbyes once they reached the train station were subdued. Marta slipped her arm through Annelise's and they walked in silence until they had to part ways.

"I don't like how that Nazi looked at you," Marta said, before she turned down her street. "Like he wants to eat you up."

Annelise didn't need to ask of whom she was speaking. "Wolves should be scared of me."

But she couldn't muster up a cheeky grin like she had in the summer and neither could Marta, who simply waved and trudged off toward home.

Before Annelise could get far, she caught sight of movement.

A flash of a dark jacket and then nothing.

She didn't think. Didn't question the instinct to follow.

When she rounded the corner where the person had fled, she saw broad shoulders and dark curls.

"Stop," she called, when she was close enough not to draw the attention of any patrolling HJ.

The man's steps faltered, but he didn't turn around.

Annelise decided to take a chance. "Eitan?"

He paused.

"Eitan Basch?" she asked, creeping closer. He shifted, his body half turning toward her, but not his face.

"Are you following me?" Annelise didn't want it to sound like an accusation. She didn't think it should be. She knew the stare of a hunter, had felt it with Felix, had begun to feel it with Hans. This didn't seem like that.

But the question got him to turn toward her fully.

Their brief meeting had been two months ago. She had thought she had mis-remembered him, had gilded her memory of him gold. But he looked even more like a Botticelli painting than she'd remembered. Soft and pretty with delicate features and a mop of rich, dark hair that seemed to absorb the night around them.

"I don't mean you any harm," he said, his voice gentle.

"I never said you did."

His eyes narrowed on the empty space behind her—she glanced over her shoulder to confirm no one had come into the alley after them. "He followed you. From the train station."

Annelise took a half step back, startled. "Felix?"

"Once he saw you were walking with the other girl, he went away," Eitan said, staring at the ground now. "I was on my way home from work. I'm not . . . I'm not following you. I wanted to make sure he would leave you alone."

"Thank you," she said, to stop the apologetic words tumbling between them. She chewed on her inner cheek, searching for something to ask him. Not wanting him to run away from her yet like he had two months ago. "Where do you work?"

He looked up, finally. "A factory."

"Only curious." When he didn't offer anything further, she reminded him, "You told me your name."

That signaled trust these days and they both knew it.

"You don't remember meeting me before, do you?" he asked, then made a face. "Before that night with the Nazi."

That made her pause.

"I work in the same factory as your mother," he said. "May Day, two years ago, there was a—"

"Picnic," Annelise finished for him, desperately searching blurry memories. She had been angry at Christina, she knew that. They had made up, of course, by a quiet little pond away from the festivities.

"A picnic," Eitan echoed. "You gave me a dandelion. Told me to make a wish."

She was furious with her past self for not making more careful note of him.

He grinned and . . . it clicked. Where other details had gone fuzzy, she remembered his smile.

"My mother had been trying out her skills with scissors," he said, running a hand through curls that would have been criminal to cut short.

"I know you," she said quietly, shocked by how true the words felt. She clarified, "I remember you."

"Yes, well," he said as he shifted back, shoving his hands in his pockets. "Be careful. You have an admirer who doesn't seem to want to take no for an answer." He paused, tilted his head. "Unless you want—"

"No," she interrupted with a near shout. Quieter, she repeated, "No."

A corner of his mouth ticked up. "Well. Then you may want to walk with a friend if you go anywhere at night."

"I can take care of myself." Proud, stubborn, even though they both knew she was in danger.

Eitan ducked his head, shot her a look from beneath lowered lashes. "I hope you don't have to."

And then he melted into the shadows.

Just before his silhouette disappeared, she cried out for him to stop. "What was the wish? Two years ago, with the dandelion."

"Now, if I told you that, there'd be no hope of it coming true, would there?"

Annelise pressed her lips together, knowing he was gone even as the words reached her.

When she got home, the house was dark, everyone asleep. Or out, more likely, in her brother's case. Though with Anders she didn't know and didn't care. She couldn't stand the sight of him these days in his Wehrmacht uniform, so neat and trim and following the regulations to a T.

She supposed it was easier to feel hope about Christina because she was so young. Anders was a grown man who was making his decisions with a clear head.

Annelise let herself in, and then slunk up the stairs. Her parents had stopped asking too much about her plans. In their eyes, she was an adult, and they'd done their job of raising her. Briefly, she wondered if Marta would want to find an apartment together. They would need to get jobs first, of course, but could it be very hard?

Her bedroom door had been left open, so Annelise easily crept inside, the lump on the mattress dear and sweet after a few days away. They were still fighting like wet cats more often than not, but Annelise wanted nothing more than to curl up next to her sister and tell her about the pretty boy she'd met.

Christina made some kind of sleepy, upset noise, but Annelise shushed her.

And she thought about that picnic where she had met Eitan.

Christina had worn Annelise's dress without her permission, the pretty blue one with the white flowers. Their mother hadn't had the energy or inclination to intervene.

Now, Annelise wouldn't have minded, but two years ago she'd been at the age where it had felt like the end of the world, Christina always copying her and stealing her clothes and tagging along behind everywhere Annelise went.

That afternoon seemed to be the first time Christina had actually realized it.

She'd brought Annelise a large slice of her favorite chocolate cake as a white flag.

I want to be like you, Christina had admitted. *Everyone loves you and you don't even notice.* She'd paused. *I love you and you hate that I do.*

That's not true. But why do you have to do everything I do?

Christina had stared out into the pond for a long time before finally admitting, *I don't know how to be myself and have people like me.*

Annelise had sighed and wrapped an arm around her shoulders. *You're my favorite person, Christina.*

But . . . why?

Because you bring me cake even when I'm mad at you, Annelise had said, not bothering with the thousand other reasons she adored her sister. *You get me the piece with the most icing even though you think it's disgusting.*

It'll make your stomach hurt.

Annelise had grinned. *Your love is quiet and sure and I never have to doubt it. You just need to find out who* you *are instead of who I am.*

Of course, Annelise could see now what she hadn't been able to predict then. After that day, Christina had thrown herself into the BDM like it had been the answer—*find out who you are.* She'd started earning badges and honors, crafting in her spare time, running and winning races and organizing charity teas.

Christina had never truly figured out who she was. She'd patterned herself after Annelise and when that had no longer been an option, she found a rule book to tell her exactly how to act to fit in and be liked. The BDM was perfectly tailored to convert girls like Christina, who didn't have a strong family life, nor a strong sense of self. With the Nazis, Christina had gotten what she'd always craved most in life and had always struggled to earn. Approval.

That might be why Annelise could still hold love in her heart for Christina despite how much she hated everything her sister believed. There was guilt and pity and fear all tangled up in her chest, threaded through with affection and duty.

She never wanted to have to choose to let her sister go, but she feared she might have to someday soon if she couldn't change Christina's views. What would it be like? Being on different sides of a war? Knowing her sister had chosen evil over her?

Annelise sighed. She didn't know. All she did know was that the picnic had been the last time her sister had brought her a piece of cake.

Christina snuffled and then settled, and Annelise kissed the crown of her head. Pushing the thoughts away for now.

Instead, she thought about Botticelli paintings and dandelions.

And she thought about wishes.

Chapter II
CHRISTINA

February 28, 1943

T hat was brave of you."

Still unsteady from the decision to help shift this gathering into a protest, Christina huffed out a disbelieving breath and turned to the woman who had spoken.

Her world tipped sideways. The woman was beautiful, with soft, sunset-copper curls, eyes that were some impossible combination of blue and green, and freckles that covered more of her skin than not. Her pert, upturned nose seemed out of place with her bee-stung lips, but somehow all her features worked together to hit Christina low in the belly.

She blamed that for why she blurted out, "I'm not brave."

"It looks like you are from where I'm standing," the woman said, her voice husky. Without conscious thought, Christina's eyes dropped to the woman's left hand and caught sight of the gold band there.

"Appearances can be deceiving," Christina said. "Especially here and now."

The woman studied her for a moment, a soft bubble of privacy forming around them as the chant Christina had started continued to rise into a crescendo. *Give us back our husbands.*

"I'm Lisbeth."

It was clever of her not to give a full name. Privacy over propriety. "Christina."

"You were scared," Lisbeth said, the simple statement stripping away Christina's carefully constructed facade. "Yet you sparked this anyway."

"They were bluffing with the guns," Christina said, not sure why she was arguing the point. "You see, it wasn't bravery but calculation."

"It was still a risk," Lisbeth said, lifting one shoulder. "One you didn't need to take."

"We're all taking a risk here." The implied compliment itched at Christina's skin, and she looked away from those bright eyes that saw all the wrong parts of her. Or, saw the right parts and misinterpreted them. "We need to keep everyone on that one message, I think."

"Why?"

"If we're going to accomplish anything beyond confirming our husbands are inside that building, we need to be clever about it." It felt good finally saying all the thoughts that had been bumping against the inside of her head out loud to someone she knew she could trust because she was in the same situation as Christina. The relief of doing so loosened her tongue even further. "Just standing here is doing nothing but guaranteeing a few of us will lose some toes."

"But we didn't come here for a protest."

"Yes, but then why not leave?" There had to be something keeping these women here even if they couldn't admit it to themselves yet. Something beyond that tether you felt to a loved one. "Why aren't we leaving?"

"It sounds like you don't know how to answer that yourself," Lisbeth pointed out, and she was right, of course.

"I keep thinking that they can't ignore us when we're standing right here, so many of us," Christina said, her eyes darting over the crowd. "So why not use that to ask for what we want?"

"Our husbands."

"Exactly," Christina said. She'd seen enough propaganda from both sides to know what they needed to do. "It's crucial that the narrative is just right. We are women who are loyal to our husbands, nothing more. We don't hate the Nazis; we simply want our husbands back. We can't make this political."

"That's all well and good," Lisbeth said. "But you can't control a crowd no matter how pure your intentions. How do you intend to keep the ocean from changing tides?"

She had a point. One of the reasons the Nazis hadn't acted yet was because this crowd wasn't a protest. That would help them avoid the wrath of the Gestapo, but it also came with downsides. They weren't a cohesive group and no one had an incentive to listen to anyone else's suggestions. Hell, Christina had even scared that other woman away with one kind word.

They didn't see each other as allies yet. But maybe they could.

"What if we spread the word?" Christina said. "What if we talk to each other?"

The suggestion shouldn't sound radical, but considering they'd been trained to do the exact opposite for the past decade, it hung in the space between them as if Christina had said they take up their own weapons.

"They won't want to talk to us," Lisbeth said, quietly. Her attention was on their closest neighbors who had picked up the chant but still were closed off, refusing to look anywhere but at the community center's doors.

She wasn't wrong. Christina tried to remember how Annelise used to be able to gently nudge anyone into a conversation, even their shyest cousin or the quiet widower who'd lived down the block from them and refused to say a word to most people after his wife had died.

What was that magic? Christina didn't have any of it, that was for sure.

But she had a plan. She could also sense a confusion, a desperation, in these women. Even if they didn't want to be thought of as a group, they wanted to be shown what to do. That's why they'd picked up the chant so quickly.

Christina looked around only to meet the eyes of the woman who had joined in almost immediately. She was watching Christina now as if waiting for instructions.

"We concentrate on the women already participating," Christina said. "They'll do the work of convincing anyone who's remaining quiet."

"Clever," Lisbeth said. "It'll be faster if we separate and conquer."

Of course, she was right, but Christina didn't want to lose her in the crowd.

Lisbeth read the hesitation on Christina's face for what it was. "Meet back here?"

Christina nodded, just one jerk of her head so as not to give away her relief that they would find each other again.

"Oh," Lisbeth said, turning back from where she'd been about to slip into the sea of women. "I do hate the Nazis. So we're clear."

On paper, Christina worked for the Abwehr. She had earned all her badges in the BDM. She dressed in pretty silk and went to dinner with handsome Wehrmacht officers where she drank champagne no one else in Germany could afford.

On paper, she *was* a Nazi.

She tried to smile reassuringly. "As do I."

NOT ALL OF the women packed into Rosenstrasse cared to listen to Christina, but the ones who did nodded in agreement.

"Give us back our husbands," they cried as she moved on to the next group and the next group. There were families here, even some brothers and fathers among the wives. There were friends who were clearly keeping each other upright.

The Gestapo relied on neighbors tattling on neighbors. It was the only way they could monitor so many people with limited resources. The mentality had been described to her over drinks one evening with an insufferably smug Wehrmacht officer. The panopticon, it was called. Some philosopher had created the thought experiment—that a prison should be built around a single guard tower. The detainees would never know if the guard was looking at them and so they would act, always, as if they were being watched.

People rarely chatted with strangers, rarely even talked to anyone they didn't know well.

There was something important, though, about that kind of connection, about seeing the people around you as real people, with names and faces and a family who loved them. It was powerful, and the Nazis liked to control anything that held power.

It took Christina two hours to work her way back to the front. She found Lisbeth holding court in front of a half circle of young women, who were all listening and nodding.

A cloud shifted above them and Christina paused nearly mid-step, caught by the way the early morning light sunk into Lisbeth's burnished curls. The hummingbird-quick movements of her delicate hands drew attention to the face that had so tipped Christina's world sideways.

In Bonn, she hadn't been able to put a name to *this*, and then she'd come to Berlin where once upon a time, there had been cabarets and magazines and films all for people like her.

Maybe had she been born ten years earlier she would better understand this simmer in her belly. But now she just knew she had to keep it hidden.

Lisbeth must have felt the weight of Christina's stare, because she glanced up suddenly, their eyes finding each other even across the crowd. Lisbeth's smile faded, her head cocking to one side, like there was something on Christina's face she was trying to interpret.

Christina swayed, off-balance, praying there really wasn't anything there for Lisbeth to read. Once upon a time was a different world from this one where she would be arrested should anyone find out this particular secret.

But as Christina considered fleeing, Lisbeth's smile returned.

When Christina made it over to the half circle of women, she got a full round of names that she didn't bother memorizing. The only one who stood out to her was Ingrid—a woman who, at first glance, looked about sixteen and was heavily pregnant. On closer inspection, Christina could see the lines at the corners of her eyes and placed her in her early thirties instead.

"Ingrid believes her husband, Nathan, is in there," Lisbeth said, wrapping an arm around Ingrid's shoulders as the other women drifted away.

"But not sure?" Christina asked, and Ingrid nodded, chewing on her lip. "Go ask for his ration card from one of the guards. They've been confirming the detainees that way."

Her eyes slipped to Lisbeth. "You could do it, too."

"I know my husband's in there," Lisbeth said, her voice breaking at *husband*. Christina had to look away, an uncomfortable tightness in her chest at her obvious distress. "But I can go with you, Ingrid, if you'd like?"

Ingrid took Lisbeth's hand and they wove through the bodies toward one of the younger-looking guards.

They didn't make it.

A woman with wild hair and wild eyes barreled past them, heading for the policemen. Ingrid stumbled, went down, and Lisbeth was immediately by her side, hands on her belly as if she could feel the baby to make sure it was unharmed.

Christina tore her attention off the pair and instead concentrated on the disruption. She had spent the past two hours trying to control the crowd, and here was a grenade waiting to send them all to hell.

The woman fell to her knees in front of one of the younger policemen. The color had drained completely out of his face and his hands trembled enough that the machine gun he'd been resting them on shook.

"Murderer," the woman sobbed, her voice otherworldly. Broken and desperate, the kind of cry that crawled inside you and wrapped your organs in barbed wire. "Murderer."

The policeman shifted his weight, his eyes darting to the Gestapo agents who hovered like the vultures they were. No one moved.

The woman clearly didn't pose a threat, but there was a crowd of hundreds watching.

Christina studied the policeman closely, her attention flitting between the trigger and his face. He was shaken, not because of the potential for this whole crowd to go up in flames, but because of the accusation itself. When the woman hurled it at him again, he flinched, shaking his head in denial.

No one saw themselves as a monster. Then someone might hold a mirror up and say, *Look, this is a monster.*

And in that moment a person's life could change.

"Murderer, murderer, murderer."

The policeman's expression hardened.

No one saw themselves as a monster.

Sometimes when someone held a mirror up, it was easier to blame them for doing so than to look the monster in the eye.

"Murderer."

Christina felt the brand against her own skin and saw herself in the policeman's mirror.

The women that could hear were nodding now, surging forward, their anger and fear transmuting into action as Christina had worried.

Stay on message, stay on message, she willed them.

"Murderer," someone beside her murmured. It carried to the next person. "Murderer."

No, no, no, no.

This wouldn't get the men freed, it would just get the women killed alongside them.

Christina darted forward, past Ingrid and Lisbeth, who were both back on their feet.

Crouching, she lifted the broken woman by her armpits and, with strength she wasn't aware she had, pushed her toward the anonymity of the crowd. The woman was swallowed up in seconds, and Christina had to hope that someone would take her out of there, away from the gathering.

Christina tucked her hands in front of herself, eyes downcast, rounding her shoulders. "She's not well, please forgive her."

There was silence at her back, silence at her front.

The policeman was no longer pale, she realized when she glanced up. Red splotches covered his neck, his face. He was embarrassed and humiliated, and there was nothing more dangerous than those emotions in a man. Not even rage came close.

His arm twitched as if he were going to raise his pistol, but before he could, a voice finally broke the taut hush behind her.

"Give us back our husbands."

It was Lisbeth. Christina could already recognize that husky tone. In the next second, ten more women joined in, then twenty, then fifty. Soon it seemed like everyone packed into Rose Street was once again speaking with one voice.

One message.

Give us back our husbands.

While the policeman was distracted by the sudden roar, Christina edged backward, but some prickle on her neck had her scanning the shadows behind him.

It was then she noticed the tall Nazi from earlier, the one who'd given the initial command to scatter. The one they'd all ignored.

And even from the distance, she could tell he was watching her.

By the afternoon, the crowd packed into Rose Street had to be more than two hundred women.

Ingrid, Christina, and Lisbeth were still camped out in the front, though Christina ducked her head every time the tall Nazi walked by. Right now, the Nazis would be desperate to find a leader for this protest. Punish the leader and the group would fall apart—that was always their mentality.

Around midday, Lisbeth disappeared for ten minutes and then reemerged from the sea of bodies bearing chunks of brown bread and a little bit of cheese.

"The café on the corner is friendly to us," Lisbeth said, ripping off a piece for Ingrid and then Christina.

Christina waited for Ingrid to finish her slice before pressing her own into the pregnant woman's hands. Ingrid tried to protest, but Christina wasn't interested in hearing it.

When she looked up, she found Lisbeth's attention on her. Heat bloomed beneath her skin and she quickly glanced away. Christina had an uncomfortable feeling that she was giving Lisbeth the impression that she was a far better person than she was.

"Give us back our husbands."

For the past few hours, the chant had rippled through the crowd like a wave through a lake, never settling, forever ebbing and flowing.

"Will this actually work?" Ingrid asked. Christina had to keep reminding herself the woman wasn't a girl. She looked so sweet, all big blue eyes and earnestness.

Christina didn't want to disappoint her with what she feared was the truth, so she pretended she hadn't heard.

Forever the coward.

"There are so many of us." Lisbeth filled the silence that followed the question. "They *have* to listen."

That wasn't true at all, but Christina held her tongue. Had they been men, had they been the Jewish wives of these detainees instead of the Aryan ones, had they been anything but good German girls showing up en masse, they already would have been bleeding out in the street from machine gun wounds.

Who they were gave them some protection, but their days—if not hours—were numbered. How long could this last? Word of the protest had to already be leaking out of the city; it would only be a matter of time until the Allies caught wind of it and had a field day with the information. That didn't give the wives leverage, it gave them a ticking clock over their heads. Nazis didn't care about what the Allies thought, they cared about what Germans thought. That's where the calculation would lie.

Homefront morale.

"Christina?" Ingrid whispered.

"What?" Christina snapped, too anxious to temper her tone. Ingrid flinched and shook her head. But it was the quick flash of disappointment on Lisbeth's face that had Christina softening her voice. "What is it?"

"Do you think this will work?" Ingrid asked, tentative now in a way she hadn't been before. Christina hated herself, though that wasn't much different than every other day in her life. "Do you think we can actually get them free?"

Lisbeth was watching her and Christina wished the other woman wasn't there. What could she say to make Ingrid feel better? This already stretched credulity. Weren't they all told that standing up to the Nazis meant certain death? Wasn't that why they all obeyed their masters?

Yet it had been twenty-four hours since the women had started gathering, and they were still alive.

"After Stalingrad, the Nazis can't afford to slaughter us," Christina finally said. *Calculation not bravery.* She had never pretended to be courageous. But she *was* clever. "We need to stay strong. They won't be able to ignore us forever."

"Then that's what we'll do," Ingrid said, jaw clenched in determination. For once, she looked her age, but in a way that made her all the lovelier. There were years of hardship there in the wrinkles at the corners of her eyes that Christina hadn't seen before. Ingrid raised her fist and cried out, "Give us back our husbands."

Lisbeth still watched Christina with enough of a smile that her dimple winked into life. Christina swallowed and looked away. She decided to use that moment to seek out the water closet in the café, and found herself waiting in line with nearly a dozen other women. She sent the owner a look of gratitude and got a smile and shrug in return.

When she made her way back to the crowd, she easily caught sight of Lisbeth's copper-sunset curls from a distance.

Ingrid was missing, though.

"I convinced her to go sit at the café. I'm surprised you didn't see her," Lisbeth said.

Christina wasn't. The crowd had grown so large they could lose themselves in it.

She was about to reply, but she was cut off when Lisbeth's palm pressed into hers. Christina stilled completely, terrified to break the moment, not sure it was even happening.

"I popped back to my apartment. It's quite close. And . . . I brought you this, in case you want to avoid any questions," Lisbeth said, and the words didn't make sense until Christina felt the cool metal against her skin. "Ingrid was curious."

Lisbeth pulled her hand back, and Christina glanced down.

Nestled in the dip of her palm was a smooth, gold wedding band.

Lisbeth met her eyes even as she opened her mouth to yell, "Give us back our husbands."

Chapter 12

EMMY

April 1946

O n Emmy's first day off work from the depot, Major Arnold showed up at her door in his open-air jeep.

"I have an errand today that I could use your help with," he said, somewhat stiffly.

Emmy didn't even need to think about her answer. She simply turned and grabbed her coat. Then she paused. He was wearing his uniform.

"Do I need to change?" she asked.

His gaze swept down her body. She wasn't wearing anything fancy—just her practical, black wide-legged trousers paired with a red blouse that tucked into the waistband. Still, she was very aware that this was the first time he was seeing her in civilian clothes.

There was nothing in his expression when he met her eyes once more, almost as if he was hiding a reaction. She tried not to fidget.

"You'll be fine," he assured her.

"Do you ever take a weekend?" she asked as they drove over the bridge to Frankfurt.

That half-slant smile. "I'm looking forward to this particular errand."

Which wasn't quite an answer.

"And that errand is . . . ?"

"Ah, yes." Major Arnold shot her a look. "I've been chasing down a Nazi bookseller who made quite a pretty profit in connecting German collectors with looted books during the war years."

Emmy swallowed the unprofessional epithets that sat on her tongue. "Chasing down?"

"So far, he's been able to elude us," he said. "We know where he is, but we haven't had enough proof to do anything about it."

"But now you do?" Emmy asked.

"That may depend on you."

"How so?"

"This man is trying to reestablish himself as a reputable dealer but won't communicate with any American men for fear of entrapment," Major Arnold said. "We have been writing to him as a wealthy American woman who was sympathetic to the Nazis' cause."

When Emmy didn't say anything, Major Arnold glanced over at her. "All I need is confirmation that he has a particular volume that was part of the French Rothschild library before the Nazis looted the collection. That's enough proof for us to search his establishment for other war spoils."

The Rothschild library would have held untold treasures. It was legend within the book world, and since she'd come to Germany, Mr. Dernbach had dropped a reference to the collection at least once per conversation.

"Ask to see the book and that's all?" Emmy clarified.

"I'll be watching from outside." Major Arnold held out a pretty blue scarf. "Take this off if the book is authentic. You won't be in a moment of danger."

She smiled at that. "I'm not concerned, Major, but thank you."

Curiosity flicked into his expression, but he snuffed it out. "This will be a first edition of Jonathan Swift's *Gulliver's Travels*."

"That's helpful," Emmy murmured.

"Why's that?"

"It's unique as far as first editions go." Emmy had even held one before, during her studies in Boston, so she knew what specifically to look for.

"It seems I picked the right person to help us." He sounded impressed and she blushed at her own pleasure in that.

They were in Frankfurt now, and navigating the destruction took most of his attention. She didn't speak again until he made it through the main square.

"I find it galling that there are Nazis who are going about their lives without being punished," Emmy said. "The trials are supposed to restore some sense of justice in the world, but so many low-level party members are going to get away with their crimes."

For once she didn't get that half smile, but a full, wolfish grin as he said, "But not today."

The Nazi bookseller's store could have passed for any ordinary shop. It was housed in a quaint and narrow building on a street that had probably once been bustling with Germans out buying trinkets and bread and new clothes. There were a few bullet holes in the brick, but for the most part it had avoided major damage. The bad seeds always seemed to skate through life that way.

Major Arnold had parked the jeep a few blocks over so as not to give away their game before it had even begun. Emmy fussed with her hair as she left the major behind and headed toward the storefront. She doubted she looked like someone who could afford a first edition Jonathan Swift, but oftentimes confidence was enough to carry the day.

A bell tinkled overhead as she stepped into the cool, dark room. At first glance, it was like any other bookstore in the world, with rich mahogany shelves and the lovely musty smell that came with paper and glue and bindings.

But on closer inspection there were empty spaces where books should have been. Some were on display, but they were arranged in a way to make it look like stock wasn't low when it clearly was.

Emmy supposed this seller wasn't making his living off the novels in the front, though.

The owner stood behind an elaborate, glass-topped counter, watching her through half spectacles. He was unusually tall, with sunken eyes and a protruding forehead. His skin seemed paper-thin and pale so that she could see the blood running in his veins.

He introduced himself as Adolph Becker. She gave him the name Major Arnold had told her to use—Mrs. Julia Johnson of Massachusetts. Widow.

"I believe you have a book for me," Emmy said, once the pleasantries were out of the way.

He stared at her for a long moment and she tried to school her expression to look both innocent and impatient. Excited, but not too excited. It must have worked, because he handed her a pair of silk gloves and set out a manuscript holder.

Then he disappeared toward the back of the shop. Emmy took a few calming breaths. This was the easy part. Major Arnold expected the authentication to go smoothly—especially after the seller saw Emmy, who didn't look at all like an army officer.

Becker returned cradling a box. A few minutes of fiddling and then the novel was properly displayed in front of her.

Everything around Emmy went silent. It had always been this way for her, the awe every time. First editions carried so much life with them. They had been held and tended and read for hundreds of years, each of their owners imbuing something of themselves in the spine and covers.

But she hadn't earned her spot on the Library of Congress's acquisitions team through good luck. She knew what she was doing here.

The title page was correct. The first editions of *Gulliver's Travels* had been titled *Travels into Several Remote Nations of the World*, and Lemuel Gulliver had been credited as the author.

Emmy continued to work in silence, checking the publisher's information, the copyright dates, everything she looked for when determining the authenticity of a book. For this particular manuscript there were also a few other requirements—including an authorial portrait of Swift as Gulliver.

She smiled idly at a coffee stain on one of the inside pages, another sign of life, a silent conversation.

Then she paused.

"The maps are wrong," she said, without thinking it through. They should show Swift's fantastical lands superimposed onto actual maps. The ones in Becker's book were nonsense.

Becker's eyebrows rose, and the corners of his lips twitched. "You can never be too careful, you understand."

So it had been a test, one a basic army officer pulled in off the street would have failed.

"I don't enjoy my time being wasted." The truth lent authenticity to her scowl.

"Forgive me, madam," Becker said, his tone obsequious now. "There are too many unscrupulous people these days."

Emmy wanted to say that the unscrupulous person here was standing behind the counter. Instead, she gave a little pout of understanding and then went through the entire process again with the real first edition.

When she got to the maps the second time, she took off the scarf.

Everything moved quickly once Emmy declared the first edition authentic. Becker had a secret storeroom full of valuable, looted books, and Major Arnold swore the man would be charged with something beyond a hefty fine.

They spent most of their day at the store, sorting through the hoarded treasure, Emmy all but lost in her own world for hours at a time.

"Tell me more about how the looting worked," Emmy said, as they drove back toward Offenbach. The sun was setting now, and Emmy closed her tired eyes, basking in its lingering warmth.

"Rosenberg was instrumental in all of it," Major Arnold said, in a historian lecture voice that she found a little too appealing. She imagined him in front of a classroom and thought he might be good at that. He was kind and patient and clearly empathetic.

"There were two competing factions for books within the Third Reich hierarchy," he continued. "Between the Reich Security Main Office—or RSHA as everyone calls it in Germany—and Rosenberg's Einsatzstab Reichsleiter Rosenberg force."

"That's a mouthful."

"ERR for short," the major said. "What's important to understand is Rosenberg was an ideologue. Others in the upper echelon were doing it for power or fame or because they were sadistic basta— Apologies."

"Major Arnold, I'm not sure there's a curse word you could dream up that I haven't heard," Emmy said.

"I *was* in the army, you know. We could get creative."

That was cute. "Have you ever been to Montana?"

"No, have you?" he asked, sounding genuinely curious.

She waved that tangent away. "There was a war within the Reich. The RSHA was the Gestapo, correct?"

Major Arnold looked like he wanted to press the point about her past, but gave in. "It was the umbrella agency that the Gestapo reported to. They had something called Office VII, which was the department for Ideological Research and Evaluation. Both Office VII and Rosenberg wanted the plundered books to, well, there's no other way . . . they wanted to study the Jewish culture."

She thought about what Lucy had said. "To kill them."

"That. But also . . ." Major Arnold's mouth was tight, his voice grim. He glanced at her as if unsure if he should keep going. She both hoped he would and hoped he wouldn't. "Rosenberg said that he knew men in the future would look back and possibly criticize the actions the Nazis had taken. He wanted to make sure they had an accurate account of 'the enemy' so that they would understand what had to be done."

Nausea struck, swift and sudden. "I hope he hangs."

"He will." Major Arnold sounded confident enough that some of the tension bled out of Emmy's shoulders.

"So there was a war . . . ," Emmy prompted again.

"Rosenberg made an ally of Göring." The major slipped smoothly back into his lecture voice. "And with Göring came the might of the Wehrmacht. Göring got all the priceless artwork he wanted—which Rosenberg had no interest in—and Rosenberg got soldiers and transportation as he looted his way through libraries and research institutes in Eastern Europe."

"So the ERR didn't simply focus on books?" Emmy asked. "It plundered artwork, as well?"

"Yes. Rosenberg knew most of the men in Hitler's inner circle coveted the masterpieces, as well, so they were his currency," the major said. "But for him their value didn't come close to books. History is written by the victors, they say."

"Rewritten, too," Emmy murmured. "It tracks back to the book burnings, doesn't it? They've always wanted to dictate what voices were allowed to speak. Whose stories were allowed to be told."

"Precisely. Rosenberg believed that he could determine what everyone remembered about the Jewish people, could control what future generations thought," he said. "He saw books as the most powerful weapon at their disposal. And they were all there for the taking, overlooked by most of the other top Nazis."

"An ideologue," Emmy repeated. "A true believer."

"It's interesting, isn't it?" he asked. "Hitler wanted land, Göring art, Himmler bodies to damage. Rosenberg? He knew the real power lay in books."

Chapter 13

ANNELISE

Winter 1938

The leaflets padded the space between Annelise's rib cage and her coat, and she kept her arms crossed over her body so they didn't spill out onto the ground.

That would be a disaster considering what was printed on the paper. She'd had too many close calls with the Nazis in recent months; if they found her standing among a pile of resistance materials they would ship her to EL-DE Haus without even asking questions first.

Something had shifted in the past six months with the Pirates. In the summer she had been thinking that they could barely call themselves anything but a hiking youth group based on outdoor pursuits. Now they were plotting acts of resistance several times a week.

The Pirates took turns distributing the pamphlets, not wanting to draw attention to any one person. They also switched the spots where they left them, both for wider reach and so as not to create a traceable pattern for the Nazis to predict.

The city's Catholic basilica towered over her now, and Annelise tucked herself behind a group of visitors as they all ducked into the entryway and out of the cold.

Bonn Minster's vaulted ceilings and magnificent stained-glass windows greeted them. It was the type of church that pulled in spectators along with the devout, so there were plenty of people both in the pews and milling toward the back, their mouths open as they gawked.

Annelise took a seat in the last pew and reached for the hymnal. As surreptitiously as possible, she slid one of her flyers in between the pages.

This one read: *We want peace not war.*

It was simple and positive, perfect for the church. The Pirates had other slogans they liked to use—including Annelise's particular favorite, which was a crude play on the fact that the Nazi uniforms were ugly and brown. But they were also careful in directing their messages to the right audience.

It took an hour to carefully move through the pews. The Catholics weren't persecuted to the extent of some of the others the Nazis targeted, but they weren't welcome in Hitler's ideal Reich either. This congregation should be sympathetic to the Pirates' cause. And if anyone wasn't, Annelise would be long gone before they could report it to the patrolling HJ.

When Annelise stepped back into the frigid evening air, it was to find Eitan sitting on one of the benches in front of the basilica.

She pressed away a smile and skipped down a few steps to get to him.

His eyes went from her face to the church behind her, a silent question in his expression. They had arranged to meet here, but she hadn't told him what she would be doing first.

He already knew she was part of the Edelweiss Pirates. They had met for coffee a handful of times over the past weeks, and he'd eventually asked why she'd been chased by the HJ that first night when he'd saved her from Felix.

"We put flyers in the hymnals," she said now, once she'd made sure there wasn't anyone listening in.

"That's dangerous," he murmured.

Annelise lifted a careless shoulder as if she didn't tremble every time she did something like this. "I have to be able to say I tried. Even if it's hopeless."

Some emotion she couldn't read flickered in and out of his expression. "Do you need to be home at a certain time?"

"No."

"I have a surprise," he said, almost shy. He held out his gloved hand instead of just taking hers. It was a small gesture—letting her decide—but she liked it.

She liked him.

Their palms slotted together and he tugged her forward. She longed for warmer weather when she could feel his skin against hers.

They didn't slink through the shadows, but they were both alert. The HJ patrols were out of hand now, the boys vicious with power. There were even rumors that the full-fledged brown- and blackshirts could get away with murder in the streets without any repercussions. Annelise wasn't sure if those whispers were fear-mongering, but considering the way the Nazis were training the young boys in Bonn, she tended to believe it.

"Do you live with your family?" she asked when they made it out of the main section of town.

"My father died when I was a child," Eitan said. "Two years ago, my mother managed to secure a train ticket for her and my baby sister to get to Switzerland. She . . . knew it was going to be bad here. They've settled with distant relatives."

Anger that she had no right to sliced through her. "She left you?"

"It's not that simple." He said it gently but there was steel beneath the velvet rumble. In the silence that followed, she heard the *you wouldn't understand.*

Annelise chewed on her lip, ashamed but still angry. He was correct, of course. She might take risks that sometimes felt big, but she was ultimately protected by who she was. That was nothing compared to the daily fear Jewish families had to live with beneath Hitler.

Still, the part of her that was already drawn to Eitan—to his quiet strength, his protectiveness, his rare smile that had made a home in her memory even when the rest of him had faded away—hurt for a boy whose mother was now gone. She simply did it in silence.

"You live on your own?" she asked, trying to right the conversation.

"A close friend of my mother's owns a bookstore near the Botanical Garden," he said. "I rent a room from her above the shop."

"Does she live there, too?"

"No, she has a small house her husband left her," Eitan said, nudging her around a puddle of slush.

"Are you lonely?" Annelise asked, and only when the words had left her mouth did she realize how impertinent they were. She was spending too much time around the Pirates. "You don't—"

"I like reading," Eitan said, cutting off her fumbled apology. "I have plenty of company within the pages."

Annelise squeezed his hand. She wasn't much for books herself. Most of the time at her desk was spent looking at the trees outside, wishing she was in the mountains instead of in a classroom. But she liked the idea of him finding comfort in stories. Of finding comfort in *something*.

"Are you taking me swimming?" she teased when she realized they were nearing the banks of the Rhine.

Eitan lifted his brows, light and happy all of a sudden. "It's perfect weather for it."

She laughed, delighted that she hadn't ruined the evening with her questions.

He pulled her into a small park that she knew well. The Pirates spent plenty of time there, especially in the warmer months.

They came to a stop in front of the frozen pond at the north end of the park. Confused, she glanced at Eitan. "I didn't bring my skates."

He waved toward the small shack to their right. "Good thing I remembered some."

She tilted her head in question, but he just grinned, pulling her along as he walked backward.

When they got closer to the shed, he pulled out a key.

"How did you get that?"

"I have a few friends left in the city still," he said, and stepped back when the door swung open. The moonlight glinted off the blades of the dozens of ice skates that hung on orderly hooks.

Annelise rewarded him with a beaming smile, and then made quick work of finding boots that fit.

The mid-February ice was thick and sturdy beneath her as she pushed off from the snow at the edge. Eitan was only a step behind.

He executed a quick spin to face her, and then held his hands out. She didn't need help—Annelise had been skating nearly before she could walk—but she took them anyway, and they glided off into a slow, steady rhythm, the only sound the swish of blade against ice.

"What are your favorite books?" she asked.

"All of them," he said on a laugh. "But poetry best."

"Why?"

"It's beautiful, moving. I love how poets play with language," he said. "But most of all I like that it's how we used to tell stories."

"What do you mean?"

"In ancient times, in the days of Homer, most people couldn't read or write," he said. "Instead, stories were mostly spoken so the words had to flow and rhyme and repeat to make them easier to remember."

"Like songs," she realized. "How I can always remember them better than anything else I try to memorize."

He hummed in agreement. "And I think a good poem can change the world."

She thought about the slogans the Pirates used. They rhymed sometimes, urging people to resist the Nazis. She wondered if that counted, but didn't want to make a fool of herself, so she only made an inquiring sound.

"For the longest time, poems are how we told the story of humanity. How could they not change the world?" he asked. "I think . . ."

He trailed off and then did a quick side step so he was no longer facing her. Annelise missed being able to watch his face. It was so expressive, made even more beautiful with his enthusiasm for the topic.

But perhaps he realized how vulnerable it made him.

"The Nazis want to erase us," he said quietly. "Jews. They want to eradicate our culture, and burn our books and steal our art and silence our great thinkers. I look around and all I can think about is how desperately Jewish people will need to tell the story of *our* humanity. They will take everything from us eventually. But poetry doesn't need paper or ink to survive. Poetry has ever only needed one thing in order to exist—the poet himself."

He spun around again, as if now that he'd cut himself open he could face her head-on instead of hiding at her side. "You must think I'm—"

"Brilliant," Annelise cut in before he could say anything disparaging about himself. She was in awe of him, of his mind and his nature and his romanticism. He wasn't pretentious about it either, she could tell he didn't judge her for not being able to rhapsodize about books beside him. This—he—was what she'd been looking for, when she'd passed up every offer from the boys at school or the boys in the Pirates. This was *wanting*, and it had been so incredibly worth the wait. "I think you're the most brilliant person I've ever met."

He slowed to a stop with enough warning that Annelise could have kept herself from bumping into him. But she didn't.

Annelise's skates slotted into place next to his, his thigh pressing between her legs, her hands resting on his chest. His fingers pressed into her hips then slid around to her back. He wasn't a tall man, so she barely had to tip her head up to meet his eyes.

He rested his forehead against hers. "And you are poetry in human form."

Something in her cracked open and warm, golden light poured out.

Then he pressed his lips to her cheekbone, to her jaw, to the corner of her mouth as if he wanted to worship each part of her. She shifted and let their mouths finally meet.

And if this was poetry, she understood how it could change the world.

Chapter 14
CHRISTINA

February 28, 1943

Christina knew enough about winter weather to know that shivering wasn't the sign of danger. It was when the shivering stopped.

As the sun dipped below the horizon on Sunday, the second day of the gathering, the temperature dropped to unbearable levels. And it would only get worse as any lingering warmth from the afternoon dissipated.

Ingrid's eyes had gone glassy, the skin around her lips white. Christina shared a look with Lisbeth, who seemed as concerned.

Christina was the one to finally say it. "We have to get her inside."

"No," Ingrid said, rousing. "My husb . . . Give us back our husbands."

It was supposed to be a shout, but the demand came out weak and wavering, the words slurring together.

"Do you have anyone who can come stay with you?" Lisbeth asked.

"No, it's just me and Nathan here," Ingrid said, blinking at them slowly as if she were trying to remember who they were. Also not a good sign. "My family. Well. We don't have anyone else."

Of course she didn't. That would be the case with so many of the women on this street.

"You have to go inside tonight to warm up," Lisbeth prodded. It would be the second night many of these women stood out in the cold. How many more could they possibly last? "You can stay at my apartment, if you'd like. It's close by. Then you can come back in the morning."

As if God wanted to help them make their point, the sky opened up. Had it been snow, Ingrid might have remained stubborn. But the frozen rain pelted them in angry little lashes against already wind-chapped raw skin, sinking into their clothes and then their bones.

"We'll stay here," Lisbeth promised. "And come get you if anything happens."

"You would do that?" Ingrid asked, her eyes flicking down to Christina's hand where the gold ring Lisbeth had given her now sat. Ingrid shook her head slightly, and Christina hoped any questions about its sudden appearance would be written off as confusion from the cold.

"Take her," Christina told Lisbeth, who was also staring at Christina's hands.

"You don't have gloves," Lisbeth murmured, almost to herself. And then she looped an arm around Ingrid's shoulders and pulled her into the crowd behind them.

Christina popped the collar of her coat up, though more to do something with her hands than because it would actually warm her up. She had grown numb hours ago, anyway.

She took stock of the women around her. They were all malnour-ished, desperate, and frayed already. These were the women who were married to some of the last Jewish men in Berlin.

They were considered race betrayers. They might be technically exempt from the Nuremberg Laws that would have them paraded through the streets with placards around their necks, but that didn't mean they were saved from public humiliation.

She thought about the way Ingrid had said, *My family. Well.*

Most of the intermarried women Christina knew of had been completely disowned by their German families. Their brothers would have faced repercussions in terms of jobs because they had a sister married to a Jewish man. Their parents would have been shamed by their communities. It took a strong character to buck all that and offer support, and most people simply weren't up to the moral chal-lenge.

But the stories Christina had found the most abhorrent were of the Nazis who threatened to remove children from the homes of intermarried couples in an effort to pressure the women into divorce. The babies would be raised in households who respected the Führer, they were told. It was heartless and cruel and exactly in line with Nazi philosophy.

"How long are we going to stay here?" a woman behind Christina asked her companion.

"As long as it takes," came the answer. "I refuse to leave while my husband is in there."

As long as it takes.

The workweek started again tomorrow. The weather would also scare a few people off. They'd all been out here for a full twenty-four hours now, if not more for some of them. Everyone was cold, hungry, scared, desperate.

The door to the Jewish Center slammed against the brick wall. It was meant to be a dramatic entrance, but with the weather only the policemen standing guard and the first few rows of protesters even noticed the appearance of the tall Nazi. The one who'd eyed Christina earlier.

His brimmed hat hid his face, but it wasn't difficult to read the anger in the rigid set of his shoulders, in the way his hands were clasped behind his back, in the bark of his voice.

Though Nazis always sounded on the brink of rage when they spoke in that clipped manner of theirs, there was a different kind of fury layered into the deep baritone. The women in the front could sense it, their chatter cutting off almost abruptly. The women in the back continued to call out, unable to see or hear through the pounding sleet.

From the sidewalk outside of the community center, the tall Nazi scanned the crowd. Despite the falling darkness, despite his hat, Christina swore he locked eyes with her.

She didn't dare move as the rain ran down her face, into the dip of her collarbone, sliding past her pounding heart.

Christina felt safe to take a breath only when his gaze moved past her toward the far side of the street, and then down right, left, and she knew what he was thinking at the sight of them hundreds strong.

Hitler's rule depended on a scared, self-regulating populace. It was the only way he could control so many people. He didn't have the resources to wage a war against his citizens while he was devoting so much time, energy, and materials to his effort to take over the world.

A protest this large could not be allowed in the Third Reich.

Each and every person on both sides of the human barricade knew that incontrovertible truth.

And yet here they were, persisting.

In the thirties, during Hitler's steady climb to power, the Nazis had killed the bravest among the Germans, the ones who had been willing to say "no" in the face of guaranteed death. What had been left—apart from the loyalists and those targeted by Hitler—were everyday people who were not exactly cowardly and not exactly courageous. They were just people who didn't want to die, who didn't want their loved ones to die. So they'd kept their heads down.

The ones who hated the Nazis had tried quiet resistance methods, slowing down factory work, sabotaging bullets and bombs where they could, even sneaking Jewish families out of the country.

It was the kind of protesting that Christina did in her work at the Abwehr. The Allies only ever semi-trusted information coming out of the leaky agency, but Christina had sent along enough airplane manuals and factory blueprints to know she was probably doing *some* kind of good.

Still, that wasn't loud resistance. That type of protest wasn't the catching kind.

This, though? This kind of protest was a pilot light. And Germany—full of people who had survived a brutal winter, who were losing their men in droves, who were watching the world close in around them—was tinder waiting to go up in flames.

The tall Nazi unclasped his hands and un-holstered his pistol.

"This is your last warning," he called out, his voice carrying to the first two rows. It didn't matter, the message made its way toward the back of the crowd, slithering through until the chanting died into silence. "Disperse."

He wasn't bluffing this time. Christina didn't know how she knew, but she did. She glanced around. The women around her were shifting, uneasy, meeting each other's eyes, clasping hands.

"You have been good German wives," he said. "You have been a testament to German loyalty and devotion, and an example of the valor that has carried us this far against our enemies. But, by order of the Führer, you must go home now."

Someone in the back started the chant again but was hushed almost immediately. This was different from the bluster of earlier. There were no threats attached to his little speech because there didn't need to be.

Nazis answered protests with blood.

Christina flinched when a hand grabbed her arm from behind.

"Only me," Lisbeth said. She'd pulled on a hat over her copper curls, the wool dyed to match the impossible mix of blue and green in her eyes. Her dark lashes were wet from the frozen rain, her cheeks flushed from the cold. She shoved something at Christina. "Here."

Christina stared down at what she now held.

Gloves.

Though they were threadbare they were blessedly warm when Christina tugged them on. Shock kept her silent, the "thank you" getting tangled somewhere on her tongue. She couldn't remember the last time someone had been kind to her like this. Or . . . she could.

Annelise would have done something similar, making sure she had water, making sure she'd gotten some fire-warmed nuts that one time Christina had camped with the Pirates.

It didn't matter that Christina had been struck mute, Lisbeth had already shifted her attention back to the tall Nazi.

She was clever enough to read the situation easily.

The Nazis needed to get control of this protest before word of it made it to the international press corps. They could control their own media, but they knew there were enough illegal wireless radios in use that if the BBC got ahold of the news, it would spread through Germany not long after.

The truth was, the fervor that had admittedly and shamefully burned bright for Hitler in the thirties and the early days of the war was fading into discontent.

The calculation was about to shift. Before, the Nazis didn't want to deal with the idea of hundreds of German women slaughtered in the middle of Berlin. But if it was that versus letting a spark of rebellion turn into a potential wildfire, the answer for them was obvious.

"He's going to shoot," Christina whispered urgently to Lisbeth, though she made sure only the other woman could hear. Starting a panic at the front of three hundred women would be incredibly dangerous for all of them.

Lisbeth's eyes narrowed in on the pistol. "He can't shoot us all."

While Christina admired the courage, she disagreed. The Nazis had proven that a high body count wasn't a deterrent.

"Maybe he can't, but they can," she said, pointing toward the men at the machine guns.

"This is your final warning," the Nazi said, pistol raised into the air. The sleet swallowed up the words, but even those toward the back of the crowd understood his stance. The women shifted, en masse.

"On my count," the Nazi directed toward the local police and SS officers who had filtered outside. The police looked as hesitant as the women, but the uniformed Nazis and the plainclothes Gestapo were nearly gleeful.

Christina cursed beneath her breath, the world going blurry and silent for a heartbeat, then another.

"One," the tall Nazi shouted.

With that, everything snapped back into action.

"Shelter," Christina breathed out and turned to the group of women behind her. "Find something to get behind. Now."

She didn't push, she didn't run, didn't nudge others to do so either. But by "two," the women around them had started to purposefully direct the crowd away from the deadly weapons at their backs.

Without thinking, Christina latched on to Lisbeth's wrist. The other woman didn't fight her. Christina's boots skidded on the slick cobblestones as they all scrambled toward elusive safety, desperate to put space between their bodies and bullets that would tear through flesh and bone.

"Three."

The crack and flash that followed came like simultaneous thunder and lightning. Everyone around them ducked, as if that would do anything.

"Zigzag," Christina screamed. "Don't make an easy target."

The *rat-tat-tat* of guns layered over the shrieks from the terrified protesters, but Christina didn't dare look back. She pulled Lisbeth as fast as she could, caught in a wave of bodies going not very far way too slowly.

Their only saving grace was that Rosenstrasse wasn't wide. Most women fled left and right, emptying out into the alleys and streets nearby. Christina, meanwhile, aimed for the sidewalk across from the community center. It was the shortest distance between the guns and solid building.

The distance to the promise of safety seemed endless, though, stretching out always, always, always past their reach.

Rat-tat-tat. Rat-tat-tat. Rat-tat-tat.

There was no pain yet. That's all that mattered.

Some distant part of her was clamoring at her to drop to the ground and hope the Nazis thought they'd hit their mark.

But just as she had the thought, she and Lisbeth reached the far side of Rose Street.

A doorway wouldn't offer much protection, but it was something.

With a quick move, Christina spun and pressed Lisbeth to the stone, covering the other woman's body with her own, gloved palms pressed to the building, shoulders rounded, creating the only barrier she could.

Out of the two of them, Lisbeth was who mattered.

Christina closed her eyes, dreading the pain that would surely come.

Why, why had she thought they could get away with this? Why, when everything they'd ever experienced beneath Hitler told her this was always how it was going to end?

The answer, of course, was obvious.

Because of Eitan.

Because of Annelise.

The guns went silent.

Christina waited for the cries of the wounded.

They never came.

Were they dead?

Hands cupped Christina's jaw, gentle, soothing, bringing Christina back from the edge of darkness and terror.

She forced her eyes open only to find herself a hairbreadth away from Lisbeth.

Christina was breathing too hard, too fast, and an alarm bell clanged in her mind. If she didn't calm down, she'd likely faint. But she couldn't stop bracing for the bullet to the ribs that would inevitably travel through her and into Lisbeth's body.

"We're alive," Lisbeth whispered, her thumb stroking the hinge of Christina's jaw, the slope of her cheekbone. "We're alive."

Like the chant they had all taken into themselves, Lisbeth repeated the promise over and over again until Christina's shoulders dropped and her legs unlocked.

She started shivering, loud and embarrassing so that her teeth clacked together. And Lisbeth held her face between two soft, warm hands, her calm, controlled voice a contrast to the harsh gunfire from only minutes earlier.

Christina latched on to it, let herself believe the words. *We're alive.*

As the fear receded, it left in its wake an awareness of how much she'd crowded into Lisbeth's space, an awareness of how they touched from breast to pelvis to thigh. Her skin felt too tight around her bones.

Lisbeth had gone still beneath her, as if she could sense a shift but wasn't sure in which direction Christina had gone. Had she known, Lisbeth would have recoiled, surely.

Surely.

The thought gave Christina enough strength to step away from the comfort Lisbeth offered so generously.

"They've stopped," Christina said, clearing her throat. She chanced a glance toward the street. She had been expecting bodies, but all she got was cobblestones glinting in the moonlight. The tall Nazi still stood just outside the door, hands clasped behind his back once more. Lisbeth pressed against her shoulder from behind, looking out as well.

"They shot into the air," Lisbeth realized only half a beat behind Christina.

Lisbeth started to laugh, and when Christina turned to her, Lisbeth only laughed harder until there were tears streaming down her face, mixing in with the frozen rain. Christina knew it was a delayed reaction to the fear that had been coursing through her, but Christina couldn't gently cup her jaw like Lisbeth had done. It would mean something more to Christina, and that wasn't fair. Instead, she awkwardly patted Lisbeth's shoulder as the women around them crept out of their hiding spots, out of the alleys, back onto Rose Street.

When Lisbeth's laughter finally trailed off, she offered a blinding smile in its place.

"What?" Christina asked, shaken and irritable in the face of Lisbeth's apparent joy.

"They shot into the air."

"So?" Christina said, still not getting it.

"Don't you see, Christina? They're terrified of us," Lisbeth said, awe laced into her voice. "Which means we're actually going to win."

Chapter 15

EMMY

April 1946

Emmy dragged her fingertips over the spines on her and Lucy's bookshelf, pausing when she got to the pilfered Rilke that she'd flipped wrong-side out to hide where it had come from. She tugged it free from its neighbors and opened it to the title page.

She'd memorized the message written there the second time she'd read it, but in the week since, she'd gotten into the habit of checking on the slim volume.

My dearest Annelise, my brave Edelweiss Pirate

Lucy came up behind her, hooking her chin over Emmy's shoulder. "Oh, naughty. Did you sneak that out of the depot?"

It was too late to tuck it away, so Emmy fessed up. "In a moment of weakness. I thought . . . I don't know, that I could find the owner myself."

"Oh, lovey, we've all been there," Lucy said, with a sad sigh. "Sometimes, those books feel like friends we haven't yet met."

Emmy turned and Lucy stepped back. She looked beautiful as always, in a slinky blue number that revealed a surprising amount of thigh—but only when she moved just right.

It was Thursday night, and apparently everyone who worked at the depot went to the one—and only—nightclub in Offenbach on Thursday nights.

When Emmy had declined to join, Lucy winked. "Shall I send Major Arnold your way?"

"Does he often attend the nightclub?" Emmy asked, trying to picture the historian at a place like that and failing.

"When he gets dragged along," Lucy said with a laugh, and she blew a kiss when a honk came from outside. "And you didn't say no."

"Because it's so absurd," Emmy shot back, but Lucy was already out the door.

There was a strange restlessness that filled any room after Lucy left, the air going stale when all that energy got sucked out of it. Emmy truly couldn't imagine summoning the strength for a nightclub—the week at the depot had been invigorating and draining in equal measure.

By the second day, she'd fully settled into reviewing what she'd been sent there to look over—books from Nazi leaders' offices and libraries. A particularly good find was an early edition of Rosenberg's *The Myth of the Twentieth Century*. It was one of those books any Nazi who considered himself an intellectual kept on his shelf. Rumor had it that Hitler had called it nonsense, but it had still sold more than a million copies and could be considered the second Bible for the Nazis. As much as she detested the content, it was still a notable find.

Sorting through the Nazis' property became like any position she'd held before. She was meticulous and unemotional, checking print editions and quality to determine how rare and valuable each book was, like she had with the *Gulliver's Travels*.

Some were interesting simply because of the fact that they'd been in certain officials' possession. On her third day she'd found a eugenics book, *The Passing of the Great Race*, annotated by Georg Ebert, a man who had been a part of Rosenberg's foreign affairs office. The content had been hard to read, but the insights the volume offered had been valuable. It went in the carton destined for the Library of Congress.

Though the work had proven to be fascinating, it was not as emotionally difficult as she'd feared. The teams that had collected the material had been fairly diligent when sorting through it for content that originated with the Nazis. But every once in a while, she would stumble on a book from a personal collection.

Earlier that day she'd found a mass-produced version of *Berlin Alexanderplatz* by Alfred Döblin. The book would be sent to Poste's local team—it hadn't been a rare copy nor had it been owned by a high-ranking Nazi official. But Emmy hadn't been able to resist flipping to the title page.

Scrawled across the top was a quote from the book:

"Berlin's a big place. Where thousands live, there's room for one more."

And then below:

Meet me there when this all ends?

It was signed simply with a *T.*

Emmy hadn't had the heart to create a story for the owner, sure that doing so would break her in a million subtle ways. There wasn't enough information to help it find its way home, anyway. All she could hope was that whoever it landed with would read those words and spare a moment for the hands that had touched this book in another life.

Now, Emmy poured herself a hefty glass of Lucy's good stuff, and settled into one of the two armchairs by the tiny fireplace with the Rilke. This one did have enough information to go on—at least enough for her to give it the old government try. She knew she was fixating on the task because she was so helpless in the face of thousands, if not millions, of books that had been orphaned.

But this volume was no less important than the priceless editions that would draw far more attention.

The knock, when it came, surprised her and it didn't.

Major Arnold stood on the other side of the door, hands shoved deep into the pockets of his fine gray trousers. There was a pink flush at the edge of his light blue shirt, which was buttoned high and tight against his throat.

He was embarrassed for showing up even though Lucy had likely sent him. For some reason, that tickled her.

"I wanted some quiet," he admitted, and, of course she opened the door to him. Without launching into any chatter as she might have with anyone else, she poured him his own glass of scotch while he lowered himself into the companion chair. He rested his cane on the armrest, brows raised at the expensive alcohol. But he took it without question.

"Am I quiet?" she teased as she settled into her own seat, her hips pressing against the sides, the arms cradling her.

"Mysterious," Major Arnold corrected.

"I think there's an expression about pots and kettles that would fit here."

His eyes flicked down to her lap, and for one strange second she thought he was looking at the wedding band she still wore.

Then she remembered the Rilke volume and flushed. It bore the easily identifiable catalog tag from the Rosenberg Institute on its spine.

A terrible image of him hauling her off in handcuffs made her stomach roll over, but his expression remained neutral.

"I knew you took it," he said. "It's quite tempting, that's why we have security."

Her blush deepened. "I wasn't going to sell it."

She'd never thought a half-slant smile would be so reassuring.

"Of that, I have no doubt," he said. "Or I would have stopped you."

"Why didn't you?"

Instead of answering, the major held out his hand. After she handed it over, he flipped the book open to the title page, studying it for a while. She knew his expert eye was noting everything that she had. The bookstore, the *J*, the mention of the Edelweiss Pirates.

"It would have been a lost cause, otherwise," he finally said, glancing up to hold her gaze. "It likely would have gone to a good home, but not the right one. We don't have enough resources to track down the owners of every personalized book."

"But if it became my pet project . . ."

"You might actually get somewhere with it," he said, handing the Rilke back to her, which was exactly what her rationale had been. "I know of your résumé, Mrs. Clarke. You wouldn't have taken something to take something."

"That's quite a bit of trust to put into a stranger," she said, a little overwhelmed by it. Or perhaps the strange flutter of something not quite unease but close to it was due to the fact that it once again demonstrated how well they understood each other in such a short amount of time. Had Mr. Dernbach told her he'd trusted her right away, she would have been nearly insulted that there was ever a question about whether he could.

"I know where you live." He winked, so quick and sly that she wondered if she'd imagined it.

"I haven't had time to start the research," she admitted. "But the Edelweiss Pirates . . . that has to be unique enough to offer some clues. Have you heard of them?"

He hummed, settling into his lecture persona. If she were being brutally honest with herself, she would have to admit that, as an academic herself, she enjoyed this look on him and she liked to provoke it when they chatted.

She had met plenty of professorial types who doled out knowledge only because it made them seem superior to those around them. Major Arnold always seemed like he simply wanted to share interesting information, and he usually only did so when asked.

"The Pirates as a concept emerged from the youth group movement in the early nineteen hundreds in rural Germany," he said, swirling his drink so that it caught the low light. "The groups were focused on hiking and camping, skiing trips, outdoor activities. It was a pushback against industrialization, if I'm not mistaken."

"For some reason, I had the impression this book was newer than that, though I don't know why."

"No, you're right," he said. "The Pirates emerged from that earlier youth movement, but they came about in the late thirties as a direct contrast to the Hitler Youth. Different regions called themselves different names—like the 'Navajos' in Cologne—but they can all be considered under the umbrella of the Edelweiss Pirates."

"The Navajos?" Emmy asked, surprised to hear the name come up in Germany.

"Germans are quite . . . enamored with the United States' indigenous cultures," he said, slowly, cautiously. "They have festivals dedicated to them, it's a main theme in popular literature and films here."

He paused and stared into the empty fireplace. "In recent months, I think it helps them with their guilt."

"What do you mean?"

"As information and pictures come out about the camps and the torture and the death chambers," he said, grim around his mouth once more, "they have something to point to. Americans were the victors here, and yet look at the blood they have on their hands. It helps Germans feel less guilty about their complicity in what happened over the past decade. At least that is what a German friend of mine philosophized over too many beers one night."

Before coming to Germany, she would have said she had a generally positive outlook on life. Now, she wasn't so sure. "I believe by the time we part ways, Major Arnold, that we'll both have ruined each other for optimism."

"It's still worth believing in the goodness of people. There's always a way to find the light. The Pirates. They started as an outdoors group, but many of them participated in resistance efforts as the Nazis were getting more and more brutal. It's hard to overstate how dangerous that was at the time, when Hitler was still trying to establish full control and power over the Germans' hearts and minds."

"It does seem like we were told to believe no Germans put up a fight," Emmy said.

"Well, the Pirates didn't storm the Reichstag, or anything as cinematic as that," he said. "But they were so young. Most of them were between the ages of thirteen and seventeen. So what they managed, to me, is impressive."

"What did they manage?"

"Much of it was getting the word out that there were resisters to Hitler at all," the major said. "They distributed pamphlets and graffitied anti-Hitler slogans on buildings. But some went as far as blowing up train tracks and sabotaging Nazi vehicles. They painted train cars with messages so that people from the countryside would see them—at least until they were washed off by the Nazis. They protected each other and the printers and suppliers who helped them."

"All from a hiking group." She wasn't sure why she was surprised. She'd dipped her feet in glacial lakes, gotten lost in books for entire days while nestled into the trunk of a tree whose tops she couldn't even see. She'd stood beneath a sky that stretched into eternity and back.

Emmy understood the magic of the wilderness, and the unique way it spoke to people who would be more naturally inclined to reject conformity.

"Never underestimate the romanticism and moral passion of the youth," he said, sounding much older than he must be. "Not everyone in this country looked away."

"It's hard sometimes to remember that," Emmy said, fiddling with her ring. She could feel Major Arnold's eyes on her, and she dropped her hand back to her lap. "It's hard to forgive a country where it seems everyone simply let this all happen."

"I've noticed Americans who come here often think in terms of forgiveness," he said after a weighted pause. "As if they have the power to grant or withhold it. As if that matters."

"You don't think it matters?"

"I don't know what role my forgiveness or lack thereof plays in the cleanup of a war," he said. "What would I do? Withhold my help until all the Germans properly groveled at my feet for their sins? Who am I to forgive them?"

Her eyes slipped to his scars. How extensive were they? "You were hurt."

"The world was hurt. Many far worse than me," he countered. "The people who lived here have paid a dear price, but they also looked away and let atrocity happen. I don't have any love for them; I hope they wrestle with that guilt for the rest of their lives, to be quite honest. But I still want them to have shelter and clean water and not have to walk over dead bodies on their way home. I want the children to have something to eat beyond the glue holding books together. What does forgiveness have to do with helping other humans survive?"

"Such a historian," Emmy said as lightly as she could, not sure how she felt about any of it. This was hard, being here. It was easier back home, easier to hope the entire country responsible for Joseph's death rotted in hell. In the quiet of the cottage, in the company of this thoughtful man, Emmy felt like she could tell secrets. "It's like a wound sometimes, that anger I have. Like it's festering and infected. And the only way to get any relief is to . . . hate them. Not only the leaders. But everyone."

He nodded, but then in a quiet, considering voice, said, "We salted the earth after the Great War. And millions of deaths later, here we are again. Yet how do we resist the urge to re-salt the earth when it's actually warranted? When what they've done—and we've only hit the tip of it, I'm sure—is unforgivable?"

She thought about the Navajos. "And yet what country has not done unforgivable things?"

"I went to school for a philosophy degree and it didn't take," Major

Arnold said, tone shifting toward amused. "I think this is all starting to get above my pay grade."

Emmy laughed, some of the tension bleeding out from the air, and she held up Eitan's book. "I want to find the owner."

"I've heard it's supposed to be lovely weather on Saturday. Perfect for a trip into Bonn. I can drive us."

Emmy pressed her lips together at the kindness he so easily offered. Only, it wasn't kindness, she didn't think. It was his sense of duty, and what was right. That's what had brought him here in the first place.

"Thank you," she said, though she knew he wasn't doing it for her.

He ducked his head in acknowledgment. "Don't get . . ."

"My hopes up, I know," Emmy finished for him. "But, at the very least, it will be nice to see the countryside." She paused. "Shall we start at the bookstore from the title page?"

"Yes, let's. Bonn is a small city," Major Arnold said. "Which is lucky for us. We'll have to see if that luck holds and the shop is still standing."

The excitement that rushed in was a tonic to the sad conversation of earlier.

"If it's not, we'll start asking around," she said, her mind gaming out the steps. She was a librarian, after all. She knew how to solve a mystery, even if it wasn't usually as exciting as this one. "Annelise is a common enough name, but I would imagine Eitan would have been memorable in Bonn in the thirties."

"We can check with the cafés around the bookstore, the grocery stores, places that people return to frequently," Major Arnold said. "Maybe a few neighbors. People create routines for themselves."

"Would you have any access to records?"

"It'll be helpful if we can get surnames," he said. "Otherwise . . ."

"Right, of course." She studied him as he swallowed the last of his drink and wondered why he had shown up tonight. With her practical demeanor and only-pretty-in-the-right-light looks, Emmy wasn't the type to intrigue men.

For her, though, there was a definite simmer beneath her skin when she thought about the ways she wanted to glide her teeth over the spot on the major's jaw that he'd missed shaving; wanted to see exactly how those rough calluses felt against skin that had been untouched by someone else's hands for five years; wanted to find and kiss the edges of his scars.

The impulses startled her more than anything, though she could sense fear lurking in the wings, as well. The only thing that kept it at bay was the knowledge that nothing would ever come of the attraction.

Major Arnold was likely only helping her because this was a cause that was dear to him. That would be obvious even if he hadn't devoted his life to traipsing around war-torn Europe doling out justice like some kind of book-themed superhero in those comic books that had become so popular in the past few years.

It was in how he held the Rilke, how anger slipped into his expression *only* when he thought about plundered books; it was how he'd so easily taken on this mission as his own because he saw the value in a beat-up Rilke even though there must be thousands of volumes of the exact same poetry collection.

He loved books. It was one more way they were similar.

But, as she saw him to the door, as she watched him give a slight bow of goodbye at the gate, Emmy couldn't help but wish that at least part of his motivation had nothing to do with a book.

Chapter 16
ANNELISE

Spring 1938

Annelise could only avoid the National Socialist Women's League for so long. A week after the Anschluss and annexation of Austria, Annelise reported to the office of Frau Erna Sommer.

"You do not look ill," Frau Sommer said.

Annelise coughed weakly into her closed fist. "It comes and goes."

"Your sister is such a fine example of how the Bund Deutscher Mädel can help young women like yourself thrive," Frau Sommer said, ignoring Annelise's obvious lie. "I see you'll be turning eighteen within the month. Have you considered your future if you persist in your antisocial attitudes? Have you considered your sister's reputation, of being associated with you?"

There were things Annelise could have said. That the BDM's definition of "thriving" was forcing the girls—married or not—to deliver Aryan babies like there was a conveyor belt beneath their hospital beds. That she knew "antisocial" was coded Nazi language for any German who didn't conform or who dared to question their strict expectations. That the adults were indoctrinating a generation of young Germans into bigotry and hate because they couldn't stand the idea that young people might live their lives outside their parents' control.

All of that would have prolonged this terrible meeting, though. And despite what teachers, Nazi officials, and Hitler himself believed, the NSDAP was not all-powerful. They could threaten her future work prospects, issue thinly veiled threats to her family, and yet they couldn't do much more than that.

Annelise smiled blandly. "It seems like it's too late for me to join the BDM, Frau Sommer. Unlucky that."

The instant Frau Sommer's expression turned gleeful, Annelise knew she must have made a misstep.

"That's where you're wrong, my dear," Frau Sommer said. "We've recently realized we were abandoning our girls the moment they aged out of the BDM. We'll be launching a sister program that will be voluntary for all young women ages seventeen through twenty-one."

"How . . . delightful," Annelise managed.

"It is called the Faith and Beauty Society," Frau Sommer said, all but preening. "It's a perfect fit for you."

"Ah, well. I have to find a work position to help my family," Annelise said, grateful for the excuse even though both she and Frau Sommer knew finding a position would be difficult. There was a price to pay for rebellion. "I shall be too busy."

"Nonsense," Frau Sommer said. "Your sister tells me you don't have any plans for future education. The Faith and Beauty Society can help you train for what you're interested in. We will be offering classes in fashion and wellness and home economics. We want you to be part of the Volksgemeinschaft, Annelise."

Annelise's mouth pursed at the word. The idea of one "German community" had gained popularity back during the Great War, and the Nazis had resurrected the slogan to stoke the fires of patriotism in even the most complacent of German breasts.

"Thank you, Frau Sommer, for all of your insight," Annelise said, standing. "You've given me much to think about."

Frau Sommer pushed to her feet as well. She was the perfect face for a program called the Faith and Beauty Society—pretty in a way that wasn't intimidating, soft and feminine but with the ramrod straight posture of someone with discipline. Her uniform was impeccable, her fingernails clipped short and without a speck of dirt beneath them.

Annelise looked at her own hands, the jagged nails, the calluses from putting up tents and carrying logs for the fires. She wondered how much Frau Sommer itched to fix everything scraggly and wrong about Annelise.

"I would hate to see where you end up if you continue down this antisocial path of yours." Frau Sommer's voice was as soft and lovely as the rest of her, her threats wrapped in silk. "Why, just last month, a group of young people were rounded up in Cologne. They had been defacing public property and distributing profane leaflets. They've been detained at the EL-DE Haus now for four weeks. I can't imagine the state of them."

Annelise didn't react, because that was so clearly what the Frau wanted. The EL-DE Haus was infamous in their region as the Gestapo's Cologne headquarters. Rumors ran rampant about what went on inside the building. Mothers used it as a warning to ill-behaved children, the Pirates whispered about how people could hear screams from blocks away. The mention of it was enough to make someone fall into line.

But Annelise was tired of this. She wasn't a child any longer, afraid to speak back to an adult no matter how wrong they were. That very impulse was what terrified the Nazis about the Pirates.

So be it.

"I would say that people more worried about the defacement of property than the health of young German citizens should perhaps spend more time on bettering their character and less time on home economics," Annelise murmured. "But maybe that's my 'antisocial attitude' making itself known. Good day, Frau Sommer. As always, I thank you for your concern about my well-being."

Christina was waiting for her in the hallway, leaning against the wall and chewing on her thumbnail, a bad habit that had reared its head again ever since she'd joined the BDM. She never seemed to acknowledge the connection between all her worrying and her participation in the group. Annelise was done trying to point it out.

"Don't talk to the Nazis about me." Annelise stormed right by her sister, then she stopped, whirled, almost too furious to see straight. "Actually, don't talk about me to anyone. Better yet, don't talk *to* me."

Without waiting for a response, Annelise took off down the hall-way once more, Christina at her heels.

"I want what's best for you," Christina said. "Who else was I sup-posed to turn to? Frau Sommer has been a wonderful role model for me, I thought she could help you."

"How much did you tell her?" Annelise asked. "About the Pirates."

"Nothing damaging," Christina hedged. "Just that I worried you were heading down a dangerous path. She needed to know so she can help you."

Annelise's frustrated scream caught behind her teeth. But she kept walking.

Or she did until Christina grabbed her wrist, yanking her back. In a hushed voice, her sister whispered, "I saw the leaflets in your bag. The paint flecks on your fingers. I know you've been coming home later and later. How much longer do you think you'll get away with all this?"

"I'll get away with it until I don't," Annelise said, not bothering to lower her voice. "And then they'll send me to EL-DE Haus like they do with anyone who doesn't parrot their awful beliefs. Don't worry, you'll be safe. You can denounce me the moment I'm arrested. In fact, why wait?"

"You treat this like it's a game," Christina said, and Annelise was actually surprised by the genuine mix of fear and anger in her sister's voice. "You *know* what they do to Germany's enemies. Please do not become one."

Annelise felt herself wavering for a split second, Christina's dis-tress a magnet that would forever pull Annelise in. She didn't like her sister anymore, wasn't even sure she loved her. But taking care of Christina had always been a cornerstone of who she was. That would be the last thing to go, right before their relationship ruptured completely.

And then Christina's words registered.

"You know what they do," Annelise repeated slowly. "You *know* what they do to Germany's enemies."

For some reason, Annelise had always told herself Christina was young and ignorant. She only read Nazi-approved newspapers, was preached at all day long at school and then at BDM about how wonderful the Party was, all her friends were good BDM girls. She didn't have access to the information that would let her form her own ideas.

But . . . she *knew*.

"That's what I just said."

Annelise shoved at Christina's shoulders hard enough for her to stumble. They were of the same height and build, but Annelise had surprise on her side. She had never laid a hand on Christina with the intention of hurting her before.

She pushed again until Christina's back hit the hallway's wall. Annelise stepped closer, crowding in on her.

"So what is it, sister dear?" Annelise said, barely recognizing her own voice. All the color had seeped out of Christina's face. "Is it that you think Germany's enemies should be treated as less than human or is it that you love the Nazis enough that you can look away?"

Christina paled and then flushed. Her chin tilted up. "You don't know everything you think you do, Anna."

The nickname from their childhood came like a kick to the gut, probably as it had been intended.

Annelise stepped away, and Christina smoothed a shaky hand down her BDM uniform.

"How did we turn out so different?" Annelise wondered out loud. They were less than two years apart, they had been raised in the same household, by the same parents, had gone to the same school. The Nazis had managed to get their hooks into Christina young, but at the same time, she'd let them.

The question landed as her own kick to the gut—also as intended. Sisters always knew how to hurt each other best.

"Do you like that our parents are working themselves into an early grave?" Christina asked, for once sounding much older than her years. "Do you like Germans starving to death on the streets because there isn't enough bread? Do you like that we have no future because the world crushed our country beneath its boots for something that happened before we were born? Do you wash Mother's feet like I do? Bandage the burns on her hands? Have you ever listened to Anders talk about how he's afraid to die because our army has been stripped of anything that would help our country defend itself?" Christina pulled her shoulders back, looked down her nose at Annelise. "No. You go gallivanting with your *Pirates*." She all but spat the last word. "You say I don't care about Germany's enemies, but you don't care about us. Your family. Your neighbors. You care more about faceless strangers than you do about your own flesh and blood. What does that say about you?"

Like everything spouted by the Nazis, the words certainly sounded righteous. But that was the beauty of the Party's propaganda machine. Christina was now no more than a cog in that. She'd probably wanted to make Annelise feel small, but all this little show had done was convince her that Christina was well and truly lost to the other side.

"Tell me, Christina," Annelise said. "If you are so suddenly wise, tell me the ways the Nazis have enacted any change to address those problems. You say these are the struggles we have now, right now, and yet Hitler has been chancellor for five years. All he wants to do is give you someone to hate and fear so that you're distracted from all the things he hasn't accomplished."

Christina made some kind of frustrated sound, but Annelise cut her off before she could start.

"You're worried about Anders?" she asked. "Hitler is going to send him to fight and kill innocent people because he wants more land to control. You're worried about Mother and Father working too much? They'll only have to work more to produce the tanks and bombs that Hitler will use to fight and kill innocent people. You're worried about starving Germans? What do you think will happen when the world cuts off all our supplies because Hitler wants to—please listen here—fight and kill innocent people? Tell me one thing the Nazis have done to make Germany better." She waited a beat. "You can't. Because they rule through finger-pointing and criticizing and creating scapegoats instead of policy. You are right about one thing. There are big issues in the world. None of them are solved by hating people who are different than you."

"I don't hate people who are different than me," Christina argued, voice trembling now.

"Right," Annelise said. "You just don't care what happens to them."

Christina opened her mouth, closed it, and looked away.

"That's what I thought," Annelise said, and turned sharply on her heel and walked away.

Her mind was staticky, her blood hot with anger. Without much thought, she made her way to the botanical gardens, knowing Eitan would likely be there if he was off from work. They had taken to meeting in the gardens in the evenings, talking and walking or sitting in silence as Eitan worked on his poetry and Annelise imagined shapes in the clouds in the sky.

She found him in the back, among the unopened tulips. He didn't hear her, and so, selfishly, she took a moment to watch him. Annelise had once likened him to a Botticelli painting, and though she found him no less beautiful now than she first had, she realized how shallow the assessment had been. He was, instead, like her beloved woods, deep and quiet and lovely and generous.

They hadn't only spent time in the botanical gardens—Eitan had also wanted to see all the things that made her smile. So she'd showed him the mountains, the frozen ponds, the ice-melt rivers of the countryside.

In return, Eitan had shown her Bonn. The cafés, the bookstores, the shops filled with strange dolls and clothing and furniture that Eitan somehow turned into fascinating stories of times gone by.

They were so different, had different loves and interests and ways of thinking and yet all their pieces seemed to fit.

They never talked about the state of the country, the hardships that were coming for him. And because of that it almost felt like they lived in a moment outside of time, like they lived in their own little world.

He sensed her, looking up from the slim volume in his hands. His immediate smile faded into concerned curiosity. "You fought with Christina."

"How can you tell?" she asked as she sat on the little stone bench next to him, her hip pressed into his, her thigh warm from where they touched.

Eitan traced a fingertip from her eyebrow to the bridge of her nose. "You wear your anger here." He touched the corner of her mouth. "And your sadness here. Together, they equal only one thing."

A pleased flush slipped over her skin, and Annelise couldn't tell if it was from the intimacy or the fact that he knew her so well now. She sighed and let her head fall to his shoulder.

"What are you reading?"

"Rilke," he said, showing her the cover.

"Read me something?"

He considered for a moment and then flipped to a section toward the end. "'For one human being to love another human being: that is perhaps the most difficult task that has been given to us . . . the work for which all other work is merely preparation.'"

Annelise straightened and pretended to glare at him. "Subtle."

Eitan laughed, and guided her back to his shoulder. She easily sunk into his side, marveling as always how well they slotted together. "I'm the last person who would tell you to make nice with Christina. But it hurts me to see you hurt."

"Do you hate me for still loving her?"

"I don't think I could hate you in one hundred lifetimes, my brave Edelweiss Pirate," he said, tugging at the braid that hung down her back. "Your big heart is the reason you are you. You don't like giving up on people."

"I keep thinking if I say *just* the right thing . . ."

"I don't think it works like that," Eitan cut in. "They're too deep in the avalanche now to tell which way is up."

"Not everyone," Annelise said. She had to believe that. He touched her jaw, her brow.

"You wear your mischief here," he said, sounding wary. "What are you plotting?"

"I'm not sure yet," she said truthfully, but she did know one thing.

Too many people were caught in Hitler's avalanche. The Pirates needed to make their own.

Chapter 17
CHRISTINA

March 1, 1943

Y ou're not married," Lisbeth said as the sun rose over the buildings on Monday. The third day of the protest. Christina had been marveling at the fact that they were all still alive. "So why are you here?"

Christina rubbed her thumb over the wedding band Lisbeth had given her. "I could be in love."

Something Christina couldn't read flicked into Lisbeth's expression. "I don't think that's it."

"Or here for someone else," Christina pointed out. There were some men in the crowd, fathers or brothers supporting their loved one. She was sure there must be others here who didn't have someone inside the building.

"You use 'husband,'" Lisbeth reminded her. "When you talk about him."

She had thought that choice would make everything easier. The real explanation was too convoluted. All of a sudden, she was too tired to play coy. Neither she nor Lisbeth had slept, though they had sat right down on the slick cobblestones and taken turns closing their eyes, their spines pressed together for support. Christina had been all too aware of each point of contact with the other woman, the hint of lemons she could smell on her, the brush of curls against her cheek whenever Lisbeth shifted to talk.

Eitan. She thought about Eitan. His life, her penance. His life, Annelise's sacrifice.

"It's my sister's husband who is being detained," Christina said. It was another lie, of course. Annelise and Eitan had never had the chance to marry. But in their hearts, they would have been. So maybe it was the truth.

Christina knew if she ever found someone to love as Annelise had loved Eitan, she wouldn't be able to call herself a wife, either. But there was something about love that transcended laws.

"Yet your sister is not here," Lisbeth said, the obvious question in her voice.

They were standing again, which meant Christina couldn't hide from Lisbeth's too-knowing eyes. They bore into her as if she could see Christina's deepest hurt, her deepest shame. If Lisbeth actually could, her open, friendly demeanor would twist into hate and disgust in an instant.

"No" was all Christina said, careful not to let any emotion slip through. "She's not here."

Lisbeth reached out, squeezed Christina's hand through the gloves. The gentle comfort seared into her soul, and Christina had to hold herself still so she didn't flinch away from the pain of it.

Lisbeth let go and Christina could breathe again. She followed Lisbeth's gaze to find Ingrid weaving her way through the crowd. The woman actually had some color in her cheeks and her eyes were bright and alert.

"Shall we trade off?" Ingrid asked as she joined them, her hands on her belly. "For a few hours each? Lisbeth's apartment is only three blocks away. You won't last much longer without a break."

"You go," Christina said, nudging Lisbeth. "I'll keep watch here."

"Not yet," Lisbeth said, and Christina heard the *not ever* even if Ingrid didn't. "It's Monday now."

"And the third day," Christina added.

Both of which were sure to bring more attention to the women gathered outside the Jewish Center. It always took a few days before news trickled out of Germany to the international press, but the Allies likely had hold of the story now.

"I shall go, only to the café, though," Christina said. "For a short time. I'll be back."

Ingrid smiled like she was relieved Christina was taking her advice, but Lisbeth watched her with narrowed eyes. Christina averted her own as she darted into the crowd.

There was a strange energy this morning. Many of the wives had stayed all night, some had gone home to children or to get out of the brutal weather. Some still hadn't shaken the fear that had swept over all of them when the Nazis had begun firing over their heads. Those ones had wide eyes, and they shook even as they stood still.

When Christina made it through the crowd—which still seemed to be growing by the hour—she paused. It was Monday, so technically she was due to report to the Bendlerblock. But if anyone there ordered her to stay away from the protest, she would be disobeying a direct command from a military official. That carried with it a certain weight.

All things being equal, Christina would like to maintain her position at the Abwehr. She'd been there four years now, and had worked her way into a few important inner circles despite her lowly position.

Of course, there were double agents much higher than her. Admiral Canaris, the head of the Abwehr being one of them. While she couldn't exactly drop in on Canaris and ask him to intervene with the Gestapo, she had identified a few others that might be able to at least give her some information.

One of those Canaris loyalists was a man named Royce Wolff, and he worked in an Abwehr office not far from Rose Street.

She flashed her credentials to his secretary and was let in to see him only a few minutes later.

"Fraulein Fischer," Royce greeted her warmly. He knew where her loyalties lay just as much as she knew what side he was on. "How may I be of service?"

"You've heard of the protest?" she asked, not bothering with pleasantries. He gave a curt nod in acknowledgment. "One of the detainees is . . . family."

"You know we can't free him," Royce said carefully. "It's the Gestapo; I certainly don't have sway there. None of us do."

"No, I—" Christina cut herself off, wishing she wasn't so tired. It had been two nights in a row now without more than a few snatched minutes of sleep. She pressed her lips together. "I wanted to hear what the Party line was. About the protest."

Royce sat back in his chair, studying her face. "Goebbels is out of town."

"So?"

"So, that might be the only reason the order to kill you all hasn't been issued," he said, as if it were obvious. "The lower-level Sicherheitsdienst are trying to keep this from him right now. But the higher-ups know he needs to be consulted. There's some internal warring going on that's leaving everyone paralyzed."

The Sicherheitsdienst—the SD for short—was the intelligence-gathering arm of the RSHA. And unlike the Abwehr, the agents were fiercely loyal to Hitler and terrifyingly competent.

She blinked, slow and stupid. "What does that mean?"

"Goebbels's directive was to round up all the Jews in Berlin," Royce said. "Goebbels's other directive is to try to resurrect some home-front morale. The orders contradict themselves and no one wants to get it wrong. Meanwhile he's in Obersalzberg right now. It's buying you time, at the very least."

Christina slotted that piece of information into the rest of what she knew and became even more convinced. "So it *is* the perfect storm."

She knew it sounded like a non sequitur but her entire mind was full of them at the moment. When Royce shook his head, she nodded hers. "Don't you see? This protest could only have happened in this exact moment in time. The defeat at Stalingrad, Goebbels out of town, the long winter, the threat of increased RAF attacks. That it's in Berlin and not some Nazi stronghold like Munich. That's why it's working."

"Is it working?" Royce asked, doubtful.

Christina made a face. "They haven't killed us yet. That screams success in Berlin."

"Fair point." He studied her. "Still, this will likely end in mass arrests. You're willing to risk your position on quite a gamble. Have you considered what's at stake here for such limited gains?"

Christina swallowed. Canaris and his loyalists were planning something big in the next few months. A potential coup attempt, she was sure, though, for obvious reasons, the rumors were few and far between about the operation itself.

She'd heard about it from the same source—a field marshal's secretary who had a penchant for ice-cold blondes—from whom she'd learned that the conspirators were desperate for help from the Allies. But the Allies thought the Germans would get cold feet.

"If any of the higher-ups have big plans that hinge on a low-level Abwehr employee, they have bigger problems than me," Christina pointed out, tired of the theatrics. *Limited gains* stuck in her throat, as well. So many of Canaris's loyalists viewed themselves as righteous, but whenever she spoke to them, they all seemed too entertained by the spy games they were playing. "And I know that we're at war, but the last time I checked, two thousand souls still weighed quite a lot."

He leaned back in his chair, and she could tell she'd struck a nerve. He was gracious in his shame. "That's another fair point, Fischer."

She didn't belabor the point. They'd all said careless, callous things. "Is there chatter about Rosenstrasse from anyone outside of the RSHA?"

"Yes, it's the only thing anyone in Berlin is talking about," Royce said. "There's interest. Doubt. Fear. Depending on what side they're on."

Christina closed her eyes. She could relate to that. "I think it might be something."

"Or you'll all end up dead," he pointed out, not unkindly. It wasn't a far-fetched possibility, though Christina thought the more likely scenario was the first he'd offered. Mass arrests. She wasn't about to linger on the possibility of either, though.

"When does Goebbels return to the city?" If he was the deciding factor, they would need to strategize around his schedule.

"Midweek."

"Does that help us or hurt us?" Christina asked, knowing Royce would tell her the truth, even if she didn't want to hear it.

"Depends if anyone over at RSHA goes rogue," he said. "If they decide it's better to ask Goebbels for forgiveness and sweep you all with machine guns, his absence might hurt you. But if they have any impulse control at all, it gives you time to build public pressure. Maybe they can pretend they really were just registering the men for work details."

Speaking of the detainees . . .

"Why haven't they simply deported the men?" That would be the easiest solution. Get them on trains, and when they were gone, the women would have nothing left for which to ask.

Royce held his hands up. "I would only be guessing. But if you want me to . . . They're not used to this and they don't have a protocol in place. You know. You have to get seventeen signatures and file four different reports just to get extra paper clips. Imagine trying to figure all this out."

Anything that had the Nazis scrambling was a good thing in her book. "What happens next?"

"They'll try to identify the leader—"

"There isn't one," Christina cut in. That was part of what was keeping them safe.

"They'll create one," Royce countered, unruffled. "They'll arrest her, or a few, whatever they decide will play best. A few women with black eyes are better than a street full of dead ones."

It was a classic move from the Nazis. But it wouldn't work now, she didn't think. Maybe if they had done it immediately, when those first couple dozen women had started gathering at the center on Saturday it would have.

Now they knew the Nazis would shoot over their heads.

This had become larger than any one woman.

"That's not going to work," she said.

"Then you better start practicing running from bullets," Royce said, though his voice was still soft. He was like any other double agent, hardened against the world. But he was nicer than some, and he seemed to care. Besides his proximity to the protest, it was why she had come to him.

"There were others rounded up. Thousands of Jewish men, beyond the ones on Rosenstrasse," Christina remembered suddenly. "Ones who aren't married to German women. Are they . . . ?"

"No other protests." Royce confirmed what Christina had already known in her gut. "They'll be deported starting today."

She couldn't care. She *couldn't*. All she could concentrate on were the men held on Rose Street.

"I was . . . doubtful," Royce said. "Before. I thought whatever was happening over there was doomed to fail. But it's day three and you haven't died yet, which was not the odds I would have bet on."

Christina snorted, though secretly she agreed.

"What I'm saying is, don't get distracted by the things you can't do," Royce continued. "Like you said, two thousand souls still weigh quite a lot. You all might actually pull off a miracle, and it's one that the world needs right now."

Christina nodded but didn't tell him the truth.

She didn't care about the world. She only cared about one man.

Chapter 18
ANNELISE

Annelise ran as though her life depended on it, her thighs burning, sweat trickling down the dip of her spine, her heartbeat a fast flutter against her throat.

Arms came around her, yanking her back so that her feet flew off the ground.

"Don't do it."

She screeched like a bird as Eitan swung her in a circle right at the edge of the sharp drop into the lake. Giggling, she swatted at the thick forearms banded around her waist. "You're a scaredy-cat."

"There's nothing wrong with not wanting to break my neck by jumping off a cliff," Eitan said, setting her back on the ground, but he didn't release her yet.

Annelise melted into his embrace, giving him a false sense of security. Then she tipped her head back and nipped at his jaw. The move seemed to surprise him enough that his hands instinctively loosened on her waist, and Annelise wasted no time in seizing the moment. In two strides, she was at the edge of the rocks. Once there, she swung her arms and dove, her body held tight as she plunged through the air.

Her hands hit the water first, but only a split second before the rest of her, the snow-melt lake stealing all the breath from her body. The shock of it was lovely after such a sun-drenched afternoon. She stayed submerged until her lungs begged for air, and stayed submerged a second longer because she liked pushing boundaries.

When she broke through the surface it was to find Eitan leaning over the cliff edge, hands on his hips. She was too far away to see his expression, but the way his entire body relaxed when he spotted her made her think he was genuinely nervous.

"You can't swim," she realized, treading water easily.

"I can swim." Said with righteous male pride.

"Do you need me to hold your hand?" Annelise taunted, amused to have found a way to ruffle him. He was usually so even-keeled it was hard to tease him into a reaction. "You'll have to wait for me to hike back up."

The cliff—which was more an outcropping of rocks, really—wasn't actually that high above the lake; it probably wouldn't take her long to get to him. But she guessed the indignity of it would be too much for Eitan to bear.

"I hate you," he called down before disappearing. Annelise laughed and moved back, out of the way. In the next second, Eitan came flying into the air above her, his arms and legs pinwheeling wildly. He hit the water at such an awkward angle that she winced in sympathy for his poor skin. When he came up coughing and spluttering, Annelise pressed her lips together so she wouldn't laugh at his wet-cat disgruntlement.

"That was graceful," she said, managing to get only half of it out with a straight face before dissolving into laughter. He glared at her before paddling closer and she shrieked knowing what was about to happen.

Fast as anything, he snagged her ankle and yanked her down beneath the water. Instead of fighting it, Annelise went pliant, sinking into the quiet, murky depths with something close to rapture.

Just as quickly, his hands slipped under her arms, pulling her back to the surface. She kept her eyes closed, her face upturned to the sun.

"Annelise." There was panic in his voice as he shook her gently.

She grinned at him then opened her eyes.

"You're going to give me heart failure one of these days," Eitan muttered.

"You're the one trying to drown me."

Their bodies drifted closer together until her belly brushed against his, a fleeting touch. He was in his pants and she in her underthings.

His eyes dropped to the waterline, where the tips of her breasts were outlined against newly transparent fabric. His thumb brushed the underside of the swell, his fingers tight against her rib cage.

"My water sprite," he murmured against her lips before closing the distance between them completely. Heat pulsed through her, yet the water stayed cool against her skin, the contrast exhilarating. She slipped her hand into his damp curls, holding tight even as they began to sink.

Only when they were fully submerged did her smile force them to part.

They both kicked to the surface.

"You are trying to drown me," she said again, laughing.

"We'll drown each other," he promised, his fingers encircling her wrist, trying to bring her back to him.

She splashed him playfully. "Mutual tragedy is only romantic in plays."

"Speaking of tragedy . . ."

Annelise kicked her feet up until she floated on her back, knowing what he was going to say and not wanting to see his puppy eyes. "No, I haven't rethought my plan."

They had been having this conversation ever since Annelise dreamed up what she should do to create her own little "avalanche." In the grand scheme of history, it might not make too many ripples, but there was only so much she could accomplish without weapons.

And as rebellious as she felt these days, she wouldn't know where to even start on that front.

What she had was words. And perhaps something even more powerful—the ability to speak out.

"What if you're caught?" Eitan asked.

"Simply by being born Jewish, you're in more danger every single day than I will ever be," Annelise said, hating that it was true.

They didn't speak about it much, Annelise following his lead. He had enough reminders; he didn't need any from her.

But for her it was an ever-present fear each minute they were apart. The Nazis didn't need much of an excuse to throw a boy like Eitan into a detention center.

"I worry that this is nothing but a lark to many of your friends." Though he softened the criticism by directing it at the other Pirates, Annelise couldn't help but think he included her in the sentiment. The words struck close to Christina's accusation from that day with Frau Sommer.

You treat this like it's a game.

With Christina, Annelise had returned the slap, angry and defensive.

With Eitan, she never would.

Instead, she let herself consider the point. It was true that the Pirates hadn't started out as a resistance group; they all just had a disobedient streak that had drawn them to each other. But over the past year, she'd noticed that urge hardening into something more foundational to who they were.

Their lives were more difficult because they didn't roll over and join the HJ or BDM. Teachers harassed them; employers turned them away. There were people in the country who had it much harder, of course, but it would have been so easy not to be a Pirate.

And it was only going to get harder. Hitler was hungry for war; it was obvious to everyone except the European leaders who were still trying to pacify him. They were to meet in Munich soon to address Hitler's aggression toward Germany's neighbors, but Annelise had read enough of the news reports to know nothing would come of it.

Hitler was going to take the ground they gave him and then he was going to take more until the world had no choice but to respond with violence. This wasn't going to simply get better because everyone was tired of war.

So maybe their resistance schemes seemed childlike now. But how else were they to get better?

This wasn't a game. It was practice.

She slipped closer to Eitan, draping her arms over his shoulders once more, bumping his nose with hers. "I've never been more serious about anything in my life."

"But why?"

"You think it's because of you?" she asked.

"You don't have to sound incredulous."

Annelise dipped down to kiss him, a chaste brush of lips. "I want to believe people are better than what Hitler thinks we are. The only way to do that is to *be* better."

And because she didn't want to think about what would happen to Eitan if people were exactly who Hitler thought them to be, she broke free, kicking into a smooth freestyle stroke heading toward the far side of the lake. She sensed more than heard Eitan follow at a slower pace.

Annelise smiled back at him when her feet hit the pebbled bottom, her attention locked on Eitan, who was struggling but still making his way toward her.

She stood up fully, water sluicing down her arms, over her breasts, the gentle waves lapping at her hips.

A gasp came from the tree line.

Christina stood there, staring at Annelise with dawning horror.

There was a flurry of movement and Eitan stepped in front of her, guarding her modesty with his own body, as if she cared what state her sister saw her in.

They were all frozen in some terrible tableau.

Then Christina's face crumpled.

"Felix was right," she whispered, and took off into the woods.

When Annelise went to follow, Eitan grabbed her around the waist in a sad mimicry of their playful tussle only a half an hour earlier.

"You'll cut each other right now until one or both of you is bleeding," Eitan said quietly, and Annelise realized he was right. The moment she stopped struggling, Eitan released her, and she immediately missed his warmth. Though she'd felt almost pretty in the lake, her translucent underthings giving her a womanly power, now she felt vulnerable. She wrapped her arms around herself.

"I don't know why she cares."

"Secrets," Eitan said, with a wisdom that sometimes infuriated her. He was only a few years older, and yet he could make her feel like a child with only a word. "She doesn't like that she didn't know about us. Who's Felix?"

It took Annelise a moment—she'd almost forgotten what Christina had said before running away.

"Felix Hoffmann," Annelise answered absently as she began searching for her clothes. They'd left them behind one of the rocks along with the remnants of their picnic lunch. She stilled then looked up at him as she realized what that truly meant. "That Nazi you saved me from."

Eitan's brows drew into a deep vee, but he didn't say anything else until after he'd stepped into his trousers and pulled them up over his wet pants. "Why is Christina calling him Felix?"

Annelise straightened, the full weight of the thought slamming into her in the same way the lake had stolen her breath. "We were friends when we were children. But now? I don't know."

They locked eyes, and he ran a worried hand through his curls.

"He wants you."

"I don't want him." It was a stupid thing to say. It didn't matter, and Eitan knew that, anyway.

This wasn't jealousy. This was about the thing they never talked about.

"Men like him, they don't take kindly to rejection," Eitan pointed out. "Especially when the other man is a Jew."

Annelise made a sound, wishing she could refute it but knowing it was true. She looked away. "You're right."

The awful truth hung between them, not quite spoken yet. She made herself say it because it wasn't fair to make him pull the trigger.

"It's not safe for us to spend time together anymore," she said. "Not if Christina is involved."

Eitan didn't argue, and Annelise stared at the ground because it hurt so much to look at him now. How had everything gone so wrong, so fast?

Their little bubble had been popped. And Annelise knew it wasn't just about Christina and Felix. She was bringing attention to Eitan when he needed to keep his head down and blend in. Christina was simply a warning that they could no longer bury their heads in the sand.

Eitan came up behind her, his arm encircling her waist. Just like in the water, she relaxed into his embrace, letting her head fall back against his shoulder. His mouth pressed against the pulse point in her neck.

A goodbye, she thought.

How would she live knowing he was only a few streets away and she couldn't see him? How would she stop her feet from finding their way to the gardens, to the shops he loved so much? To his apartment.

By telling herself that it could mean his death, that's how.

Annelise shuddered out a breath and turned in his arms.

She ached with how much she wanted him. "Can we?"

It came out a whisper, one he could have ignored. But he tugged at her braid until her mouth was positioned perfectly to accept his.

As they kissed, they moved closer, her breasts against his chest, his leg slipping between hers and pressing up against her warmth. His hands gripped the soft flesh of her thighs and lifted, supporting her so that she could wrap her legs around his waist. They sunk to the ground, Annelise in his lap.

She pulled back and pressed her lips to the corner of his eye, to his cheekbone, to his jaw, exactly as he'd done to her that night they'd skated on the frozen pond. Wanting to worship him as he had her.

When their eyes met again, his were full of unshed tears. "I love you, Annelise."

Annelise rested her forehead against his because it hurt too much to look at him. "If only that was enough."

He pinched her, and it startled a giggle out of her, disrupting their somber mood.

"All right, all right," she said. "I love you, too. You know I do."

"It's nice to hear," he said, with a pleased smile. "Goodbyes don't have to be forever."

Except this one might be. Neither of them had to say that out loud. For now, she was being held by the boy she loved. She wasn't going to ruin that.

Everything went hazy and soft and golden after that. Though she couldn't deny there was a layer of desperation beneath their skin, they took their time, exploring the dips and valleys and landscapes of each other's body. Eitan held her gaze when he finally pushed into her and she no longer *wanted*.

Because she had everything she'd ever needed, right in that moment.

They didn't talk on their walk back to town and parted ways long before they could be in danger of being seen.

Annelise was too upset to notice the extra weight in her bag until she got home. She locked her door, and curled up on the floor by the window, pulling out the Rilke volume Eitan must have slipped inside when she was getting dressed.

On the title page was a message, written in his familiar scrawl.

My dearest Annelise, my brave Edelweiss Pirate,

"We need, in love, to practice only this: letting each other go. For holding on comes easily; we do not need to learn it."

Forever yours,
Eitan

Annelise was careful to catch her tears before they ruined the ink.

Chapter 19

EMMY

April 1946

Frankfurt and its surrounding areas had become the de facto American capital of postwar Germany, so Emmy had to flash her papers at several different checkpoints on the way to Bonn.

Every time Major Arnold slowed the jeep, they attracted a gaggle of gaunt-faced children running at their wheels. And every time, Major Arnold reached into a bag he'd stowed behind her seat to toss out bread and cigarettes.

They drove by two entirely leveled towns and one that was perfectly intact, which seemed to serve as a cruel reminder of the destruction's fickleness.

Beyond the reminders that they were traveling amid the aftermath of war, the countryside was as beautiful as she'd expected, the pastoral landscape painting-perfect. Gentle mountains rose in the distance and, as they crept closer, towered above the fields below.

"The Seven Mountains," Major Arnold said, as she stared up at them in wonder. He hadn't spoken overly much on the trip beyond inquiring about her comfort, but she hadn't minded the silence.

"Are the Seven Mountains somewhere the Pirates may have gone camping?" Emmy asked, trying to picture a young Annelise.

"Yes. And Bonn as a whole would have been a haven for outdoor-oriented groups," Major Arnold said, smoothly navigating the ruins as they got closer to the city. He had an appealing confidence about him, borne out by his clear competence whenever dealing with any situation.

"I grew up in the mountains."

His quirked brow was the only thing that gave away his interest. "Would you have been a Pirate?"

"No." Emmy laughed. "We never stayed anywhere long enough to make friends."

That had come out more revealing than she'd meant it to. But he just hummed, a question if she wanted it to be one, an acknowledgment if she didn't.

"My mother was a train car librarian," she said, because for some reason she wanted this man to know her.

"I'm not sure I knew such things existed," Major Arnold said. "I assume it's exactly what it sounds like?"

Emmy shifted to face him, drawing her leg up a bit on the seat. "Yes. My mother talked a wealthy railroad magnate into donating one of his cars. He got publicity for it, and the logging company owners provided money for the books."

"Your mother sounds quite brave."

"She was," Emmy said, smiling softly at the memory of her. Looking back now, she realized how strong her mother had been, living in the American West on her own with a daughter to take care of. She had made life bend to her will, rather than the other way around. "We traveled to logging towns in Montana. The men were usually there without their families, with nothing but work to entertain them. So we brought them books. We had a route, so even if they didn't return them during our stay there, we would collect them on the next pass."

"You must have been a godsend."

"It certainly seemed that way with how they greeted us every time," Emmy said. "It was a painful life for those men. They had work, which was more than everyone could say. But it was lonely and harsh. Many of them died because of lax safety measures. Their bosses took most of their profit and left them in rustic conditions where they had to pray to survive the winters. I always thought of the books we brought them as candles in the dark, providing a little bit of light and warmth."

In those circumstances, books became a connection to others.

Even if it was just to the author, even if it was just to curse their name or laugh at a joke they told. How did you ever walk away from a book without one of your tapestry threads forever tied to someone else?

"Sometimes, if we were particularly friendly with the men, we'd join them at their fire," Emmy said. "There were plenty who couldn't read in the camps, but the ones who could always took turns reading out loud."

Emmy realized the picture she was painting was too romantic for what life had actually been like for her and her mother. There were those fond memories of nights by the fire, filled with the simple, primal joy of someone telling a story to an audience.

But there had also been the men who stole from their tiny library to sell the books in the next town over; the close encounters that her mother had experienced and Emmy had been too young to understand; there had been the shotgun tucked under the bolted-down checkout desk in case the bandits who saw trains as an easy jackpot ever wandered into their car.

She glanced at Major Arnold and again felt that tug in her belly, the urge to tell him all that. And so she did as they drove ever closer to Bonn.

"Your mother must have been quite hearty," Major Arnold said when she finally trailed off, and Emmy hiccupped out a laugh.

"That's certainly one way of describing her."

"You wouldn't agree?"

"Oh, she was the toughest lady I've ever met," Emmy said, with a sigh. Her mother had died more than ten years ago, when Emmy had been only seventeen. That's when Emmy had headed to Boston, and met Joseph and her life had changed forever. "I was picturing her face hearing you call her a descriptor best used for a soup."

Major Arnold actually grinned at that. Emmy had to look away and watch him from the corner of her eye, unable to deal with the full onslaught of his subtle charm.

"Fair enough," he said, his face settling back into neutral. "Your father . . ."

"Didn't exist," Emmy confessed. It had never bothered her. She'd asked about it once, her mother had given some terse reply and then the subject had been dropped for good. How could she miss something she'd never had? "And by that I mean, of course he did, but my mother never named him. She put a wedding ring on her finger the night she left Boston and her family behind. In the West, no one asks questions about your past." She smiled. "Her family had been old, established wealth. The kind who'd come over on the *Mayflower* to hear her tell it. I can't imagine being thrown out of a life of luxury and deciding to head to Montana to bring books to men who lived in the wilds."

He shot her a look. "Can't you?"

It was a line she had used before, and most people nodded in knowing agreement. They didn't often see past her soft body and the city veneer she'd picked up from ten years of living in Boston and Washington. But her thighs, though thick, were strong and carried her up mountains; her temperament had been crafted by precarious survival.

"Well, I suppose I can imagine it," she said, with a wry smile. "Here I am, spilling out my whole history to you and you have the audacity to call me mysterious."

"I think there might be a saying about icebergs that seems appropriate here," he said, mirroring her own gentle jibe from Thursday night.

Emmy hummed in acknowledgment. She might have told him more than she had any other stranger she could think of, but she hadn't told him the big secrets. The ones that still felt like tender bruises under her skin.

"Still. Now you must divulge something, as well."

"I never agreed to this contract," he protested, but his lips twitched. "I'm an orphan. I didn't know either of my parents."

Something clicked into place with that tidbit. "That's why you chose history."

Her observation surprised him if his sharp glance was anything to go by.

"When you don't have any of your own, you go looking for someone else's," he said. "Not many people have made that connection."

And yet it seemed so obvious to her. Had his thinking become so familiar in just two weeks that she could follow it without batting an eye?

"Did you find what you wanted to?" she asked. "From history."

"I believe so," he said after a thoughtful moment. "So much of history is long, sweeping arcs—the wars, the empires, the time periods divided up into hundred-year spans. But that's never what appealed to me. I liked the human moments."

Another piece of the puzzle. "Like Eitan and Annelise."

He smiled, pleased. "Just like Eitan and Annelise. A Jewish man who fell in love with a German rebel." He waved a hand toward a burned-out vehicle on the side of the road, and then to the cratered field they were driving by. "It makes all this seem real in a way that simply knowing about the bare facts doesn't."

"Do you think we'll find them?" she asked.

"I want to say yes."

"I know you do. You're an optimist," Emmy said, unable to keep the affection out of her voice. How did they have inside jokes already? Softly, she said, "I think we will, too."

They didn't speak again until they made it into the middle of Bonn, Major Arnold parking on a street that had only half its houses standing. He flagged down an American soldier and tasked him with watching the jeep. These days, that kind of vehicle could be stripped for pieces in less than five minutes.

Major Arnold had both secured a map of Bonn and located the bookshop from the title page of Eitan's Rilke. The store's name was in German, but Emmy could read—if not fluently speak—the language.

One More Page Books.

Through some kind of fate, the store was still standing. Its neighbors had not been so lucky.

A middle-aged woman looked up from the counter when the bell rang announcing their presence. She had Coke bottle–thick glasses and long, silver-threaded hair twisted into a braided updo around the crown of her head. "Guten Tag."

Major Arnold rattled something off in what sounded like flawless German, and the woman smiled.

"Hello," she said in English this time. "May I help you with anything?"

"I'm trying to find the previous owner of this Rilke collection," Emmy said, pulling the book out of her bag.

The woman's eyes narrowed. "Why?"

Emmy actually appreciated the suspicion. This woman had spent more than a decade living under Hitler's rule after all.

"I'd like to return it to them," Emmy said, hesitating for a moment before holding the slim volume out to her.

"All books are safe with me," the woman said, before taking it and flipping open to the title page. She stilled completely.

"You recognize the names," Emmy said. It wasn't a question.

"Eitan," the woman breathed out, and Emmy wasn't even sure she realized she'd said it. She looked up, meeting Emmy's eyes. "This belonged to my nephew."

Chapter 20
CHRISTINA

March 1, 1943

Christina's mind was foggy from exhaustion and the cold, but she'd been a double agent in Berlin for long enough that she almost immediately spotted her tail after leaving Royce Wolff's office.

There were two men, both dressed in nice trousers with good shoes. That was always a giveaway for these sadistic ghouls. It was one of the tricks every Berliner had picked up over the past decade or so. The Gestapo didn't wear uniforms while in Germany, so learning how to spot them became a matter of life and death.

Christina shoved her shaking hands in her pockets and kept her head down, hoping it was a coincidence they were there. She knew, though. She knew they were following her.

For a brief moment, Christina considered abandoning the protest altogether. They weren't going to win. They were deluding themselves that this would end in anything but them taken away in those horrific trucks. At best.

She could just leave. Go back to her apartment, go back to her life.

Christina wasn't actually married to Eitan. The only thing drawing her back to Rose Street was a promise she'd made when she was sixteen.

Then she pictured the flash of disappointment that would inevitably cross Lisbeth's face when she slowly realized Christina wasn't coming back.

And she trudged on, toward Rose Street.

Sometimes, when she wasn't careful, Christina started thinking of herself as a kind of hero. A flawed one, of course, but reformed sinners made the most interesting characters, didn't they?

Then she would have a moment like this that humbled her completely. She was a coward. Maybe she was working off her debt to the universe, trying to atone for her mistakes, but that didn't change who she was at her core. Who she would always be.

She wasn't Annelise. She wasn't some brave, rebellious spirit that couldn't be caged.

She was just some woman who was failing at the one thing she'd promised herself she wouldn't fail at.

The edges of the crowd came into view, and Christina exhaled her relief.

She hadn't received any formal training when she'd signed on as a double agent for the Americans, and she'd always gotten the distinct impression that they didn't know what to do with the spies who worked in the Abwehr, the organization already so leaky they were never sure what was good intel or not.

Still, there were things she'd learned along the way—things beyond managing the fear that sat lead-heavy in her belly.

The crowd would protect her, but she needed to reach it. The Gestapo were still half a block behind her, and Christina was only a few strides away from the closest women. She didn't want to bring them down with her, but she didn't need to.

All she needed to do was liberate the crocheted hat carelessly stuffed in a coat pocket. She nabbed it as she passed the young woman, smiling as she did. Her target didn't so much as frown at her before going back to her chants.

With a quick jerk, Christina undid her plait, which had frozen sometime overnight. She brushed some slush and ice out of her hair and shoved the cap on over the mess. Still pressing through the crowd, she shrugged out of her coat, inverted it, and slipped it back on. The lining would look strange to anyone up close, but if the Gestapo agents were scanning the crowd looking for dark fabric, their eyes would skim over the tweed.

The small adjustments might not have worked had the crowd been any smaller, but she soon became another blond woman in a sea of them.

By the time she made it to the front, she no longer felt the agents' eyes on her back.

It didn't bode well that they'd been following her in the first place, but that was something she would worry about later.

Lisbeth greeted her with the same narrow-eyed suspicion from earlier. Ingrid smiled, one hand pressed against her enormous belly.

"Did anything happen?" Christina asked. The women in front of them had started marching in a line along the human chain of police. She heard a few variations on the theme, but for the most part the wives were still sticking with that one message:

"Give us back our husbands."

Christina studied the faces of the men guarding the Jewish Center. Some seemed bored or cold, but some seemed impressed, their mouths ajar, their eyes wide as they watched the women.

"The man in charge keeps coming out to check on us," Ingrid answered. "That tall man."

"Has he done anything?"

"No, he just glared at all of us," she said.

Christina turned to study her closer. "Are you feeling well?"

"I am," Ingrid said, rubbing her stomach. "But truly, how long can this go on?"

She was staring at the women marching through slush and ice. The frozen rain had let up around midmorning, but it had done its damage. Wet clothes in winter meant death. Moving about must be helping some of the women, but their closest neighbors all had blue-tinged lips.

And yet the crowd only continued to grow. Hundreds of people crowded into the narrow space—it had been almost impossible to navigate her way back to Lisbeth and Ingrid. This protest wasn't going to break up anytime soon.

Mass arrests, her mind whispered viciously.

She pushed that thought away.

It would either happen or it wouldn't. Right now, they had to stick with the message that had so far kept them alive.

They would also have to figure out a way to make this more sustainable to the wives who refused to even take breaks inside.

"I've been thinking about collecting some blankets from my neighborhood," Lisbeth said, as if she'd read Christina's mind.

Her cheeks were flushed a painful-looking pink beneath her freckles. But her eyes were alert. She also bounced on the balls of her feet, a sign that she could still feel the cold. Paradoxically, perhaps, that made Christina feel better.

"I'll help." Maybe it was a bad idea to leave so soon after returning to the protest, but they wouldn't have a protest to hold if half the women froze to death, the weather doing the Nazis' dirty work for them.

When they broke free of the crowd, Lisbeth glanced around and dropped her voice.

"Any information you'd like to share?"

When Christina shot her a questioning look, Lisbeth rolled her eyes. "Oh, please. Don't try to bullshit a bullshitter."

Christina squawked out an unattractive laugh at the language and Lisbeth grinned.

"My father owned a nightclub," she said. "We learned some colorful phrases from the Americans who stopped by."

"A nightclub?" Christina was desperately intrigued, picturing sticky floors and brassy music and rowdy dancing.

Lisbeth's smile dimmed, her expression shuttering, and Christina wondered what she had done wrong.

"Did you find anything out?" Lisbeth asked, returning the conversation to the matter at hand.

"Goebbels won't be back in the city until midweek," Christina said, letting Lisbeth keep her secrets. "If we survive long enough for him to get back to Berlin, we might have a chance of getting out of all this alive."

"If we don't?"

"There are power games being played that probably won't end in our favor," Christina said, and she knew Lisbeth could fill in the blanks.

"The one and only time I'll ever wish for Goebbels to prevail."

Christina couldn't say that honestly. Once upon a time, the man had been an idol of hers—she'd wished for him to prevail many a time. So she changed the topic. "Tell me about him. Your husband."

Lisbeth's smile went dreamy and fond, and Christina immediately chastised herself for the lick of pain she felt seeing it.

"He's kind and brave," she said, without having to think on it at all, extinguishing a tiny flame of hope that the pair's relationship wasn't a love match. Of course it was. Lisbeth wouldn't have stayed married to him otherwise. The Nazis had made it laughably easy over the past few years for Aryans to divorce their Jewish spouses. The second they did, the Jewish partner would be immediately deported, though. "And smart as a whip. He's my dearest friend. And he's the best man I've ever known."

"How did you meet?"

Lisbeth shoved her hands in the pockets of her coat and didn't answer. Again, Christina tried to figure out what she'd asked that was wrong, and this time she realized what it was. One glance at Lisbeth confirmed her guess.

"You didn't meet before the Nuremberg Laws."

"Shhh," Lisbeth all but hissed, looking over their shoulders. No one was following them.

The Nuremberg Laws had banned intermarriages between Aryans and Jews, but hadn't dissolved ones that already existed. Christina had heard tell that sometimes, instead of smuggling a Jewish man out of the country, it was easier to forge a marriage license to an Aryan woman granting the man some degree of protection. Christina supposed that possibility existed for couples who were actually in love, as well.

"I won't ask again," she promised.

Lisbeth shot her a grateful look and took a sharp turn down a narrow side street.

They started knocking on doors. Some were shut in their faces, but most were held open to them. The women pressed blankets and food into their arms, even though their linen cupboards and pantries must have been nearly bare coming at the end of the impossibly long and hard winter they'd all had.

When she and Lisbeth struggled with the weight of what they'd collected, they were given bags. Two women offered to help bring the supplies to the protesters. Another offered them the last of her tea.

After they were finished asking at each house in the neighborhood, Christina had to lean against a building and breathe.

Lisbeth was in front of her in an instant. "What is it?"

"They have next to nothing themselves, and yet they're giving us what they do have." Christina couldn't even identify what emotion had her voice quavering. It had been so long since she'd seen the good in people, since she'd thought of them as anything but enemies or allies.

"It's hard to hate people whose name you know, who you see every day at the bakery," Lisbeth said. "One of Hitler's best strategies was isolating us from each other so we didn't realize he was the one causing all the pain we blamed everyone around us for."

"Some people realized," Christina said, not thinking of herself, of course, but of Annelise.

Lisbeth smiled sadly. "Not enough."

"No."

"Well, this is also a historic Jewish district," Lisbeth said. "Even if those women aren't married to Jewish men, they still view us as a part of their community."

Christina pushed off the building and grabbed the last of their bags. They turned in unison back to Rose Street.

"How do they look away, though?" Christina asked, not expecting an answer. What she really wanted to say was *How had she?* She'd been a child, that much she acknowledged in the quiet of her own mind. It alleviated the guilt, but only slightly. Annelise had been young when she'd said no to joining the BDM.

Christina knew she wasn't special. Almost every girl in her school had joined the BDM; almost every girl in Germany who had qualified for membership had.

Annelise had been the special one.

"I think we underestimate how hard it is to be brave," Lisbeth said. "I think we read stories as children about heroes and think everyone—including ourselves—would be able to save the day, if given the chance. Most people are just people, though. Not heroes."

"I think these women are heroes," Christina said as they neared the edges of the protest.

Lisbeth bumped her shoulder against Christina's. "You know you're one of these women, right?"

Christina nearly recoiled at the implication that she was heroic. Her horror must have shown on her face, because Lisbeth stopped, studying her.

"You don't like yourself very much, do you?" she asked, and Christina's heart raced in her throat. But Lisbeth didn't force her to answer. She turned and pushed her way into the wall of people, somehow finding spaces to slip through. Christina stayed on her heels, both of them handing out the last of their supplies as they headed back to the spot where they'd left Ingrid.

Except Ingrid wasn't there. Christina told herself not to worry. The women had become something of a collective, more united now than the strangers they'd been only three days prior. Ingrid would be looked after.

Christina turned to the group next to her. "Has anything happened?"

"They're letting in some packages," the woman said. "Food for the men inside."

"And another truck came," someone else added. "The men were beaten but able to walk."

"Any more threats?" Christina asked.

"No, just the same blustering."

Christina smiled her thanks and turned back to Lisbeth.

"I suppose now we wait."

"For what?" Lisbeth asked, and though Christina knew it was rhetorical, she answered anyway.

"For one side to break."

"Hopefully not ours," Lisbeth murmured, her eyes scanning the faces around them. "It feels like we should be doing more to nudge it in our favor."

"But if we do, we could tip the scales in the wrong direction." They were on a tightrope right now, hundreds of feet off the ground with thousands of lives in the balance. Right now, the status quo was what they needed to maintain.

And so, they waited.

The day passed uneventfully. At some point, Lisbeth disappeared to create a package for her husband. She spoke quietly to one of the young SS officers by the door, handing over the small bundle.

"I don't know if he'll actually get it," Lisbeth admitted when she returned. "But I had to try."

Christina went next, finding a small store a few streets over that still had some bread left. She didn't put a note inside. Eitan didn't need to know who was helping him, just that someone was.

Hope was a powerful force when it came to survival.

By early evening, the SS officers were kept busy delivering items to the detainees, and Christina had to wonder if it was to maintain the illusion that the husbands were only being kept there to be registered.

The Nazis were walking on a tightrope, too.

Christina had spent the better part of the day thinking about what could push them one way or the other.

But when the sirens started to wail, she realized she hadn't once considered an air raid.

Chapter 21

EMMY

April 1946

The woman who owned One More Page Books was named Ursula Braun—no relation to Eva, she'd rushed to assure them. She closed up the shop immediately after realizing she was holding her nephew's book and led Emmy and Major Arnold up to a small apartment on the second floor.

Major Arnold paused at the bottom of the long, narrow steps, but only for a moment. When he eventually lowered himself into the chintz chair in the sitting room, he surreptitiously massaged the top of his leg. Emmy wondered if it was enough to help, or if another pair of hands would be more beneficial.

She blushed at her own inappropriate thoughts and tore her eyes away from him.

"Eitan wasn't my nephew by blood," Ursula told them as she handed out weak tea and stale cookies. It was more generous than she had to be, so Emmy took one even though she knew it would surely taste like sawdust. "His mother was a dear friend of mine when we had been children. And I helped her get out of Germany with her baby daughter."

"Eitan stayed behind?"

"There were only the two visas," Ursula said, her tone blunt but not defensive. "Eitan had a good job in a factory in town. We had hoped that would keep him safe."

Emmy didn't want to ask, but she forced out the question. "And it didn't?"

"I wish I knew the answer to that." Ursula sighed. "In truth, I lost track of him when he left Bonn back in 1938."

"Where did he go?"

"He wouldn't say. Told me that the less I knew the better for me." Ursula shrugged. "He was scared and devastated, acting like he was being chased out of town. I thought maybe he could outrun whoever was after him, but I was naive. No one outruns Nazis."

"Do you know what happened to upset him?"

"He left the second day of Kristallnacht." Ursula's throat bobbed as she swallowed. "I assumed that was the reason."

The Night of Broken Glass. Emmy distinctly remembered being horrified at the news reports. There had been riots all over Germany, Austria, and the Sudetenland where violent mobs had destroyed synagogues and Jewish businesses and homes and schools. Around thirty thousand Jewish men had been arrested and sent to concentration camps and nearly a hundred had been murdered over the course of the pogrom.

"The Nazis called it 'a night' but in reality the terror went on for two days," Ursula said. "I didn't know if he was alive or dead. And then he showed up with his bags packed. I wept for the first time in years when he left because I had promised his mother I would look after him."

Emmy wasn't in a position to offer absolution or comfort, so she waited. Major Arnold didn't rush to fill the silence, either. This was such a thorny place to live, in this slice of time right after so much devastation. Emmy looked at this old woman, with her arthritic hands and her somber eyes, and wanted to reassure her and also wanted to ask why she didn't do a better job.

"Did his mother make it through the war?"

Ursula shook her head. "She and the baby died in an accident. An overturned automobile of all things. You wouldn't think normal tragedies happen during war, but they do."

Normal tragedies. Emmy turned the phrase over in her mind, and as much as she hated it, she had to agree with the sentiment. The husband of one of her neighbors in Washington had died from heart failure in 1942, and the widow had been forced to explain every time that he hadn't been lost in combat. It had created an odd dissonance. War was already too big a grief to bear, no one had room left to think of life's little cruelties on top of that.

"And Annelise, did you know her?" Emmy asked. Ursula still held the Rilke, and Emmy had been fighting the urge to yank it back since she'd handed it over.

Flipping to the title page, Ursula stared down at the name.

"No," she said. "He was an adult; I wasn't his mother."

"He didn't mention anyone to you? A girl he was courting?"

"Once . . ." Ursula squinted off into the distance. "I think there was a girl that summer. In thirty-eight. Her mother had a position at the factory where he worked."

"Could it have been Annelise?"

"Perhaps," Ursula said, though she didn't sound at all certain. "I don't recall a name."

"May I?" Major Arnold held out his hand for the Rilke volume and Emmy's entire body relaxed in relief. She was finding it hard to put into words why she didn't want Ursula to keep the book even though the woman had—at least once upon a time—considered Eitan family. This might be their best chance at returning the thing to its rightful owner.

But Ursula had been so careless with Eitan when he had been here. This was the memory of him made tangible. Who was to say she would do any better by the book than she had the boy?

"You never tried to find Eitan after he left Bonn?"

"Where would I have started?" Ursula snapped. "In the mass graves?"

Emmy drew in a sharp breath.

"You don't understand what it was like," Ursula said, her body going taut with defensive anger. "You weren't here. You aren't allowed to judge me."

Major Arnold stood. "We've taken enough of your time, ma'am."

Quickly, Emmy scrambled to her feet. Ursula had that feverish look in her eyes that horses had when they'd been pinned to a fence. They were terrified but that didn't make them any less deadly.

Emmy told herself this woman had lived in a war zone, was surviving in the chaos left behind. That experience stripped a person down to raw materials. Still, Emmy wanted to leave the cramped apartment as quickly as possible.

"One more question, if you don't mind, though," Major Arnold said, his tone polite and pleasant despite the new tension in the room. "What was Eitan's surname, please? I have records I can check to see if we can locate him."

Ursula's mouth worked for a second like she was wrestling with herself about whether to give out the information. Then, as if her strings had been cut, she slumped farther into the chair and stared at the floor. "Basch. Eitan Basch. His mother's name was Sarah. He worked at the metal factory on the edge of town."

"Thank you," Major Arnold said, and handed the book back to Emmy before guiding her out of Ursula's presence.

Back on the street, Emmy inhaled, not realizing how claustrophobic Ursula's place had felt.

"That was productive," Major Arnold commented, sounding far more chipper than she was able to be at the moment. When Emmy stared at him, he shrugged. "We got Eitan's name on our first try."

Ever the optimist.

The rush of affection caught Emmy off guard, so much so that she laughed. "I like you, Major Arnold."

He flinched in a startled kind of way and then, to her delight, blushed and ducked his head. He scratched at the skin above his scars and cleared his throat. Cleared it again. "Yes. Well."

Emmy laughed once more, the storm cloud that had blown in with their visit to Ursula's dissipating completely. "Shall we try to find Annelise?"

"I don't believe our luck will hold on that front," Major Arnold said, glancing around at the shops, not looking at her. His ears were still pink. "Her name is too common, and we have so little to go on. But if Eitan spent time around here, perhaps someone will remember the two of them. It doesn't hurt to try, since we came all this way."

Major Arnold's prediction proved accurate. Four hours later, Emmy was exhausted and dejected, the earlier thrill of finding Eitan's name having faded into disappointment. A few store owners had remembered Eitan, but none of them could give them any information about Annelise.

"Don't look so downcast," Major Arnold said, as they made their way back to his jeep. A different young officer stood guarding it now, and he saluted in response to their greeting. "I'll be able to pull any records on Eitan Basch, and we know that Annelise's mother worked in the same factory as he did."

Emmy brightened at that. It had started to feel like the day had been pointless, but it had simply been so front-loaded that she hadn't managed to keep the right perspective.

After climbing into the jeep, she pulled one of her legs up beneath her and rested her elbow on the window frame, chancing a peek at Major Arnold through her lashes. "Thank you for helping me today. I know you must have so many demands on your time."

"It was a good reminder."

"Of what?" Emmy asked.

"Why we're doing this," he said simply. "There's been so much to organize over the past few months that it has become easy to forget there are people and stories behind each of these books. A lot of them have come to the depot from research libraries or state collections. Those are important but feel less . . . personal."

She'd had that thought many times about the Library of Congress. She loved her work there, felt privileged to handle masterpieces, but she sometimes missed smaller libraries. The ones where children would come in with big eyes and eager grins, the ones where mothers would desperately ask for parenting pamphlets, the ones where Emmy could spend time helping a reluctant browser find exactly the perfect book to open their eyes to the pleasure of reading.

"Some of the officers I work with"—he slid her a look—"the Monuments Men, I believe they're called."

"You're called," she corrected with a little grin.

He tipped his head in agreement. "They don't think we should waste time on personal collections. They like to focus on the big artifacts, the priceless paintings, the historic buildings that might be salvageable. Why spend so many resources on a book that can be reprinted?"

"Not all of them can, though," she said, thinking of Lucy and her Yiddish folk songs.

"Those they care about," he acknowledged. "But they wonder why I would try to save a Rilke." He gestured toward her bag. "We could reprint that volume. You can't bring back an original van Gogh, but a book isn't one of a kind. The heart of it is in the story, not the physical copy itself."

Emmy could see their point, almost. If she squinted.

That mentality only worked, though, if people collected books just for the sake of collecting them. Instead, the value was rooted in emotion rather than consumer demand. The books that people held on to—the ones they read so many times their spines became creased and their ink smudged—were a glimpse into someone's soul. Those were the books that had gotten them through their deepest grief, the ones that brought back their happiest memories, the ones that helped raise their children and guided them through life's hardest questions.

"I wish they could see the messages, the bookplates," Major Arnold continued before she could say any of that. He knew as well as she did, though, clearly. "I think on a day-to-day basis, it's hard for us to understand the sheer magnitude of this war, the atrocities too big to really make sense. But then you come across a book that was owned by a boy named Eitan who loved a girl named Annelise.

Or one owned by a man whose mother had an irreverent sense of humor. Or one that was shared back and forth between two friends who dreamed about a world bigger than their small rural town. And you see each of the human beings behind those terrible numbers in headlines. I care about a looted van Gogh masterpiece because I care about preserving culture. But I care about these books because I care about humanity."

Emmy blamed the glint of the sun off the Rhine for the tears in her eyes. They were headed back to the countryside now, into the mountains.

"I want them to be alive," she confessed so quietly she wondered if the wind would steal her words before they reached him.

He didn't say anything for a long time, so long she thought he wouldn't say anything at all.

But then he glanced over.

"If they're not, their memory will be our blessing to carry."

Chapter 22

ANNELISE

Summer 1938

Annelise would deny it to anyone other than herself but heartbreak made her reckless.

"I'll throw the pamphlets," she volunteered, interrupting the boys' discussions about who would take on the extra risk for their grand scheme at the Cologne station. The eight of them who'd come were packed into one train compartment, shoulders pressed tight to fit.

The plan was to climb various structures in the train station's lobby to get as wide a distribution as possible for the flyers they'd made for the occasion. Stefan would take one side, Hans the middle, and Annelise the ticket booths.

Their avalanche would be made of paper.

No one fought her, everyone a little scared. Hans had to be cajoled into it in the first place. Eventually, he'd had to admit he was one of the best climbers in the group.

They had been careful with how they'd dressed and Annelise was proud of them. If not for the fact that they were a mixed group, Annelise would have pegged them as HJ boys out of uniform.

The Pirates lingered in their compartment when the train pulled into Cologne until one of the porters nudged them along. The girls peeled off toward the toilets, and the boys slouched by a newspaper stand, flipping through comics and magazines.

"Are you sure about this?" Marta asked, once they checked they had the water closet to themselves. Annelise dug out the bundle of papers from her bag and shoved them into her top.

"We could hardly call ourselves Pirates if we didn't face a little danger once in a while," Annelise said, more flippantly than she felt. She handed her bag over to Marta. Three of the Pirates would "steal" the purse from Marta, who would be properly—and loudly—distraught about the loss.

"Don't forget, this isn't worth your life," Marta said, more serious than Annelise had ever seen her. "Run and hide if you need to."

Annelise leaned forward and placed a sloppy kiss on Marta's cheek. "There are things worse than landing in the EL-DE Haus."

"You say that now," Marta said, but her tone was lighter. "Let me know what you think after they yank all those pretty nails off your fingers."

Instinctively, Annelise curled her hands into fists, but then laughed and shot Marta a rude gesture. She sailed out of the toilets before Marta's concern could weigh too heavily on her shoulders.

The Cologne train station looked like a cathedral. It had high, vaulted ceilings and wooden ticket-selling booths with spires that reminded Annelise of confessionals or choirs. Light poured in through the circular windows above the arched entrance, people streaming in through the beams, not looking around, not looking up.

Stone and mortar would never impress Annelise like the forest, but there was that same muffled sense of beauty here that she felt when she sunk beneath water. She basked in it for one, two seconds, and then she mentally nudged herself.

Now was not the time to linger.

There were wrought iron gates creating lines to the ticket-selling booths that would act as a perfect foothold to launch herself toward the top of a booth.

The distance would be the challenge, jumping high enough to grip onto the edge. It might have been easier for one of the tall boys to do it, but Annelise knew her light frame was an advantage here. As long as she could reach, she'd be able to haul herself up with mostly her arms alone.

She sidled closer, trying to look like she was checking train times. The guard near the entrance watched her, but not in a suspicious way yet. Annelise considered actually buying a ticket somewhere, but it wasn't as if she had money to waste. Especially after the flyers had taken so much of her savings.

And she'd given Marta her coin purse along with her bag. She couldn't purchase anything even if she wanted to.

An old woman tapped her on the shoulder, asked if she was in line, and Annelise waved at her to go first. The guard still hadn't looked away. She wondered if the bundle of paper beneath her shirt was obvious, and guessed that maybe it was since the guard was now walking toward her.

Annelise chewed on her lip and tried to find Marta and the other Pirates out of the corner of her eye. She didn't want to look directly at them in case it alerted the guard to their presence, as well.

Run and hide if you need to.

Marta's voice echoed in her head, but then she caught sight of Hans. He lingered near the stalls, the ones that were meant for passengers waiting on trains. The wooden structures resembled the ticket booths, yet were likely harder to scale, hence the assignment falling to Hans, the best climber of the group.

She had to time her ascent with his, otherwise she would throw off the entire plan. They couldn't have half an avalanche.

Annelise pictured Eitan, pictured his quiet eyes as he watched Nazis march around Bonn as if they owned the town. And they practically did. There was already some talk about Jews having to carry special identification papers. There were rumors about those awful camps that were popping up all over the countryside. There were the "work-shy" men who were punished harshly because no one was able to hire the Jewish residents in town.

Annelise had the luxury of running and hiding.

Eitan did not.

Taking a deep breath, Annelise turned to face the guard head-on as he took the final two steps to close the distance between them.

"Sir, I've missed my train. I'm trying to get to my grandmother's in Berlin; she's going to be so upset with me. She told me I was too scatterbrained to come visit her by myself but my brother is in training with the Wehrmacht and my parents couldn't spare the day from work—"

He held up a hand, his face hard. He had small, dark eyes and a mouth so thin that she guessed he always looked angry.

"Where are you coming from?" he asked, his staccato cadence harsh.

Annelise switched tactics. "What right do you have to ask me that? I've done nothing wrong. Who is your supervisor? I'd like to file a complaint about you harassing me."

The guard's eyes narrowed, and she wondered if she really would have to run.

A scream sliced through the air.

Marta.

"Stay here," the guard barked. Annelise didn't bother responding, the man was already rushing toward the far end of the lobby. Marta had fallen to her knees, wailing and pointing to some side door as several guards converged on her.

Annelise wasted none of the small window Marta had bought them. In two strides, she was at the closest metal barrier. A young man watched her from behind the glass of the ticket booth but didn't seem inclined to alert the authorities. In fact, he went back to the newspaper he had been flipping through even as Annelise hefted herself up onto the gate.

She positioned her feet like she would if she were crossing a thin log over a rushing stream, then she bent her knees and leaped. If her fingers didn't make contact with the top, she risked a painful fall to the marble floor below.

But her hands touched flat wood and she exhaled a shaky, relieved breath.

Gripping the corner edge of the booth, she used her foot to feel for the decorative knob she'd noticed in the wood paneling.

It took two tries to gain purchase on what she thought might be a globe. The next foothold turned out to be a gargoyle that was too high. She breathed out, re-gripped the corner, and pressed up from the globe for a weightless moment. Her shoe scraped against wood. She'd landed the little leap.

With that, she was high enough to use her arms to boost herself up the rest of the way.

She scrambled for balance as she glanced around. Most people were still rushing for the trains. It was early enough in the day that there were plenty of commuters in the station. A few had stopped to gather around Marta, a few stared up at Annelise even as they continued toward the platforms. No one had blown the whistle on her yet.

Annelise found Hans, then Stefan. Both had made it to their perches. A rush of nerves and excitement flooded through her, and she yanked the bundle of papers out of her shirt.

Stefan held up three fingers. He put one down. Then another.

The three of them took one collective breath and Stefan put his final finger down.

Annelise threw her head back, and with the voices of all the Pirates that were still in the train station backing her, she yelled, "'Every nation deserves the government it endures.'"

As the quote from Joseph de Maistre echoed off the stone walls, Annelise flung the pamphlets into the air with all her might. Stefan and Hans followed suit.

The world seemed to still, the busy commuters stopping, their faces upturned, the light catching it all, holding the moment so that Annelise could burn it into her mind.

Then one woman reached up and snagged a flyer from the air.

The world inhaled.

Chaos erupted.

Annelise didn't let herself pay attention to it. She was already shimmying back down the ticket booth, her feet hitting the metal grate. She locked eyes with the boy behind the glass once more and he held his fist up in solidarity. Annelise grinned, leaped lightly down to the floor, and took off running, her shoes skidding on one of the papers now on the ground.

The guards whistled and called out behind her, but there were too many Pirates heading for exits they had mapped out the week before.

The more confusion, the better chance they had of escaping. The only one not dashing away was Marta, who they'd all decided should stay in character.

By some miracle, Annelise made it clear of the lobby without anyone yanking her into custody. She took the left and right she'd memorized, and found the narrow door that had been a lucky break in their explorations over the summer. It led to stairs, which led to an underground hallway that seemed reserved for workmen who had to service the trains.

It was nearly pitch black, but Annelise didn't slow. Cobwebs caught on her face, in her hair, and she kept going, taking another right.

Light framed the door at the end.

Annelise ran like she'd run for the cliffs at the lake with Eitan, her thighs burning from the exertion. With the next inhale, she pushed out into fresh air, the hallway dumping her into an alley behind the station.

She only stopped running when she hit Lohsepark, a green space on the north side of the city.

An arm came around her waist, and she nearly yelped. But she quickly realized it was Dietrich, the boy who had "stolen" Annelise's bag from Marta.

"Here," he said, thrusting it at her. His presence would already help. If the police were looking for Annelise, the guards would have described her as a blond girl on her own. Likewise, Dietrich would have stood out more by himself. As a couple, they blended in with the rest of the Germans strolling through the park on a warm summer afternoon.

With a few more adjustments to her clothing, they should be able to completely escape notice by anyone searching for them.

Annelise wrapped a bright blue scarf around her hair—people trying to hide tended to think a muted shade would work best, but Annelise wanted to look like she *wasn't* trying to hide. Then she stripped out of her white blouse, with Dietrich blocking her movements with his body. Beneath she had on a tighter, pale yellow shirt that might mark her as an antisocial youth, but was certainly different than any description from the train station.

Dietrich stood back, considering. "Passable."

"Did it work?" he asked, looping his arm around her shoulder.

Annelise didn't know how to answer that. Dietrich had left the building before they'd tossed their flyers, so the easy answer was yes. Their plan had gone off without a hitch—at least the execution of it had. It remained to be seen if all the Pirates had made their way out of the train station safely.

Did it work?, though, was more complicated. She'd thought she might have seen something flicker into an expression or two. Hope or pride or grief or longing. An odd mixture of all of them?

The pamphlets listed off the atrocities that Hitler's Reich had committed so far—the ones they knew about, at least. And those were enough.

Most of the pages would probably end up in the trash.

Instead of wondering if any of the people in the train station changed their minds about Hitler, Annelise thought about how her own resolve had hardened into something unbreakable. With the guard first, and the moment that had seemed frozen in time, while the papers hung suspended in the air.

Maybe resistance wasn't always about results.

Maybe it wasn't a prayer or a plea.

Maybe, instead, it was a promise.

"Yes," Annelise said softly. "Yes, it did."

Chapter 23

CHRISTINA

March 1, 1943

The distinct whine of fast-approaching airplanes layered into the wails of the air raid sirens, the two tangling into something terrifying.

Christina had forgotten that March 1 was a public holiday honoring the Luftwaffe.

Clearly the RAF had not, and they wanted to help the Germans celebrate.

Lisbeth stared at the sky and cursed. Christina echoed the sentiment as the women around them began to shift uneasily.

The policemen were watching the sky, as well, everyone nervous. The RAF wouldn't have planned something so symbolic just to hit a few targets and leave.

In a flurry of activity, the Nazis exited the Jewish community center, the Gestapo agents shedding their viciously mysterious air as they hustled, awkward and very human, to safety. The last one out padlocked the doors to the center.

There would be no way for the detainees to seek shelter. The Nazis probably were hoping the building would get leveled and all of their problems would be solved with the help of one well-placed bomb.

The local police watched the higher-ranking Nazis take off down the street running, glanced at each other, and followed at a quick clip.

"Bastards," Christina screamed at their backs. Her voice was swallowed up by the noise overhead, but it wasn't as if they would have cared to be painted with that brush anyway. They'd locked innocent men inside a building that could be flattened in the next hour. The accusation would land about as hard as "murderer" had.

"We have to go, too," Christina yelled at Lisbeth.

"No," Lisbeth said, her eyes on the center, as well. "We can't leave them."

"There's nothing for us to do."

Even as she said it, a handful of women near them fell to their knees and began to pray. Their words were drowned out, but there was no need to hear for Christina to understand. These women would stay with their husbands through the bombing and accept God's fate.

Christina was not one for God's fate. His fate had a way of upending her life and causing her untold amounts of pain. She preferred taking matters into her own hands.

But she couldn't leave Lisbeth. So she made the one argument she thought might work.

"If we die, then who will be here to protest?"

Sacrificing themselves to an RAF attack was no way to get their men free. And it was no way to die for women who had been hoping the Allies would come save them all.

Lisbeth's expression of absolute certainty wavered, and Christina pounced on the weakness.

"Either they die tonight or they don't. Us being here with them isn't going to change that. But if they don't, we need people back in the streets as soon as the Nazis return. Not corpses."

As Lisbeth thought, Christina considered how far she was willing to go for this beautiful stranger. They had only just met, and yet something in Christina recognized a kindred soul. They couldn't stay here in the open, but she couldn't shrug and leave Lisbeth behind. If necessary, she would drag her away, kicking and screaming.

"You're right," Lisbeth said. "I hate that you're right, but you are."

Christina didn't waste time celebrating her victory. She simply turned and took off toward the neighborhood where she and Lisbeth had collected blankets.

They weren't alone.

While some women remained, prostrate in prayer, a good majority of the crowd scattered in all directions. At this point in the protest, there had to be more than three hundred women in the street, and they spilled out to surrounding alleyways and squares. Christina tried to picture what it would look like from above, wondered how much the RAF pilots could see.

Wondered if they cared.

Were German women simply another variation of evil to them? Would their deaths be as inconsequential as stepping on ants?

"Come," Lisbeth said, and it was only then that Christina realized she'd stopped. She shook herself and followed Lisbeth, who was keeping them flowing along with the crowd, not trying to fight the tide or get in front of it, but rather riding the wave.

Christina wished she knew where Ingrid had ended up. Lisbeth kept scanning the faces they passed, as well, and Christina guessed she was thinking the same thing.

When they broke free of the throng, they stopped, met each other's eyes.

"I don't think there's any way to find her," Christina said.

"Any other night I would have welcomed an air raid," Lisbeth muttered, and tugged at Christina's wrist to get her to keep moving.

They stopped in front of a narrow town house, and Lisbeth glanced at her once, hesitating.

"It's not much," Lisbeth admitted as she slid the key in the lock.

Christina nodded, speechless that Lisbeth would be worried about something so inconsequential when she was so generously offering her home as shelter. Christina followed her into the dark hallway.

Berlin was pitch black at night these days as protection against the bombings. Maybe it would help, maybe it wouldn't. How precise were the RAF coordinates? Or did they simply want to see Berlin destroyed, indiscriminately? The Brits probably thought the city deserved it.

Fair turnabout and all that.

The fact that it was justified didn't make it easier to calm her heart when the sirens pierced through the dark.

"It couldn't have been last week," Lisbeth said, mostly to herself, as she continued to climb the stairs. "No, it had to be tonight."

By the time they hit the third set of steps and kept going, Christina realized they were heading toward an attic apartment.

She started noticing things about Lisbeth she hadn't before. Like how threadbare her coat was, how her shoes were worn down, how her gloves and hat were handmade and a bit sloppy if one was being particular. Which Christina wasn't. But it was information that she should have gathered sooner—would have if she wasn't trying *not* to look too closely at Lisbeth.

When they finally reached the top landing, Christina bumped into Lisbeth's back. Outside, the moon had helped somewhat. But here, in this narrow hallway, Christina couldn't even see her own hand. She pulled away quickly, not wanting to seem like she had enjoyed the press of her body against Lisbeth's.

A second later, the door creaked open and then Lisbeth lit a candle that was worn down almost to the stub.

The first bomb hit as Lisbeth closed the door behind Christina. The walls shook, the ground shook. Christina's nerves shook.

Everything went silent. Only for the time it took to inhale. Then the sirens rushed in to fill the void.

"Come." Lisbeth held out her hand and Christina took it.

An attic apartment was not an ideal place to shelter, but they did what they could, sitting against the wall farthest from the window, beside a sturdy beam that would hopefully hold even if other parts of the building were torn away.

It was better than the street.

And so, too, was the weight of a person next to Christina. Better than sheltering alone.

Maybe she didn't deserve the comfort, but she took it anyway, because she was selfish like that.

The building shook, the ground shook. Christina's hand shook in Lisbeth's.

When she opened her eyes, they were still there, the candle was still burning. The sirens were still wailing.

Christina squeezed Lisbeth's fingers tighter.

And Lisbeth started to sing.

She had a raspy, beautiful voice, one that seemed born from the depths of Annelise's beloved forests of the Seven Mountains back home. Her thumb traced over the bone of Christina's wrist as she spun a story of a beautiful mermaid and the sea and a bargain and a prince, none of it mattering as much as her soothing cadence.

A bomb dropped.

The walls shook.

The ground shook.

Christina held on to the comfort she didn't deserve, and the only thing inside her that trembled was her heart.

The bombing lasted an hour and an eternity. Their candle burned down to the metal plate, only a hint of wax holding the light.

The walls had held.

The ground had held.

Christina didn't know if she could say the same was true about herself.

"We don't know it's over," Christina said, hearing Lisbeth's thoughts in the silence. She wanted to go check on the Jewish Center. But now, in the pitch dark of a city targeted by the RAF, was not the time to leave safety.

"How can I not know if he's alive or dead?" Lisbeth asked, voice used up from singing.

"Putting yourself in danger won't help him," Christina said, her jaw tight. She pulled her hand out of Lisbeth's, refused to look over. She didn't want to see the devastation on Lisbeth's face. "You know that."

"You're so rational about it."

"It's not my husband," Christina said, thinking back to the moment in the street where she'd had to convince Lisbeth to leave. The stakes were high for Christina, because of her promise to Annelise, but that was nothing compared to wanting to save the person you cared for the most in the world. She forced the words out. "You love him so much."

"I—" Lisbeth started.

Something rumbled in the distance—a building that had held on just long enough for the planes to leave.

When the night went silent once more, Lisbeth pushed herself to her feet. "Come."

It was the third time that night Lisbeth had said it. And like with the others, Christina was helpless to resist. She let Lisbeth pull her up and they crossed to the mattress that was laid out on the floor. It was tidy, the sunny yellow quilt pulled up. Christina recoiled at the idea of sleeping in their marriage bed, but her other option was cold hardwood.

And she was so tired that the world was blurring at the edges, her limbs heavy. The fear from the raid had bled out and all that was left was a shell too cold and too weary to do much beyond swaying toward the idea of warmth and softness.

"Let's get you out of . . . ," Lisbeth murmured as efficient hands tugged at her coat, then her sweater. Christina was nudged down onto the bed, Lisbeth's fingers making quick work of her boot laces. She hated that Lisbeth was taking care of her and loved it at the same time. Then she hated herself for loving it.

Then her mind went a little blank as she was pushed back toward the wall, her head hitting a pillow that wasn't exactly cloudlike but was *something*.

"That's my side," Lisbeth said, and for some reason that let Christina relax into sleep rather than fighting it.

Lisbeth climbed in afterward, practicality the enemy of squeamishness. They didn't feel like strangers anymore, anyway. And that wasn't Christina's infatuation talking. They had gone through enough in the past three days that Christina knew who Lisbeth was.

Christina tucked her knees up, rounding her shoulders, her body going lax beneath the thin quilt. There were parts of her that she hadn't felt in three days that were now warming up. Everything in her tingled and pulsed and still she sunk toward sleep, Lisbeth curled behind her, protecting her.

"I don't," Lisbeth whispered into the dark. Christina tried to hold on to the words, sensing they were important. But she couldn't. Her mind was already fading to dark so that she almost missed the rest of the confession. "I don't love him the way you think I do."

Chapter 24
ANNELISE

Summer 1938

The Pirates camped out in a local student's small apartment a few streets off the Rhine. They celebrated with beer and songs and laughter that felt just on the right side of nervous.

It wasn't until they were walking into the entryway of the train station that Annelise finally asked Marta the question that had been bothering her since the night before. "Did Hans come in late yesterday?"

They both glanced over their shoulders to find the stout boy toward the back of their small group. He had been quiet last night. This morning, he hadn't been able to meet Annelise's eyes when she'd asked about how he'd escaped.

"Now that you mention it . . . ," Marta said, her fingertips pressing into Annelise's wrist hard enough to bruise. Moments ago, they had been relaxed. Now, they were tense.

Annelise identified the location of each of the guards in the room.

"You two look like you've seen a ghost," Stefan said, slinging his arm around Marta's neck and pulling her close, away from Annelise. Stefan's smile was teasing rather than questioning, but when Marta didn't fling back some witty rejoinder, he studied their faces more closely. "What is it?"

"Was Hans acting strangely yesterday?" Annelise asked.

"No, he's . . . ," Stefan started, but then glanced back at Hans. More slowly, he said, "He wouldn't."

"If he was caught. He wouldn't protect us, not if they threatened him." Annelise could feel her pulse in her palms, in the soles of her feet, in her throat. "We have to split up."

"But—"

"Now." The directive came out harsher than she'd intended. But the guard near the door, the one who'd talked to her yesterday, was staring at them. She didn't think he'd recognized her yet, but it would only be a matter of time. Meanwhile a man in a business suit was pretending to read the newspaper over by the grandfather clock, but his attention was on the Pirates.

Marta reached out to squeeze Annelise's arm one more time before she let Stefan tug her into the wave of morning commuters headed toward the platforms.

Annelise turned to the Pirate behind her and gave him the message, which spread to the rest of the boys. She didn't bother to wait for Hans's reaction, she simply fell into step behind an older couple, walking close enough to give the impression she was with them, but not close enough to draw their attention to her.

Still, she felt the eyes of the guard from yesterday on her back. It was bad luck, that. Maybe they should have waited another day before heading back to Bonn. Maybe they should have chosen somewhere other than the train station to stage their act of protest.

The pamphlets were already gone. Had they all been swept into the trash?

The guard was closing in on her.

A woman pushing a pram and holding the hand of a young boy stepped into Annelise's path, forcing her to stutter to a stop to avoid crashing into the little family. The woman's expression was harried.

For one terrible moment, Annelise was certain the woman was going to grab and hold her until the authorities could get there. It was what so many people were being trained to do these days.

"Trudie, silly girl," the woman said, looking directly at Annelise. She spoke in German but with a heavy English accent. "If I have to tell you one more time not to dillydally, you'll be looking for a new job. Now take James while I push Rose."

Annelise didn't hesitate, and neither did the boy, offering her that special type of smile only children with lovely lives could give to strangers.

"Apologies, Mum," Annelise murmured, earning herself a curt nod before the woman headed toward the platform. By some miracle—or simply the fact that there were only so many trains leaving at this hour—the woman was clearly going to Bonn, as well.

"Hello?" Annelise half said, half asked the boy to see if he spoke German.

"Hello," James said, beaming up at her. She didn't have a good sense of children's ages but she would guess he was around five. "Do you like treacle tart?"

"I've never had it," Annelise said. He clearly hadn't known the translation for the dessert's name, so it came out in English. Treacle tart.

"Mum said I could have some if I'm a good boy on the train ride," he said, swinging their hands together, not an ounce of fear in his little body.

"Are you going to be a good boy?" Annelise asked, most of her attention on the guard who was fading back to his original station. Even if he thought she looked like one of the rebels, he didn't have enough authority to challenge a clearly wealthy English lady's claim to the truth.

Her heart still beat too loud in her own ears, but the terror that had held her in its grip began to recede.

She didn't dare look for the other Pirates. They would all fare better if they pretended they were here alone.

"Do you have a ticket, dear?" the woman asked almost beneath her breath when they were a few feet away from the doors. She was digging around in her own purse, and anyone not watching them closely would just think she was looking for something.

"I do," Annelise said quickly, still unsteady. This woman had saved her, but wasn't there always a cost? Looking down at James's happy little face gave Annelise a false sense of confidence. Surely no mother who'd raised this precocious, kind child would hurt her.

She took a nervous half step back, which the woman noticed. Her eyes were as sharp as the rest of her.

"Don't turn skittish on me now, dear," the woman said, with a tiny smile. "We've almost gotten you out of here."

And she was right. Just because the guard had given up the chase didn't mean any of the Nazis had. The Gestapo agents were far more astute than others when it came to conspirators. If they had her description, they wouldn't hesitate to stop her, English family or no.

The four of them made their way through the narrow, crowded hallways until the woman maneuvered the pram into a compartment about halfway down the train. It was empty, and Annelise sighed in relief.

She helped James up onto the bench, near the window, his attention caught by the bustle on the platform.

They sat in a charged silence until the whistle blew and the train lurched into movement. Annelise closed her eyes and offered a quick prayer for the rest of the Pirates. Then she handed her ticket over to the woman, who smiled approvingly. When the conductor came by, Annelise kept herself occupied with James, her hair shielding most of her face, as the woman dealt with him.

"Well done," the woman said, after the conductor had left. Thankfully, no one else had joined them in their compartment. "Now. What is your name, dear?"

Annelise calculated all the ways offering the truth could lead to disaster. But in the end, she owed the woman that at least. It was all she had to return her kindness.

"Annelise," she said. "Annelise Fischer."

"Well, Annelise Fischer, it's a pleasure to meet you," the woman said, her voice husky. Annelise enjoyed the way her plummy English accent wrapped around the harsh German syllables. "My name is Lilian Harris. You've met James, and this is Rose."

She said the last with a wave toward the pram and the baby who was presumably sleeping.

"And please call me Lilian," she said. "I insist."

Annelise dipped her head, but wasn't sure she'd be able to manage that. This woman was posh, her clothes all extremely well-made, her hair impeccable.

"I saw you yesterday," Lilian said, studying Annelise closer now, her dark brows in a tight vee over her eyes. Assessing. "You and your compatriots."

Annelise flushed, but didn't say anything. Trusting Lilian to offer her some protection on the way back to Bonn was one thing, admitting to participating in yesterday's show was another.

"We're in Germany because my husband is thinking about a partnership with a munitions factory in Bonn," Lilian continued. "But you and your friends have confirmed what I've suspected since we came into the country. We should not be doing business with the NSDAP."

When Annelise still didn't say anything, Lilian gently nudged Annelise's shin with the tip of her shoe. "I know you have no reason to believe me, but I will make sure you make it back to Bonn safely. If I can."

"Thank you," Annelise said, this time at something more than a whisper. She knew she shouldn't ask, shouldn't make Lilian think too deeply about it, but she did. "Why are you helping me?"

"You have to understand, no one in England is eager to provoke hostilities," Lilian said, instead of answering. "We're quite war-shy, if I'm honest. So there's a good deal of press around the idea that Hitler can be pacified."

Annelise hated that the Nazis had convinced the world of that. Hated that creating their own version of truth seemed to be one of their greatest skills. "It's a lie."

"Yes, that's becoming clearer by the day," Lilian said on a sigh, glancing at James with something close to grief. "I'm not eager for war." After a pause, her expression cleared, and she clapped her hands together. "But needs must, I suppose."

She said it with startling practicality, as if she could call up the prime minister at her will. Maybe she could; Annelise didn't know who she was. But she was traveling alone, which seemed to speak to a class station lower than what Annelise had originally thought.

"My brother and the nanny accompanied me to Cologne," Lilian said, seeming to read Annelise with the ease of a book. "Both fell dreadfully ill and had to stay. I have to return to Bonn, though. James has medication he must take at certain intervals."

"Needs must," Annelise murmured, not sure if Lilian would take it as cheeky.

But Lilian grinned. It transformed her whole face, and all of a sudden she looked a lot younger and more vibrant than she had only seconds ago. "You're a clever one, aren't you?"

There was no good way to answer that. And anyway, Annelise wasn't clever, not like Eitan.

"Well." Lilian reached into her bag and pulled out a pamphlet Annelise recognized all too well. "This little stunt was certainly clever. Tell me about what you and your friends get up to. I'm old and stodgy, I want to live vicariously through you young people."

Annelise was barely listening, though. Lilian would be safe if she was found carrying it around—she could easily say she didn't know better. But if she was bandying it about like that, there was a chance it could fall into the wrong hands. Plenty of Lilian's countrymen had ties to the Nazis. Her husband, even. Though she seemed sure she could stop whatever partnership had brought them to Germany, Annelise still found it difficult to believe a wife could have so much sway over a business decision.

Lilian squinted at her, seeming once again to sense Annelise's apprehension. "Ah, shall I destroy this, then?"

"Please." A cold layer of sweat had dried on her skin, the ghost of the fear she had felt not so long ago. That she still felt for Stefan and Marta and the others. It was so easy to be brave in theory, to sit around a campfire and pretend you could be courageous. But it was more natural to be cowardly, Annelise thought shamefully. No one actually wanted to die, no one wanted to be tortured, or even to be detained.

There were things that were worth all that—and so she had to overcome the fear. But it wasn't natural to be brave, she didn't think.

It took practice.

"Never fret," Lilian said, tucking the paper away. "The whole show was quite persuasive, though. And coming from people so young."

"Someone has to," Annelise said.

"It is the beauty of youth to believe no one else in the world knows what they're doing," Lilian said, a sly amusement in her voice. Annelise hated when adults talked to her that way, as if she just didn't know better.

"I wish I could just be young," Annelise said, a sharpness she couldn't help turning the words jagged. "I wish I could hike my days away, lie in the sun, have silly romances, and eat chocolate and have not a single worry besides how I should style my hair. Do you think I want to be climbing ticket booths? Do you think I want to be chased by Nazis? Do you think this is what I imagined when I thought of these years on the cusp of becoming a woman?"

Lilian watched her, those thick, unruly brows of hers pinched. But she didn't seem angry, merely thoughtful.

"The beauty of youth," Annelise said, the words sour in her mouth. "We will never have that, Mrs. Harris. Because the mature adults in charge have let that be stolen from us. I would love, more than anything, to believe one other person in the world knows what they're doing."

"You're right," Lilian said after a loaded moment of silence. "My husband fought in the Great War. I was a volunteer ambulance driver; he was my patient. It is almost a cliché story now, where we come from."

Annelise sat back, at a loss following her tirade. Lilian kept surprising her.

"He was only a boy when the war ended, I was only a girl, neither of us much older than you must be," Lilian said, and the deep, profound grief that sat in the lines of her face, in the nooks of each word, left Annelise breathless. And in that space where she had no air, she saw her future. "If you had been there you would also believe anyone who promised you it wasn't going to happen again."

"But we can still stop it."

Lilian smiled at her and it was gentle in its condescension. Then her eyes went to James. "I do hope so."

Maybe they both knew it wasn't true. But Lilian was right. When the truth was as horrifying as it was, why not believe the lie?

They spent the rest of the ride in silence. When they arrived in Bonn, Annelise helped Lilian disembark with James and Rose.

"Thank you," Annelise said. "You saved me and I was quite rude to you."

Lilian leaned forward as if about to share a secret. "I think had I not come along you would have saved yourself, my dear."

Annelise blushed at the implied compliment, and Lilian patted her hand.

"And I deserved your rudeness. That was me told. Now, if you ever need real help, my brother is here for . . . hmm . . ." Lilian trailed off, squinting into the middle distance. "He's told me many times, but I do always forget what he does with himself. Liaison for something or other. Bernard Wicklow. Here is his address. He'll be in Bonn for the foreseeable future, unfortunately."

Lilian handed her a slip of paper that Annelise carefully tucked into her pocket.

"You never know, one day that might save your life."

Though Lilian said it lightly, they both knew it wasn't a joke.

Chapter 25
EMMY

April 1946

While Emmy understood the Library of Congress's reasoning for acquiring enemy literature and propaganda, after two weeks of combing through such material, she was beginning to long for the simple ache of the personal collections.

That pain felt real and honest. Going through books that Rosenberg had deemed relevant to the "Jewish Question" made her sick.

One thing had become clear in her work sorting through the bounty—the Nazis had been attempting to rewrite history in their favor. There seemed to have been no shortage of Nazi thinkers putting out articles and books even in the midst of paper shortages.

"Lovey," Lucy said, appearing at her shoulder seemingly out of nowhere. "You'll go blind if you keep working."

Emmy squinted, her eyes searching for a window that didn't exist. She looked back down at the book she'd been assessing.

Geist und Macht. Mind and Power.

It had been written by a man named Walter Frank—a prolific ideologue and protégé of Rosenberg's. She'd come across several volumes published by him before, though none in such good shape.

After some research, she'd realized he had been put in charge of presenting a unified view of the history of Germany with focus on the enemy.

She closed the book and placed it in the crate that would eventually be shipped back to the Library of Congress, with Poste's approval, of course.

"Time to leave?" Emmy asked, though she already started gathering her things.

"You look sad, today, duckling," Lucy said on the bicycle ride home.

"I see the benefit of my work here . . ."

"But you don't love it." Lucy finished the thought for her. "Yours is not a task I envy."

"Yours is," Emmy admitted. "You're saving a culture that would have been eradicated otherwise."

"Helping save," Lucy corrected modestly.

"What you're doing matters," Emmy continued as if she hadn't heard. "What I'm doing matters, too, I'm sure of it. But it's the personal collections that speak to me the most. They are heartbreaking but there's a tiny bit of hope in them, as well."

"Like that sneaky Rilke that's hiding on our bookshelves," Lucy said with a sly smile.

"Yes," Emmy said, as they parked their bicycles against the cottage. "I wish I had more time to work on those. Or was allowed to."

"The Monuments Men—"

"Are prickly about the rules," Emmy said, laughing. "I've heard that a time or two hundred."

There was good reason the Library of Congress mission wasn't allowed close to the restitution efforts—no one wanted to be accused of plundering plundered books. But that didn't mean she couldn't wish she was on a different team.

"Anyway, enough of that, who is in the box tonight?"

The two of them had fallen into a comfortable evening routine. They alternated nights cooking, while the other tidied the small cottage or mended clothing or pruned the bushes outside. If nothing needed doing, they simply kept each other company through dinner.

Then Lucy would pour them both some sort of expensive liquor and they'd settle in for the wireless reports on the Nuremberg Trials.

At home, Emmy hadn't listened to the daily play-by-plays of the trials that had started back in November, sickened by even the most sanitized roundups. But Lucy was determined to know exactly how horrific the Nazis' actions had been.

"Rosenberg's testifying." Lucy answered what Emmy realized she'd already known. The days were blurring together apparently.

This was the one they'd been both anticipating and dreading.

The announcers began with a short biography of Alfred Rosenberg, but Emmy knew it well already. It was his institute she was combing through, after all. She tuned back in when they got to his charges—conspiracy, crimes against peace, war crimes, and crimes against humanity.

"I wish we could come up with more inventive ways to kill them," Lucy mused, more than halfway through her drink already. The liquor hadn't softened her words even a little bit.

Emmy plated the chicken and rice and they sat at the tiny, rickety kitchen table that tilted no matter what they shoved under the short leg.

After a few bites, she dared to ask the question she'd been wondering since she'd realized Lucy listened to the trials religiously. "Don't these make you . . . ?"

She struggled for the right word and settled on the one Lucy had tossed her way earlier. "Sad?"

It was the same concept, after all, whether it was reading or listening, they were both having to experience these men's twisted minds firsthand.

"So few will face repercussions for what they've done," Lucy said, after a minute or two of contemplation. "Actual war crimes, crimes against humanity. And they'll walk away and have fruitful, fulfilling lives."

"You want to witness at least some of them getting punished," Emmy realized.

"Tzedek, tzedek, tirdof," Lucy murmured.

"What does that mean?"

"Justice, justice, you shall pursue," Lucy said. "Deuteronomy."

The radio crackled, interrupting anything Emmy might have said in response.

The Allies had presented their cases over the winter, and now it was the Nazis' turn to offer their defense.

Like the other war criminals, Rosenberg blamed the Führer and the men who had already committed suicide. He demurred over accusations he'd ever touted a "master race," and said that he was merely "protecting" and "safeguarding" the artifacts he'd plundered with such abandon.

"Tell that to our block-long, five-story warehouse," Lucy shouted at the wireless before downing the rest of her drink. In a more contained voice, she said, "He'll swing. I wish more of them would."

Emmy agreed with a salute of her glass.

"Have I told you of the Kazet Theater yet?" Lucy asked.

Emmy was starting to get used to Lucy's brand of conversational whiplash. Sometimes the path her thoughts took seemed random, but she always had a point to make in the end. "No."

"In the Bergen-Belsen concentration camp, there was a troupe of actors who would perform for their fellow prisoners," Lucy said. "They were starving themselves, had worked fourteen-, fifteen-hour days. They were beaten-down and exhausted, and yet they put on these plays for the others."

"A light in the dark."

"Yes," Lucy agreed. "But also a way to preserve a culture they were watching be destroyed and erased in front of their eyes. They held the plays in Yiddish."

"That was very brave of them." Stories of courage were inevitably going to trickle out over the next few years, and maybe the next few decades. All Emmy wished was that people wouldn't have had to be so brave. "Why was it called the Kazet Theater?"

"The initials Germans used for concentration camps," Lucy said. "'KZ.' Kazet. But it didn't end there. The troupe has carried on the tradition into the displaced persons camps. They perform original plays about their time during the war to thousands of people who went through it, as well."

Emmy tried to imagine being in that theater and couldn't, like she couldn't imagine what their lives had been like in the camps. Even if she saw the plays she would never fully understand.

"One of the plays I watched depicted a German guard ripping a baby from its mother's arms and slamming it into the train to kill it," Lucy said, her voice flat, not like she didn't care but like any emotion had been sucked into a dark abyss within her. "Which is, of course, horrific. The plays are filled with moments that make you gasp like that. But do you know what I found worse, almost?" She scrunched her face up. "Or equally bad. Can we really compare the horrors?"

"Tell me," Emmy said before Lucy could get tangled up in that philosophical knot.

"Well, it was how they portrayed the daily indignities they'd suffered," Lucy said. "The Nazis never let them forget they were viewed as animals. Every single moment of the day."

"They held on to their humanity through the plays," Emmy realized. "And through each other."

"They did. And that is a blessing. But I can't help thinking about those performances every time we listen to these assholes lie and lie and lie," Lucy said, pointing her refilled glass at the wireless. Rosenberg's voice grated against Emmy's skin. "They knew exactly what was happening. This bastard orchestrated it. And he doesn't feel an ounce of shame. He only cares that he didn't win."

She let out a shaky breath, emotions flicking across her face too fast to catch and decipher. "There's a concept in Judaism. Teshuva."

Emmy made an inquiring sound to show she was listening. From the very first day, Emmy had realized that Lucy's well of grief was deep, nearly bottomless, beneath her bright mask. She was honored she'd made her way past that defense, and could be someone Lucy allowed herself to actually talk to.

"We're very big on forgiveness," Lucy said. "But only if it's earned.

Teshuva is the process of repenting for the hurt you caused someone else. If you're sincere, the injured party can forgive you, which brings both people closer to God's divinity."

"Repentance." That was what was missing, not only from the war criminals, but from everyday Germans as well. She thought of Ursula's defensiveness. It had clearly been driven by guilt, but the woman had lashed out instead of admitting her shame, or at least sitting with it. Emmy was no one's confessor, and Major Arnold was right that she wasn't in a position to be offering forgiveness, but so many would never admit what they'd done wrong.

Maybe this was all too big to heal from anyway. Lucy would certainly carry this wound with her the rest of her life.

The world would—should—carry this wound for the rest of time.

Lucy finished her drink and went for the liquor cart again. When she came back it was with the whole bottle.

"I think admitting to hurting someone might be the second hardest thing in the world," she mused.

"And the first?" Emmy prompted.

"Forgiving them."

Chapter 26

CHRISTINA

March 2, 1943

Golden light poured in through the portrait window, announcing a new day. Christina and Lisbeth had lived through the night.

Sometime during the early hours of the morning, Lisbeth had curled around Christina, palm pressed to her belly, leg thrown over her thigh. The warmth of the quilt kept the chill at bay, and Christina barely breathed, not wanting to break the spell.

I don't love him the way you think I do.

Surely that didn't mean what Christina's brain wanted her to think it meant.

There had to be another explanation. And one for how Lisbeth stilled but didn't retreat when she woke. Maybe also one for the flex of Lisbeth's fingers, the way they stretched just enough to brush the sensitive spot along Christina's pelvic bone.

Terrified and exhilarated at once, Christina slowly brought her own hand up to cover Lisbeth's. She traced a fingertip over one of Lisbeth's knuckles then along soft skin up to the bone of her wrist.

In the next heartbeat, they'd shifted so Christina lay flat on her back. Lisbeth hovered over her, her lovely curls a riotous mass of fire-laced sunset around her face. This time when Christina reached out, she traced a constellation in the freckles splattered like paint over Lisbeth's nose, her cheeks.

Lisbeth's eyes dropped to Christina's mouth and she chewed her own bottom lip.

Their hips pressed together. Heat pooled between Christina's legs for the first time in as long as she could remember, and pressing them together did nothing but remind her Lisbeth's thigh was now slotted between her own.

The world had gone silent and all Christina could hear was the rush of her own heart.

"Tea."

With that one word, Lisbeth rolled away so quickly Christina was left blinking at the ceiling, her arm still outstretched. Lisbeth was on her feet adjusting her clothes, her back to Christina.

"I . . . I have some tea," Lisbeth said, her voice remarkably steady, despite that initial hitch.

"Please," Christina said, and of course it came out as an unattractive croak.

For a moment, all Lisbeth did was lean against the tiny stove, head bowed, and Christina wanted to go to her. She wanted to replicate the position they'd woken up in, to press a palm into Lisbeth's belly, to press a kiss into the knob at the top of her spine.

But Christina stayed in the warm, rumpled bed that smelled of lemons and Lisbeth.

She touched the pillow beside her, and realized that's where Lisbeth's husband slept.

The knowledge had her sitting up, swinging her legs over the side of the mattress, all of a sudden wanting to be out of there as quickly as possible.

Christina glanced down at her rumpled clothing. She looked a mess, there was no doubt about it. Not only was she wearing the same clothes she'd dressed in to go to work on Saturday, she'd then stood out in icy rain, marched back and forth on mud-slicked cobblestones, sweated through her blouse in odd moments of exertion and fear. Surely, she did *not* smell of lemons. How had Lisbeth managed it?

A bookshelf caught Christina's eye, and, relieved for something to do other than sit in the leaden silence of *almost*, she crossed the room to examine the titles.

"We could get arrested for half of those," Lisbeth called over, sounding equally happy to have something to say. "But we could be arrested for existing. So."

Christina didn't point out that the "could be" was no longer theoretical—Lisbeth's husband was detained as they spoke. They would have to face reality again soon enough. Right now, Christina wanted this morning, this moment, in a cozy attic with tea and books and a woman who made Christina feel almost brave.

It was heady, intoxicating.

Foolish.

Christina never said she was anything but.

She ran her fingertip along the spines of the books—Fitzgerald, Mann, Trotsky, Wilde.

"*The Soul of Man Under Socialism*," she read, loud enough for Lisbeth to hear.

Lisbeth made a soft sound of amusement. "Right to Dachau."

There was truth in the humor, which made it so dark. Christina was about to chide her for being careless, but she noticed the edges of a photograph sticking out of the pages.

She flipped the book open and found a picture of two men, the taller of whom had his arm thrown around the shoulders of the shorter one. They beamed at each other; a rare feat given the limitations of cameras in those days.

Something clenched in Christina's stomach when she recognized the emotion on their faces. It was so clear.

Love.

A line on the page where the picture had been tucked was underlined in pen.

To live is the rarest thing in the world. Most people exist, that is all.

Christina had to swallow against the unexpected emotion that rose in her throat. Grief, longing, hope, sadness.

"My father," Lisbeth said. She was so much closer than she had been, a solid presence at Christina's back.

"Who is he with?" Christina asked, not quite understanding. Maybe she was reading the picture all wrong. Maybe the obvious love between these two people was fraternal rather than romantic. But her eyes kept flicking down to where the shorter one's hand rested on the taller man's hip. The grip seemed unmistakably possessive.

Lisbeth set both mugs of tea—which Christina knew was simply water with the hint of flavor—on top of the shelf.

Then in a move so swift Christina could never have anticipated it, Lisbeth pressed her up against the wall, a hand slipping into Christina's hair to cup the back of her head.

With steady pressure, Lisbeth brought Christina's mouth down to hers.

Christina's mind whited out to anything but the pressure of Lisbeth's lips, the taste of her, the weight of her body holding Christina steady even as the ground shifted beneath her feet.

She had been kissed before only a few times, only enough to know she liked her partners to be women. But all of those occasions paled in comparison to this.

This heat, this pleasure that pulsed from her core, this feeling of absolute *rightness*. Lisbeth kissed like she meant it, like this was all she'd ever wanted to do, as if this was where her home was now.

Lisbeth ripped herself away, and Christina, embarrassingly, chased her, swaying forward until Lisbeth placed a gentle hand on her shoulder to hold her still.

"I needed to know," Lisbeth said, almost apologetically, and Christina just stared at her, not comprehending. "I needed to be sure, before I told you."

Christina shook her head, her brain sluggish, her soul left wanting.

"I thought . . . the way you looked at me," Lisbeth continued, as if she wasn't wrecking Christina. "The way you stop yourself from touching me, even casually. I thought . . . you would understand."

"Understand what?" Christina asked, though she knew.

"That I couldn't simply risk everything because of a guess," Lisbeth said. "It's dangerous times for people like us."

Christina stared at her dumbly as she realized what this had been. Nothing but insurance.

"I wouldn't turn you in" was all Christina could manage, her lips numb now. Where a moment ago she had felt as light and happy as she had before Bonn and Annelise and Eitan, now she wanted to sink to the floor in mortification.

"I'm sorry," Lisbeth said, sounding both like she meant it and like she didn't. That's how they all lived these days, hurting each other constantly with paper cuts and knife wounds. Lisbeth pushed up on her tiptoes and kissed her once more, this time chaste and sweet and short. A reassurance. "I also wanted to. We . . . can't. Not now, maybe not even anytime soon. I still wanted to make sure, though."

Christina nodded and realized she was still holding the book and photograph in her hands. She hadn't even been able to touch Lisbeth in the short moment she would have been allowed. Disappointment crashed upon her like waves.

"Those are my parents," Lisbeth said, stepping back and grabbing one of the mugs of tea. She looked far too composed for what had just occurred, but there was a blush riding the ridge of her cheekbones beneath her freckles. Maybe not so cool and unaffected, then. "My mother is the blonde."

It took a moment for the words to make sense, and when they did, Christina brought the photograph up for closer inspection.

The blond one was pretty in that way men could be, with delicate features that would have inspired Renaissance painters in days past. His ears were a touch too big for his face, but that was the only flaw Christina could see.

Now that she was looking more closely she could see his suit wasn't tailored as closely as the taller man's.

"I know you weren't here in Berlin then, but before Hitler rose to power, people were allowed to live how they wanted," Lisbeth said, her eyes on the photograph, her expression wistful. "People like my parents, there were plenty of them who lived and loved in this city. Now the Nazis call us deviants."

She spit the last word, and Christina wanted to recoil from it, like she always did.

Christina had known since she was young exactly who she was. She'd been terrified of it back then, so scared that she would say something to give herself away, that she would linger too long while glancing at a friend, that she would simply exist and everyone would be able to tell. In desperation, she'd tried to mimic her sister, and when that hadn't worked, she'd thrown herself into the BDM. It was easy to hide there. With so many guidelines to follow, it became simple to know when she was being good.

She had let herself disappear into the model NSDAP girl. No one had ever suspected she was perverted. No one had uncovered the terrible darkness in her heart, in her body.

If everything with Eitan and Annelise hadn't happened, Christina had no doubt she would have married a patriotic German boy to make sure no one ever rooted out her secret.

But everything had happened, and Christina had landed in Berlin. Way past the days Lisbeth spoke of, but she'd heard the rumors of how it used to be. Something about Christina must read as bent, because Lisbeth wasn't the first woman to guess where Christina's inclinations lay. When they'd kissed her in dark rooms at Nazis' parties, they'd told her of a time gone by. Of nightclubs and champagne, of lavender nights and salons and a city where love beat in its soul.

"My father owned a cabaret for men like him," Lisbeth continued, unaware of the path Christina had taken back toward self-hatred. At one time, that hatred had been toward this thing she wanted so much that so many thought made her damaged. Now it was for her younger self who had been so scared that she'd become a Nazi to avoid it. "He met my mother there."

"Did your mother always go about as a man?" Christina asked.

"Yes," Lisbeth said, like it was simple and easy. Maybe it had been. "That's who he felt he was. Living any other way would have made him miserable."

To live is the rarest thing in the world. Most people exist, that is all.

"They're not here." Christina almost didn't want to ask. "Did they . . . ?"

"They were deported. Both of them," Lisbeth said. "I don't know if they're alive or not. The last letters I received were from over six months ago."

"I'm so sorry," Christina said, and the words felt so empty and useless.

"They called my mother an asocial and arrested her," Lisbeth said. "They didn't need to call my father anything. It was already illegal that he existed."

"You were spared," Christina said.

"Because my parents saw what was coming, and wanted to make sure I was safe," Lisbeth said. "They spent the last of their money protecting me."

Something clicked at that.

I don't love him the way you think I do.

"Your husband," Christina said.

"He needed a German wife; I needed a husband. There was a church willing to magically find some lost records when we went to the government office. For the right donation amount, of course." She paused, as earnest as Christina had ever seen her, then continued, "We do love each other. Please, I hope you understand."

Of course Christina did. Love didn't come in only one form. She was well aware of that fact.

"I wanted it to mean something," Lisbeth said slowly. "It would have been easier for me to marry an Aryan man, of course."

It wouldn't have been an exchange, though. There would have been expectations of Lisbeth, ones she might not have wanted to fulfill. Christina didn't bother saying what they both knew.

"You saved someone," Christina said instead.

Lisbeth shook her head. "No. We saved each other."

Christina opened her mouth and shut it as some alarm rang in her head, one that sounded like the air raid siren.

Something felt . . . off.

She ran back through the conversation, going over every word, and she realized what had her on edge.

Lisbeth seemed to notice the change in her demeanor, her open, friendly expression shuttering. "Christina?"

"How did you know?" Christina pushed the words out with a tongue gone clumsy with suspicion and fear. She couldn't *think*. "How did you know I wasn't in Berlin then?"

"What?" Surprise slipped into her expression before it went carefully blank. "I didn't. Or, I suppose I knew you'd have been too young."

"No," Christina said slowly. "You said it like you knew where I was instead."

The book she'd been holding dropped to the floor, but she didn't let go of the photograph. She knew that was too precious to drop, even in her state of heightened emotions.

"Lisbeth?"

The woman stared at her for a long minute and then sighed.

Keeping her movements slow and predictable, she reached toward the bookshelf. When Christina flinched, Lisbeth frowned. "I don't want to hurt you."

Christina wanted to believe her, but she knew she couldn't. So she just waited and found herself staring at a book.

It was Edgar Allan Poe, an English version. Christina hadn't known what to expect, but it hadn't been that.

"Annabel Lee."

A photograph stuck out of the pages, like with the Wilde.

When she flipped the book open, she noticed the underlined words first.

We loved with a love that was more than love.

Then she saw the photograph.

The tips of her fingers tingled as blood rushed out of her head. She leaned against the wall, the world going sideways.

Desperately, she stared at Lisbeth, willing any of this to make sense. The woman was braced for the question she knew was about to come.

Christina forced it out, though all the words sounded strange through the buzzing in her ears.

"Why do you have a picture of my sister?"

Chapter 27
ANNELISE

Summer 1938

All the Pirates made it home safely from Cologne.

To Annelise, it seemed like a miracle, but maybe her worrying back in the train station had been foolish. Had the guard really been headed in her direction? Lilian had seemed to think so, but what if it had been to check her papers and nothing more?

For the week after they'd returned, Annelise had dreams in which she'd been captured, thrown in a tiny cell at the EL-DE Haus, and been beaten, starved, ridiculed, threatened. Hans always lurked in the corners, sometimes crying, sometimes laughing, but always *there*. No matter how many times Hans had sworn he hadn't given them up to the Nazis, no matter how many of the other boys defended him, Annelise didn't trust him anymore.

She wondered if she ever fully had. Out of all the Pirates, he was the one who complained the most about how hard it was to go against Hitler. Hans had been made for the easier path in life—the only question in her mind was why he remained with the Pirates. She hoped it wasn't going to be a difficult lesson the rest of the boys had to learn.

Annelise often woke sweat-drenched after the nightmares, clutching her blanket and assuring herself it wasn't real.

The latest one forced her out of bed as dawn was breaking. She quickly changed into suitable clothes and snuck out of the house. She wasn't worried about anyone caring what she was doing except for Christina.

Her little shadow. Although, that had changed ever since Christina had caught her and Eitan at the lake. When Annelise had finally confronted her sister about it, Christina swore she hadn't told Felix Hoffmann.

But could Annelise believe that? Christina had a history of tattling. A few months ago, she'd told Frau that Annelise hadn't really been sick. Who was to say what else she'd reported back to the people she so desperately wanted to impress?

How could she trust someone like Christina?

The answer, of course, was that she couldn't. Annelise sighed out all her last expectations. It was time to let go.

Her mind—if not her heart—settled on that matter, she turned her attention to the way the early morning light hit the water of the Rhine.

The footsteps behind her didn't come as a surprise. She rolled her eyes and glanced over her shoulder expecting Christina.

Only it wasn't her sister. It was a boy, younger but much taller than she. He wore an HJ uniform and a cruel smirk.

Annelise ducked her head, wrapped her arms around herself, and started forward once more at a brisker pace.

Another boy fell into step beside her. And then another came to a stop in front of her.

She was surrounded.

Don't panic.

They were just boys, not even men yet, their skinny frames swimming in their bulky uniforms.

But they had that malicious, hyena air about them, the one most of the boys in the HJ carried.

"Leave me alone," she said, and she was proud of the fact that her voice hadn't quavered at all.

"What have we got here, boys?" one of them asked, ignoring her demand completely.

"It looks like we've caught ourselves a Pirate, gents," another one said, and Annelise froze.

She was wearing conservative clothes, she hadn't pinned on her edelweiss flower. They shouldn't know that she was a Pirate.

Hans, she thought bitterly and wondered how much he'd spilled to his Nazi friends.

Or . . . had it been Christina?

Annelise met the eyes of the head boy. "You haven't caught anything. Leave me be."

The boy stepped closer, garlic heavy on his breath, spots covering his face. His features were all wrong, too big or too small. If he were a jolly fellow, maybe that could have softened him, but his ugly soul made him all the more repulsive. She struggled not to step back.

"I think I *have* caught something," he said. "I think I've caught a Pirate."

He was about as clever as he was attractive. She guessed he was in love with the way the uniform bought him respect and admiration for the first time in his life. What a weak man, what a weak mind.

"Annelise." It was Christina, running through the early morning fog in her BDM uniform. "Annelise, you left without me."

Christina didn't bother addressing the boys at all, just rushed to Annelise's side. "You forgot your schoolwork for the day."

"So foolish of me," Annelise murmured, eyeing the baby Nazis surrounding them. They were caught off guard by Christina's uniform, that was clear.

Christina pretended to notice them. "Why are you bothering us? Disperse, please."

It was said with such an incredible amount of authority that two of the boys started backing away. But the older one narrowed his eyes.

"She's a traitor to our country," he said. "This is not your business."

Christina scoffed and looped her arm through Annelise's. "She's my sister. I would thank you very much to watch your tongue, Paul."

The boy was taken aback by the fact Christina knew his name. He hesitated. "I cannot in good conscience let you walk away with a criminal."

"And I cannot in good conscience ignore the fact that you are patrolling outside your designated area," Christina said, nose in the air, her rule-follower voice crisp and superior. "I wonder what Scharführer Heydrich would think about that."

Paul's mouth worked, but he clearly didn't know what to make of Christina—who'd never met a rule she hadn't immediately memorized. He grumbled, but after only a few more fraught seconds, all of them faded back into the alley from whence they'd come.

Annelise slid a glance at Christina—her little shadow, always following her. For once, it had paid off.

Christina's fingers were tight on Annelise's arm. "You shouldn't be out here this early by yourself."

"I gathered," Annelise said mildly, studying Christina's profile. "Thank you for helping."

Christina's eyes went wide. Had Annelise really been so terrible that simple gratitude was enough to shock Christina?

Apparently so, because her sister went shy with pleasure.

"Skip class today," Annelise said, the words escaping before she'd given them any real thought. But there was something about glimpsing the sister she loved in this girl who had become such a stranger that made her impulsive.

"Frau Sommer wouldn't be pleased if she heard," Christina said beneath her breath. "I'm supposed to be setting a good example for the younger girls."

That wasn't actually a no, so Annelise waited.

"What would we do?" Christina asked, hesitant but clearly interested. Maybe she was picturing all the unfettered access she'd have to Annelise to try to convince her to ditch the Pirates.

"Picnic in the Seven Mountains?"

Christina's shoulders rounded in, and her almost-pleased expression went neutral. "All right."

The shift in demeanor made Annelise pause. Maybe even a few days ago she wouldn't have noticed or cared, but there was a reason she'd suggested spending the day together. She wanted to know Christina away from all the trappings of the Nazis. Wanted to figure out who Christina was as she began to head into adulthood. She'd only ever known her sister as a child, and then a good BDM girl. There had to be more to her than that.

Annelise ran through what she'd said that could have caused the change.

The Seven Mountains.

Those were Annelise's. Christina didn't enjoy hiking the way Annelise did. She only tagged along when she felt like she had to. How many times had Annelise inadvertently done this? She had told Christina to figure out who she was without copying Annelise's life, and then she hadn't been interested in what Christina had found there.

She tried to remember what Christina had liked before the Nazis had taken her mind hostage. "Or . . . the Museum Koenig?"

The natural history museum had opened four years ago, and her parents had surprised them with admission tickets that very summer. It had been one of the last things they'd bought the girls that wasn't a necessity.

Christina had loved looking at the animals from far-off lands, studying the butterflies and landscapes and dinosaur bones.

Christina lit up, and in that moment, Annelise realized how miserable her sister had been for years. She couldn't remember her smiling like that since they were young.

"You wouldn't be bored?" Christina asked, almost shy.

"No," Annelise said, picturing herself trailing Christina from exhibit to exhibit, delighting in her delight. "It'll be my treat."

The Museum Koenig was an impressive building standing at the edge of a park south of Bonn.

Inside, they lingered the longest in the great hall with its impressive glass ceiling. The tableau that took up the most room was of the African desert, featuring two stuffed giraffes, their long necks stretched high as they reached for vegetation.

"This place was taken over by the government in the Great War," Christina said. They were moseying their way toward the Villa, which housed Alexander Koenig's bird collection.

Annelise knew that—she'd been at the reopening in 1934, as well. But she made a humming sound to show she was listening and following along.

"It was used as a military hospital," Christina said, a skip in her step. She was still so young. Annelise knew their parents might view her as an adult at sixteen, but Christina was just a girl, really.

"Maybe it will become one once again," Annelise said carelessly. "With how Hitler's behaving, it probably won't be long."

Christina tensed and dropped silent. Annelise didn't know why she'd said it. How often did she lob barbs like that, completely shutting down any conversation they might be having?

Annelise scrambled to find a topic that would let them return to the camaraderie they'd almost recaptured from before Hitler had taken over their lives. "Are you interested in any of the boys at school?"

Pink touched the ridges of Christina's cheekbones, but she shook her head and stared at the ground.

"Was that boy in the mountains . . . was he a Pirate?" Christina asked.

"No," Annelise said, trying to ignore the well of grief the memory brought, the depth of it taking her by surprise. While she had never doubted she loved Eitan, they hadn't actually known each other very long, certainly not long enough to feel like this. She swallowed, wondering if she should ask what she wanted to know. "At the lake . . . Why did you say that about Felix? About him being right?"

Christina's flush was far more obvious now, spreading from the nape of her neck to her cheeks, marking the path of embarrassment.

It was their light coloring—neither of them had ever been able to hide mortification well.

"He asked me to the cinema," Christina admitted, and Annelise bit her lip before she could say something hurtful and unwise. Felix only wanted Christina because she looked so much like Annelise. But hearing that would do nothing but push Christina further into his clutches.

"He's not a nice man, Christina," Annelise murmured. "He hurt me. He grabbed my hair, he wanted to do more."

That seemed to startle Christina out of her embarrassment. She glanced over sharply. "Felix wouldn't do that."

"How well do you think you know him?" Annelise asked, knowing, knowing, knowing she sounded condescending and not able to do anything to temper it.

"We played with him when we were children," Christina said, as if the question were absurd. "Of course, we both know him well."

"That was when we were young," Annelise said, as patiently as she could manage. "People change."

"Yes, I'm aware," Christina said, her back straight as she dragged her eyes over Annelise in disdain.

Why, oh why, had Annelise picked this fight? Why couldn't she leave it be, ever?

Christina probably thought Annelise believed herself perfect, but she was so far from it that it was laughable.

"I'm sorry," Annelise said. "Who you spend time with is none of my business. But . . ."

"But what?" Christina asked, eyes narrowed.

"What did he say about Eitan?" Annelise asked. "What did you?"

Eitan was still in Bonn, still under the purview of the roaming HJ, and Annelise had no idea if he was being harassed by Felix or his cronies because of her.

"I didn't say anything, which I've already told you," Christina said. Gone was the girl who delighted in the animals. Here was Christina

Fischer, role model at her local BDM. "Felix was . . . interested in how you were spending your time."

How could her sister not find that odd? Disturbing even? Annelise hadn't spent time with or talked about Felix in years. "Christina."

"He cares about you and wanted to make sure you were staying out of trouble." The words rushed out in one breath. "A lot of people are worried about you, Annelise. I know you think I'm an insufferable prig when I criticize the Pirates, but what you're playing at is incredibly dangerous."

Annelise closed her eyes, wondering if this message would *ever* get through. "When something is right it doesn't matter if it's dangerous."

Christina pursed her lips, and Annelise knew she was marshaling all her arguments about the Pirates and how they weren't *right*. But Annelise wasn't interested in having that debate for the thousandth time. What she cared about was this feral wolf, and the ways he'd latched on to her family. And her loved ones.

"Felix is angry at me, Christina," Annelise tried again. "I rejected him and now he wants revenge."

Christina looked away, deliberately hiding her expression. "You think I'm some foolish girl who doesn't know anything about the world."

"No." None of this was going as she'd meant it to. But when had any conversation with Christina been productive?

"You think a man like that could only want someone like you," Christina continued anyway. "Never someone like me."

Annelise did think that was true, not because Christina was lacking in charm, but because men like Felix Hoffmann only wanted women who fought back. Christina wouldn't be a challenge for him, she wouldn't get him *aroused*.

"You know that's not what I mean, Christina." Why did they always assume the worst intentions of each other?

Christina studied her, and then all at once seemed to deflate. "He hasn't mentioned you or that boy for weeks now."

Annelise dropped her hand to her side, not sure how she felt. She knew she should be relieved, but a large part of her doubted Felix Hoffmann's ability to move on past the indignity of her rejection.

It did seem to confirm her decision not to see Eitan anymore, at least.

"He's not as bad as you think," Christina murmured, starting to walk again. They had been caught in some tense tableau in the entry-way of the Villa. "But I won't be going to the cinema with him again."

It was a kindness, a peace offering, and Annelise took it silently. Instead of saying anything that might push Christina further away, Annelise simply slung an arm around her shoulders, pulled her close, and pressed a sloppy kiss to her temple, like she would do with any of her Pirates. "Thank you."

Christina once again blushed with pleasure.

They continued on through the rooms filled with long-dead birds, Annelise marveling at the fact that Christina would rather be sur-rounded by stuffed animals than in the woods with live ones.

"Why do you like it here?" Annelise asked, and she made sure that it came off as genuinely curious instead of judgmental.

It took several minutes for Christina to answer, but she appeared thoughtful rather than defensive.

"Bonn is so very small," Christina finally said. "I like knowing there is more to the world than this place."

Annelise stopped walking, caught staring at her sister—who had always seemed so content with the idea of living here forever, marry-ing well, and building a family. Christina wasn't the type to dream. She wasn't the type to know what *wanting* was.

But why had Annelise thought that?

Because she didn't do so in the same way Annelise had done?

"Would you like to go to these places?" Annelise asked, tentative now that the world had trembled, even slightly, beneath her feet.

"It's silly."

"It isn't," Annelise rushed to say. Just because it was unlikely didn't mean it was impossible.

"I don't . . . I don't fit in anywhere," Christina said, shooting tiny glances at Annelise. "There are a million places out there, and sometimes I tell myself that I must fit in one of them. Just one. That's all I need."

Annelise could do little but blink at her dumbly, almost unable to fathom that there were things about her sister that she didn't know. "I thought you fit in here."

"I know you think that," Christina said, bitterness creeping into her voice. "But truly, you don't actually think about me all that much."

"What?" Annelise felt like her sister was all that was on her mind most days. Christina and Eitan.

"You think about the BDM and all the ways you want to scream at me about the NSDAP and Hitler and Felix. But you don't think about *me*."

Annelise opened her mouth, closed it. Christina was right. At some point Annelise had started associating those things so strongly with her sister that they became all that defined her.

"All right," Annelise said slowly. "Tell me more, then."

"You wouldn't understand," Christina finally said, her eyes frantic, trying to find someone hiding in the shadows perhaps. Her gaze finally seemed to land on a tiny colorful bird labeled as a Malachite kingfisher.

"'Do you know why swallows build in the eaves of houses?'" Christina asked. "'It is to listen to the stories.'"

One side of Christina's lips pulled up in a smile. "That's from *Peter Pan*. But I always loved the idea. I come here to listen to stories, I think."

Annelise wasn't one for books, but she thought she knew what Christina meant. That she listened to the stories these animals told, that she imagined herself in them. Watching giraffes walk across the setting sun on a safari with a rich lover; watching dolphins play at the bow of a ship bound for America; watching the penguins toddle and slide on some Antarctic expedition, Christina a female scientist stunning the world with her brilliance.

They weren't actually whispering gossip for Christina to overhear, just by existing they created a space to be filled with stories.

Annelise finally understood why Christina liked it here.

Finally understood the way Christina *wanted*.

But she was so taken aback by this side of her sister that she teased her instead of admitting to any of that. "To the stories of dead animals?"

Christina laughed, actually laughed. Full-bodied, her head tilted back. "You have no imagination."

Annelise joined in her laughter and soon they were leaning on each other, not even sure what had started them off. A guard came through, eyeing them sternly, and they giggled as they walk-ran back through the museum toward the sidewalk.

It felt like they were young again. And Annelise realized they still were.

When they calmed down, Annelise shot Christina a look. "Life is bigger than Bonn, you know."

Color flooded into Christina's cheeks again and Annelise desperately wanted to know *why*. On paper, Christina was the perfect little Nazi, content to be a part of the Volksgemeinschaft and further populate their country with children of the Master Race.

But there must be more to it than that. Otherwise, Christina wouldn't long for something else.

Annelise bought Christina an ice cream at the next shop, and they took a table outside beneath the colorful striped awning.

"What is it you aren't saying?" Annelise finally asked outright.

Christina looked away, her attention snagging on a girl walking toward them on the sidewalk. The breeze lifted the girl's skirt so that it fluttered against her thighs as she moved, her blouse shaping to her body so that the outline of her undergarment was visible.

Christina's mouth flattened to a line before she dropped her eyes to the table.

Annelise looked between her sister's distressed expression and the girl several times before something finally clicked into place. Years of Christina blushing for no apparent reason, of her showing interest in only the most popular boys, as if she needed someone to tell her who to admire, of her face when she stared at the bird.

There are a million places out there, and sometimes I tell myself that I must fit in one of them. Just one.

"Oh, darling," she whispered, and Christina's eyes darted up to hers. They were filled with panic.

"No."

Before she knew what she was doing, Annelise found herself nodding, soothing Christina. "All right."

But Annelise couldn't help but think of the murder of Ernst Röhm, who had been in Hitler's inner circle during the rise of the Nazis. He'd been killed along with other SA leaders who were considered deviants. Being a good member of the Party didn't protect you.

Annelise wanted to wrap Christina up, hide her away, protect her so that this never came back to harm her.

"If I do everything I'm supposed to . . . ," Christina murmured, and Annelise's heart cracked. She remembered last summer when she'd stood in the forest and mentally berated Christina for toeing every line she'd ever met. "If I follow the rules no one will look at me too closely."

In that moment, Annelise realized how much she herself must be a liability for Christina. Annelise did things that could get them all investigated. She brought the Nazis' attention to her family.

She didn't regret anything she'd done. But she had made those decisions thinking only about herself. Not only that, she had judged Christina harshly for making what she thought were different ones.

Even with this new danger, though, Annelise couldn't back down. Not now, as Hitler plotted how much land he could seize, how many indignities he could force onto Germany's Jews, how much everyday Germans would take of his madness.

"I'm not going to quit," Annelise said slowly, though neither of them really thought she would.

Christina smiled, and for once it was world-weary and knowing. This girl who was no longer a girl, but someone Annelise might like to get to know again.

"I was wondering when you would notice that I stopped asking you to."

"But . . . Frau Sommer," Annelise said. She understood why Christina wanted to play the role she did, but if that had been all there was to it, why had she tattled to the Frau about Annelise's delinquent ways? Annelise wasn't about to let her sister rewrite history.

Christina chewed her bottom lip for a long while, but Annelise didn't rush to fill the silence. She needed to know. It was all well and good for Christina to make pithy little statements over ice cream, but that wasn't where courage was tested.

"Do you remember the conversation in the hallway? Afterward." Christina's eyes darted up to Annelise's before returning to the table. "It's burned in my mind. You said—"

"There are big issues in the world and none of them are solved by hating people who are different than you," Annelise said. "More or less."

"Mostly spot-on," Christina said, her lips twitching for a moment. "Perfect, as always."

"I'm not perfect."

Christina didn't take the bait for an easy argument. "I said I don't hate people who are different than me. You didn't know when you said that . . ." She paused, her gaze slipping past Annelise to where the girl had disappeared. "That I'm the one who is different."

Annelise waited, and Christina took a deep inhale, as if she were bracing herself.

"It wasn't only about *that*, though," Christina admitted. "You were always right; I didn't simply parrot the Party's beliefs as a cover to fit in. I . . . I believed them. Or at least enough of them."

There had been a line pulled taut between her and Christina ever since her sister had donned the BDM uniform. Annelise expected in that moment for it to snap, a bond broken for good. But she heard the past tense even if Christina wasn't aware she'd used it. So Annelise waited, still, the most patience she'd granted her sister in quite some time.

"I told you in that conversation that I don't hate people who are different than me," Christina said again. "And I believed it."

Past tense.

"You said—"

"That you just don't care what happens to them."

Again, some kind of bitter amusement slipped into Christina's expression as she tipped her head in acknowledgment.

"I was so angry that day," Christina said. "And for the weeks after. Then I saw you at the lake with that boy, and I was furious. So furious I . . ."

For the first time, alarm bells rang in Annelise's head. She nearly lunged across the table to grip Christina's wrist, but that would take them back into a fight they'd been waging for years now.

"I almost ran straight to Felix," Christina finished. "I wanted to hurt you for lying to me. I wanted to hurt you because I knew how much you hated me and that—"

"I didn't hate you," Annelise cut in.

Christina made a disbelieving sound. "I knew how much you hated me, and I wanted to hurt you because of that. And some part of me knew telling Felix about the boy would hurt you."

"It would," Annelise agreed softly, her breath caught behind her teeth.

"But I went home instead," Christina said. "And I saw you. With . . . the book."

We need, in love, to practice only this: letting each other go.

"I watched you cry for hours and then you fell asleep, and I . . . took the book."

Annelise straightened despite the fact that she knew—with absolute certainty—that the Rilke was safe, tucked beneath her mattress. She'd looked at it yesterday.

"I gave it back," Christina rushed to say. "But I read his note. I read the poem. It's about a dead woman."

Christina said it in that blunt, direct way of hers, as if it would come as a surprise.

"Yes," Annelise said. She'd read every word of the volume, had nearly memorized all of the poems. "And about grief and love tangled together."

"He wrote you that because of me, right?" Christina asked. "Because you couldn't trust I wouldn't tell Felix."

Annelise let her silence be the answer, the echo of *I almost ran straight to Felix* hanging between them.

"Right," Christina said, and there was something close to shame in her eyes. "I thought about what you said that day with Frau Sommer then. That I didn't care about what happened to other people, people who weren't my family, people I didn't love already. And I realized you were right. Because I didn't care about Eitan until I realized he loved you and would grieve you, and then he became mine, in a way.

"I should have cared even when he wasn't," Christina said, her eyes finally meeting Annelise's gaze and holding. "It's not my instinct. I thought a single person couldn't possibly care about the whole world, about everyone and their problems, there's not enough room in here." She tapped her chest. "There's not enough room to hold all of that, there's only enough for the people who are *mine.*"

Thought. Annelise held her breath, feeling like she was watching the moment a flower bloomed, or glimpsing the tip of a butterfly wing as it broke free of its cocoon. Or seeing her sister shrug off the selfishness of childhood and become a caring woman.

"But if everyone thinks that way, what happens to the people who aren't someone's to care about?" Christina said. "I'm not . . . I'm never going to be like you."

Perfect, as always, Annelise heard. She wondered if Christina really believed that. It seemed outlandish that anyone would think Annelise perfect.

"I'm trying to be better, though," Christina said, sitting back, her truth spilled out between them for Annelise to accept or reject. "I'm trying."

A butterfly, flawed but beautiful nonetheless. Annelise started laughing, because she didn't know what to do with the emotion that clogged up her throat, her chest.

Christina's expression took on a wounded edge, and Annelise shook her head. She reached over and grasped her sister's hand.

"I'm thinking of something Eitan said once," Annelise confessed. "He said he believed poetry could change the world."

How many fights had she had with Christina? How many debates that only ended in them bleeding all over the floor, emotionally speaking? How many times had Annelise tried to change Christina's mind?

And all it had taken was a poem.

Christina's smile was tentative, but it held within it a lifetime of hope. "I guess he was right."

Chapter 28
CHRISTINA

March 2, 1943

"You look just like her," Lisbeth said, almost sadly.

Christina stared down at Annelise as she'd been back in that summer of thirty-eight and her heart ached, her bones ached.

Everyone had said that back then. *You look just like her.*

Christina had never seen it. Or, she had, but she had been the dull version, the copy that wasn't quite right. Annelise had been bright and vibrant, her hair silky and her smile wide. She'd charmed everyone she met with such ease.

"Why do you have a picture of my sister?" Christina knew she was repeating herself, but she couldn't find any other words. Her voice sounded thin and far away even to her own ears.

Lisbeth licked the lips she'd kissed Christina with five minutes ago. A lifetime ago.

"When I first saw you, you were standing on Rose Street looking like this photograph come to life," Lisbeth said, still not answering the question. "And I knew who you were; of course I did."

"You hated me," Christina realized. Not a question this time.

The guilt was easy to read in the flick of Lisbeth's eyes. Away. Back to Christina.

"I wasn't going to talk to you," Lisbeth said, instead of agreeing. It still felt like agreement. "And . . . then . . ."

That was brave of you.

The first thing Lisbeth had said to Christina, after she'd tipped her head back and yelled for that first time. Shifting the gathering of strangers into a protest.

"I had to talk to you then," Lisbeth said. "Because . . ."

"Because why?" But Christina knew. There was only one reason Lisbeth had a photograph of Annelise in the apartment she shared with her husband.

"Because we were there for the same man," Lisbeth said.

Christina's knees gave out at the confirmation. She forced the words out. "Eitan is your husband."

Lisbeth folded herself down onto the floor across from Christina. "Eitan is my husband."

Annelise smiled up at Christina, laughing almost at the absurdity of the situation.

"Once I realized you weren't there as some sort of Nazi spy, I had to know what you were like. But . . . I was expecting something else," Lisbeth admitted. "A selfish, terrible woman, perhaps."

Christina closed her eyes against the very words she whispered to herself every night.

"But you aren't that, are you?" Lisbeth gently tugged one of Christina's hands into her lap to hold with both of hers. "I wanted to hate you."

"You don't know me well enough not to," Christina said, the words jagged against her throat.

"Did you lie to me?" Lisbeth asked. "When you said you hated the Nazis?"

Slowly, Christina shook her head.

Lisbeth's eyes crinkled at the corners even though she didn't smile. "How old were you? In Bonn?"

"It doesn't matter."

"To me it does," Lisbeth said. "How old were you?"

"Sixteen," Christina said, because she didn't have a choice. Or, at least that's how this felt. Lisbeth had been kind to her even though she'd known everything. She'd known what Christina had done to Lisbeth's husband. Christina owed her answers at the very least.

"After I married Eitan, he began teaching me about his religion," Lisbeth said, as softly as the pink-tinted light streaming in the window. "There was a philosopher that he told me about by the name of Maimonides who preached about forgiveness and repentance. It requires four steps. Do you want to hear them?"

No, Christina thought. "Yes."

"You must recognize and discontinue the improper action."

Christina huffed out a breath. That she had done.

"You must verbally confess to the action," Lisbeth continued. "You must regret the action and determine never to do it again."

"Done."

"And there must be restitution," Lisbeth said. "Which, pardon me for presuming, but that seems to be your life, considering where I found you."

Christina blinked quickly against tears, but it was no use, they finally spilled over. Lisbeth shifted closer, brushed at one with her knuckle. Her gaze was soft, understanding.

It shouldn't be.

"It can't be that easy," Christina said. But maybe it wasn't. Hadn't she thought about her mistake every day for the past five years? Hadn't she lived a life deliberately stripped of anything that could make her happy because she knew she didn't deserve it?

"Oh, darling," Lisbeth murmured. "Don't take this the wrong way, but you're small potatoes in this big, terrible war. At the end of all this, there will be people who will never be able to apologize for all the wrongs they did. I can't speak for your sister or Eitan, but from where I sit, you are not one of them."

Christina's laughter was wet, but it was there in the space between them. "You're—diplomatically—telling me I'm being self-centered."

"Only a pinch," Lisbeth said, and then she sat back. "I've been thinking a lot about forgiveness. Who knows why."

The last bit was loaded with sarcasm.

"There are times when I want to be a lunatic and find a gun and shoot everyone," Lisbeth admitted. "These people who did nothing when my parents were taken away from me, who would have cheered had I been arrested. Who would gleefully murder my dearest friend and me with him since I won't jump at the chance of divorce." She paused. "I think it would be easy to focus on my hatred toward all of those people. But instead I like to think about the women who gave us blankets yesterday. And the women standing in Rose Street right now. God can deal with the rest."

Christina knew more than she ever wanted to about the camps because she worked at Abwehr. Not everything, she was sure, but enough to be a daily reminder of how ashamed she should be for ever defending the men who created them.

It wasn't clear how much the everyday public knew about them. They knew Jews and political enemies and antisocials and deviants were deported and never came back. But did they really know? If Lisbeth did, she couldn't still believe there was a God who would hand down final justice. If he existed, which Christina had long ago stopped being sure about, then he owed his people those four steps.

He owed it to them on his knees.

"It's the only way I survive," Lisbeth whispered, seeming to read Christina's doubt on her face. "Believing that someday these people will pay for their fear and their cowardice and their hatred and all that it led to."

"How did you meet Eitan?" Christina asked, wanting to erase the pain she read in the creases of Lisbeth's face.

Like she'd predicted, Lisbeth glowed. She always did when speaking of Eitan. "At a bookstore. There used to be shops you could go to where you knew the owner kept banned books beneath their counters. I called it the Berlin Book Club, which is silly, but I was young."

"You say it as if you're old now," Christina said, kicking her leg out until their ankles pressed together. A point of contact.

"Thirty in three months," Lisbeth admitted. She laughed, but for the first time since Christina had met her she seemed self-conscious. "I was looking for Thomas Mann's *The Magic Mountain*."

"I don't know it," Christina admitted.

"The main character is in a sanatorium," Lisbeth said, without a hint of judgment for Christina's ignorance. "And he meets people that personify prewar Europe. Not this war. The last one." Lisbeth rolled her eyes. "So many wars. But Mann's book is quite entertaining. And it has some of my favorite quotes. 'What good would politics be, if it didn't give everyone the opportunity to make moral compromises?'"

"Apt," Christina noted.

"I have an even better one. 'Tolerance becomes a crime when applied to evil.'"

"Ah. Germany."

"Germany," Lisbeth agreed. "You were patriotic once. Do you still love your country? Now that you've seen what it is capable of?"

Christina had thought about this too much and wasn't sure her answer was the one Lisbeth wanted. But it was the one she had to give.

"Who am I forsaking when I say, yes, I still love Germany? Who am I forsaking when I say I don't? Your parents? Eitan? They are the best of Germany, though. They are the best of the Germany that I want to see live beyond this war. How do I say I hate Germany without saying I hate them? How do I say I love it without saying I hate them?"

Lisbeth stared at her for a long moment and Christina's stomach clenched. She always thought the wrong things, she had known that. It still hurt to have it confirmed.

But then Lisbeth lurched forward, her hands cupping Christina's cheeks, her mouth finding Christina's. This kiss was urgent, desperate, searching.

Christina met Lisbeth where she was, their tongues brushing as they sunk into each other. Sparks lit behind the velvet of Christina's closed eyes and she wanted to live here in this moment forever and not think about Germany or the war or forgiveness or grief.

Once again, Lisbeth was the one who pulled back, the one who broke the spell.

"We can't," she panted, and Christina nodded because she knew that was what she was supposed to do. "We can't."

"All right," Christina said mindlessly. She looked away, searched for some tether to return them to normal. "You didn't tell me how you met Eitan."

Lisbeth's warm palms were still cupping Christina's face, as if it was beloved.

But she sat back once more and laughed. "Right. Um. The Berlin Book Club. I was looking for *The Magic Mountain*, and I had heard one store in the Bavarian Quarter might have a copy. When I went, the owner told me he'd sold the last one. But the gentleman had only just left if I wanted to chase him down."

"You didn't."

"I did." Lisbeth grinned. "Eitan was halfway down the block and about bolted when I tapped him on the shoulder. I asked if we could set up a lending system. He asked me if I wanted a coffee."

"Did he . . ." Christina trailed off, not sure how to word it. She tried again. "Does he know . . . ?"

"About the fact that I have no interest in consummating our marriage?" Lisbeth said dryly. "Yes, he managed to pick up on that."

A blush heated her cheeks, though Christina felt silly about it.

"He was in love, anyway," Lisbeth said with shrug. "He always will be. It didn't matter who I was. I wasn't Annelise."

Christina brought her knees into her chest, resting her chin upon them. "I know Romeo and Juliet fell in love in the blink of an eye, but I always wondered at that. Love that came so quickly."

"You don't think Eitan and Annelise . . . ?"

"No, no," Christina rushed to interrupt. "I know they loved each other. But sometimes I wondered how deep it ran. Everything happened so quickly."

"Some people simply know."

"I think love, for me, has always been hard," Christina admitted.

"So I didn't believe that it could ever be easy. As easy as an introduction."

"Oh, sweetheart," Lisbeth murmured, and Christina hid her face. She didn't want sympathy. "I wish you could have been here for the cabarets. You would have had so much fun."

"I don't remember how that feels."

"Fun?"

Christina nodded. "I think the last time I had fun was at a picnic. I was fourteen, and I had filched Annelise's dress so I felt pretty for once. She was mad at me, but I brought her cake and after that we played sports all afternoon. When night came, we sat by a lake and made wishes on dandelion stems."

"That sounds nice."

"If I had grown up in the cabarets I think I would have been different. Better," Christina said, trying to imagine a life like that. She couldn't; all she had was her own, for better or worse.

"But then you wouldn't be you," Lisbeth said, as if that wasn't the very point Christina had been making. "All of your choices, good and bad, have led you to this moment, this precise moment in history." Lisbeth drew in a breath. "Who would say you would be one of us if you erased every choice you'd ever made?"

And that was true. Even if Christina hadn't done what she had, Eitan would still be a Jewish man living in Hitler's Germany. Christina didn't see herself as overly important to the protest—that had a heart and soul of its own. But she was one more person in the street. One more German woman to kill if the Nazis wanted to get their way.

One more bullet they would need to waste, one more name in the newspaper articles written about the slaughter, one more grave they would have to dig.

Lisbeth was right.

If every decision she'd made had led her here, to this moment, to this fight, then maybe hers really had been a life worth living.

Chapter 29

EMMY

April 1946

Y ou look like you're going to a funeral, lovey," Lucy said from her chair by the fireplace. Emmy glanced down at the dress. It was the best one she'd brought to Germany.

She tried not to wince as she remembered the last time she'd worn it.

"Oh, shit," Lucy muttered, realizing her faux pas at the same time. "Well. We can't have that, can we? Let's go shopping in my closet, shall we?"

"I don't think we share a dress size, as flattering as that offer is." Emmy laughed, following her into their room and sinking onto Lucy's bed rather than her own.

Emmy had let herself be talked into going to the single club in Offenbach, mostly to raise Lucy's spirits. The Nuremberg Trials had taken a toll on her, and Emmy longed to see Lucy returned to her joyful—if sharp-edged—self. Even if it meant socializing after hours. Truth be told, the Monuments Men and the other Offenbach workers were generally her type of people—quiet and studious—with the rare exceptions like Lucy. So it might not be a terrible night out.

Lucy spun now and evaluated Emmy in the detached, professional manner of a salesgirl at a department store. Then she cupped her own chest that wasn't nearly as generous as Emmy's. "Obviously, you are far more blessed than I am."

She said it like she actually believed that and Emmy laughed. She had long ago become comfortable with her body. It had kept her warm in Montana's winters, it had been what had drawn Joseph's eyes to her in the first place. She always had a nice cushion on bus seats, too. But Lucy was stretched-out saltwater taffy, long and gorgeous, and Emmy was the lump of it in the packaging.

"But . . ." Lucy turned back to the closet, and then whirled around with a cherry-red dress that was perhaps the exact opposite of what Emmy was currently wearing.

"Oh, heavens no," Emmy muttered instinctively. "I won't fit into that. And even if I did—"

"You'd give Major Arnold heart failure," Lucy cut her off. "And you will. The material stretches at the bust and hips, which is where you need the extra fabric. For me, lovey?"

Emmy rolled her eyes, but did as she was told and headed into the bathroom. Lucy had been right, the dress was tight over her curvy bits, but did actually zip in the end, the cinched waist creating an hourglass silhouette that hid the soft swell of her belly. The skirt's hem flirted against her legs as she swished her hips, and the color contrasted stunningly with her inky black hair and pale skin. There was too much décolletage on display for her taste, but Lucy was right. They weren't attending a funeral.

When she stepped back into their room, Lucy eyed her with that same intensity from earlier and then beamed.

"You're missing one thing," she said before handing over a lipstick that matched the dress exactly. By the time Emmy slipped into her boring black pumps she felt more like she was going to a costume party than a night on the town.

Lucy looped her arm through Emmy's and tugged her out of the cottage. "Our chariot awaits, Snow White."

Their chariot turned out to be an open-air jeep—the kind that crawled like bugs all over Frankfurt and Offenbach. An officer who couldn't have been older than twenty sat at the wheel, while the other boy held the door open for them.

"They're babies," Emmy whispered into Lucy's ear. Lucy cackled, and swatted Emmy on the rump as she climbed into the back with uncoordinated movements, more focused on not giving the young private a show than caring about being sensual.

"I know you like them more mature," Lucy said with a wink. "But there are benefits to the young ones as well."

"Incorrigible," Emmy said, certain the men had heard the whispered conversation. But if they were bothered by it, they didn't let on.

And Emmy had to admit it was nice to have two handsome, young soldiers on their arms when they walked into the nightclub. Something deeply feminine in her purred at the way the men's eyes lingered, even if it was mostly the dress's doing.

The nightclub was packed with boys like their escorts, dressed in their uniforms, but also with the Monuments Men and other librarians visiting the depot, like Emmy. There was a grand piano in one corner, manned by an older officer, three women in slinky dresses crowding around him.

A few gaming tables were set up toward the back, a small stage acted as a dance floor, and a frantic man behind the bar was trying to keep up with everyone's orders.

Emmy was reminded of the scenes of Rick's Cafe in *Casablanca*, a movie she had watched so many times during the long, hard nights of the war that she knew most of the lines. It had turned out she'd found a fellow fan in Lucy, and, in their sillier moments, they would go long stretches of simply reciting the dialogue to each other.

The boys deposited Emmy and Lucy at a table in one of the corners, while they disappeared, presumably to procure cocktails.

"You know, it certainly won't hurt for Major Arnold to see that pup worshipping at your feet," Lucy said, eyebrows waggling.

"We're friends," Emmy protested. "Nothing more."

"Why not more?"

Because Major Arnold had shown no real interest in doing anything about the spark she sometimes felt between them. That sounded pitiful, though, so she simply shrugged, looking away.

"Is it because of your late husband?" Lucy pressed. "No matter how brave and wonderful he was, he wouldn't have wanted you to throw away the rest of your life."

For one second, Emmy wanted to snap that Lucy didn't know anything about what Joseph would have wanted. But that wasn't fair. Emmy had only ever spoken about Joseph as a good man, and a good man *would* want Emmy to be happy.

"No, he talked about me remarrying in some of his letters. He encouraged it," Emmy admitted quietly. "He . . . he wasn't doing well toward the end."

Sometimes in the darkest parts of the night when she couldn't sleep she wondered how hard he'd really tried to live that day they'd stormed the beaches in France. She doubted his emotional state would have made the difference. Emmy still couldn't listen to the details, but she knew many of the men had been slaughtered simply because they'd stepped off the boats.

Still . . . there had always been some doubt in her mind.

"The boys all told themselves they were fighting for us, I think so they could cope with all that horror. Joseph said that he was fighting for my chance at a happy life."

"Pretty words, but it sounds to me as if you don't believe that," Lucy said.

It wasn't fair to give away Joseph's secrets as if they were her own. She shook her head, hoping Lucy would take the hint.

Of course, Lucy knew about silences and when to offer the grace of a new topic. She leaned in and batted her lashes like a film star. "Don't look now, but someone's watching you."

That was as effective as telling someone not to think of a pink elephant. Of course Emmy looked.

Major Arnold was in his uniform, leaning on his cane at the end of the bar. He didn't even try to hide the fact that his attention was locked on her.

There were so many beautiful people in the nightclub, they shimmered like finely cut jewels scattered by the handful. But everyone else dimmed to background noise. Her skin tingled under his gaze, heat gathering at her center.

"Yes, yes, yes," Lucy chanted quietly when Emmy stood.

"Incorrigible," Emmy tsked again, but made sure it sounded as fond as she felt.

Major Arnold wasn't like the young pups who had escorted her and Lucy there. He kept his eyes on her face as she navigated her way over to him.

"Mrs. Clarke," he said, with a not-quite smile. "May I buy you a drink?"

"Whatever you're having," Emmy said, as a stool freed up. He gestured for her to take it and then waved down the harried bartender.

The seat put her at eye level with him, and she leaned her elbow against the bar, knowing the way it would help the dress drape just right.

"I haven't forgotten about Eitan," he said, as he handed over a tumbler with clear liquor in it. At her raised eyebrows, he grinned. "Vodka. I should have clarified."

Emmy shot him a look and then took the drink in one swallow, the only proper way to consume vodka. Major Arnold laughed.

"Prost," he said—cheers, in German—and then downed his own.

He switched them over to something gin-based and fizzy after that, and she enjoyed the bubbles against the roof of her mouth.

"Most people would have made me take the seat," he said, when she thought he'd direct them back to their conversation about the Rilke volume.

"Erm," Emmy said, shifting. "Did you . . . ?"

"No," he said, smiling down into his glass. "Those are less comfortable than standing for me. But when someone makes a big show of it, sometimes I'll just go along."

"How long has it been?"

"Two years," he answered without hesitation. "Two months and nine days."

"So what you're saying is that you don't remember it well," she teased.

He studied her for a long moment to the point that she thought she might have taken a misstep.

"I like you, Mrs. Clarke."

It was exactly what she'd said to him in Bonn, but it struck her differently on the receiving end. Her cheeks burned as she swirled her glass. "Was it an air raid?"

She asked it mostly to deflect, half expecting him to dodge the question himself.

"No, a land mine."

Her eyes slipped to the scars that peeked, as always, over his collar.

"There were rumors of an abbey in Italy at the feet of the Apennines that had a perfectly preserved incunable."

While Emmy didn't specialize in early typography, she knew that those manuscripts from the birth of the printing press were extraordinarily valuable.

"There was a village at the bottom of the cliffs where the abbey was located," he continued. "When we got there . . ." He trailed off, glanced around. No one was paying them any attention. The man at the piano switched over to "White Cliffs of Dover" and more than one or two soldiers were wiping their eyes, leaning on each other and swaying. People laughed and flirted and danced, and an older officer with a row of heavy medals on his chest kept shooting disapproving glances at the gaming tables.

"The village had been punished for partisan attacks in the area," he said. "There weren't any survivors, but we still had to check to be sure."

Emmy didn't let herself picture the scene. Didn't let herself picture him, this quiet historian with so much faith in the long arc of history, stumbling upon an entire village full of bodies that must have been desecrated. How did he survive that and come out the other side as thoughtful and kind and hopeful as he was?

"The man I was with, we had been traveling behind the army, trying to rescue as many artifacts as we could," Major Arnold said. "He triggered a land mine."

His mouth pinched in as he stared down at his now-empty glass. "I was still on the other side of the village. I woke up in a hospital in Rome two days later, not remembering any of it. They never found his body."

Emmy reached out, covered his hand with hers. "I'm so sorry for your loss."

She couldn't help the guilty thought that she was glad it hadn't been him. The mercurial hand of war.

"When I was able to get out of the hospital bed, I caught a transit plane home to tell his wife. Hardest thing I've ever done."

"She must have appreciated that," Emmy said, squeezing his hand one more time and letting go. "The man who delivered my telegram got Joseph's name wrong."

Major Arnold stilled.

"I don't blame him," Emmy rushed to say. "That job must be unbearably difficult. But it would have meant quite a bit to me had one of his friends visited as you did."

His eyes were on her face now, searching for something—what, she didn't know.

"Your husband . . . he died?" Major Arnold finally asked.

"At Normandy," Emmy said slowly, sure that they'd already talked about this. But . . . she reviewed the past few weeks. Their conversations had wound through philosophy and religion, ethics and forgiveness. They'd also touched on sillier topics, like the best food days in the Offenbach Depot's cafeteria, what baseball teams they rooted for—the Boston Red Sox for her, the Orioles for him. During the cigarette breaks that she now always joined him for, they compared notes about the books they'd worked on that day.

But she hadn't told him about Joseph.

Oh.

She would never have thought that had been a deliberate choice, but it *must* have been. Major Arnold hadn't asked, outright, but she had managed to tell Lucy that first night all on her own.

Emmy had deliberately been putting distance between them, a wall with a sign that said Keep Out.

When Lucy had asked why nothing romantic had transpired, Emmy had put the responsibility on Major Arnold's shoulders. He wasn't interested in her and that was that. But she'd been the one holding him at a careful arm's length.

Like how she still called him Major Arnold, when he'd told her to use his name almost immediately.

He was simply following her cues.

There was still a chance he had no interest in her. But that might not be the only reason he made sure never to touch her longer than necessary, never to flirt beyond what could be written off as friendship. Never to overstay his welcome.

She could see him making the same calculations. She still wore her wedding ring, and had never once disabused him of the idea that it might be more symbolic than anything else.

Why hadn't she?

Emmy wasn't actually sure. It certainly hadn't been something she'd thought through. But now forced to face her decisions, she realized that it was because she could tell that Major Arnold, for all his optimism, still had ghosts in his eyes. How could he not? From that one Italian village alone, he would be haunted for the rest of his life.

Joseph had been haunted, as well. Not by war, but by life. And Emmy had sworn long ago that she couldn't put herself through that again.

All of their men were going to come home scarred and battle worn. Emmy had read enough books from the Great War to know what exposure to that much violence and death did to a man.

Major Arnold might be an optimist now, but there was a difference between living in a war zone and living with the daily monotony back home. What could fuel a person through atrocity quickly shifted to corrosive acid when faced with normality.

"Oh, hello." The puppy from earlier chose that moment to find Emmy, a drink in his hand clearly meant for her. She took it and downed it while holding Major Arnold's eyes. And then she smiled brightly at the young man who'd brought it to her.

"Hello, shall we dance?" Without waiting for his reply, she hopped off the stool, and grabbed his hand.

"Oh, sure, yes, ma'am," he murmured as he trailed behind her.

Emmy didn't usually dance. But she could fake it, especially to a slow song. She settled into a gentle rock back and forth with the young man, his palm sweat-slick against hers. Her eyes were prickly with tears she didn't fully understand, and she refused to glance over to see if Major Arnold was watching them.

When the song ended, she turned deliberately back to her table with Lucy. The other woman was cozied up with her young admirer, taking advantage of Emmy's absence and the shadows. But Lucy straightened the second she saw Emmy; there must have been something obvious on her face. Lucy didn't ask questions, simply clapped once and said, "All right, time to leave."

The men glanced at each other, but they were far too used to taking orders—and far too polite in general—to argue with a lady.

Somehow, Emmy held it together until they got back to their little cottage. Then she headed directly for her bed, curling up so that her back was to the room.

"Oh lovey," Lucy said, sitting on the edge of the mattress. Emmy had never had a friend who would ignore all the ways she was screaming to be left alone, and she realized how lovely it was. Just to have someone comfort you even when you thought you didn't want it. "I thought you said Joseph wouldn't have minded."

"It's not him," Emmy murmured mostly into her pillow. "It's me."

Chapter 30
CHRISTINA

March 2, 1943

B erlin was on fire.

Or so it seemed when Christina and Lisbeth stepped outside on Tuesday morning to the ruins left as a gift from the British Royal Air Force. On any other day, Christina would have been celebrating. Now, she looked around and saw the neighbors who had given Lisbeth and her blankets and food and care standing outside their bombed-out houses.

The ones who'd made it out uninjured, at least.

Christina wasn't one for prayer, but she found herself desperately begging a higher power that the Jewish community center with nearly two thousand men locked inside had stood through the night.

The two of them cut through a destroyed shop and Christina had a strong memory of doing the same three days ago on her way to the Bendlerblock. So much had changed since then, it nearly took her breath away. She wondered if she'd ever see the inside of that building again. Even if they didn't know where she'd gone off to, Christina had still missed several days of work.

It didn't matter right now, though. Christina would deal with the fallout later. Hopefully after Eitan and the other men had been freed.

As she and Lisbeth neared Rose Street, a swell of noise crashed into them. Christina closed her eyes and listened.

Not screams of grief, not wails of loss and desperation.

"Give us back our husbands," came the chant like an answer to their prayers.

When Christina opened her eyes it was to find Lisbeth beaming. The sight stole Christina's breath, and for one wild, crazed second, Christina wanted to grab her, kiss her.

Lisbeth's smile softened into something private, her fingers brushing the back of Christina's hand before she charged ahead. "Let's go."

They reached the edge of the crowd and Lisbeth pulled the first woman she saw into a tight hug. The woman didn't even hesitate, she simply wrapped her arms around Lisbeth in return, tears of relief streaming down her face.

Christina remembered the woman she had tried to talk to days ago, the one who'd flinched away from a stranger offering a kindness. How far they'd come in so short a time.

"They lived," this woman said to Lisbeth now. "They lived another day."

Christina kept her distance, watching Lisbeth hug the next woman and then the next after that and the next after that as they made their way toward the front of the protest. Still, she could feel the bonds of this community tug at her heart, a thread that wove them all together.

They were one now, they spoke as one, they moved as one, they celebrated as one.

They were the women of Rose Street.

Their community wasn't the type the Nazis forced—the kind where people united not out of love and solidarity but out of fear and hatred. Those communities were weak and brittle, prone to rot and infighting.

This community had come about from a decision made by each one of these women to risk their lives because it was the right thing to do. They might hate the Nazis, but that wasn't the singular thing holding them together. They might be afraid, but it wasn't fear that this community was built on.

And that made all the difference in the world.

The Nazis, who had risen to power by driving wedges between Germans, by singling out "enemies," by convincing people that isolating themselves from anyone different was the only way to be safe, would never understand the women of Rose Street.

Humans' worst instincts caused them to hunker down against the *other*. But their best made them seek connections through joy, through hope, through a shared goal that was good and right and meaningful.

Lisbeth's lashes were a damp soot-black by the time they made it to the front, her cheeks flushed with a mixture of emotion too complex for one name.

The community center stood before them, boarded up but whole. Women had begun scaling the building next door to try to get glimpses inside.

"God was on our side," someone murmured as the sight fully hit them all.

The police were back standing guard, but the Nazis were few and far between. Perhaps they were busy regrouping from their flight to their bunkers. Christina smiled at the image of them gathered in the darkness, pressed together like the men they treated as no better than animals. Scared and trapped.

As Christina scanned the scene, a thought scratched at the inside of her skull.

"I haven't seen Ingrid yet," Christina said, turning to Lisbeth. The crowd was the thinnest it had been since Saturday, but there were about a hundred women in the street, with more flooding in by the minute. There was no reason they *should* have seen Ingrid. But still, Christina worried.

Lisbeth tensed and Christina felt guilty for destroying the jubilant mood. "Let's start asking about."

Christina turned to her neighbor. "Have you seen a woman, she's pregnant, short, with a pretty face?"

She got a blank stare in return, a headshake. She moved to the next woman and the next until she felt a tug on her sleeve.

Lisbeth.

"Someone saw her take cover in a house near the Spree," she said. And then by some kind of miracle, added, "They gave me an address."

Without needing to speak further, both of them pushed their way back through the crowd, this time ignoring the celebrations around them, an urgency sparking between them for no real reason. Ingrid was fine, Christina was sure of it. Just . . . she needed to check.

The houses near the Spree would have been attractive targets, the river an easy path for the bombers to follow.

Christina and Lisbeth had to detour three separate times before they got to the stretch where Ingrid had been seen heading.

Lisbeth stopped so suddenly that Christina bumped into her back.

The row was razed nearly to the ground, the smoke and stone and dust still thick in the air.

"No," Lisbeth whispered.

Christina didn't waste time arguing with her. Instead, she headed straight for the address they'd been given, judging the right number by the houses opposite on the street. All of those had survived.

She started digging, mindlessly, knowing that if she was going to find anything it would be a body. Dust coated her throat, her lungs; her fingernails broke; her skin ripped so that blood dotted the stone; her knees throbbed and her head throbbed; and still she dug.

Arms wrapped around her, pulled her back.

Christina fought the hold, but Lisbeth was surprisingly strong, her voice soft with reassurances. After a few wild minutes of struggle, Christina finally slumped, letting Lisbeth take the weight of her body, the weight of her disappointment.

"You wouldn't answer me," Lisbeth said, gentling her hold. "I called your name so many times."

"I didn't hear you," Christina admitted, staring at the blood in the beds of her nails. "Why does this hurt so much? I barely knew her."

"Because she was ours," Lisbeth said.

The answer rang like a clear bell in her chest. Of course that was it. These women were hers now, hers to love and celebrate with and protect.

Except she could never seem to get that last one right.

Why was she always failing to protect the people who needed her the most?

"Why don't you hate me?" It came out a broken, childish whisper.

"One day you'll stop asking me that." Lisbeth was holding Christina up now, though she didn't seem to mind. Her palms pressed against Christina's ribs as if she was making sure Christina was breathing and not breaking.

Christina wanted nothing more than to turn into her arms, to burrow into the warmth of her, the comfort. But a shout from the other side of the street had them stepping quickly apart.

A hefty woman hung out a second-story window. "Are you here for the girl?"

Ingrid wasn't a girl, but hope crackled to life in Christina's chest. She'd thought Ingrid much younger at first glance, as well. "Is she pregnant?"

"Come up," the woman grunted before retreating from the weather and dust.

The house was cold, as so many were in Berlin, the only light coming from the windows, and Christina carefully gripped the handrail as she navigated up a staircase that wasn't much wider than she was.

The woman met them at the second floor. "She lost the babe."

"Oh," Lisbeth breathed out behind her, distraught. Christina tried to muster up some emotion but she still couldn't get past the relief that they weren't digging Ingrid's lifeless body out of a stone grave right now.

"Come on, then." The woman still hadn't introduced herself, though Christina didn't blame her. This wasn't Rose Street. They were back in the real Berlin, the one where strangers could only be trusted so much.

Ingrid was curled on a thin mattress in the corner of a tiny room, her back to them. Blood and soot were caked on her chemise, in her hair, on her bare shoulders. Christina made a pained sound and then rushed to drape her coat over the shaking woman.

She didn't react at all.

Lisbeth sat at the foot of the bed, one firm hand wrapping around Ingrid's ankle, the threadbare blanket only reaching her shins.

"You couldn't have given her a quilt?" Christina asked, and Lisbeth shot her a warning look.

"She's lucky I didn't leave her on the street," the woman said, her voice brusque, defensive. It was how they all dealt with each other these days—feral creatures mostly focused on survival.

"Thank you," Lisbeth managed, because she was the better of the two of them. "May we see to her now?"

The woman grumbled but left them alone, and, as gently as possible, Christina tugged at Ingrid's shoulder. Her body went with the pressure so that she lay flat on her back, but her eyes remained locked on the ceiling, unseeing, her palms pressed to her womb.

A quick glance beneath the blanket showed that at least the older woman had helped clean up Ingrid's legs.

Lisbeth, visibly burying her distress, rubbed warmth into Ingrid's feet.

"She was a girl," Ingrid finally said.

Lisbeth was at a loss for words at that, it seemed, and Christina, emotionally clumsy even in the best scenarios, could only reach for the glass of water that had been left out on the side table. A kind gesture, really.

Ingrid swallowed the water obediently, but then went back to blinking at the ceiling.

"She was what I had left of Nathan," Ingrid whispered, and it seemed to break the dam. Tears streamed out of the corners of her eyes, the salt soaking into her hair, into the pillow. "What if I've lost everything? My entire world."

Christina wanted to say *You'll go on*. Because they all did. If humans didn't carry within them the innate ability to *go on* then the whole world would simply lie down and stop, overwhelmed by a grief that was so beyond anything any one person could be expected to bear.

Even she knew better than to say that.

Like she had a few dozen times over the past few days, Christina met Lisbeth's eyes. It was almost startling how easily they could communicate now without needing to speak, how they always seemed to have the same thought at the same time.

Lisbeth shook her head, not enough to catch Ingrid's attention but to make her position clear.

Christina ignored her—because sometime in the past seventy-two hours she'd begun to hope.

So she promised Ingrid something she had no business promising her.

"We'll get your husband back."

Chapter 31

ANNELISE

Summer 1938

A flash of dark curls near the flower cart caught Annelise off guard.

She stumbled to a stop, her eyes darting from face to face, as though through sheer force of will she could make one of them become beloved and familiar. But she'd blinked and whoever had caught her attention was now gone.

It didn't matter. Eitan never went to the market, of course it hadn't been him.

He was still in Bonn, she knew that. Sometimes she thought she saw him in crowds like this, but then wondered if it was a trick of her imagination—her desire to see him so all-encompassing she'd conjured him out of a stranger's similarities.

Every sighting, real or not, came like a punch to the belly, a reminder that even though they lived so close, they couldn't be together. To soothe the pain, she found herself returning to the Rilke he'd left as a parting gift. She could tell what pages he'd lingered on, the ones he'd come back to. When she traced the passages with her fingertips, it was as if she knew him better than she had even after hours of conversation.

Find out the reason that commands you to write; see whether it has spread its roots into the very depth of your heart; confess to yourself you would have to die if you were forbidden to write.

The ink had faded like he'd pulled the very words off the page into his own heart. She wanted to do the same.

She wondered how anyone could hate this man without ever knowing that he held stars within him; that he skated with careless grace; that he smiled at dogs and children and little else besides

Annelise; that he loved Bonn and its people even when they didn't love him back; that he was terrified of jumping off cliffs but not enough that he wouldn't follow Annelise over the edge; that he wasn't terrified of anything else, including the men who wanted to steal all his words from him. How could they hate so easily a man who saw so much poetry in the world?

Annelise swiped at a stupid, silly tear.

"Anna," Marta called out, panic in her voice.

Annelise dragged her eyes from the spot where Eitan *hadn't* been and turned toward her friend. Marta's normally pink-kissed cheeks were ice-cold marble.

"What is it?" Annelise asked, her tone sharper than it should be. But her mind was tangled up on Eitan and all she could picture was him being surrounded by the HJ, all of them with their whips in hand.

"The boys" was all Marta said, but that was all she needed to. The HJ's scrapes with the Pirates were near weekly occurrences, the smallest sign of "disrespect" enough to start an all-out brawl in the street.

She could now identify the sound of knuckles pounding into flesh from at least half a block away.

Grown men and women gathered around the small park where the chaos had unfurled. Stefan was at the center of it, his arms held by boys in HJ uniforms. Blood trickled into the divot beneath Stefan's nose, pooling in the dip of his lip. He was running his mouth, but Annelise couldn't make out the words, not with everyone shouting as they were.

It didn't matter, she knew what he would be saying. Taunts, insults, anything to get under his attackers' skin because Stefan never knew when to quit and that's what they all loved about him.

In the next moment, the biggest boy caught Stefan right under the jaw with his fist. Stefan's head snapped back, and all Annelise could see were the whites of his eyes before he crumpled to the ground. Marta cried out.

One of the Pirates broke free of her own attacker and ran toward Stefan. She didn't make it far, though. A short man with beady eyes grabbed her braid from behind and yanked her off her feet in a vicious jerk.

"We have to do something," Marta said, even as the adults around them shifted back, shifted away.

Like always.

Annelise whirled on the closest pair—a man and woman who sold lavender and lemon soap at the market. On her last birthday, Annelise had splurged at their stall, a purchase she now deeply regretted.

"They're children." Annelise hurled the accusation at them, and the pair averted their eyes, trying to blend into the gathering audience. "This isn't fair, they're children."

"They're riffraff who've brought it upon themselves," an older woman threw back, the only one who dared to meet Annelise's hard stare. There was no kindness or understanding in her face, just hardened antipathy. They were all used to the sound of knuckles on flesh. They had all *let* themselves become used to it. Why would it be any different now?

"If they'd just followed the rules," the soap-seller added, quieter but still confident. "If they'd just listened to what they were told to do . . ."

Marta grabbed Annelise's arm. In a voice loud enough for everyone to hear, she said, "Come on. History will be their judge. We don't need to waste our time on them."

"No," Annelise said, making sure the words dripped with disdain. "We don't."

And then she dove into the fray.

THE MOUNTAIN LAKE nearly stole Annelise's breath away, but that was the point.

Her body ached down to her bones. Bruises bloomed, yellow and purple and blue along her hip, over her knee, on her shoulder, as if a painter had taken a particularly cruel brush to her. Her broken lip pulsed with every heartbeat and her head still felt echoey and heavy from where it had connected with cobblestone.

Ice would have helped, as well, but this was more efficient. The cold water was already seeping away the pain.

The fight had not lasted long after Marta and Annelise had joined in, but they'd both gotten battle scars from it. The HJ boys didn't care about hitting girls, not if those girls were Pirates. Within the first minute, Marta had taken an errant fist to the cheek, and Annelise had caught the tail end of an elbow to her side. From then on it had been a blur trying to pull everyone apart.

Annelise dipped under the water, letting her mind go quiet. She didn't want to think about men who loved the smell of blood, who craved the taste of it on their tongue. But more than that, she didn't want to think of the bystanders who had simply watched the scrum, not willing to risk even a single punch for someone in need.

Germany was worth fighting for, it was why her left knuckle—caught on the ground, not on someone's face—was ripped right now. But if the Pirates and other anti-Nazi factions ever prevailed, how could she look her countrymen in the face when they hadn't even been able to meet her eyes when girls were being beaten into the ground?

While she had always believed cynicism was for the weak-minded and cowardly, she couldn't help the way reality chiseled away at her optimism. She knew people were scared, she did. But she didn't understand how they'd gotten to the point where they could watch such an unfair fight and think, *They brought that on themselves.*

Annelise waded back to the shallows, letting the air caress her naked skin. It was late, so late that she didn't worry about anyone being out here but her. The full moon felt like a friend lighting her way, the water a lover who cradled her wounded body.

She imagined Eitan on the beach with a book of poems forgotten in his lap, his eyes flicking up to her again and again and again—every part of them drawn to the other.

If only he were here with her . . . but even at night, protected by Annelise's woods, her mountains, her sky, it wouldn't have been safe.

So she turned away from the beach, away from the fantasy, and she dived, cutting through the surface, leaving barely a ripple in her wake.

And this was why she'd come up here.

Despite all the ways her body and heart and soul hurt, there was still joy in this darkness, in the memory of the way Eitan had held her, played with her, kissed her here.

If she thought only of their parting, she would begin to forget all that had become before. And that was unacceptable.

In the moment that she surfaced, Annelise thought not of Rilke, but of an American poet who had caught her attention.

Emerson was his name. Ralph Waldo Emerson. He had written of woods and ponds and dirt like he'd known her innermost thoughts. She hadn't shown Eitan because it had felt like a piece of her heart was right there on the page. Now she wished she had, because of course Eitan had already known her heart.

The poem that had stuck with her the most felt like it had been written about them.

> It is not only in the rose
> It is not only in the bird
> Not only when the rainbow glows,
> Nor in the song of woman heard,
> But in the darkest, meanest things . . .
> But in the mud and scum of things
> There always, always something sings

Chapter 32
EMMY

E mmy clutched a clipboard to her chest as she surveyed the crates lined up along the far wall of the main floor of the Offenbach Depot.

They were all bound for Washington, D.C., and some silly urge in her wished she could crawl into one of them.

She hadn't spoken to or seen Major Arnold since the debacle on Thursday night. That had been nearly a week ago now, and it forced her to acknowledge that she usually spoke to him most days she was working.

It had been lucky she'd been incredibly busy since or she would have spent far too many hours wondering if he was avoiding her or if she was avoiding him or if she was overthinking it all and they just hadn't crossed paths.

Emmy turned her attention back to where it should be—on the books in front of her.

This was the first shipment she was overseeing so she was being extra careful. The last thing she needed was for some valuable treasure to have slipped in under her watch. She had no interest in provoking an international incident.

She paused by one of the last open crates full of copies of books that had been printed in America and England during the war and positively focused on Jewish culture. Her fingers brushed against the worn blue cover of *A Book of Jewish Thoughts* by the United Kingdom's Chief Rabbi Joseph Hertz, published in 1943 in London. It was a collection, more than anything, of lessons and poetry and proverbs and prayers—and it had been annotated by a researcher at the institute. The decision to acquire the volume had been an obvious one, and so Emmy hadn't been able to justify spending too much time on it. But two of the lines close to the beginning had stood out to her.

This wonderful and mysterious preservation of the Jewish people is due to the Jewish woman. This is her glory, not alone in the history of her own people, but in the history of the world.

It had been credited simply: *M. Lazarus.*

The Nazis had not enjoyed that particular section, but Emmy had.

Mr. Dernbach stood at her shoulder now, all but rubbing his hands at their bounty of books. He'd proven to be a lax supervisor for the most part, which Emmy appreciated. When left to her own devices, Emmy tended to accomplish more than when she had someone hovering over her at all times.

"Well done, Mrs. Clarke," Mr. Dernbach said, his breath smelling of onions and mustard. Emmy took a discreet step to one side. "What's in this box?"

"These were curious finds," Emmy said. "Rosenberg must have had quite a system in place to get his hands on so many books that were published outside Germany during the war."

"Some kind of courier network through Switzerland, I'm sure," Mr. Dernbach said. "Well done, Mrs. Clarke, well done. How many books total are we sending to our colleagues?"

"Three thousand." The number seemed staggering even in the face of the hundreds of thousands of books at the depot.

"Director Evans shall be quite pleased, quite pleased," Mr. Dernbach said. He had a tendency to repeat himself, a strange affectation that made him seem a tad cartoonish.

"Yes, I believe so," Emmy agreed. "I'll start on the next shipment after lunch."

The next cache of spoils she would be working through included not just books but film reels and journals and even sheet music. While any type of manuscript would always be her first love, she was looking forward to the chance to get her hands on something different, as well.

"And you'll be with us through the next month, is that correct, Mrs. Clarke?"

"Another month, yes," Emmy said, hardly able to believe she'd been in Germany as long as she had.

"Wonderful," Mr. Dernbach said. "I'll see to getting these loaded on the trucks. You take your lunch."

Emmy hesitated, wanting to see her work through, but then accepted that this particular shipment was now out of her hands.

She stowed her clipboard at her makeshift workstation and then turned toward the door. She needed a breath of fresh air more than food.

Major Arnold found her leaning against the side of the building in the location she was coming to think of as their spot. Emmy wanted to run, to hide her flushed face. To jump into the river, really.

She wanted him to press her up against the wall.

For the past few days, she'd prayed that the next time she saw him he would simply pretend Thursday night had never happened. But when that was exactly what he did, she had to acknowledge her disappointment.

Oh, how fickle and flighty she was, even in her own head.

"You've had a busy morning," he said.

She nodded, unable to manage anything more.

"I was away," he explained, and something ugly and self-conscious in her dissolved in relief. "There was a dealer who has been operating out of Munich."

"You're becoming more of a book detective than a historian," Emmy said, trying to slip back into their easy give-and-take.

He offered her his half smile and she warmed at the sight of it. "They won't be tried at Nuremberg, but they'll face some punishment."

"Because of books." How curious their world was now. There would be plenty of Nazis who would leave their atrocities in the past, walk free, and never face consequences. But not the ones Major Arnold had set in his sights, the dealers who had profited from genocide.

Tzedek, tzedek, tirdof. Justice, justice, you shall pursue.

"Speaking of books," Major Arnold said. The tone shift had Emmy straightening. He never sounded overly joyful, but this was grim even for him. "When I was in Munich, I was able to visit a friend who had access to records from this area before and during the war."

No.

"Eitan?" she asked.

He sighed, an answer in itself. "Perhaps you can come to my office?"

Major Arnold didn't wait for an answer. Emmy trailed after him, hoping she was reading him wrong.

But when they were seated on either side of the desk in his broom cupboard–sized office, she knew from his expression it was bad news.

"Eitan Basch was part of the final roundup of Jews in Berlin in 1943," he said. There was a document in front of him, but the words were a jumble to her. "It was a sweep of intermarried Jews and people categorized as 'part-Jewish.'"

Her eyes darted up to his. "Intermarried?"

"It seems he was protected through the early years of the war because he married a German woman when he fled to Berlin," Major Arnold said, and Emmy cursed the flutter of hope in her throat.

"Annelise?"

"No," he said, crushing it out before it could even think about taking flight. "A woman named Lisbeth Wagner."

Emmy tried to do the math. "But he left here in thirty-eight. The race laws were put into place years earlier, weren't they? She wouldn't have been permitted to marry a Jewish man."

"It's murky," he said. "But I'm guessing they bribed a church and a local official to get everything documented. Their official wedding date was in early 1935."

Which would have had them skating in under the wire—at least on paper. But she bet plenty of couples had rushed down the aisle when they'd sensed what was coming with the Nuremberg Laws. That wouldn't have looked odd in and of itself.

"And they lived in Berlin until 1943?"

"Yes." Major Arnold slid the document over to her. "He was detained February 28, 1943. He was held for a week in Berlin, and then put on a train to the Auschwitz concentration camp in Poland."

Emmy touched the paper with shaking hands, blinking back foolish tears. Some part of her had always known it was silly to believe he'd made it through. His best chance had been if he'd somehow managed to leave the country in thirty-eight, but clearly that hadn't happened. "When did he die?"

"I couldn't find any information on him after he left Berlin," Major Arnold admitted. "They're still sorting through all those camp records. The ones that still exist. My friend is looking into it, though."

"Thank you," she said softly, still staring at Eitan's name, undeniable proof in black and white. She cleared her throat, picturing the Rilke. It was for Annelise, but perhaps this Lisbeth Wagner would appreciate having something of her husband's. Maybe Eitan had told her about Annelise, how she had been his childhood love. "Would it be insensitive to try to track down Mrs. Basch, do you think?"

"She'll certainly be easier to find than our mysterious Annelise," Major Arnold said. "Shall I try to procure a current address for her?"

Emmy put herself in Lisbeth's position. What would she think if someone showed up on her doorstep with a book that Joseph had dedicated to another woman?

Would it hurt?

Perhaps a little, in that sore tooth sort of way. A dull ache that made itself known when you prodded at it.

Mostly, she would be excited to see his handwriting again. To see words he'd written, that beloved scrawl that had become so familiar to her as they'd traded notes during the war.

It would be a gift, she realized. Not a tragedy.

She nodded, not lifting her eyes from Eitan's name on that terrible roster. "Please."

At the start of this, she'd wanted to find this book its rightful home. What better place than with someone who had loved the man who'd owned it?

IT TOOK MAJOR Arnold only two days to find Lisbeth Basch—née Wagner—in Berlin. She lived in a historically Jewish neighborhood in the old part of the city.

Emmy stared down at the address, hardly able to believe they'd located her. Hardly able to believe the woman had made it through the war. Even though Lisbeth was German, that still wasn't a sure thing. Berlin had been bombed like the cratered countryside they were now so familiar with.

"It's in East Berlin," Major Arnold said. They were standing on the front stoop of Emmy's cottage, his hat dangling from his fingertips. There was something about the way he said it that had her pushing the door all the way open, inviting him in.

By silent agreement, they headed through the house and stepped outside once more, the view of the river calming in the early morning light. There was still a crispness in the air, but they were headed toward late April now and so she didn't need her cardigan as often.

Emmy wrapped her arms around herself as she braced for whatever bad news Major Arnold had. He grimaced as if aware that he was the messenger who was hoping not to be shot.

"When the Soviets marched into Berlin last year . . . ," he started and then trailed off.

She tried to guess what he was nervous to tell her. The fall of Berlin had occurred at the same time she'd been coming out of the daze she'd sunk into since hearing about Joseph. She hadn't paid much attention to details.

Major Arnold huffed out an aggrieved sound and Emmy turned to him.

"Tell me," she said.

He studied her as if trying to verify that she meant it, and she kept still under his attention.

"The Soviet soldiers acted as a victorious army often does," Major Arnold finally said. "The German women in Berlin were looked at as spoils."

Emmy exhaled, not surprised but saddened. "It's all so very bleak, isn't it?"

"Living in the aftermath of hell? Yes."

"'All murderers are punished unless they kill in large numbers and to the sound of trumpets,'" Emmy murmured, knowing out of anyone he would get the reference.

"Voltaire," he said, proving her right. "'Only the dead have seen the end of war.'"

"Plato," she said and shot him a half grin. "We are not good for each other, Major."

He laughed, though it was a hollow sound. "I would have said the opposite."

Before she could react to that—how she would have, she didn't know—he shook his head.

"I wanted to make sure you were prepared," he said. "For what we may find."

"We?" she asked, though of course she had taken it for granted that he would accompany her.

"I'm not one to give up in the middle of a mission."

"No," Emmy said. "I wouldn't think you are."

"But Mrs. Basch might not actually be there," he said, grim again.

Emmy tried not to imagine that kind of fear, an army that had every right to be vengeful closing in, nowhere to go. Her body becoming a thing to be plundered. Even if Mrs. Basch was there, and had survived all that, she might not have any interest in talking to foreigners.

"When do you have a free day next?" Major Arnold asked and then pursed his lips. "Though we should probably plan on two days."

Emmy didn't let herself think about what they would do for the night in Berlin. He would likely book her a room in a proper establishment and then bunk down at whatever barracks the military had set up.

"Tomorrow," she said, reminding him, perhaps, that it was Saturday. He rarely stopped working from what she could tell. "That might be too short notice, though."

"How about next Saturday?" he said. "That gives me time to sort out our paperwork and lodging."

When she agreed, he left with a tiny bow of his head. But she stayed outside staring at the river.

She thought about the Nuremberg Trials, and the crooked Nazi bookdealer and the women in Berlin. She thought about the ruins in Frankfurt and the hollow-cheeked children and the dogs who were destined to become meals. She thought of Eitan on a crowded train headed to certain death and thought about Lisbeth hiding in her house so as not to be dragged out into the streets to face the fate of conquered women all throughout history.

She thought of Joseph, his body likely buried in the sand, beneath the waves off a beach in France.

Emmy sunk onto the steps of the back stoop, the dew from the morning soaking into the hem of her skirt. She could no longer bear the weight of so much while standing.

This was the land of monsters. You didn't forgive monsters. You didn't care about what happened to them.

She wondered what Major Arnold would say to that.

Perhaps he would once again point out that monsters had always walked among them. In America, they had their crooked bookdealers and the people who painted swastikas on temples. They had separate drinking fountains for their Black citizens and had been quite content with chattel slavery for most of their history. She'd even read about a terrible lynching just before she'd left for Germany, and it was 1946, not the 1800s.

Weren't there people who looked at *her* as if she had come from a land of monsters?

Could anyone say they hadn't?

Why was this all so complicated? Why couldn't everything be simple?

A small, childish part of her wished this was a film, where the good guys wore white hats, the bad guys wore black hats. At the end of the war the curtain fell and the lights in the theater came back on and no one had to think about how to navigate the aftermath of hell.

But she'd spent the past month reading the inner thoughts of the Nazis' most devoted ideologues. They wanted to control people by having them think like that. Here is the villain, they said, here are the heroes. Enjoy the story we're telling and don't think too deeply about the painted canvases and hollow props and shallow banter, because isn't it entertaining?

Emmy wanted to grapple and struggle with tough ideas and *feel* the weight of unimaginable grief, the weight of difficult decisions, the weight of love and hatred and hope. She wanted to understand others who had lived vastly different lives than her and see the humanity in them even when it was the hardest thing she'd ever had to do.

The whole world was staring on in horror, wanting to know: *How did this happen?* Emmy didn't have all the answers, but she did know one thing. The Nazis had put an immense amount of effort into making sure their people did none of that.

They had all paid the price for too many wanting life to be as easy as a movie.

Emmy should be grateful it wasn't.

Chapter 33

ANNELISE

Fall 1938

The Pirates were turning eighteen—the dreaded age that came with conscription into the Wehrmacht.

It was far easier to dodge the Hitler Youth than a formal notice to report to the army.

Some of the boys donned uniforms, some defied the orders anyway. Stefan packed a bag with clothes and bread and a tent and then headed into the forest with plans to hike to France if he had to. Marta had cried for three days over how proud she was that he hadn't become a Nazi. Annelise thought he would likely die within the week, but she kept her mouth shut about that prediction.

The ones left behind continued to be thorns in the sides of the HJ in Bonn, but they were all coming to realize that pamphlets were no longer enough. The air crackled with war and no amount of graffiti—or even brawls in the street—would stop Hitler's mad march to the east.

The time had come for real resistance plans, not just their youthful rebellions.

Camps had started popping up in their region, barbed wire doing little to block out the sight of rail-thin men with gaunt cheeks and hungry, desperate eyes. They were worked hard, to the point where their bodies had to be breaking down.

They were deviants or Germany's political enemies or foreigners who were threatening the safety of this great country, that's what all the papers said. But those were a mouthpiece for Hitler these days.

Annelise knew the truth. Those men didn't threaten the safety of Germany. They threatened the safety of Hitler's iron grip on the masses.

"Are you free tonight?" Marta asked one unseasonably warm day. They were taking a rare afternoon in the park, lounging in the sun and whispering about their grand ideas to thwart the Nazis.

"You know I am," Annelise said, rolling her eyes. When was she ever busy with anything but Pirate business?

One of Stefan's friends—a boy named Max—had invited them to meet at a barn on the outskirts of town.

When the time came, Marta and Annelise caught a streetcar as far as they could ride it and then walked the rest of the way, keeping to the woods. They couldn't be caught out here. They would be hard-pressed to explain this away as a casual jaunt in the middle of the night.

But no one knew these woods like they did, not even the HJ.

Some new energy thrummed beneath Annelise's skin. They had never attended such a clandestine meeting before. This was going to be serious, whatever it was.

That was confirmed when Max led them all to the back room of a drafty, otherwise empty barn and lifted a heavy tarp.

Annelise took an involuntary step back even as a gasp escaped. She wasn't weak-kneed usually. She had stood on top of a ticket booth in Cologne and shouted down the Nazi regime blocks away from the EL-De Haus.

But this . . .

She locked eyes with Marta. Despite the fact that neither of them had ever seen explosives before, they both knew instinctively what was on the floor.

"We know the train lines," Max said. "Let's start making noise."

Most of them cheered in a hushed kind of way, but there was a current of nerves that threaded through the fervor. Annelise felt very young and very old somehow simultaneously. This was a line that they were about to cross, here, a moment in time where they went from children to fighters.

Where they went from peacetime to war.

No one wanted to linger, so they quickly made plans to come back to the barn in a few days to figure out where best to use the explosives.

They would start with train tracks and go on from there.

Marta stayed behind with Max, who lived only fifteen minutes away from their rendezvous point. The barn wasn't his—he was smart enough to keep this far away from his family.

One of the Pirates offered to walk Annelise back to the streetcar, but she didn't want the company, her thoughts too scattered, her pulse too fast. The woods had never scared her, even at night.

The other boys put up a token protest, but they all lived in opposite directions and no one was eager to draw extra attention to themselves if Annelise assured them she was fine.

The moon was full, anyway, guiding her steps easily. The forest was alive with sound, comforting her.

The confidence made her complacent, which she realized only too late.

A hand reached out and grabbed her wrist, tugging her out of stride.

She stumbled, cursed, tried to right herself, her mind jumping right to Felix and all the ways he could overpower her out here in the dark.

And then familiar lips brushed against her ear. "Shhhh."

Annelise sagged into Eitan, all the tension seeping out of her body at once.

"You are the most foolish woman," Eitan said, but he sounded so fond and familiar and beloved Annelise's soul burst with joy.

Without thinking too much about it, Annelise reached up, cupped his face, brought his mouth to hers.

Oh, how she'd missed this boy. His fingers dug into her hips, pulling her flush to him. Her bruises from the fight had faded, so she didn't wince at the touch.

His heart beat against hers.

They pulled away, but barely, so they were still breathing the same air.

"You followed me." It seemed like that was a recurring theme for them.

"I saw you waiting for the streetcar," Eitan said, not sounding at all apologetic. "I got in the compartment with a group of older women, no one looked at me twice."

"It's dangerous."

"As is everything in my life," he countered. "At least this danger is worth it."

She hated that fact, but couldn't deny it. "You need to leave town."

"And go where?" he said, anger slipping into his tone. "Not all of us have options."

"Maybe your mother—"

"You know she can't help me," he cut her off. "You know that."

He had made that clear but Annelise was so worried about him she couldn't think straight. Their world had been bad before, but it was steadily sliding into something worse. They hovered on the brink of war, and she couldn't walk down the street in Bonn without seeing hateful signs plastered in every window. Eitan hadn't been safe in Germany for a long time, but she had a sense that now his life was truly in jeopardy.

"I don't want to fight," he said. "Not when we have so little time."

All Annelise could think was how true that fact was.

All Annelise said was "Neither do I."

ANNELISE WALKED CHRISTINA to school the next day. Her sister was still attending classes and Annelise was desperately searching for a job. Because she hadn't participated in the BDM it was proving incredibly difficult to find someone who would take a chance on her.

Many of the adults in the Pirates' lives had warned them of this very truth and it turned out that the lectures hadn't been scare tactics. No one wanted to hire young people who weren't in good standing with the NSDAP.

Even still, Annelise would not have done a single thing differently. She'd rather join Stefan on his death march into the woods than bend to the Nazis' will.

"You were with that boy last night," Christina said.

Annelise's chest tightened as she froze and stared at Christina. In the space between breaths, she dragged her sister into the closest alley. "You followed me."

The words were the same as she'd uttered to Eitan, but they were sharp now, all jagged edges and points. How many times did she have to warn Christina not to follow her. This wasn't simply sisterly annoyance at her little shadow. Felix could be trailing Christina. Annelise had been vigilant about him ever since he'd tried to follow her from the train station the winter before. Christina was far easier to track.

"No, you were just . . . happy," Christina said, halting and awkward. She sounded like she was actively trying not to lash out. "I could always tell because you came home with a smile you only had for him. Even before I knew who he was, I could tell."

The tension bled out of Annelise's body until all that was left was a twinge of guilt. "I'm sorry. I . . . It's dangerous." Again, what she'd said to Eitan. "It's best if you don't follow me anywhere without me knowing."

Christina stared at her, clearly surprised by the apology. But she accepted it. "I won't. I promise."

Perhaps they *could* change.

"You would like him," Annelise said, as they headed back to the street. "'The boy.'"

"Why do you think that?"

"He finds the bigness of the world in Bonn," Annelise said, which had always been one of her favorite things about him.

"What do you mean?"

"He has favorite shops in town that sell wares from Egypt and Asia and America," Annelise said. "He picks out books for me to read from his aunt's store that take place in fantastical lands. He shows me the flowers in the botanical gardens that come from the Netherlands or the South of France. You said you want to believe the world is bigger than Bonn, but sometimes all that takes is looking where you already are."

"Like with the museum," Christina realized.

"Which is why you would like him," Annelise said, and imagined a different world. Her sister and her lover as friends, none of them having to worry about anything more than finding jobs and finding their way in life.

They started walking again, Christina kicking a loose pebble out in front of her. "Would you marry him? If you could?"

Annelise nearly laughed at the question out of sheer surprise. Of course she had thought about marriage constantly growing up, but it had always been how she didn't want to get trapped into one. She'd seen plenty of girls from their neighborhood saddled with a mean drunkard or seven children or, more likely, both. Annelise had never looked at them and thought, *I want that.*

But marriage to Eitan would surely be different.

"Hitler has made that decision for me," Annelise said, letting the bitterness lace her voice. Her sister should hear it.

"And me," Christina said, almost timidly, shooting Annelise a shy look.

Annelise wondered if Christina had enough courage to protest the very party she had shown such devotion to for the past three years. Especially now, when it was becoming truly risky to do so.

She didn't know the answer to that, wasn't sure she wanted to. It was easy to hint at a shift in loyalties, it was another thing to do something about that change. Annelise had watched plenty of people mock or deride Hitler as a madman and then shrug and go about their days, doing nothing to try to stop him.

When she asked her father about it once, he'd brushed her off. *It's not going to change your life either way. Why pay attention to it?*

Christina seemed to have a grudge against the Pirates, and Annelise didn't think she'd get over that resentment anytime soon. But the world was bigger than the Pirates. There were other resistance groups. The ones that were cropping up at universities seemed particularly appealing.

Sometimes Annelise wished she could join those without actually having to be admitted to the schools. If only she hadn't skipped so many days, if only she hadn't spent the time that she had been in the classroom staring out the window and dreaming of *more*.

She hadn't told anyone yet, but she had been starting to truly plan a move to Cologne. There were hundreds of Pirates in the big city, including the ones she'd spent the night with after their protest at the train station. Annelise was fairly certain there would be someone to take her in and help her find her feet.

There were only two things holding her in Bonn now. The first was the idea of Eitan, even though she knew they couldn't repeat last night. It had been foolish and careless, and if Christina had noticed, surely someone else could have, as well. Still . . . the heart didn't always listen to reason, and there was something reassuring being in the same town as Eitan even if they could never speak.

The second was Christina, of course. Always Christina.

This seemed like a moment in time, though, an important one where she might actually be able to nudge Christina in the right direction. If Annelise left now, all Christina would have was two parents who were gone from sunup to sunset and a brother fully devoted to the Wehrmacht. Christina didn't have close friends and all the girls she knew were from the BDM.

She would be pulled back so easily into their cult.

"Shall I pick you up from school, as well?" Annelise asked, earning a pleased smile from Christina.

But her sister was sixteen, which meant she had to protest. "I'm not a child."

"Maybe I want the company." Annelise nudged her playfully. They were tentative with each other, even more so than when they were rooted so firmly in their own positions. Annelise liked the delicacy of it, though, the way their relationship had the potential to become a precious thing worth being careful about.

After waving Christina off, Annelise popped into a few shops to ask about menial positions that might be available. No one was outright mean to her—she had lived in this town her entire life—but there was a chilliness in their responses that nearly had Annelise giving up.

Cologne was looking all the more appealing by the day.

Her last stop was a newsstand.

She rarely even glanced at the papers anymore—they were all puppets to Hitler's regime—but today the headlines were hard to ignore. They were big and bold, the kind that screamed something important had happened.

Ignoring the seller's aggrieved shout, Annelise grabbed the closest one, her stomach clenching. The world went blurry around her and all she could see were those damning words that she had a feeling would change life as they knew it.

GERMAN DIPLOMAT SHOT IN PARIS BY POLISH JEW

Chapter 34
EMMY

May 1946

Major Arnold and Emmy got an early start to Berlin, the drive more than five hours even on a good day. They were also headed into Soviet Union territory, which meant checkpoints and scrutiny. That didn't even take into consideration sometimes nearly impassable roads and forced detours.

Still, they made it to the American Zone in Berlin by noon.

The sprawl of the devastation took Emmy's breath away. Berlin was both huge and destroyed.

A line of about a hundred children wrapped around one of the blocks, all of them clutching bowls as they waited for a small portion of some type of soup served from an oil barrel. Crutches were a common sight on the streets, as were people carrying what looked like all of their possessions on their backs. Women begged on corners, their babies crying in their arms, or worse, silent. Prostitutes solicited customers in broad daylight, and Emmy tried not to wonder if they had been here when the Red Army had taken the city.

The military presence was strong. Emmy had gotten used to seeing the streets crawling with U.S. Army uniforms, but in Offenbach there was a relaxed air about it all. Half of the people wearing them were librarians and historians, archivists and scholars. Here, they actually seemed to serve a purpose, their hands on their weapons, their eyes alert and bodies tensed.

Emmy made a note to thank Major Arnold for securing them passes and smoothing their way. She wondered if he'd hinted that their mission seemed more important and urgent than it technically was.

They drove straight to the address they had for Lisbeth Basch, only stopping to get through the Soviet checkpoint into East Berlin. When Major Arnold parked, Emmy stared up at the town house tucked in between its neighbors. There were skeletal structures down the way, the remains of what used to be, but this stretch had made it through.

She clutched the Rilke to her chest and hoped this wouldn't turn into a fool's errand.

The address they had been given included an apartment number, which turned out to be essentially the attic. Major Arnold barely winced at the sight of the stairs, but by the top he was favoring his good leg more than he usually did.

Emmy didn't draw attention to his pain. Instead, she knocked.

The door opened a crack. All Emmy could see was the hint of eyes, the barest suggestion of hair.

"Who are you?" the person asked in German.

"I'm Mrs. Clarke, with the United States Library of Congress," Emmy said, feeling silly. This person wouldn't know what that was, but she had no better answer. She'd deliberately worn her uniform today for this very reason—as much as she'd hated it in the beginning, she had to admit it served a purpose. "I'm looking for Lisbeth Basch."

The door slammed in her face and Emmy, startled, took a step back, the disappointment that had been hovering in the wings rushing over her.

A second later, the inside chain jangled and this time the door opened fully to reveal a middle-aged man. He was unnaturally thin, his face so devoid of softness that she could see the bones beneath, the cheeks, the harsh jawline.

It didn't take much to guess where he had been for at least part of the war.

A glance down at his exposed forearm confirmed her theory, the numbers black and stark against flesh that should never have been desecrated so.

"What do you want with her?" the man asked, dark eyes defiant even in his weakened state. He'd switched to English, but his northern German accent was thickly layered over the words.

"I have a book," Emmy said and then shook her head. She should have prepared a more eloquent speech for this interaction, but at such proof of obvious suffering she had lost her tongue. "It belonged to her husband. I wanted to return it to her."

The man's brows shot up. "You came all this way for a book?"

Emmy didn't know if he was referencing her journey from America, or if he could tell she hadn't been stationed in Berlin somehow. Or even if he meant going through the Soviet checkpoint. But she would have traveled farther to complete such a task so she simply nodded.

"It's not simply a book," she said quietly. "It's something that belonged to her husband."

His lip twitched at the word *husband*, though she couldn't tell if he was amused or distraught. Either way he stepped back. "She's gone. But you may come in."

Emmy's breath hitched even as she forced herself to step over the threshold, worried that if she dallied he might rescind the offer. Major Arnold followed behind her, silent, letting her take the lead.

"Gone?" she asked, forcing the word out past dry lips.

"Not dead, I don't think," the man said carelessly. She imagined he had seen far more death than one human should ever have to experience. "Just not here."

"Do you know where she went?"

He crossed the single room to whatever passed for a kitchen counter and picked up the tumbler full of clear liquid that he'd left there. "When I got to this apartment it was abandoned."

"So you knew Lisbeth Basch?"

"Her father. He owned a cabaret. I spent some fun"—his smile turned mischievous—"indiscreet years there in my youth. He gave this apartment to his daughter, from what I can tell."

That had certainly not been what Emmy had expected. Without waiting for him to offer, she sunk onto the threadbare sofa. Major Arnold remained standing.

"How did you know it was abandoned?" Major Arnold asked. He was alert, carefully watching the man as if he was expecting him to lunge at them. He was more accustomed to danger than Emmy, though, so she followed his lead, making sure she would be ready to move if directed.

But the man simply sprawled out on his mattress, one elbow holding him up, sipping his vodka with practiced ease. He looked incredibly graceful, somehow. If she were an artist she would have longed to paint him like this.

"The dust gave me some idea," he said.

He certainly would have had to break into the place, though, Emmy now realized. That's why Major Arnold was still on his guard.

"Did she leave anything behind?" Emmy asked. "Anything that might tell us where she is?"

"This book of yours must be important," the man muttered in German. Emmy was about to remind him it had belonged to Lisbeth's husband, but he waved that away, switching back to English. "Yes, yes, sentimentality." He studied her face with uncomfortable intensity. "You're with the United States Army?"

"If we're being technical about it," Emmy said. "But I work for the Library of Congress." She nodded toward the major. "And he's an historian."

"A bunch of intellectuals then, are you?"

"Something like that," Emmy said, with a rueful smile. An image of her standing in the Frankfurt train station's water closet flashed into her mind. *She was a librarian not a soldier.*

The major cut in. "We're not here to harm or arrest you."

Emmy glanced at him, surprised by the reassurance. Neither she nor the major looked aggressive or physically intimidating, she was mostly certain about that. But he didn't acknowledge her reaction.

He was busy watching the man, whose mouth twitched like it had before—amusement or distress, she still couldn't tell.

"We're not going to hurt Lisbeth, either," the major continued. "We're not here to expose anyone."

Expose.

Emmy knew better than to voice her confusion in that moment, but the two men were having a conversation she was clearly not privy to.

The man stood and paced. He kept tossing suspicious looks at the major, who simply held his ground, his expression serious but sincere. Emmy was biased, but she would trust the major with her life and she hoped this man would sense the integrity that was baked into his very bones.

"Let me see the book," the man finally said.

Emmy quickly handed it over, sensing that he was teetering on whether to trust them or not.

He stared at the title page for a long time before finally asking, "What is an Edelweiss Pirate?"

Major Arnold explained once again who the young resisters had been, and Emmy watched the man's face transform, soften.

Then he headed toward a mostly empty bookshelf. There were a few novels, lying scattered about, though, and from one he pulled a small slip of paper.

"Ask around there," he said, handing it and the Rilke back to Emmy. "I can't guarantee anything, but they might be able to point you in the right direction."

"Is this someone you know?" Emmy asked.

"It's more of a place," he said, with a secretive smile. "Now, I do believe it's time for you to go."

At once, Emmy got to her feet, grateful that he'd offered even this much of his time. "Thank you."

Major Arnold lingered. Then she realized he was searching in his inner pockets for a small notepad and a pencil. "If you ever need any help, please go to this lieutenant in the American Zone. Tell him Major Wesley Arnold sent you."

The man seemed like he was going to reject the slip of paper Major Arnold held out, but reluctantly he took it with a nod. Nothing else was said.

Emmy held her tongue until they made it to Major Arnold's jeep. They hadn't dallied, both eager to get back to West Berlin.

"What was that about?" she asked when the major pulled away from the sidewalk.

He slid her an assessing look but then seemed to decide to tell her the truth. Practical to the core.

"I suspect he's a homosexual," he said. "That lifestyle is still illegal under German law. He could be arrested and put in prison if the wrong person found out."

Expose. That word made more sense now.

"I have a friend who still talks about the cabarets in the early thirties," the major continued. "I . . . I took a guess that's why the man was nervous about us being in the army."

"Do you think that's what he was sent to the camps for?"

"Likely, yes," the major said. "I have heard of men who were freed from them only to be sent to jail under the still-current law."

She thought about what Lucy had said about the camps, how the horrors there had been unimaginable but so had the daily indignities. To be taken from there and put into a cell instead of given freedom . . . the idea was so terrible Emmy couldn't even finish the thought.

"Do you think Lisbeth is . . . ?" She couldn't finish the question; it felt invasive all of a sudden.

"I don't know," Major Arnold said in his standard calm, neutral tone. He never judged anyone, she realized. Maybe that was the side effect of studying humans through so many empires and civilizations, their foibles, their flaws, their strengths. The way they loved. She had a feeling very little would ever shock him. "The regime couldn't prosecute women because the law only covered men. But they were arrested for other things, for being work-shy or antisocial. It didn't take much to make a trumped-up charge stick."

The major jerked his head toward the address the man had given Emmy. "I believe we'll find a pub of some sort there. It'll have become a fairly tight-knit community out of necessity. The fact that we know about the place will buy us some goodwill."

His prediction proved correct. They pulled up to a glass-fronted establishment that had a simple Food sign hanging over the doorway. Emmy could see booths inside, though not many people. That wasn't surprising given it was midafternoon, but overall it had a passed-over quality, like people's eyes slid from the grocer on one side to the newsagent on the other.

An older woman with glasses stood behind the bar, her rag covering the same twelve or so inches, back and forth, back and forth.

When they introduced themselves and explained who they were looking for, the woman simply shrugged and spit in the bucket on the floor. "Not going to kick you out, am I?"

Emmy shared a glance with Major Arnold, who simply ordered two beers and fish-and-chips for both of them, taking advantage of the fact that restaurants got special food rations to help feed the Americans in this zone.

They took a booth near the front of the pub, and the lady behind the bar proceeded to ignore them as the place filled up.

"Did the shipment go off without a hitch?" the major asked, a frothy line of beer giving him a mustache.

Emmy smiled at the table. "Yes. It's almost unimaginable to me that there are still thousands of items to sort through even after we sent all that off. I thought I was going to have little to do for the next month."

"It feels like a tidal wave, sometimes." The mustache was still there, and Emmy continued to find it unbearably endearing.

"I have heard that I might be assigned to films, next," Emmy said, and reached across the small space to rub her thumb against his top lip, an absent gesture, mostly. He stilled the moment her fingers made contact, his breath hot against her hand. Their eyes locked, and Emmy froze, all but cupping his jaw. Heat flooded her, and she had the sudden, foolish urge to lean into him, to press her mouth to his.

Someone dropped a glass behind them, and Emmy jerked back, her fingers tangling themselves on her lap so she didn't do any other mortifying thing.

She fought through the flushed embarrassment, and continued blathering on as if that would make him forget she'd groped his face.

"I'm not exactly an expert in films, but I'll be looking for the same thing in the reels—propaganda, strategy, anything to help us better understand the Nazis' war and home-front morale plans," Emmy said. "It sounds quite interesting, but I'll miss the books."

"You've enjoyed working with the used volumes," the major observed, the tips of his ears pink. But they were both gamely charging forward, and she appreciated that. "Would you ever leave the Library of Congress for a used bookshop? Or something similar perhaps?"

"I like the idea of lending too much, I believe," Emmy said, though she had taken a moment to consider the question because he'd read her correctly. "But I could see, eventually, shifting to a smaller public library, even if it would mean a step back in my career. This experience has reminded me why I love working with common books so much."

She made a face, and he laughed.

"I know what you mean by 'common,'" he reassured her. "I understand. The books that are most used and borrowed."

"I like knowing everyone who has read them is connected in a tiny way," Emmy said, and then confessed to what she'd been thinking about the other day. "Nazis certainly weren't the first ones to ban or burn books, and most censorship fights have tried to sever that connection. Books help you care about and understand people who are different than you, they create a shared experience, they give you something in common with a person you might never have had something in common with otherwise." Her cheeks heated. It didn't take much to have her climbing up onto a soapbox when it came to this issue. But it was what she thought about in the long, quiet hours of her work. "I think those types of bonds, thin though they may be, will help us prevent this from happening again. It's harder to hate someone or something when you're connected to them."

"That's very true," the major murmured, and there was something in his eyes, in his expression, that she couldn't look directly at.

Emmy quickly asked what he was working on, and he went with the shift in topics easily. When he got back to Offenbach, he was planning to travel to a castle where they suspected a cache of rare books was being kept. Then they chatted about the people they both knew, and the interpersonal dramas of the rest of the teams Emmy only encountered at a distance.

She had never talked so easily with someone, their conversations always half finished because they took three left turns into different topics and didn't mind not finding their way back. She thought she could talk to the major for days, weeks even, and never grow tired of it.

Around the time the light changed from afternoon to dusk, a woman slid into the booth beside Major Arnold.

"I hear you're looking for Lisbeth Basch," she said without preamble. "You have one minute to convince me not to kill you."

A tense silence fell between them, filled only with background chatter.

Then the woman laughed until tears gathered at the corners of her eyes.

"I apologize, you both looked so serious," she said. "Like spies, but draped in 'Property of the United States Army' uniforms."

Major Arnold had that tense, watchful air that meant he wasn't sure what to make of this interaction.

Emmy had no clue either. "Erm?"

"I'm sorry, I find my humor where I can these days," the woman said, some of the amusement fading, and Emmy found that she immediately missed it. But then the woman giggled again. "Your faces are so funny right now."

She looked young when she laughed like that. No one seemed young anymore, not here. Not even the children. But this woman, for one brief moment, did. And Emmy liked her for that.

"So what does the United States Army want?" the woman asked.

"Mrs. Basch?" Emmy checked.

The woman lifted her brows, and Emmy wasn't sure if she should actually take that as confirmation. But she pulled out the Rilke anyway.

"We work at a depot in charge of returning the plundered books from the Nazis," Emmy said, and most of the lingering good humor dropped out of the woman's expression.

"Surely the army has better ways to spend its resources than sending two soldiers to return a single book," the woman said, her voice light. But her eyes were locked on the slim volume.

Emmy didn't say anything more, just slid it over to her.

The woman's hand trembled, and Emmy only realized in that moment she might have lost more than her husband. "It's from the personal collection of Eitan Basch."

"Eitan," the woman whispered, not looking away from the cover.

Everything had gone so tense, so quickly. Emmy couldn't take her eyes off the emotions flickering in and out of the woman's expression. They settled into something that Emmy recognized from her own mirror as profound grief when the woman flipped to the title page.

A single tear slipped over her cheekbone.

"I can't," she said. In the next heartbeat, she was out of the booth. The door to the pub slammed against the outside brick as she flew out into the street, a blur of hair and arms and fabric.

She had left the book behind.

Chapter 35
CHRISTINA

March 5, 1943

I cy rain sliced against Christina's cheeks but she couldn't even feel it any longer. She was so cold she had swung around to hot and then numb, both of which she knew were bad signs.

In the days since they'd found Ingrid, Christina and Lisbeth had taken turns sitting by her bed. They'd moved her to Lisbeth's place, after a few too many hints that the woman who'd rescued Ingrid wanted them gone.

Lisbeth's apartment was by no means warm, but it was enough to bring pins and needles to Christina's skin, the sensations subsiding just before she was about to return outside to start the cycle over once more.

All throughout Tuesday the women of Rose Street returned from where they'd fled during the air raid. The Gestapo agents and SS officers were also back, and they kept threatening to shoot if the women didn't disperse. Sometimes their warnings sounded serious enough to send everyone running, but they failed to act on them, and Christina knew there must be orders from above staying their hands.

Goebbels, perhaps? He must have been informed about the gathering at some point, because on Wednesday he ran an opinion piece on the front pages of his mouthpiece newspapers about how women were in the streets protesting the RAF bombings.

Quite the alternative narrative—but he was the king of that, wasn't he?

For once, Christina was grateful for it. The Nazis had given them more cover—they couldn't very well slaughter the women they had praised for protesting the Brits' barbarity.

Monday's bombing had been catastrophic. The dead, the wounded, the destruction. It was a stark demonstration that they were no longer safe beneath Hitler's umbrella, so far away from planes that needed to refuel. The Brits hadn't appreciated the Blitz, and they were about to dole out revenge tenfold.

If the Nazis ended the Rose Street protest with more bloodshed, it would surely send a spark through the rest of the country that was waiting to ignite with panic.

So the women made it through Tuesday and then Wednesday and Thursday alive.

Now, on Friday morning, Christina could see signs of restlessness among the police guarding the community center. The tall Nazi who had watched her a few too many times was standing outside the door, narrow-eyed, his gaze scanning the crowd.

He looked like he was waiting for something.

A shoulder knocked into Christina's and she nearly yelped. Then she swallowed her embarrassment and turned to greet Lisbeth.

She was pink-cheeked after coming back out from her apartment into frigid air, but it made her look young and fresh and happy. Her curls had lost some of their bounce, but that didn't stop Christina from wanting to run fingers through the soft strands.

They hadn't talked since Tuesday morning, not really. Since they were dividing their time between the apartment and the protest, they had barely spent any time with just the two of them.

Maybe they would always pretend their kiss, the confession, all of it, hadn't happened. That was for the best, it was. No matter how Lisbeth and Eitan defined their relationship, they were legally married.

"What's that?" Lisbeth asked, cutting into Christina's grim thoughts.

A roar of an engine.

Christina automatically looked up, even though that was foolish. There wouldn't be an air raid in broad daylight.

Not a plane, then.

A truck.

Christina was tall enough to see the vehicle over most of the heads of the crowd.

It rumbled toward them, machine guns lining the top. A Nazi stood behind the weapons and yelled for the women to move out of the way.

The women were used to this, though, they'd had nearly a full week of being ordered to leave with little consequence when they refused. They were no longer the people they had been on Saturday, shaking and terrified of saying no to Nazis.

For the first time in a long time, they understood their own power.

So the protesters stood their ground.

Christina did, as well, but she couldn't suppress the shiver that ran along her spine.

It was Friday. This had gone on far too long. International press outlets were reporting on the gathering with glee.

The Nazis needed to put a stop to this. Now.

"Give us back our husbands," they cried out in defiance.

The engine revved. Revved again. Then the truck started forward.

"The sick bastards are going to run them over," Lisbeth murmured in disbelief.

The truck wasn't creeping carefully, but rather moving at a clip. A ripple of panic rolled through the crowd as the protesters at the front tried to scatter, the fear of being pulled beneath those big, lethal wheels real and daunting.

The women had gotten used to fleeing from threats, but this was different. They weren't as surefooted, didn't have the instincts to dive left or right. Lisbeth took three steps toward the community center, realized her error, and then started encouraging the women around them to head toward the far streets, away from the truck.

Rat-ta-tat-tat-tat-tat.

Christina froze—a potentially deadly decision in the middle of a skittish crowd. She was shoved once, and then shoved again. Her feet skidded on wet cobblestones, the ground coming up to meet her face far too quickly for her to get her hands down.

She hit the street, but somehow she'd managed to avoid cracking her head against the stones.

Pain radiated from her thighs, her stomach as women scrambled over her, their fear making them senseless.

Then someone was pulling her up, up, up.

Lisbeth's face was blurry, but her grip firm. "Now's not the time, Christina."

She said it in such a no-nonsense, practical way that Christina almost laughed—as if she were being silly and rolling around on the ground for the fun of it. Christina's response was drowned out by cries from the sidewalk on the far side of the street.

"The doors are all locked," someone yelled. Lisbeth passed the message to the women behind her but met Christina's grim stare as she did. They both knew what that meant. The storekeepers had all been surprisingly supportive of them all week; it wasn't the proprietors who had done this.

The Nazis had trapped the women in a narrow space and had eliminated at least some of the places where they'd been scattering to hide throughout the week.

For the first time, she saw real fear in Lisbeth's eyes, and it chilled her already frozen bones.

"The park," Christina said, once, twice, three times, each louder than the last. The women around them heard, shifted directions toward the small park on the end of Rose Street. It wouldn't hold them all, but maybe the women who had already been packed in there would have fled by now.

The crowd all seemed to have the same idea, the wave turning as one.

But Christina caught sight of something.

The tall Nazi was on the move.

She stopped, pushing Lisbeth into the tide of moving bodies even as she did. Lisbeth was swallowed up, unable to fight against the momentum even as Christina ducked out of the flow, toward the community center.

The Nazi grabbed a woman by the arm, hauling her away from the group that tried to hold on to her.

She yelled and kicked and cried out. It did no good. The Nazi was strong. He held her with one hand as he waved to his lackeys.

That must have been some kind of prearranged signal, because the men all started grabbing protesters, snatching them from the crowd.

The screaming stopped, the engine cut off, the women who were still left in the narrow street all turned to watch the new spectacle.

The silence that dropped was almost unbearable. No one chanted. No one said a single word.

They watched as one by one, ten women were plucked seemingly at random and thrown unceremoniously into the back of the truck that had tried to run them all down.

In her braver fantasies, Christina would have thrown herself at the feet of the Nazis and volunteered to take one of the women's places. In real life, she stood paralyzed, unable to move or make a sound. Like the rest of them.

One real, true show of force and their bravery crumbled like the cheap facade it was.

Where would these women be taken? What would be their fate?

Why couldn't any of the other protesters *move*?

This, Christina realized. This was how the Nazis had taken control of an entire country.

The truck reversed, its bounty safely tucked away. Over the past week, whenever space had been made on the street, the protesters had always rushed to fill it in. No one did so with the hole left behind by the truck.

The echo of it as powerful as the thing itself.

The tall Nazi returned to the stoop wearing that same self-satisfied smirk all the members of his party wore.

"Bastards." It was Lisbeth, of course it was Lisbeth.

She had made her way back to Christina, because that seemed to be their pattern—they were pulled to each other like magnets. Christina was starting to accept that as their fate.

"Is this just the start?" Christina asked. "Will they arrest us all?"

"They can't," Lisbeth said. But for the first time Christina heard the silent *Can they?*

The truck was gone, the guns quiet, and yet there was a new hesitancy in the women's movements now.

No one started up the chant this time.

"Will they kill those women?" Lisbeth asked, so quietly Christina almost missed it.

She could see the question on the faces of every person around them.

Christina stared at the space the truck had left. This was how the Nazis had been so effective. They hadn't needed to arrest a thousand women—they'd made their point with ten. Now each person here was questioning if they were brave enough to risk being put up against a firing wall.

This right here was a moment. It could break the entire protest, could send women scuttling back home. The cost would be the lives of two thousand Jewish men.

And . . . Christina was so goddamn tired of the Nazis winning. They were terrible, evil people and they just kept winning.

"We hold the line," Christina said, and then louder, "We hold the line."

It was so silly, a battle cry in the middle of a block full of women who'd never been to war.

Except every single day of their lives since Hitler had risen to power might as well have been.

She turned to the stranger next to her, who had heard, who was now watching her. "We hold the line."

The woman stared at her for a long moment and then something strong and determined slipped into her expression. She nodded once. "We hold the line."

The message swept over the crowd. Christina wasn't arrogant enough to take credit. She was sure other women had reached the same conclusion she had. But she was glad the mood seemed to be shifting once more, the timidity lifting.

If the women were going to die, they would do it their own way. Proud, livid, courageous, not cowering in fear.

The chant that rose from the crowd was not the one that had filled the street all week.

Instead, it was one that seemed torn from their souls, the last seven days of anguish and terror and boredom and discomfort and camaraderie vocalized as a sharp condemnation of the men trying to retain their stony indifference in the face of a lion's roar.

"Murderers," the women yelled for their men.

"Murderers," the women yelled for their country.

"Murderers," the women yelled for the world.

Christina met Lisbeth's eyes. "Well, I think we've officially become an anti-Nazi protest."

Chapter 36

EMMY

May 1946

M ajor Arnold had arranged a room for them in a private lodging establishment.

"I'm not certain Berlin's a safe place for you to be on your own right now," Major Arnold said, with the same tone he'd informed her that Red Army soldiers had raped the women in the city.

Emmy didn't argue.

The host's shoulders relaxed when her eyes dipped down to Emmy's ring, and without further ado, she handed over a thick metal key.

"I'll sleep on the sofa, of course," the major said once the door was shut firmly behind them.

The tips of his ears were pink, and Emmy sighed, her heart and head at such odds that she was dizzy with the sensation.

"What should we do about Lisbeth Basch?" she asked, instead of telling him that he didn't have to.

"We go back tomorrow."

Affection rushed in, threatening to tip the scales. "Optimist."

He gave her that half-slant smile she loved so much. "I think she'll regret fleeing. We show up tomorrow, give her another chance. Someone was sent to tell her that we were there today, someone will be sent tomorrow."

She nodded in agreement, distracted by the fact that he'd started rubbing absently at his thigh. Even though they had done quite a bit of sitting all day, it had been on uncomfortable surfaces and in odd positions.

"Sit," she directed him.

He quirked his brows at her, but then did as he was told. She noticed a decanter of brown liquor on the side table—likely because this establishment seemed frequented by Americans. She poured him a hefty dose, and stepped into the vee of his spread knees to hand it to him. He seemed to be waiting for her to shift back, to sit beside him, but instead she stayed where she was, bracketed by his thighs. She studied his face and liked it so much.

His features had become so familiar and dear over the past month, it felt as if she'd known him for decades.

"Did you have a book?" she asked. "That got you through this."

She nudged his bad leg very gently with her knee.

"It was poetry," he said without hesitation, though curiosity lingered in his expression as if he wanted to ask if she'd taken leave of her senses. Perhaps she had. "Churchill gave a speech in 1941. It was a few months after the Blitz. At the end of it, he paraphrased a couple lines from a Victorian poet. They stuck with me."

Emmy waited. She wasn't familiar with the speech.

"I was in the hospital for a time," he said, clearly downplaying his recovery, which must have been arduous. "I ended up looking up the poet, and it turned out that he'd had his leg amputated when he was young due to tuberculosis. We still hadn't been sure at the time if the doctors could save mine."

"What a strange little connection," Emmy said.

He smiled. "Yes, I thought so. I became enamored with his poetry, but especially the poem Churchill borrowed from."

"Which was?"

"Invictus." He said the word like the prayer it probably had been for him.

> "Out of the night that covers me
> black as the pit from pole to pole
> I thank whatever gods may be
> for my unconquerable soul."

He held her eyes, reciting the poem as if it was as natural as breathing.

> *"In the fell clutch of circumstance*
> *I have not winced nor cried aloud*
> *under the bludgeonings of chance*
> *my head is bloody but unbowed."*

Tears gathered in her eyes, but she refused to look away or let them fall.

She had never been one to gravitate toward poetry for no other reason than she loved being swept up in a novel. But now she understood. Each word felt tattooed on her skin, on her bones.

And when he got to the last line, when he finished with "I am the master of my fate / I am the captain of my soul," every single one of Emmy's worries, her hesitations, her fears melted away.

If he had been brave enough to weather all that he had, she could be brave enough for this.

As slowly and gracefully as she could, she dropped to her knees. His eyes widened, but he didn't say anything, didn't shift away, didn't stop her.

"Your leg must be sore," she said, and then pressed a hand to his thigh. He groaned in pleasure-pain, his head tipping back to rest against the sofa.

Praying she didn't hurt him, Emmy worked the ropy muscle, glorying in the feel of him beneath her palms. But it wasn't enough. She wanted to see him. She sat back on her heels, bringing his foot into her lap. He watched her through hooded eyes, his drink forgotten on the seat beside him.

Emmy held his gaze for as long as she could as she untied his shoes. Once those were gone along with his socks, she asked herself if this was really what she wanted. But why not? Why shouldn't she take a chance at life?

He was her dearest friend, her confidant. He had become so after such a short amount of time.

She breathed out, and went up fully on her knees, reaching for his belt. This time, she couldn't look up at him, her blush too fierce. But he simply let her undo the buckle, pull the supple leather from his trouser loops.

"It'll be easier," Emmy said, staring at his lap instead of his face. It was a miracle her hands weren't trembling. She and Joseph had enjoyed their marriage bed, but she had always let him take the lead. This was all her. She had to own every move she made. Somehow that made her feel powerful and vulnerable all at the same time. "Without these in the way."

As she said it, she tugged at the waist of his trousers, and he obediently lifted his hips. It was the only sign he gave that he was all right with what was happening.

When he was down to his drawers, Emmy sat back once more. The damage to his leg was severe—thick white lines of scar tissue twisted along his thigh, over his knee, to his calf. He didn't try to hide the injury, just sat still beneath her scrutiny. Trusting that she wouldn't—would *never*—flinch away from something that was such a part of him.

Emmy couldn't help herself. She leaned forward and pressed her lips to the slick-looking skin at the edge of his boxer shorts.

That seemed to be his undoing.

He swore and the next thing she knew she was being hauled into his lap, her knees settling on either side of him, her army skirt rucked up around her waist.

His hand cupped her cheek, his eyes searching her face for something.

Emmy hated that he still wasn't sure what she wanted.

She leaned down, and right before her mouth brushed against his, she murmured his name. Simply his name.

It came out a sigh, a plea, a promise. "Wesley."

EMMY MAPPED THE scars on his back with her fingertip. Wesley's face was smooshed into his pillow, but he watched her lazily, his eye half shut.

"What changed?" he asked softly, as if he was giving her a chance to pretend she hadn't heard.

But she owed him an answer, especially after her behavior at the nightclub.

Emmy was still naked and hadn't bothered to worry about covering up. Something about spilling out her insecurities, though, made her grab for the sheet to wrap around her breasts. His disappointed groan had her laughing.

"When I first met Joseph, he was all sunshine," she started. "He was funny and sharp and the life of every party. It was so different from me, but I was drawn to him like everyone else was. You couldn't not love Joseph."

Wesley sat up then, arranging himself against the headboard. He was less shy than she, and instead of reaching for a blanket, he just reached for his bag, pulling out his cigarettes. She waved a hand for him to go ahead when he lifted questioning brows before lighting one.

"It wasn't until we were married that I realized that of course Joseph's highs had to be matched by his lows," Emmy said. "We called them his blue times. I wasn't . . . unaware of those kinds of trouble. In Montana, in the winter, when the workers would be their most isolated, their most miserable, there were always stories of ones who ended their suffering by their own hands."

Wesley blew smoke out away from her. "Did Joseph try . . . ?"

"No, but he started doing foolish things," she admitted. "Walking into the street without looking. Staring at train tracks for too long. When he was issued his service revolver, I wanted desperately to ask the army to take it back."

"The war must have appealed to that side of him," he said, understanding and kind but not sugarcoating it.

She smiled without humor. "It did. I was so tired at that point, which sounds like such an awful thing to say. But waiting for the person you love most in the world to die is . . ." She sniffed, not sure how to finish that thought. Unpleasant? Torture? No word seemed right, too melodramatic or not serious enough.

"I knew never to tell him to be careful after he'd shipped out," Emmy said. "I used to sign my letters that I missed him, but I never pretended he wouldn't take unnecessary risks. He never reassured me he wouldn't."

Wesley hummed to get her to go on, his eyes locked on her face.

"Everyone who knew he was serving would try to comfort me, and I had to pretend I was worried in a different way than I was," she said. "Do you know the horrible part? Whenever I imagined him surviving the war, him coming home, all I could think about was how terrible that would be for him. He struggled incredibly, getting up some days was so hard for him, and then add a war on top of it . . ."

She swiped at her wet cheeks. "And I loved him so much. Not only on his happy days, either. I loved every part of Joseph, even the blue times."

"You loved his scars because they were a part of him," he said, and she remembered that pressing a kiss into *his* scars had been his undoing. "But love isn't always enough."

Of course he understood. He always seemed to.

"I won't say loving him made me whole, because I think I was whole without him," she said slowly. "But I will say it made me who I am today and I wouldn't do a single thing in my life differently even knowing how it all ended."

"But you didn't want to go through it a second time," he said, shrewd and unselfconscious.

"You've seen war," Emmy said with a small, helpless shrug. "And I knew that whatever was between us could never be casual. I was so scared to let myself fall in love again with someone who might prefer the company of their ghosts to me."

He held her gaze and snuffed out the cigarette. Once again, he asked, "What changed?"

She smiled, almost sadly. She had already bared the darkest parts of herself to him, why not bare this as well? "I realized I no longer had a choice in the matter."

It took a second for understanding to hit. When it did, something akin to reverence slipped into his eyes.

Emmy bit back a grin. She had been fairly sure her admission would be welcome, but hadn't been completely certain.

In a quick move, he tugged the sheet away and then pressed her onto her back, holding most of his weight off her with his forearms.

This time it was her name that was whispered between them.

"Emmeline."

Chapter 37

CHRISTINA

March 6, 1943

The sun rising over the rooftops on Saturday morning somehow became symbolic in Christina's mind. The women had held their ground for one week. A full week.

The unprecedented protest was starting to spread beyond the wives of the men inside the community center.

Berliners who had been passing by on their way to work, or to run errands, or to gawk were joining the crowd. The shouts of "murderers" had only grown in ferocity. The Nazis were well and truly losing any control they'd had of the gathering.

That morning was frigid, worse than it had been in days. It wasn't raining, at least, but their defenses had been worn thin.

She leaned against Lisbeth and felt the shivers and couldn't tell whose they were anymore.

Christina exhaled, watched her breath as a tangible thing dissolve into the sky.

"I think it's today," Christina murmured, mostly nonsensically. She'd said that every day since midweek. "They need to break."

Lisbeth didn't bother to argue. They'd both read reports about Stalingrad. Persistence was not one of the Nazis' weak points.

"Tell me something," Lisbeth said.

Christina waited for more, but nothing came. She nudged Lisbeth with her elbow. "About what?"

"Something to keep me warm," Lisbeth said, amusement lacing her voice. But the request was real. Christina wasn't sure how much longer any of them would last in this weather. The Nazis were able to switch in and out of the community center, but some of these women hadn't once left the street since the protest had begun.

"I thought your hair looked like the sunset when we first met," Christina admitted in hushed tones, though there was little danger of them being overheard. Everyone was sleepy in the early morning light and bundled as deeply into their coats as possible.

Lisbeth laughed gently. "Sweet-talker."

They rested against each other in silence once more. Christina wondered if Lisbeth returned the sentiment—not about her hair, Christina was well aware hers was not in a state to be admired. But . . . the idea. The interest, the attraction.

"Tell me something," Lisbeth said again, her head lolling against Christina's shoulder, the words slurring together from the cold.

"About what?" Christina played along.

"When did you start hating the Nazis?"

"You believe that I do," Christina observed instead of answering. "Even with everything that you know about me? You don't think I was lying when I said I didn't?"

Lisbeth made an impatient sound. "Don't question my intelligence, Fischer."

Christina grinned, though no one else saw it.

"I want to lie and say I've always hated them," Christina said, just loud enough for Lisbeth to hear. There was a new tenseness to Lisbeth's body to show she was listening. "But that's not the truth. I was fourteen when I first joined up with the BDM. I barely knew what those letters stood for let alone the Party's philosophy."

"I wouldn't be able to think much about anything past those horrendous uniforms," Lisbeth said lightly.

"They flattered no one," Christina admitted. "Were you always a resister?"

"Oh no, not at all," Lisbeth said, surprising Christina. "I was in my own world, to be fair. By the time I realized how dire the situation was, I was trying to keep my head down. I married Eitan and we tried to escape notice for the past four years. We did fairly well, if I do say so myself."

"I would have pictured you at the barricades," Christina said. "Or at least at underground meetings."

"I think your idea of me might not fit who I actually am."

"You're brave," Christina said, stubborn with it. She had witnessed Lisbeth's courage firsthand so many times over the past week.

"Maybe so, but there are all kinds of bravery." Lisbeth paused and then tapped her elbow into Christina's ribs once more. "When did you start hating the Nazis? I swear, there's a point to my question."

But Christina struggled to put it into words. "It was never one thing. The BDM was all I knew for so long. They didn't sound evil when they spoke about their mission. They sounded patriotic and feminine in a way I longed to emulate. They prized intelligence and loyalty and conformity, all things I very much liked. Annelise always spoke about how terrible they were, but she was a wild child. She ran barefoot in the forest and wore scandalous clothes and cavorted with boys who had long hair and played guitar. She wasn't exactly a role model."

Lisbeth smiled gently. "She was a Pirate."

"When she spoke, I thought her deranged. Everyone else I knew—everyone else besides the Pirates—was in the BDM or the HJ," Christina said, still marveling at how organized the Nazis were. They'd planned well to indoctrinate the youth of the country. "It's like if a pig who could talk all of a sudden told you all the humans around you were actually villains and that you were evil for listening to what they said. It was simply incomprehensible to think she made sense. But I don't think that way ever works anyway—someone who hates you telling you all you believe is bad."

"She didn't hate you," Lisbeth said, and Christina wondered how much Eitan had told her.

"She hated everything I thought, which was close enough," Christina countered. "It's a strange paradox, though. When you're in the BDM, they warn you that enemies will tell you that your beliefs are heinous and harmful and that's what makes them the enemy, right?

So when Annelise told me all the things the Nazis said the enemy would say—"

"You deemed her the enemy," Lisbeth breathed out, as if seeing it clearly for the first time. "Whereas she thought she was persuading you to see reason, she was really driving you deeper into their clutches."

"I never saw her as the actual enemy," Christina rushed to say. "I saw her as someone the Nazis would consider the enemy. So I knew I had to save her."

"But you changed your mind eventually."

"That came from my own realizations, not someone trying to convince me," Christina said. She had spent many a night trying to pinpoint an exact moment, action, event, anything. "It was the small contradictions within the Party that made me begin to doubt. Which is where the cracks always start, I think."

"Like what?"

"The Hitler Youth ran an anti-smoking campaign," Christina said. "They said cigarettes were terrible for your health. And then, as propaganda, they issued cigarette cards that glorified the German military." She paused. "They preached to us that motherhood was the highest, noblest calling—that it was our way of serving the Fatherland. But they encouraged girls to fall pregnant as if they were broodmares. There was never any actual respect given to the mothers. I know it sounds like an inconsequential thing compared to the horrific acts they were committing. But those were the moments that caught me off guard. Those were the moments that made me question if they really were as brilliant and perfect as they called themselves."

Lisbeth hummed like she understood. "I think . . . we're going to win. Not us, on Rose Street. That's still undecided. But, this war. I think the Nazis will be defeated in the end. And I believe people will look back on this time and wonder what we were all thinking."

Christina grimaced at the truth of that. At least she hoped it was the truth. The alternative, the Nazis winning, wasn't worth imagining.

"And there will be people out there who will take every opportunity to excavate the courage of war from all the rest of this muck," Lisbeth continued. "They will make it their religion. I have seen it happen with the Great War; all those Americans who came to my father's cabaret were full of stories. Everyone will point to the examples of the few who always knew Hitler was as bad as he is, they will hold them up as icons. As saints. And they are, they were, don't misunderstand me."

Of course, Christina couldn't help but think of Annelise. Annelise who would have benefited greatly under Hitler's regime, and yet had never once been swayed to join the popular movement.

"But most of us aren't saints," Lisbeth said. "Most of us are just people. And when you tell a story, and you say, the righteous, the pure, the good-hearted will *always* recognize evil when it walks among us, it makes people vulnerable to thinking they will never fall prey to terrible men. Because if they can't recognize it right away, they must be bad or broken. No one wants to think that of themselves," Lisbeth said. "And saying all that does a disservice to those who are trying to learn from the mistakes of the past."

Lisbeth let that sit for a second between them before turning to look at her fully. Her eyes raked over Christina's face, looking for what, Christina didn't know.

"I like that it was never one thing for you," Lisbeth continued. "I like that it was a slow process, both ways, both falling into it and falling out of it. That means there's hope for others to pull themselves out of the darkness."

Christina easily picked up the thread. "I like that you weren't at the barricades or at underground meetings."

"That's right," Lisbeth murmured. "It means that you don't have to be a saint, you don't have to be an icon. Sometimes you can simply be a person who realizes there's an injustice being done. And you can stand on the street and become a hero."

A wound deep inside of her ached, and then started to heal. "Even if you've never believed you could be one."

THE RUMORS STARTED a few hours later. A handful of women had heard that some of the Mischlings had been released from the community center the day before. Another said her sister's husband had shown up in their house, exhausted and bruised but mostly whole and healthy.

The men stationed outside the community center hadn't budged, nor did they give any sign that a release of the prisoners was imminent. The tall Nazi stood in his position on the stoop, scanning the crowd.

Christina was close enough to the front that he caught her eye. A smirk sat in the corners of his lips.

Smug. He looked smug, despite the fact that he'd clearly lost control of this protest.

Before she could study him further, he executed a sharp turn and went back inside the building.

Lisbeth's fingers curled around her wrist, gave a tug. "Do you think it's true? Are they being released?"

"I don't know," Christina said, her brain fuzzy. She was so tired she couldn't think, but she did know one thing. "He doesn't look like someone who lost."

"But the rumors . . ."

The "murderers" chants died down as everyone exchanged whispered versions of the conversation she and Lisbeth just had.

"Do you think . . . ?"

"Is it true . . . ?"

"Would they really . . . ?"

Christina chewed on her nail, wishing she could go ask Royce Wolff for information. But she didn't dare leave in case something happened while she was gone.

The Nazis didn't blink. That was a fact they all knew.

But what if that mythology had simply been Goebbels's propaganda machine in action?

The Nazis didn't blink. Except at Stalingrad. Except in North Africa. Except, except, except . . .

The Nazis didn't blink except for when they did.

Lisbeth's fingers gripped her wrist once more.

"Christina," she breathed out. When Christina glanced over, Lisbeth's eyes were locked on the building, her expression filled with awe and doubt and love and fear.

Christina's attention snapped to the community center.

A detainee stood there on the sidewalk, blinking into the sun, into the crowd of hundreds of women who had spent the week begging for his release.

The protesters were absolutely silent as the realization began to sink in.

These women had gathered in desperation, and had stayed because there hadn't been another option. They had started out as strangers who wouldn't even talk to each other and ended up as a movement that had accomplished something no one in Berlin, no one in Germany, no one in the world, would have thought possible.

They had faced down bullets and threats, they had persevered through icy weather and British bombs and their own doubt. They had shared their strength with each other when one of them faltered, they had shielded the most tired among them from the rain, they had fed the hungriest with their portions of bread and cheese.

Together, they had cried tears of fear, tears of hate, tears of frustration. Together, they had slowly, so slowly, found their voice.

Together they had said no.

They weren't like Annelise and her Pirates, brave and youthful and rebellious.

They were just women.

And it seemed like, maybe, that had always been enough.

Chapter 38

CHRISTINA

March 6, 1943

The first group of detainees was greeted by a roar.

The men ran into the crowd and were swallowed up immediately, as if they would be snatched back by the Nazis if they weren't protected.

The roar became a constant crashing wave as man after man after man came through the community center's door. They were dirty, clearly weak from their time crushed together in a building far too small to hold nearly two thousand men.

But they were free.

The women around Christina were openly weeping, in relief, in joy, in some kind of nuanced grief for all those men who hadn't been saved.

What would their world look like if more of them had done this earlier? There had been resistance efforts in the thirties—Annelise had been part of them—but those had been small groups of people who would have been hurt the most by Hitler's rise to power.

What they hadn't seen were people who would benefit from Hitler's policies speaking out. They were the ones who pursed their lips over some of his wilder rhetoric but ultimately decided that him in power was better for them than the alternatives.

That was a dangerous game to play, but she couldn't help but play it as she watched nearly two thousand Jewish men be released after a peaceful protest that had required only tenacity, grit, and some moxie for one week. So many had suffered so much more for so much less.

"Who is to say it would have succeeded at any other time," Lisbeth said, but she sounded hesitant. The idea that some of the clear crimes against humanity the Nazis were committing could have been averted by three hundred German women was nauseating. It was simply easier to believe this was a unique situation, a perfect storm that the Nazis had wanted to avoid.

With all the commotion, Christina decided to risk slipping her hand into Lisbeth's. Lisbeth squeezed in acknowledgment, and they held on to each other for a good minute. From the outside they wouldn't look like anything but two women who had formed a friendship throughout the week.

Christina's heart beat in her palm, though, as she wondered what would happen to them when Eitan came through those doors. There was no reason to think Lisbeth wanted to see anything but the back of Christina as she walked out of their lives.

She didn't even allow herself to think about Eitan's reaction to her presence. The cowardly part of her wanted to flee. But she had to see this through.

Morning eased into the afternoon, as the crowd began to disperse. It took time to discharge nearly two thousand prisoners, and some of the wives made noises about waiting for their husbands at home instead of in the street so as to clear the way for the men coming out.

The news of what had actually happened worked its way through the remaining women.

Earlier that day, Goebbels, in his role as Gauleiter of Berlin, had ordered the intermarried men and women being held at the Rose Street center be released. The gossip was that he'd finally made the decision that the fuss had grown into a disaster for the Party. There was talk that Goebbels would give the situation a few weeks to cool down and then try to round up the same men once more, but, at the very least, they had bought time.

And . . . Christina didn't think Goebbels would want to risk this embarrassment again. He wouldn't want another protest by women who had just learned how effective their voices could be.

What she guessed was that Goebbels would convince Hitler to categorize these men as "privileged" Jews and then leave well enough alone.

Soon after the first man had stumbled into the street, Lisbeth ran back to give the news to Ingrid, and then returned to wait for Eitan.

Christina didn't start to worry until early evening.

The flood of men from the building had become a trickle. Was Eitan still there? Or was he one of the men who'd been released from the back entrance? Maybe he'd already made his way back to that cozy attic apartment, maybe he was even now lying down in the bed where Christina and Lisbeth had slept. Maybe he had missed Lisbeth when she'd gone back to talk to Ingrid.

She told herself over and over that's what had happened even as the sky darkened into blue velvet.

But she couldn't quiet the nerves that had her stomach clenching.

One of the freed detainees passed by them, and she decided to take a chance. She called out to get his attention, and when he turned she asked, "Are there many more men left?"

Lisbeth hovered at her shoulder, tense now, as well.

The man cleared his throat, looking between the two of them. "Only a few. But . . ."

Christina resisted the urge to shake the words out of the man. "But?"

"There were a handful who were deported this morning," he said. "Two dozen or so, maybe."

"What? Why?" The words came out too sharp, but Christina couldn't gentle her voice.

"I don't know." He looked so apologetic, as if it were his fault. "Perhaps they were sent before the order came to let us go?"

"What, what do you mean—?"

"Thank you," Lisbeth cut in, ushering the man along.

"Christina, he was a detainee," she murmured. "You looked like you were about to slap him."

"What if it was Eitan?" Christina knew her voice bordered on manic, but she couldn't help herself.

"What if it's not?" Lisbeth shot back, but they both knew.

They both knew it was him.

Christina's neck prickled and she glanced up.

For the first time since that morning, the tall Nazi was back at his spot by the door.

The world shifted beneath her feet as he met her eyes once more and he smiled.

"He found out that I asked for Eitan." It was a guess, but it made sense.

"No," Lisbeth said. "You don't know that. Even if he was deported, it could have been random." When Christina didn't say anything, Lisbeth growled in frustration. "Stop this. Blaming yourself for everything has become such a habit for you, you don't even see it for how self-centered it is."

"This was a monumental failure for him," Christina said, ignoring Lisbeth, even as the words sliced along her skin. "He needs someone to hang this on, and he's always thought I was the leader here. Ever since the second day."

Christina knew how men like him worked, knew how the Nazis worked. They didn't bear humiliation well. He wanted to punish someone, and his attention had found her throughout the week. He'd only need to ask the guards from the first day what man she'd been inquiring about. She'd even shown that guard her papers. They could have her real name.

She breathed out, her mind racing.

"This isn't about the Fatherland anymore," Christina said. "It's about him, personally. He'll need a victory to bring back to Goebbels, even if it's a private one."

"What are you talking about?" Lisbeth said. "None of this would be a victory for him."

"Not yet," Christina said, and even from a distance she could tell the Nazi still watched her. Waiting for her to come to the realization of what he wanted. "They're going to start pointing fingers soon and he can't be the one everyone blames. He needs a scapegoat and he needs a victory."

"Christina, no," Lisbeth said, finally catching on. She grabbed both of Christina's arms, shook her. "No."

But Christina laughed at the beauty of fate. Her penance had never been served by simply lingering in the wings, watching over Eitan's life like some impotent guardian angel.

Penance only meant something if it was actually paid.

"No, there's another way," Lisbeth said, her fingers digging in now, leaving bruises.

"What other way?" Christina asked, almost giddy now, too many emotions rushing in at once. "He'll die otherwise."

"You say otherwise as if you can negotiate with Nazis," Lisbeth said. "If you turn yourself in as some 'ringleader' then you'll both die. This isn't some noble sacrifice, this is martyring yourself for no reason."

"I have to try," Christina said. The Nazis never blinked . . . except when they did.

"You don't deserve this, Christina," Lisbeth said, gripping her shoulders hard now. "I know you think you do. I know you think the world should hate you as much as you hate yourself. But whatever happened in the past, you're a different person now. You don't deserve this."

"'If anyone saves a life, it shall be as though he has saved the lives of all mankind,'" Christina said. She had heard that so long ago, when she'd first moved to Berlin and was trying to unlearn everything she'd been taught to believe. Now she finally understood its meaning could be more than metaphorical. "'Save one man, save all mankind.'"

Of course, Lisbeth recognized the passage from the Talmud. She had told Christina that she'd studied Judaism after meeting Eitan.

"Christina," Lisbeth whispered, because she knew she'd lost the battle.

"I'm so glad I met you," Christina said.

"No, we're not doing goodbye speeches. You're not dying." There was a desperation in the words, though, as if Lisbeth could force them to be true by will alone.

"Thank you for this week," Christina said, once again ignoring her. She wanted to say more, but couldn't think of anything else beyond Eitan right now. "I couldn't have made it without you. I'm so lucky you found me."

Lisbeth sighed, stepped back. "One day you'll realize that I'm the lucky one."

Never, Christina thought. But right now was the time for pretty words if ever there was one, so she almost let herself believe it.

"Did you mean it?" she asked instead. It wasn't fair, but she'd never called herself a good person. "When you kissed me. Or was it to prove a point?"

Lisbeth's eyes dropped to her mouth. "I meant it."

Christina breathed out, grateful for the answer that Lisbeth hadn't really owed her. "Thank you."

Then she half turned to the Nazi, ready to fulfill a fate that had been put in place when she'd been sixteen.

But she stopped, needing one more thing.

"Tell Eitan I'm sorry," she said, because there was no room in her mind to think this might not work.

Lisbeth tilted her head, her smile sad. "I think he knows."

Chapter 39
ANNELISE

Fall 1938

Glass shattered beside Annelise, the cascade of broken pieces almost pretty in the moonlight.

She flinched at the sound, wanting to cower but there was no time for that.

Flames licked into the dark night sky, men went to their knees in the streets pleading to be spared, goods and possessions were tossed through the destroyed windows. Slurs were flung toward the prostrate men with just as much ease.

Screams came from so many directions they blended into each other, as if the city itself were terrified.

Chaos had come to Bonn.

Under Hitler's reign, there had to be punishment for the death of the German diplomat in Paris. It was a perfect moment for the Nazi Party—a way to point to the Jews as dangerous, as unlawful, as a problem that needed a solution.

Down the street, Annelise saw Felix leading his former Hitler Youth brigade, hammers and hoes and rocks held at the ready.

They were smiling with the macabre grins of demons unleashed on earth, and Annelise wanted to drop to the street right there, retch until her body felt anything other than dirty.

But she had to find Eitan.

His shift was set to end at the factory, so Annelise headed in that direction, praying that the Nazis hadn't reached the far side of town yet.

In front of her, a group of boys in HJ uniforms dragged a shopkeeper by his hair onto the sidewalk.

Annelise's hands curled into fists and before she could think, she struck the lead boy in the head, screaming as she did so. He flinched, but she didn't stop, simply kept beating him, knowing she couldn't be causing much pain but needing to do as much damage as she could.

There were cries of "Fraulein" and "stand down."

But no one tried to hurt her. The difference was stark.

In all the commotion, the shopkeeper managed to break free from the boys. When he was no longer in sight, Annelise finally relented.

"You should be ashamed," she shouted at them, but didn't have time to waste on these boys. And from the way they were smiling and carrying on, she guessed they didn't have time for her or her disdain.

What had become of the young men of her country? How could they have embraced violence so easily, so readily? So . . . joyfully?

Annelise didn't stop again, she couldn't. She had to get to Eitan. The image of him in the same position as the shopkeeper haunted her.

The factory was in the distance, and Annelise sprinted toward it.

Her legs burned and she remembered the lake with Eitan, that summer afternoon that had been so misleading in its sweetness. She should have known then that would be one of the last good days she would have.

The factory's stacks came into view and Annelise almost bent over in relief. There were several small figures fleeing the building and Annelise could only hope one of them was Eitan.

Despite the pain in her side, Annelise took off running once more, leaving the frenzied mob well behind her.

Through the smoke in the air she could make out a figure of someone barreling toward her.

She recognized him immediately.

Without slowing, she threw herself at Eitan, trusting he would catch her.

He did, his hands sure and easy on her thighs as she wrapped her legs around his waist.

Their mouths met in some kind of urgent communication that couldn't be spoken with words. It was quick, over too soon.

Annelise didn't hop to the ground, though, just stayed where she was, cradled by his strength.

"We need to get you out of here," she whispered.

"Where though?"

Annelise thought through their options. They could go back to his apartment, but what if the Nazis had a list of all the Jewish men and women in town? They could go back to her house, but that didn't feel safe. She still didn't completely trust Christina's shaky new loyalties—she hadn't even quit the BDM yet. Not to mention, Annelise's brother was a full-blown Nazi.

There were the lakes and the Seven Mountains, but too many people knew about them. The Pirates had been going there for years, and Hans had been acting strange and distant ever since Cologne. She hadn't been able to shake the suspicion that he had been picked up by the Gestapo and had never told them. It wouldn't have taken much to get him to switch sides.

The obvious answer came to her in a flash.

The barn.

Only Marta, Stefan, Max, and three other trusted Pirates knew about the place. And they all would have been careful about who they told. There were explosives being kept there, after all.

"We have to go," Annelise said, unhitching herself from his grasp. She took his hand and began running once more. Trying to fit in among the HJ and SS would be a foolish risk. Instead, they had to simply get to the streetcar as fast as possible.

Eitan didn't question her, nor did he hesitate. He simply followed, and the weight of that unspeakable trust pressed down on her shoulders.

A roar, a fireball, to their right. Annelise dodged left. Eitan kept a close pace.

Someone yelled after them, but a window shattered, distracting their would-be pursuer. Still, Annelise swore she could feel eyes on her back, so she ran faster.

Men were out with paint and brushes, leaving hateful scars on their city. These had been the very men who had been the first to complain when Annelise and her Pirates had left messages of love and peace on buildings.

"I hate them," she breathed out and let that rage fuel her steps.

Some high deity was looking out for them. Not only did they get to the streetcar stop unharmed, but one glided to a halt as they reached it. This would be tricky—a contained space, where tensions could boil over and they'd be trapped.

Eitan clutched her hand, and in that moment she remembered how young he was. Really, he was on the brink of adulthood—he should be thinking about nights at the cinema, and other frivolous things.

They embraced, both of them tucking their faces into the other's neck, her fingers toying with his loose curls, his clutching her hips. From the outside, they looked like any other young lovers, oblivious even in the face of a riot outside the streetcar's doors. An older woman tutted at them, disdainful of their show of affection, but that was the most attention they drew.

The crowd on the streetcar thinned until it was just the two of them and an older couple who had been clutching their bags of groceries, their knuckles white, their eyes wide. They had surely not been prepared for what they'd encountered when they'd decided to go into the heart of town that day. Annelise spared them a commiserating smile, which they returned.

Once Annelise and Eitan hopped off the car, they ran in unison toward the tree line.

With each step she found purchase on rich soil that was so much more her homeland than any flag or uniform. This was Germany. The woods, the earth, the protection from those who wanted to hunt them.

The barn came into view and Annelise almost collapsed right there on the ground. She felt like she had been running for so long now.

"A little further," Eitan murmured, and she nodded.

The barn smelled of wet hay, of safety. Of explosives.

"No one knows about this place?" Eitan asked, already scouting around for hiding places.

"Only a few Pirates," Annelise said. She spied a ladder and a loft, and tilted her head in that direction. "Come on."

They settled down, wrapped in shadows, with him leaning against the barn wall and her cradled in the vee of his legs.

"I wish I could have done more," Eitan admitted. "For everyone back there."

He hadn't seen much, she knew. He'd been in the factory and the streetcar had skirted the edges of the riot. But he'd seen enough.

Annelise squeezed his hands, which were pressed into her belly. She didn't say it, but she was glad he hadn't been able to do more. That might have put him at the business end of a Nazi's revolver.

"The people who should be doing more were sitting there on the streetcar as if nothing was happening outside," Annelise said, some of the terror bleeding away to reveal the rage underneath. "Does no one see beyond their own noses anymore? How do you watch people being targeted like that and not intervene?"

"That's the problem, isn't it?" Eitan said. "They don't see us as people."

The breath rushed out of Annelise. She couldn't deny the truth of his words. Hitler and Goebbels and the newspapers they had complete control of had been seeding that idea for at least half a decade if not longer.

"I wish we could leave Germany," Annelise said, thinking he would quickly agree. But he didn't respond for a long time.

"Where do you think it would be better?"

Annelise exhaled, knowing what he was implying. All those leaders who were appeasing Hitler weren't exactly champing at the bit to defend the Jews in their own countries. Despite the great myth of America, no one there was eager to welcome refugees. They had quotas and they were tightening by the day. She read the resistance papers enough to know that excuse kept coming up when anyone sought help from the country that billed itself as the home of the free.

She swallowed hard against the knowledge. Annelise had lived the past few years on a hope that Germany was better than it was showing it could be. But was there hope in this cruel world at all? Was anywhere else much different? Ready to blame all their problems on a group of people they'd decided were *less than* and then do everything in their power to make sure those people suffered for that imagined injustice?

"Shall we make this barn our home?" she asked instead of crying.

"Will we be owls?" he teased, his thumb brushing the underside of her breast.

"We'd be able to fly into the mountains," Annelise said, playing along. What harm was it to dream? It was better than thinking about the riot back in Bonn. There had been such frenzied glee in the air, Annelise could still taste the rotten slick of it on her tongue. Would they even be able to return to the city tonight? Tomorrow? How long did that kind of hysteria burn bright before it burned out?

"We'd be able to fly to the seaside, make a day of it."

She almost laughed, leaning back into him so that he could nose along the line of her jaw to the sensitive skin by her ear.

He stilled, newly tense.

"What?"

"Did you hear that?" he asked, his voice not even a whisper.

Annelise gripped his hands as she listened. At first all she heard was the cold November wind slipping through the cracks in the barn.

And then . . .

There it was. A muffled sob. Boots against tightly packed dirt.

They both shrank back as far into the shadows as they could, knowing that they didn't need to confirm their worst fears out loud to each other.

Annelise closed her eyes. If she was responsible for Eitan being caught or harmed, she would never forgive herself for as long as she lived.

The hinges of the barn's door protested as it was yanked open with vicious enthusiasm.

Whoever was down there wasn't trying to hide. They wanted their presence known.

Another sob came, so at odds with the confident, striding footsteps that Annelise had to fight the urge to peek over the edge of the loft.

"Ah, the little barn rats are hiding."

Annelise recognized the voice immediately.

Felix.

There went any hope that someone had simply stumbled upon them by accident. Annelise wondered if she would be able to throw herself on his mercy, pretend she was here by herself trying to escape the chaos of the city.

"I know you are here," he called. "Come out and bring your little Jew with you."

Annelise willed Eitan to remain still. It was clear Felix didn't know where they were, and they'd pulled up the ladder behind them when they'd climbed into the loft.

Felix tutted below, and he sounded far too cocky for Annelise's comfort.

"Shall I give you some incentive?"

It was then Annelise thought about the sobs, which had petered into sniffles.

He had brought someone with him, she realized, just before the girl let out a wild wail that pierced into Annelise's chest.

No.

Sounding as calm as if he were discussing plans for dinner, Felix said, "Annelise, my dear, you have until the count of three before I put a bullet through your lovely sister's head."

Chapter 40
CHRISTINA

March 6, 1943

The tall Nazi watched Christina approach with a cool expression, but she could read the triumph in the pinch of his mouth as if he was trying to swallow a grin.

"What can I help you with, Fraulein?" he said as soon as she got close enough.

"A trade," Christina said, no-nonsense. He wouldn't respect fake tears or runarounds. "You deported a man that I have an interest in. Free him, like you did the rest of the detainees here."

"Why ever would I do that?"

Christina took a breath. The cowardly part of her, the one she'd thought was her loudest voice, screamed at her to turn and run. Lisbeth was right, there was only the smallest chance that this would save Eitan. But she couldn't ignore that sliver of hope. She had to try.

"I'll take the responsibility for this protest," she said. "Your superiors are less than pleased with your performance this week, are they not? Wouldn't you like to be able to hand them someone to blame?" When he remained silent—not shooting her down immediately—she pushed on. "You can create whatever story you wish for me. Call back the men you deported."

"They're already on a train east, Fraulein," he said.

"You have enough power to call them back," Christina returned, unwavering. "And it would be following Goebbels's order to a T."

"What is to keep me from simply arresting you right now and leaving the men to their fates?" He sounded curious more than anything, like he knew she'd already worked out a backup plan and just wanted to hear it.

"Forgive my bluntness," she said. "But you have quite the mess on your hands. Herr Goebbels must be livid and looking for someone to blame. I am a good German woman. I participated in my local BDM chapter; I work for the Wehrmacht. If I say you arrested me in a fit of spiteful panic, are you certain you will be the one they believe?"

He cocked his head. "Why are you here if you are one of us?"

She tried not to flinch at the question. "It can be for whatever reason you want me to be here."

"Curious," he said, more to himself than to her. He barked out a sharp order, and all of a sudden she was surrounded by the policemen who had been standing guard at the community center for the past week. Rough hands were on her, pulling her arms back behind her and then pushing her toward a waiting car. They were exhausted, like the women had been. They weren't going to handle her gently.

Her head knocked into the top of the Mercedes when they tried to shove her into the back seat.

She didn't cry out, simply ducked down, and in an undignified move managed to right herself into a semblance of order.

It didn't matter, none of it mattered. Christina hadn't thought this was going to be easy.

Their destination turned out to be the Gestapo office a few streets down from the community center, the very one that could have put a brutal stop to the protest at any time during the week.

Christina was all but dragged into a tiny interrogation room and pushed down into one of the two chairs.

The tall Nazi lounged indolently in the one across from her.

"We're writing up a confession for you now," he informed her. "Unless you'd like to pen your own."

"No," she said, spreading her hands wide. "Tell me where to sign."

"This man must be important to you," he mused, long, skeletal fingers tapping away on the tabletop.

"No," she said again. Because it would be far better to keep him curious and guessing than to simply give up the fight.

He narrowed his eyes. "You're lying."

"Am I?"

"Why else would you be here?" he asked.

"Like I said, for whatever reason you want me to be here," she replied coolly.

"You think you will be treated well because you have made this deal?" he asked.

"No," she said again. The word seemed to slip under his skin with ease, to stick there like a burr. How must he hate hearing it after a week of *women* making his life hell.

That's why she wasn't surprised when he stood and, in one quick, vicious gesture, slammed her face against the table.

Pain bloomed out from her nose, which had cracked on impact; tears welled in her eyes, an unavoidable side effect. She would die before she let them fall.

Blood slid over her lip until she could taste copper on her tongue. Yet when she straightened back up, she simply met his hard gaze, undaunted.

"I've been wanting to do that all week," he said softly. "Would you like to see what else I've been thinking about doing?"

It was a risk, but at this point Christina didn't have much to lose. "No."

Another man might have laughed, charmed by her quick wit. But this one was bruised and battered and feeling like all the women in the world—and Christina especially—deserved to be begging for his forgiveness on their knees.

He smiled without any humor. Then he reached out and took one of her hands, in a parody of a lover's touch.

Christina sucked in a breath, knowing what was coming.

The snap of a broken bone was loud in the quiet room. She bit the inside of her cheek hard enough that more blood pooled in her mouth, but she'd managed not to react otherwise.

"I could throw you in a dark cell right now and forget you existed," he whispered, moving on to the next finger.

Snap.

Christina blinked hard as the world went dark at the edges. The pain in her face had become a persistent throb, punctuated by each finger break like it was an exclamation point.

"I could rape you day and night and no one would care or even know," he said, in that same carelessly neutral tone. Snap. "What do you think it would feel like for every bone in your body to be broken at once? Would you die from the pain? Do you think that's an interesting question, Fraulein?"

She knew what he wanted. Christina gritted her teeth and then spit the word at him. "No."

He huffed out an amused breath and moved on to her thumb. In an efficient move that made her sick thinking about how many times he must have practiced it, he dislocated the joint.

Christina couldn't help the thin wail that slipped through her clenched teeth. The entire world went black, and when she could once again focus she was sure she had lost some time.

He was sitting back in his chair, now, somewhat mollified by her obvious show of pain.

"No one knows you're here," he said. "No one even knows your name besides myself and one guard. Think about that while you wait."

With that he stood and walked from the room.

Christina waited a beat, two, three. Then she curled over her hand, her breathing gone ragged and uneven. When she closed her eyes bright pinpricks of pain danced like stars against the nothingness.

She cursed her own arrogance. Why had she thought she could control this? Control him. His rage had been simmering for too long, and here she had served herself to him on a silver platter.

Christina stared at her crooked fingers that were already shaded purple and black. Her face was likely smeared with blood, she could feel it sticky on her skin.

And she had to admit to herself the truth.

This was what she'd wanted. She'd wanted the pain, wanted to be punished. Wanted to martyr herself for a mistake she'd made when she'd been practically a child.

Of course, she'd made the offer on the chance it could save Eitan, but once again—always—in her heart she'd been selfish. She had never been able to properly pay for what she'd done, and so she'd jumped at the chance.

Why don't you hate me? She'd kept asking Lisbeth because she hated herself so much she couldn't imagine how someone who knew her whole story *wouldn't*.

No matter how the Nazi hurt her, it would never be enough, she realized. Even though she'd lived with the self-recrimination for so long, it was still a deeply shocking thought. Did she really think she was such a monster to deserve the fate the Nazi had described?

Did she really think her sin warranted that kind of penance?

Did she really think her life should be nothing but pain and guilt and despair in exchange for one mistake?

She had thought she had kept herself going because of Eitan, but maybe she'd simply learned to love hating herself. Because hating herself was easy, as Lisbeth had said. If she didn't, what would be left but a shell of a girl who had never learned who she really was?

What would that be like? To want to be herself?

Christina's head was too fuzzy for this, every inch of her body aching from both the brutal assault and from a week spent on the street in icy weather. Christina desperately longed for a warm bath and three full days of sleep. She would be getting neither here.

The door swung open and the Nazi marched back in. They all walked like that, sharp, jerky movements that were probably a result of the drugs Hitler had them all on—if the rumors around the Bendlerblock were true.

How much time had passed? She wasn't certain. Maybe an hour, maybe five.

"Christina Fischer," he said, sitting down once more in the chair.

"A low-level secretary at Abwehr. Born in Bonn, moved to Berlin five years ago. No obvious connection to Eitan Basch."

"Except," the Nazi continued, "he was born in Bonn, as well."

"Small world," Christina said, with a jaunty smile that must have looked unhinged when combined with the blood.

The Nazi hummed. "He also moved to Berlin five years ago."

"Funny that." What did it matter if he sussed out their connection—though she didn't think he had the imagination to do that. If he wasn't calling Eitan back from Auschwitz it didn't matter that he knew about their past.

"This makes me curious if you really are running an underground resistance network right under the noses of those incompetents at the Abwehr."

It wasn't a question, so Christina just lifted her brows.

"Perhaps I can entice you to give up your other comrades?" he said, and she realized he really did think he had a bigger fish on the line than he'd realized. Christina almost laughed in his face. She gave information to the Allies, but they ignored her most of the time. She'd helped smuggle Jewish families out of the country, done her best to warn the ones still in the city if they ever had to go into hiding. But she was hardly the head of some kind of double-agent spy ring.

Would it help Eitan's cause, though, if she pretended to be?

"I want to see Eitan," she said. "Then you can have all the information you want."

He stroked his thumb over his mustache as he studied her face. "You're not in a position to negotiate."

She did laugh at that. "It seems I am."

"Actually," someone said from the door, "you're not."

Another Nazi. Gestapo, Christina was fairly certain. "You're to release the prisoner into my custody, Obersturmbannführer Baur."

So the tall Nazi had a name.

"I think not," Baur snapped.

The man remained unruffled in the face of Baur's clear anger. "It's above your head, Obersturmbannführer. I'm only informing you as a courtesy. The directive comes from the office of Gruppenführer Müller."

Baur's nostrils flared, but there was little he could do about that order. Gruppenführer Müller was the Gestapo chief. His name had been bandied about in the Abwehr plenty—mostly because he was so ardently and relentlessly suspicious of the intelligence-gathering arm of the Wehrmacht. He thought it a hotbed of resistance activity. For good reason, but no one said that part out loud.

He was someone even the ghouls in the Gestapo were terrified to cross.

If Müller was choosing to intervene, it also meant that Christina's fate was surely sealed.

The papers the new Nazi handed over clearly held up to Baur's scrutiny, if his increasing irritation was anything to go by.

"She's a traitor to the Reich," Baur finally said, pushing the folder away.

"My office will deal with any investigation that's needed, Obersturmbannführer." Though his words could have been read as conciliatory, his tone made it clear they were not. He didn't like this man, nor did she like the fact that Baur hadn't asked how high when he'd been told to jump.

Baur yanked Christina up hard enough that her shoulder cried out in protest. She managed to keep her whimper behind the tight press of her lips as Baur thrust her at the new Nazi. She crashed into him, but he was steady on his feet, barely flinching. His nose wrinkled, as if she were a piece of rotting trash that had dirtied his uniform.

Two younger guards stood behind him, and when he snapped his fingers, they grabbed her arms, their grip tight enough to leave bruises. Her pulse was so fast she could feel it in the soft spots of her body, and she tried not to panic as they pushed her from the room.

They dragged her through the hallways of the Gestapo building, and then shoved her into the back of a Mercedes. Then the Nazi who had collected her waved the two young guards off and slid behind the wheel.

Christina's breathing went ragged. Everyone on both sides of this war made dying sound so noble—they had to if they wanted the boys to fall in line, little toy soldiers who knew they were cannon fodder but told themselves they were worthy sacrifices.

Death wasn't noble. It was terrifying and cruel and, in the case of so many wars, done just to sate the hunger of powerful men.

Would they hang her body on Rose Street, a warning to anyone who had seen the protest's success and gotten ideas?

Would she be used by the Party she had so defended when she'd been young to warn others off resisting? Perhaps that was a fitting end for her particular story.

Christina didn't bother asking where he was taking her, and she found out soon enough anyway. The Mercedes slid to a stop in front of a darkened town house. This time when she was dragged from the back seat, she couldn't silence the pained whine.

She wondered if her hand would ever completely heal. She wondered if she would live long enough for it to be a problem.

The Nazi shoved her through the door and then toward a steep set of stairs.

Halfway up, she realized they could be used as a weapon. But even as she tried to think of a way to knock him down to the floor below, she remembered his sturdiness in the interrogation room. If she failed, he might take pleasure in drawing out whatever torture awaited her at the top.

The opportunity came and went.

When they reached the second floor, the Nazi pressed a massive hand against her spine and pushed her through the doorway of one of the rooms. Christina tripped, her knees hitting the floor.

Her vision went dark at the edges, as she braced for the press of a pistol against her skull. Or maybe he'd use his whip, as Nazis so loved to do.

No bullet came. No sting of leather on flesh.

Nothing happened.

Nothing except a shadow shifting out of the corner. The room hadn't been empty, after all.

Christina blinked up at the person, trying to understand through the haze of fear.

A single candlelight flickered over features that had once been as familiar as her own.

Standing there looking beautiful and powerful and untouchable was Annelise.

Chapter 41

ANNELISE

Fall 1938

I n her safe perch in the loft of the barn, Annelise could only picture the pistol pressed to Christina's temple. But she knew Felix wasn't bluffing.

"One," Felix called out.

"I'm sorry, Annelise," Christina cried, but Annelise tuned her out. She was viciously angry at her sister. If she listened to her now, she would be too enraged to save her.

But how could she choose between Christina and Eitan? Because she knew without a shadow of a doubt that's what would happen here.

"Two."

Eitan pressed a kiss to the nape of her neck, a comforting gesture, a goodbye. And then, because he was who he was, he stood, nudging her away from him as he did.

"Wait."

His voice carried throughout the barn, a decision made for all of them.

"Don't shoot the girl," he said, stepping toward the edge of the loft.

Annelise scrambled to follow him, but he put an arm out, keeping her in the shadows.

"Shut your mouth," Felix said, adding on a slur, so casually cruel. Annelise could see he had an arm wrapped around Christina's throat. Her sister's face was splotchy, tear-soaked, and miserable. "Where is Annelise?"

"Here," she said. "Let Christina go. You have no quarrel with her."

"Yes, but she is proving oh so useful," Felix said. "Now come down here."

"If you let her go."

"That's not how this works," Felix said, cocking his gun. "I believe we were at 'two.'"

Beneath her breath, Annelise murmured, "You stay here."

But when she climbed down, Felix narrowed his eyes at the dark space above. "Your Jew lover, as well."

"No. You want me," Annelise said, but she already heard Eitan's boots on the ladder.

"It's interesting you think you're in a position to tell me anything at the moment," Felix said, his grip tightening on Christina.

For the first time since they'd come into the barn, she let herself meet Christina's eyes. They were pleading, miserable.

Annelise looked away, and Eitan came to stand beside her.

"What are you going to do?" Annelise asked. If he was planning to kill them all, there was a good chance he could get away with it. The court system was unbearably sympathetic to the Nazis.

Felix tossed Christina aside like a rag doll. Her sister hit the ground hard, but the message was clear. She had served her purpose.

Now the gun was pointed squarely at Eitan, who could do nothing to defend himself. Annelise and Christina, at least, had the protection of being considered full Germans. Eitan might just be one more victim of the riots who, in the eyes of the Nazis, had brought his death on himself purely by being born Jewish.

"I need a wife," Felix said, and Annelise's stomach heaved at the unexpected turn.

That he had thought marriage and not rape shocked her. But she supposed she had known he was like this. She had rejected him and so he'd been seething with humiliation ever since. Now that it was within his power to punish her, to bend her to his will, he would do anything to get his desired outcome.

"Are you going to hold a pistol on me for our entire marriage?" Annelise asked. Even if she understood why he was doing this, she was still incredulous that he thought he could get away with it.

"Not on you, my dear," Felix said. He flicked his wrist, calling attention to his current target. "One word from me, and your lover will be sent to a work camp for the rest of his days—which will be numbered once his body gives out."

Annelise's fingernails bit into the soft flesh of her palms to keep from lashing out.

"But you see, I'm quite magnanimous," he continued. "You get to decide if he dies tonight or not. All I need is an answer."

Desperately, she met Eitan's eyes. He shook his head. "You can't do this, Annelise."

"If I refuse . . ." She trailed off. This wasn't a false threat. Annelise had seen the chaos in Bonn. She was sure there would be men who were killed tonight. Felix would say Eitan was just one more.

"Take me instead."

It was Christina. The first real words she'd spoken. They trembled and were thick with tears, but she was standing once more, her shoulders pulled back in a straight, proud line. Her chin was tipped up and she looked like she could fight Felix through sheer stubbornness alone.

"You think I want a coward as a wife?" Felix asked, his derisive laughter slapping at Christina. He didn't even bother looking at her. "Weak-spined women hold no appeal to me."

Christina might as well have been slapped, but Annelise could have told her that. Felix was the type of man who wanted to bend people to his will through violence and power. He needed someone to say no to him so that he could *make* them say yes.

"Annelise," Christina tried.

"Don't speak to me," Annelise snapped. "Don't speak to me ever again."

It didn't matter what coercive force Felix had used to get Christina to bring him here. Likely pointing a pistol in her face and threatening to shoot had been enough. Felix was wrong about so many things, but one thing was true. Christina was a coward.

"It was a mistake," Christina whispered. "I lost my head when the rioting started. I saw Felix in town and I thought he could help me make sure you were safe."

The patience she'd been gripping with all her might slipped, and she turned fully to Christina, let her see the absolute fury on her face.

"I told you he was dangerous, how many times, Christina? How many times did I warn you?" Annelise's voice shook with her rage, the words choking up her throat.

Felix made a happy sound—pleased, she was sure, that he was on her mind even if it was because she thought him a cad.

"I didn't mean to." The weak plea for understanding only further fueled the fire burning through Annelise. Annelise had granted her sister understanding before. Look where it had landed them. "I remembered as soon as he said he would find you. I remembered you didn't trust him."

"But it was too late," Annelise said.

Christina had planted the idea of Annelise in Felix's head, had planted the idea that she was hiding. There would have been no reason for Annelise to leave her home besides Eitan.

"I ran away from him," Christina whispered, as if she couldn't help herself from confessing the whole of her sin. "I was on my bicycle, I saw you board the streetcar, and I caught up to it when it made stops."

Annelise wanted to rake her nails over Christina's face, wanted to see the blood pearl on her skin. "Why were you following me? Why are you *always* following me?"

"I wanted to make sure you were safe," Christina said, her voice trembling. "Like before when I stopped those boys from harassing you that day."

"I didn't need your help," Annelise all but spat at her.

"I know, I know. Once I saw you go in the barn, I left, I knew you would be safe here," Christina said. "But Felix found me on the way back to town."

"He didn't know where I was," Annelise realized. "And you drew him a map."

"I didn't need a map," Felix cut in. "She was happy to tell me."

"Not happy." Christina's chin trembled. "Annelise, he had a gun. I—"

"Stop. Talking." Annelise finally gritted the words out through clenched teeth. She no longer cared what Christina's excuses were. She'd told Felix, and it didn't matter that it hadn't been out of spite or because she wanted to be welcomed back into the Nazi fold. She had sent them all careening down this path. And then she'd followed Annelise, two things Annelise had told her not to do.

Christina, it seemed, would abide by any rule except one laid down by Annelise.

Her sister curled in on herself as if Annelise really had slapped her. Part of Annelise wanted to soften. But she thought about that time so long ago now when Christina had trailed her to the campout in the Seven Mountains. Annelise had given her food and protection and warmth. She'd cuddled around her as they slept. And Christina hadn't acknowledged any of it. She never realized how much Annelise took care of her.

And now Annelise was once more in a situation where she had to protect Christina, to shield her from the consequences of all her foolish, weak choices.

Annelise couldn't even look at her anymore.

She turned back to Felix, who seemed amused more than anything else.

"Terms," she spat out. "You have to promise to let Eitan alone."

"As long as you do not do anything foolish," Felix said, lifting one careless shoulder. "Then I could not care less about the Jew."

"Annelise, no," Eitan murmured. But he knew she wasn't going to let him be shot to death in front of her. Maybe she could figure out a way out of this later, but right now she needed to neutralize the immediate threat.

So she ignored Eitan and stared down Felix. "Why do you even want me?"

"To prove I can have you," he said, confirming what she'd already been thinking. "Plus, my little Pirate, you'll be able to provide me with the names of all your friends who are enemies of the Reich."

Of course. If Felix took down the Bonn ring of Edelweiss Pirates he might even catch the attention of the Führer. Or Göring at the very least. He would get a passably pretty Aryan wife, and a promotion at the same time. Once he started up the ranks, his rise to prominence would only gain speed.

She didn't bother telling him that she wasn't like her sister. He couldn't wave a weapon in her face and expect her to betray her friends. But he didn't need to know that now.

"Eitan leaves now, and you stay in this barn with us for the next hour," she bargained. "And I'll be cooperative from here on out."

"Deal." He lifted his pistol a fraction of an inch and pulled the trigger. Annelise ducked and Christina screamed. Eitan didn't even flinch.

"Run," Felix said to him.

But Eitan didn't flee, he simply turned to Annelise.

"Leave," she whispered. She knew he would understand that she meant leave Bonn. Even if he couldn't get out of the country, at least he could lose himself in Berlin. Felix was young, a nobody, in a small, rural town. Right now, he held little sway outside their city.

Eitan looked like he was going to stand his ground, fight for them.

She shifted, blocking Felix out as best she could. "'We need, in love, to practice only this: letting each other go.'"

He exhaled and it was a shaky thing.

"Forever yours," he murmured, and Annelise hated that they both had memorized those lines he'd written months ago because they'd known how true they were.

Then, without looking at Felix, Eitan walked toward the barn doors.

He stopped only once, next to Christina, whose face was flushed with shame. She stared at the ground, cowardly even in this moment.

Eitan didn't say anything, merely touched her shoulder, gently. Then he was gone. Into the night. And Annelise knew she would never see him again.

Christina's knees buckled and she once again crumpled to the ground, her shoulders heaving in silent sobs.

Neither Annelise nor Felix spared her more than a single glance.

"I'm thinking a spring wedding," Felix said.

"I'm thinking of ways to kill you."

The truly tragic thing was that Felix simply laughed.

FELIX ESCORTED ANNELISE and Christina home.

"There are riots happening, you know, you can't be too safe," he said, and she wondered if he was truly deranged.

When he left, Annelise didn't waste a single second. She sprinted up the stairs to her room.

She knew she had it somewhere.

Christina followed on her heels.

"Annelise, let me explain."

Even when Annelise ignored her, Christina trailed her to the far side of the room, stood over her shoulder while Annelise dug in the chest that they shared.

"I thought I could help you hide; I thought I could help you like I had before. That day that I helped you." Christina was babbling. "And then you liked me again because I helped you. You know I don't believe in the Nazis anymore."

"They're not dragons." Annelise finally broke. "You don't believe in them or not believe in them. They exist and they are out there killing people and destroying lives because . . . because—" She cut herself off with a frustrated scream. How many times would they have this conversation? She couldn't do it anymore.

Her fingers brushed against the thin book, buried beneath her winter sweaters and trousers and skirts. Annelise sighed in relief and sat back on her heels.

"I have only one thing to ask of you," Annelise said, her eyes on the cover. If she was forced to marry Felix, she couldn't risk bringing this volume into their household. He would likely burn it and she would rather lose it first.

"Anything," Christina breathed, as if she could so easily be forgiven.

"Take this to Eitan," she said. "He lives above a store called One More Page Books in the north part of town. Near the gardens."

Christina held her hand out for the Rilke. But Annelise didn't hand it over yet.

Instead she riffled through the pages until she found the small piece of paper—what she had actually been looking for when she'd come into the room. She tucked it into her palm. Was this mad? Was this an exercise in futility? She didn't know, but she had to try. The alternative was too unbearable to think about.

"I'll watch over him," Christina promised, and it was so unexpected Annelise blinked up at her. "I don't know how. But I will. I'll keep him safe."

The words barely made sense, and Annelise shook them away as so much nonsense.

She stood and raced back down the stairs.

"Where are you going?" Christina asked, and Annelise finally whirled on her.

"I don't want you to ever speak to me again, do you understand?" Annelise asked. She kept her voice low and serious so that Christina would get that this wasn't a frivolous threat. "I don't ever want to hear your voice again."

Christina swallowed, her eyes wide in the darkness. But then slowly she nodded and Annelise exhaled, some of the tension bleeding from her body. A part of her wanted to comfort Christina then, and that's how she knew that no matter what tonight brought, she wouldn't come back to this house for longer than to pack her things.

She was too weak when it came to Christina. She would break, she would forgive her. And then she would resent her, hate her, even, with everything in her being.

We need, in love, to practice only this: letting each other go.

Annelise stepped forward, pressed her forehead to Christina's. And then, silently, she let her go.

Chapter 42

CHRISTINA

March 6, 1943

As the Nazi's footsteps receded down the town house stairs, Christina tried to make sense of the fact that Annelise was standing above her.

Christina's eyes tracked to the empty doorway. If Annelise was working with the Nazis, Christina couldn't let emotion take hold. She needed to escape while she was evenly matched.

The corner of Annelise's mouth twitched up like she could read every thought, every plan that Christina would never enact. Because it had always been Annelise running away from her, never the other way around. That wouldn't change now.

Christina shifted so that she was sitting against the wall. She rested her hand on top of her knees and tried not to stare at the mangled skin and crooked bones.

Annelise's attention dropped to it, though her face remained blank.

"You're in Berlin," Christina said, almost startling herself with the observation. Her own attention dropped to Annelise's hand, looking for the wedding band she feared would sit there.

She had hoped and prayed it wasn't the case, but Christina had always believed Annelise was back in Bonn, married to Felix, stuck in a life that was slowly killing her soul, all because of Christina's mistake.

But here she was in the same city as Christina, working with Nazis.

"I'm in Berlin," Annelise agreed.

Christina almost didn't want to ask how. She never thought about that night, couldn't let herself or she would never have survived.

Now, she forced herself to remember, to search for any hints of how it had led here, to this moment, to Annelise in Berlin.

THE POUNDING ON *the door startled everyone at the dining table.*

"It's too late for visitors," her mother whispered, unnecessarily. The ferocity of the knocking made it clear this wasn't a social call. When Christina's father crossed to the entryway, his hand was already curled into a fist.

Outside, a handful of men stood in a half circle, one of them the Fischers' neighbor. He wore a feral grin and carried a hammer, while the men around him hoisted torches into the night sky.

"We're getting revenge for Paris," their neighbor said. "You must come."

The words didn't make sense until they did. Annelise had told Christina just yesterday about the German diplomat who had been shot in France. Her sister had believed that Hitler would use the shooting as an excuse to enact more legislation against the Jews. Christina hadn't argued—too enamored with Annelise's tentative friendship to rock the boat—but she'd privately rolled her eyes. The crime had been committed by a madman an entire country away. Most Germans wouldn't even hear about it.

But . . . revenge for Paris. The words sent a chill over Christina's skin. She had been wrong. Again.

"Your women will be safe here." Mania unlike Christina had ever heard before had slipped into the man's voice. "It's the Jews who will pay for what they've done."

Her father demurred, shutting the door against their cries of protest. He had never been one for violence—for starting it or stopping it. Sometimes Christina wondered where Annelise had gotten her bravery.

Annelise.

She wasn't home. She was out there with the men who had torches and hammers. Christina stood, anxious and jittery with it, one certainty pounding in her chest. She needed to go out and find Annelise, to help her, like she had that day with the HJ boys. Annelise might be brave, but she had no self-preservation instincts.

"What are you doing?" her mother asked, voice thin and shaking. She

had to be worried about Annelise. They all knew she was probably out with her Pirates, and they never backed down from a fight. Their brawls with the HJ were becoming legendary around Bonn.

Yet her parents weren't going to go out there and find Annelise. They weren't going to try to bring her back home. Christina shook her head and kept walking. She didn't have to wonder where she got her own character.

"Sit down, girl," her father yelled, and the edge of panic in his voice only amplified her own.

"We have to save her."

Her father lunged, but Christina was nimble, more so than Annelise ever gave her credit for. She slipped by him and then fumbled with the lock on the door, breaking free into the night just as his fingers brushed the air behind her.

Christina grabbed for the bicycle leaning against the fence, not even thinking straight enough to know where to go.

But it turned out, she didn't need to think. The cries, the roar of fire, the shattering glass were like a siren, pulling everyone toward the center of town.

A man stumbled into her, sending her flying to the ground. Pain bloomed in her knees and hands, her cheek hot where it had caught the road. The man loomed over her, fists raised as if she were the attacker.

At first, she thought the marks on his face were freckles. But then she realized . . .

Not freckles. Blood.

Christina froze, trapped prey.

"I'm not . . ." What was she going to say? That she wasn't his enemy? How could she not be this man's enemy when he had blood on his face, and the blank expression boys sometimes got after their first hunts.

Tears burned her eyes.

"Please," Christina tried, though he didn't seem to hear her. "Please."

He stepped closer, but then stopped, his head cocking. In the next moment, he was gone, Christina forgotten.

Christina's breathing was coming too fast, she knew that, but couldn't seem to help it. Sparks danced in her eyes as she stood and tried to wrangle her bicycle into working order once more. Her fingers shook so hard that she could barely keep the handlebars straight.

The roving gangs of men clogged the streets near the center of the square, and she dismounted as she tried to calm herself down enough to think.

Where would Annelise go?

A small crowd formed around Christina, all of them marching in one direction, their mouths wet with saliva, their deranged smiles that of hyenas.

Christina tried to keep pace, to use them as camouflage until she could make her way through the worst of the insanity. But she had her bicycle, and she stumbled, flailed, and then got shoved once more to the ground.

Her palms stung, but she managed to keep her face from hitting the street this time. A warm trail of blood crept down her shin from where her leg had snagged on the pedal.

The worst of it, though, was that the new angle allowed her to see the girl.

Or, not a girl. She was older than Christina, but she was a slight thing.

And she was a Pirate. Christina didn't know her name—it wasn't Marta, Annelise's friend from the woods—so maybe that was why all she could see was Annelise standing there with her chin tipped up as the mob descended on her.

What had this girl done other than attempt to stop these madmen?

Christina tried to get to her feet, but she was tangled once more in her skirts, the metal frame of the bicycle heavy on her. She couldn't move, she couldn't stop this from happening.

Annelise, Christina's mind wailed. Even though this wasn't her sister, it so easily could have been.

Three boys led the way. The tallest one slapped the girl's face, and she spit in his.

The girl absorbed the punch that came next, but wasn't able to stand through the second. Someone kicked her in the stomach, another in the back, in the legs.

The crowd shifted as oceans were wont to do, and the girl's body somehow landed beside Christina, her nose cracking against the road. Blood spattered Christina's face, and she thought of the man from earlier with copper-wet cheeks and blank eyes.

Christina started screaming and screaming and screaming and just couldn't seem to stop.

"Christina." The voice was calm, and she turned toward it, instinctively seeking the warmth and safety it offered. "Are you hurt?"

The voice was soft and impossibly gentle and it broke through her defenses. He was backlit but she recognized the shape of him. "Felix?"

"Where are you hurt?" he asked, more urgent now, but no less kind. The hyenas circling Christina and the girl were forced back by the breadth of his shoulders.

"Annelise."

"What?" For the first time there was an edge to his tone, but she knew it was because he wanted Annelise safe as well.

"No, this isn't her. I don't know where she is," Christina said in a rush, still hunched over the broken and beaten girl. "That boy, I think . . . she must . . . I think she went to him."

It was then the light shifted and her mouth went dry. His face wasn't kind, she realized. It was stone. His eyes weren't gentle, they burned with rage.

Felix. This was Felix. The same man who Annelise had said attacked her.

"Ignore me, please. I hit my head, I don't know what I'm saying," Christina said, though she knew it was too late. Too late. She tried to distract him. "We need help here . . ."

Without looking away from her, Felix waved down two HJ boys.

"Help," he directed, with a jerk of his chin toward the girl. "Take her to hospital."

Christina had to force her hands to let go of the girl's arms. But the boys seemed calmer than the rest of the mob. She had to trust they would listen to direct orders. It would be more than Christina could do for her anyway.

Felix remained crouched in front of her and Christina tried not to cry.

What had she said? It was only that she had been so scared of the men and then Felix had shown up and she thought she might have said too much, but she couldn't remember now.

Annelise.

"Christina, I want to help Annelise, as well," Felix said, sounding so reasonable she almost swayed into him, almost let him comfort her. He had never been anything but kind to her, and her body didn't understand that he was the enemy.

Her mind did, though. Now that she no longer saw that girl as Annelise, lying there with her face cracked open.

Christina closed her eyes and tried to think.

Annelise called her a little shadow, which she had always hated. But she was thankful now, because she knew things she wouldn't have otherwise. She knew Eitan worked in the factory with their mother on the edge of town. Knew that he worked the evening shift.

That's where he would be, which meant that's where Annelise would be.

"The bookstore," Christina forced out through chattering teeth. She wasn't even sure why she was shaking. "He lives above a bookstore. That's . . . that's where Annelise must be."

Felix stared at her for one long moment and she let her eyes fill with tears. It wasn't hard to call them up, it was as if they'd simply been waiting for permission.

"Good girl," he finally said, and then kissed her forehead. "You need to get home."

She nodded, though he wasn't looking at her anymore. "I'll go now."

"You will be all right."

Christina nearly laughed at that. As if he could simply decree something and it would be true. But he'd always been arrogant. "Yes."

He took off then, in the direction of the bookstore.

She didn't stand immediately, in case he looked back.

He never did.

A surge of energy coursed through her, the noise in her skull quieting to just one thought. She had to get to Annelise and Eitan. She had to warn them, help them.

And now she knew where to go.

She pedaled through the streets of what could only be described as hell on earth. Torchlight guided her way, as did buildings that were consumed by fire. Demons lined the path toward the edge of town and Christina couldn't look away from the road, lest she succumb to the terror nipping at her heels.

Finally, finally, finally, Christina broke free from the crowd.

She could see the factory in the distance, and—

There. A flash of blond hair and dark curls.

Annelise. Eitan.

The two of them embraced and then headed toward the streetcar, and Christina followed at a distance. She needed to make sure they knew Felix was trying to find them.

That he was trying to find them because of her.

The train was slow enough that although Christina lagged behind, she could catch up at the stops. It didn't take long to realize Annelise was headed to the end of the line.

To the woods and the farmland beyond them.

By the time they reached the final stop, Christina's legs burned, her skin was slick with sweat. She gladly ditched the bicycle and followed the lovers on foot.

Annelise was easy to keep track of in the moonlight, her bright white shirt, her blond hair, both beacons in the night. Christina followed, a shadow. She told herself to call out to them. That's why she'd come, after all.

But then she would have to admit to what she'd done, the way she'd told Felix about the two of them just like Annelise had feared she would.

If she could simply watch them, make sure they had a hiding place, then she would never have to see Annelise's disappointment. She wouldn't have to rupture this fragile thing that was growing between them.

So she ran as quietly as she could.

When the trees opened up into farmland, Christina realized exactly where they were headed.

Her knees went weak with relief and she let herself stop. She hit the ground for the third time that night, the weight of her guilt gone now that she knew they would be safe, for now at least.

Her cheeks were wet again, but this time it was with tears, not blood.

Christina scrubbed her face as clean as possible and then began the long trudge back to her bicycle. With the panic gone, the path seemed to go on forever. She tripped a handful of times, her legs heavy and uncooperative.

The bicycle lay where she'd left it and she nearly cried again at the thought of having to ride it all the way home.

She would take the road that led around the city, she would lock herself in her room, and she would never talk to anyone wearing a Nazi uniform again.

Just as she had the thought, the barrel of a pistol pressed against her spine, and a voice too close to her ear whispered. "Hello, my little liar. Now let's try this again."

LOOKING BACK, CHRISTINA couldn't understand how the words *the barn* had slipped out of her mouth even under the threat of a gun. But she had been exhausted and numb and drained of every rational thought. She'd also been sixteen, and soft.

That Christina hadn't lived through a war. That Christina had no idea that when she'd called Kristallnacht *hell on earth*, it had been only an outer ring, the start of the descent.

That Christina wouldn't have been horrified by the idea that Annelise was working with the Gestapo.

Pirates can never be serfs, Annelise had told her one time when Christina had asked why she couldn't just go along with the Nazis. She'd said it with the pure arrogance and swagger she'd worn back then like a well-fitted coat.

If the consequence of Christina's cowardice had ended in Annelise becoming *this*, someone who worked with the Nazis, Christina wasn't sure what she would do.

"Are you going to kill me?" Christina asked, no longer terrified but just tired. So tired.

Annelise's brow wrinkled in confusion before it smoothed out. "Oh, my little shadow. We have so much catching up to do."

Chapter 43

ANNELISE

Fall 1938

The riots hadn't burned out. In fact, they seemed to have only grown in intensity since Annelise and Eitan had left the city several hours ago. Bonn was on fire, its residents frenzied with bloodlust.

Annelise pulled her hat lower and turned up the collar of her coat. She kept her head down as she took back alleys she knew from her nights with the Pirates, when they had been desperately trying to get anyone to stop this. Those days seemed foolish now—though at least for the rest of her days she would know she had tried.

She would never have to wonder what kind of character she had, never have to guess about what she would do in the face of terror and violence and hate.

A group of men hollered in the distance as glass shattered. Annelise kept to the shadows. This was dangerous, and she knew she shouldn't have sent Christina out into the night alone. As furious as she was, if anything happened to her sister, she would never forgive herself.

But it was too late to go back and stop her.

All Annelise could do was try to avoid the larger clusters. The rioters had lost all sense of humanity, their canines glistening in the moonlight.

There be wolves in these woods, she heard in Marta's voice.

How right she'd been.

Despite having memorized the address when it had been given to her, Annelise checked the slip of paper again. She was thankful she hadn't thrown it out.

Annelise didn't dare let herself hope yet. All she could think about was getting to the house in one piece.

But in the back of her mind she held on to the *possibility*. There was a reason Felix believed he could threaten and bully her into marriage. Annelise was a poor girl with overworked parents and no other protectors beyond a brother who would gladly do Felix the favor of marching her down the aisle at gunpoint.

He saw her as vulnerable, as a young girl who would have to bend to his will.

There was a secret Felix didn't know, though. One that might save her.

It took her thirty minutes longer to reach the address than it would have any other day, but eventually she stopped in front of a grand row home on the south side of Bonn. The residential street was actually quiet, though she could hear the cacophony not too far away. She considered going around to the back, but she didn't want to startle a maid into screaming.

All of a sudden, her courage deserted her. Was this ridiculous? Why had she thought this was a good idea?

You're here, she told herself, and then started up the steps.

She took a final, steadying breath and knocked.

The door swung open only a heartbeat later, the man clearly having been either waiting in or pacing the lobby. Perhaps deciding whether he should go out on the streets and intervene.

The sight of her seemed to catch him off guard.

He was younger than she'd thought he'd be, though she wasn't sure why she'd imagined him as old. He was also handsome, with a hint of silver in his dark hair.

"Mr. Wicklow?" she asked, thanking the fates for introducing her to Lilian in the train station in Cologne that day in the summer. "Mr. Bernard Wicklow?"

"Yes," he said, curious and careful.

"Your sister Lilian gave me your address." Annelise hoped he wouldn't laugh her off his front stoop. "I need your help."

Chapter 44

EMMY

May 1946

E mmy and Major Arnold showed up at the pub fairly early, staking out a table not long past noon. The same bartender from the day before nodded in their direction.

"You've convinced me." Emmy dug into a pretzel two times the size of her head. "I'm fairly optimistic she'll show."

"I told you we were good for each other," Major Arnold said. For some reason, despite their intimacy from the night before, Emmy enjoyed continuing to call him Major. That's who she'd fallen in love with, after all. "Either way, I think you've done that book justice."

He nodded to the Rilke sitting on the table. She smiled down at it, hardly believing their little mission had turned into this. That first day when she'd slipped it beneath her coat, her heart pounding at the idea of being caught, she couldn't have imagined ending up in Berlin possibly about to meet with Eitan's wife.

Who was not Annelise.

She wondered if Lisbeth would know what had become of the woman. Probably not. Probably Annelise and Eitan had simply been young lovers in a cruel world, passing ships in the night.

"It doesn't make it any less important," the major said, seeming to read all that in her expression. It should be terrifying how well he knew her. "When something happens for a short amount of time."

"I know it's childish and selfish of me, but I wanted it to be simple," Emmy admitted. "Everything here is hard and horrifying and full of complexity right now. And I do, I do, I want to live in a world where there are shades of gray. But I also wanted this one thing to be simple."

He reached across the table, swiped at the back of her hand with his thumb in a comforting gesture, and then retreated. Even now that the barrier was down between them, he wouldn't be overly demonstrative. That wasn't who he was in public.

"Hello."

Emmy had been so wrapped up in Major Arnold that the greeting made her jump.

The woman standing by their table laughed. "I didn't mean to scare you."

The first impression Emmy had was that this woman was beautiful. Not like the woman from yesterday—who was cold perfection. This woman was warm, with curly red hair that framed a round face that had more freckles than not. Her eyes were deep green in the shadows, and her mouth seemed like it was used to laughing.

Where the first woman was the moon, here was the sun.

"I hear you have something for me," the woman said, and Emmy realized she had been staring at her, gape-mouthed.

She scrambled to her feet. "I have something for Mrs. Basch."

"That would be me," the woman said. "Though Lisbeth is fine."

Emmy glanced at the major, who hid his confusion better than she.

"Ah," Lisbeth said. "You'll have to forgive me. Yesterday you met someone else."

"Me." The woman they'd met yesterday swooped in behind Lisbeth. "I may have misled them." She smiled at Emmy and Major Arnold, but there was still a coolness about it. "I'm Christina Fischer. You'll have to excuse my abrupt departure yesterday. You caught me off guard."

Lisbeth shot her a look, and then turned back to them. "You'll also have to excuse her lie of omission. She didn't want me meeting with strangers before she knew what they wanted from me."

"Of course," Emmy said, and then hurried over to the major's side of the booth so the women could sit on her bench. From the way they slotted into each other easily, Emmy guessed Christina's protectiveness was rooted in something that went beyond friendship.

"Can I see the book?" Lisbeth asked after they'd all formally introduced themselves.

A soft smile tucked itself into the corner of Lisbeth's lips when she stared down at the Rilke.

"'Are you still here? Are you standing in some corner? . . . You were able to do so much; you passed through life so open to all things, like an early morning,'" Lisbeth read softly. Emmy had paged through the volume so many times she recognized the lines from the same poem quoted in the inscription on the title page. "Requiem for a Friend."

Emmy swallowed. "Would you like to keep it?"

Lisbeth shot Christina a glance, the latter lifting one shoulder in a shrug that seemed to say, *Your decision.*

"You're American?" Lisbeth asked instead of answering.

"Yes," Emmy said tentatively.

"You live there?"

"I do," Emmy said.

Lisbeth pressed her palm to the top of the book for a heartbeat, two. And then she slid it back across the table.

"Then I think you better take it all the way home."

"What?"

"It doesn't belong with us," Lisbeth said, and a fond smile broke through Christina's marble facade. "It belongs with him."

Chapter 45
CHRISTINA

March 6, 1943

Annelise cradled Christina's injured hand. "I don't have anything to fix this with now."

"It's not important." The agony had settled into something of a dull and constant throb. But there were plenty of people who had gone through much worse and survived.

"We should talk," Annelise said. "But not here. I don't trust Hans, no matter what anyone says."

"Hans?" Christina blamed her exhaustion for not being able to follow along. It had been an interminably long week, followed by an interminably long day.

Annelise's mouth twitched as if she'd told herself a joke. "An old friend who owed me a favor. He's working for the Yanks now, in theory, but I've always had my doubts about his loyalties."

"I don't understand," Christina admitted.

"I know, darling," Annelise said, cupping her cheek and rubbing a thumb along the bruise Christina knew was there. "Do you have somewhere safe we can go that's not your apartment?"

The answer came easily, and she rattled off Lisbeth's address. Only when she thought it through did she realize she'd given a possible Nazi the location of a Jewish man's house. Even if that Jewish man had been deported, it still felt reckless.

Annelise seemed to read her following wince for what it was, perhaps putting that together with Christina's earlier question. *Are you going to kill me?*

"Do you know me at all?" Annelise asked.

"I thought I did," Christina whispered. "But you thought you knew me once upon a time, too. And now I'm an entirely different person."

"Are you?" When they were younger, the question would have come out sharp and disbelieving. This had been soft, almost affectionate.

Christina met her eyes, and for the first time in five years she actually believed it. "Yes."

"I suppose none of us are who we used to be at the start of this," Annelise said, after a moment. "All right, let's be quick about it. Someone could have followed you and Hans."

Annelise gripped her elbows and pulled her up to standing. They hurried down the stairs and then turned right, heading toward the back door through the kitchen.

An automobile that didn't look like it could possibly function was parked behind the town house. Annelise didn't hesitate, just directed Christina into the passenger seat and then through some miracle got the engine turning over. She winked at Christina, and for the first time Christina saw her sister in this stranger who was wearing her face.

"You didn't marry Felix?" Christina asked, because she could no longer pretend she wasn't desperate for that answer.

Annelise shot her a startled glance. "What? You don't know?"

Christina shook her head.

When Christina had come home from delivering the Rilke to Eitan—who had taken it silently before shutting the door in her face—it had been to find Annelise's things packed already. She never knew where her sister had gone, and, at the time, part of her had assumed that Annelise had run away with Eitan.

That night had changed Christina, even more than the slow slide that had come ahead of it. She had been starting to question the Nazis before Kristallnacht, of course, but she didn't know anyone who could have seen what happened that night and gone back to their lives afterward.

Her own guilt had played a role, but she had barely been able to look at her mother and father again. She had finally understood how

Annelise must have felt, trapped in a houseful of people who didn't blink at the Nazis' actions.

Christina had dug out the pin money she'd been saving for years and had bought a train ticket to Berlin as soon as the riots had subsided. She'd made sure to say goodbye to her parents, something she knew Annelise hadn't done. They had stared at Christina with empty eyes and the resigned faces of two people who had been worked into ghosts of themselves.

When she'd told them she would never return to Bonn, they hadn't tried to persuade her otherwise. Christina was fairly certain they were relieved they had two fewer mouths to feed.

Two years later, she'd received word from her childhood priest that they'd both died three days apart from illness. Anders would be taking over the logistics of their burials and also taking ownership of their possessions.

That had been the only news Christina had heard from home, so she'd been left to make assumptions about what had happened to Annelise.

Once Christina had gotten a position with the Abwehr, and tracked down Eitan, she realized that her fantasy of them together was just that.

She remembered one day following him at a distance—always following people, she'd heard in Annelise's voice. He'd stopped at a coffee shop, the light catching on his wedding ring. She looked up his marriage license that day.

If only she'd remembered the woman's name . . . although she doubted she would have connected Elisabeth Wagner to her Lisbeth of Rose Street five years later.

Christina's scar tissue had reopened in that moment, though, thinking that Annelise really had been forced to marry Felix. She had been too much of a coward to seek out their marriage license. Better to hope Annelise had found a way out of it than to be proven right.

That wound had never healed properly again. Anytime she became too satisfied with herself, Christina simply had to think of Annelise tied forever to that bastard, forced to bear his children, forced to live a life she despised, all because of Christina.

Annelise interrupted her thoughts when she pulled the car to the side of the street outside Lisbeth's apartment. "Can we go up?"

Christina thought so, though she had to admit it was presumptuous. "Yes, but, you should know . . ."

"I should know what?" For the first time, Annelise sounded wary.

"This is Eitan's apartment."

"Well," Annelise said, with a soft laugh. "Of course it is."

"I should have thought . . ."

"No, it's perfect," Annelise said, though she looked like she was forcing the words out. "This should make for an interesting story that I'm eager to hear. But I'm also eager to get inside. Who knows if the RAF is feeling frisky tonight."

And then she was out of the automobile, heading toward the building.

Lisbeth stared at the two of them for a full thirty seconds.

"Well." Then she opened the door fully.

"Precisely what I said." Annelise didn't hesitate, just strode in.

"What happened with Eitan?" Lisbeth asked, not one for dilly-dallying about.

Annelise's mouth pinched as if she were realizing this woman had a right to that knowledge far more than Annelise did.

"He was deported this morning," Annelise said.

"Yes, we gathered," Christina said, drawing Lisbeth's careful attention. Before, she'd been focused on Christina's face, but now Lisbeth's eyes dropped to her hand.

She made a small sound at the sight, but Christina just shook her head. Lisbeth didn't argue, though she looked like she wanted to.

Christina glanced over at Annelise, who was studying them both thoughtfully. Once she realized she was being watched in turn, she shifted, taking in the apartment instead.

"This morning, Goebbels issued his proclamation that the men at the center on Rosenstrasse should be released," Annelise continued. "*All* the men, including twenty-five who were already on a train east."

Of course, that was the fair thing to do, but when had the Nazis been fair? "What?"

"When the group, including Eitan, arrives at KL Auschwitz they will be separated from the rest of the deportees," Annelise said, checking her watch. "It might take some time, but they should be on a train back to Berlin within the next few weeks."

Christina and Lisbeth traded glances. It was Christina who voiced their collective doubt. "Why would they make that effort?"

Annelise lifted one shoulder. "Goebbels's orders are Goebbels's orders. Not to sound like a riddle, but that's all there is to it. When he says something, everyone else has to execute the directive. And his directive was that all of the intermarried detainees were to be released."

"Are you saying Eitan will be freed?" Lisbeth asked.

"If all goes as it should, yes," Annelise said, and then flicked a glance at Christina. "Your sacrifice was never necessary."

The sting came and went. Christina hadn't known that, who could have known that? It wasn't as if the Nazis had a reputation for being magnanimous in their losses. The explanation barely made sense—no one came back from the camps. That was something everyone in Berlin knew, even if they buried their heads in the sand about the rest of what was going on there.

At the same time, Annelise spoke with such authority it was hard to doubt what she was saying.

"It wasn't necessary," Annelise said again. "But it is appreciated. At least by me. Thank you."

Christina pressed her lips together, unsure of how she felt. She would have given anything to hear that from Annelise when she'd been younger. Now, it felt unnecessary. She didn't need to be thanked for something she'd had to do for herself.

"Eitan may face problems when he returns to the city," Annelise continued. "If he's seen anything at Auschwitz they won't want him to be able to tell anyone. Most likely, the men will be met in Berlin by the SD or SS and given some trumped-up charge. But the important thing is that he'll be back under jurisdiction that we have some footholds in."

"Who is 'we'?" Lisbeth asked, skimming Annelise's threadbare coat, her too-long hair and worn-thin shoes.

Annelise glanced down at herself. "I know I don't look it at the moment, but I do have some connections."

"You didn't answer the question," Christina pointed out.

"Fair," Annelise said, a tiny smile riding in the corners of her lips. "I'm sure you're both aware there's no true organized resistance in Germany. But there are pockets, small groups working on their own to try to shift the tides."

That sounded right to Christina. They got briefings on political enemies at the Abwehr, which sometimes made her laugh. The biggest threat to Hitler in Germany was the organization itself.

"I'm a liaison, shall we say? Between them and Churchill's men," Annelise said, with a little shrug. She didn't elaborate—she hadn't survived this long by being careless—but something unlocked in Christina's chest as relief washed over her.

Annelise was neither a Nazi nor a collaborator. She was a resister, as she'd always been. Of course, she had found a way out of an impossible situation. Why had Christina ever doubted it? There was still the question, though . . .

"If you're not a Nazi, how did you know I was being held?"

"You thought I was a Nazi?" Annelise asked, sounding surprised even though she must have known Christina had worried about that possibility. The concept was just that foreign to her, clearly. "Oh, because of Hans?"

"Yes, you were working with someone who had enough power to get me freed," Christina pointed out, and Annelise looked thoughtful.

"Do you not work with Nazis?"

Christina flushed. "That's different."

"Is it?" Annelise asked, gentle again. "You think it so strange that there are double agents in other places than the Abwehr?"

The idea felt hard to wrap her head around, but she had to admit that Annelise had a point. Still, Annelise hadn't answered her question. "How did you know I needed help? Were you watching this whole week? Were you watching us? On Rose Street? And seeing how it would play out?"

"No," Annelise said, but there was something newly guarded in her expression that Christina, even after all this time, could read as her lying. "I spent the week visiting every contact I knew to try to get Eitan out of there. I had no idea you were involved until Hans contacted me. He recognized your name from Bonn. That was foolish to use your credentials to try to see Eitan."

Christina swallowed back a retort. Annelise had always been like this, superior and all-knowing, as if she weren't capable of making mistakes. Christina loved her sister, but she hadn't missed this part of her.

"He was a Pirate," Christina realized. "This Hans."

She tried to picture him, but his face was nothing but a smudge in her memory now.

"Yes, once upon a time," Annelise said. "I won't call him a hero by any means. I think he plays both sides and is waiting to see who the winner is before declaring his loyalty. He also does unspeakably heinous things to maintain his position with the Gestapo, but he did help me save your life. So."

They sat with that for a moment, all of them having experience with people exactly like Hans in this long, terrible war.

Lisbeth was the one who broke the silence. "How did you become . . . this? The last I heard, you were being forced to marry a Nazi."

"Oh," Annelise said, sighing as she sat back against her chair. "I don't suppose you have any tea? It's a long story."

Chapter 46

ANNELISE

Fall 1939

Annelise had never thought she'd find solace in a library surrounded by books. Her church had always been the woods, the mountains, the lakes.

But Annelise had come to love the small room at the back of Bernard Wicklow's London town house.

She was going over his diary for the next day. Ever since she'd shown up on his doorstep the year before, she'd been acting as his secretary. It was a role she wasn't suited for, but neither of them mentioned that.

When what became known as Kristallnacht had ended two full days after it had started, Wicklow had called in a favor to have Felix transferred to the outer reaches of Prussia. It was surprising how few phone calls it had taken to rectify a situation that had felt world-ending to her only hours earlier.

That had been her first real experience with power, and it was a lesson she knew she would carry with her for a long time.

Wicklow couldn't get Eitan out of the country, although he'd tried. He also couldn't promise Eitan would be safe from Felix forever, but it was unlikely the young Nazi would cause any trouble soon. The Germans were preparing for war after all.

Despite the fact that the consequences of Christina's foolishness hadn't been as dire as feared, Annelise had no intention of forgiving her sister anytime soon. And anyway, Wicklow had offered Annelise a place in his household and a ticket to London once he'd realized he needed to escape Germany—something much easier to do as an Aryan.

Annelise had fled, knowing that even if she wanted to, it wouldn't be wise to chase down Eitan. She would only draw attention to him, and if there was any chance of Felix holding a grudge it would be better if Annelise was far away from Eitan when the Nazi got to Berlin.

So far, she had been in London for eight months, and she hated it.

There were parts that she loved, of course. The bigness of the city, the way you could meet someone new every day and never worry about knowing everyone. The entertainment, the fact that there were several countries between her and Hitler.

But she loved Germany, her Germany. Fleeing had been smart, but part of her longed to be in her homeland fighting to wrench it back from the deranged madmen who held it in their grasp.

What were the remaining Pirates doing? Were there resistance groups even now forming and making plans?

She had never been one to hide far away from the barricades.

"Darling, you must come," Lilian said, poking her head into the library. "You need to hear this report."

The entire household—plus Lilian, who had been visiting for the evening—huddled around the wireless, which had been tuned to the BBC.

Lionel Marson's calm, soothing tones filled the quiet space of the staff's kitchen.

"Germany has invaded Poland and has bombed many towns. General mobilization has been ordered in Britain and France. Parliament was summoned for six o'clock this evening," he started. A loud buzzing filled Annelise's head and she missed the next bit, until she heard, "Hostilities have been going on since early this morning along the frontiers between Germany and Poland. There is no news about the progress on either side."

Despite saying that, Mr. Marson went on to describe the various towns that had been reportedly bombed. Then he summarized Hitler's speech.

"'From now on I have no other choice than to meet force with force,'" Mr. Marson quoted.

The report lasted for just under fifteen minutes, and not one of them made a single sound the entire time.

Annelise had known this moment was coming for years, though she found no satisfaction in being right.

War had been brewing for so long.

Now it was finally here.

"I HAVE TO go back," Annelise told Wicklow that evening as they sorted through the next day's tasks.

Wicklow sat back in his comfortable leather chair steepling his fingers on his chest as he stared at her over his half spectacles. She held her ground.

"I was waiting for this," he finally said, and then got up to cross the room to the globe, which held his most expensive liquor. He poured them both glasses, and then tapped them together before handing hers over.

She only rarely drank, but when she did it was whatever this brand was that slid down her throat like silk. She'd never even bothered asking him what it was.

"You'll be going back into a war zone," Wicklow said, though he didn't sound discouraging.

"I'll be going back to my country," Annelise corrected.

"You could live here in relative peace, though," Wicklow pointed out.

Annelise pulled her legs up underneath her. They had never stood on ceremony, the two of them. She thought it might be because he had never shown interest in her—or the opposite sex in general—and so she hadn't had to be on her guard around him. For his part, he seemed to appreciate her implicit understanding of his true nature.

"When I was sixteen, I joined an organization called the Edelweiss

Pirates." She had never told him about this, though she knew Lilian must have divulged how they'd met. "We were young people who liked hiking and skiing and listening to music. None of us took ourselves too seriously."

Wicklow settled in, his attention unwavering. That was something she would always appreciate about him—his ability to simply listen.

"Neither did anyone else, by the way," she said. "We were thorns in the HJ's backside for a year before they even classified us as a group." She smiled, remembering their earlier, harmless antics, pranking the Hitler Youth brigades by dumping sugar into their gasoline or making up silly lyrics to their favorite patriotic songs. "One night, when we all started realizing that Hitler was a serious threat, we asked each other why we would resist him, why put a target on our backs when all we were was a youth hiking group. And the answer was because we could." The woodsmoke-tinged memory was so sharp in her mind. "There were going to be so many people who couldn't, who had to hide to survive." She thought about Christina. "And go along so as not to be killed. But the Pirates could, and so we did."

Wicklow's lips twitched up. "Simple as that."

"Sometimes the good fight is."

CHURCHILL'S SPECIAL OPERATIONS Executive kicked off in the summer of 1940. The training grounds were set up at Inverailort House, which had been converted from an 1800s-era farmhouse to a hunting lodge. Bernard Wicklow had talked Annelise into staying in the United Kingdom long enough to get some actual training.

It was at the castle that Annelise learned how to shoot, and how to hide a message on her person—usually sewn into her clothing in some brilliantly clever way.

She was a unique case—a German girl who could be trusted not to be swayed by her homeland. Her past as a Pirate might have been a bigger mark against her had it not been in Bonn, a small rural town in the shadow of Cologne. If anyone came to her with anecdotes from there, she could say they had gotten her confused with her traitor sister.

They looked so similar after all.

Everything had been fairly simple after that. Annelise was shipped back to Germany and was integrated into a ragtag group of resisters. She was pretty and Aryan, and so she was sometimes given assignments where she had to hobnob with top Nazi officials. And that's where she'd seen Christina the one and only time in the early years of the war.

It was in one of the fancy restaurants Hitler and his ilk so loved. Christina was draped in a silk dress and cozied up to a Nazi.

It had made sense to Annelise, so she hadn't questioned it.

Still, she'd looked for far too long and wondered if she could have done something more.

Then she'd turned to her own Nazi and downed the drink he'd offered.

SHE HAD ONE love affair after Eitan, only one.

It was with a German communist who had been running a resistance press out of his basement.

When he touched her, he smeared ink on her skin.

After the first night they'd made love, she'd gotten dressed, went home, crawled into her bed, and cried.

She had slept with Nazis because that was the dirty secret of being a female spy—it wasn't all pure and noble and righteous. Sometimes it was bartering your body for information you could only get from pillow talk.

But the communist printer had awoken something in her she hadn't felt since Eitan, and it made her doubt.

How could you feel the same intensity about two different people?

How could you love so fiercely and quickly twice?

She'd gone for a drink then, and realized she'd loved Eitan as a girl.

But she was a woman now.

On the first day of fall in forty-two, Annelise went to Bonn.

She didn't bother stopping in town, just took the streetcar south.

Then she walked toward the trees.

Despite the woods' thick canopy, the sun cut patterns through the leaves, kissing her cheeks, her chest, her arms. She lived for this moment, for this freedom.

The air was cooler in here, the sounds of nature waking back up as they always did once the creatures of the forest became accustomed to her presence. She wanted to take her boots off and press the soles of her feet into the soil, to feel the earth beneath her.

She walked up the familiar trail that was now overgrown. By the time she reached the summit she was breathing hard.

Annelise had gone soft in the city.

There was a rock that jutted out to the sky and she sat on it, her knees pulled to her chest.

As a woman who had seen and heard about some of the worst crimes a person could commit against humanity, it almost hurt to stare out at the beauty spread at her feet.

Sometimes, Annelise got bogged down in the machinations of the Third Reich. She was so used to thinking three steps ahead that she didn't always realize where she was in the present.

But it helped to stop. To come out here and remember that when she'd been stuck somewhere between girlhood and maturity, she'd looked at the world and said, *That's not as good as it could be.*

Annelise pictured the Pirates, frolicking through the woods in their wild outfits and long hair. Stefan with his guitar strapped to his back, Marta with her short skirts and flirty smiles.

She thought of a quote from a man she'd discovered while drifting through Wicklow's library.

"Youth is happy because it has the capacity to see beauty," Franz Kafka had said.

The Pirates had seen beauty—in each other, in their country, in the fight against evil men.

What did Annelise see now? There had been so many times she'd compromised her morals in ways her younger self would have been appalled by. But it had helped her turn over sensitive information that the Allies would never have gotten otherwise.

Did she love her fellow man now? She couldn't say.

Did she love Christina? That was a far more interesting question.

Now that she'd lived so deeply in the shades of gray, could she forgive her sister?

Christina had meant well, Annelise could admit that much. She'd broken under the threat of a gun, but now that Annelise had seen plenty of grown men break far more easily than that, she couldn't muster the disdain she'd felt that night. That night, which had been so tinged with fear for what her future held, what Eitan's future held. Annelise had barely been able to breathe let alone think clearly and it had been far simpler to lash out at Christina than direct her anger to where it belonged. The Nazis, Felix.

Herself.

She never should have gone to find Eitan that night in the first place. It had been her own weakness that had started them all down that terrible path. Her own arrogance thinking she could somehow protect Eitan when all she'd ever brought him was more scrutiny.

In her memory, she had always viewed that night through the lens of a young, self-righteous rebel who'd thought she knew better than the whole world. She felt a fondness for the eighteen-year-old version of her who painted anti-Nazi slogans on the HJ headquarters and created an avalanche of pamphlets in a Cologne train station. But that girl hadn't really known about life, about compromise, about weaknesses and strengths, about sacrifice and loss.

Three years of war later, and she let herself think about it through the lens of a woman who had slept with Nazis to get bread crumbs of information; who had chosen to save a family of four over a family of six because the larger family had an infant who would endanger the escape plan; who had given away information on a fellow spy to buy the trust of a despicable man.

She looked back at Christina's misstep, her moment of cowardice that had changed three lives so profoundly. And she realized how inconsequential that act had actually been, especially in comparison to the sins Annelise had committed in the years that followed.

How stubborn of her not to grant Christina the grace, the forgiveness, she offered herself. She had always been tougher on Christina, though, than she had been on anyone else.

A knot that had lived between her shoulder blades for four years loosened. Christina was a Nazi, she had no plans to make nice with her sister. But, this? This she could let go of.

Once she did, she felt freer than she had since they were girls by a pond with a handful of dandelions and wishes that were painfully small.

Annelise stood and brushed the dirt from her skirts. And then she took off running, her legs pumping as they had so many times in her life. The wind kissed her cheeks as she laughed all the way down.

By the Monday of the Rosenstrasse protest, every spy in Berlin was on edge.

Spies were generally good with unexpected situations, but this had come out of nowhere and threatened to disrupt other long-standing plots. Of course, they were secretly cheering on the women, but most, thinking surely the protest would fail, hoped that it would wrap up without any impact on their own missions.

Annelise could only be thankful it was buying her time to try to save Eitan.

Ever since she'd come back to Germany, she'd been keeping track of him. In those earlier days, she hadn't had enough leverage to get him out of the city, and no one wanted to risk their lives for a Jewish man with protected status. Everyone told her he would be fine, he was married to an Aryan woman.

But she knew the Nazi Party, had seen the darkness of it from every side. Eitan would be safe for a time, but he wouldn't be safe forever. She'd started laying groundwork, hoarding the favors she could while making sure not to put anyone else in jeopardy if she could avoid it. The plan wasn't ready, but it would give him a better chance than what he was facing as part of the final roundup in Berlin.

The last piece, now, was getting him out of that damn detention center.

Most of her hours that week were spent visiting every single person who held any power in the city. She slept for hourlong snatches at a time, ate just enough so that she didn't get light-headed. Every ounce of her energy was poured into getting Eitan freed.

Each time, she was greeted with the same answer—there was nothing to be done about it. Whatever happened with the protest would be determined by Hitler's tightest inner circle. This was a live grenade, and the world was watching on with glee.

In the moments between the meetings and the clandestine drinks and the desperate attempts to get in touch with her handlers, Annelise had been drawn to Rose Street.

The sight of the crowd tugged at her so that she ended up huddled at the back of the gathering more than was safe.

Over the weekend, she had barely paid any mind to the women hovering near the door of the Jewish Center as she'd crisscrossed Berlin, frantic and desperate.

Surely the wives would grow tired and go home. The frigid weather, the threat of guns, the roiling waves of anger coming from the Nazis—that would be more than enough to send them running.

When was the last time Germans, en masse, had proven her worst assumptions wrong?

Monday came, and the women stood their ground. They seemed

less tentative, as well, clumping closer together as their voices rose as one.

But then the RAF helped Berlin celebrate the Luftwaffe's birthday.

Annelise had hunkered down through the night, but instead of praying for herself, all she'd been able to do was think of those women. Had they fled the street? Would any of them be alive come morning? Would they abandon the protest now?

As soon as the sun crept over the horizon, she was out of her bed, headed to Rose Street to check.

The women were still there.

Not all of them, but a handful, and the crowd grew by the minute. By midmorning, it was once again robust, the protest only gaining strength the longer it went on.

Annelise watched women reach out tentatively to their neighbors, watched them offer up water and comfort with a hesitancy born from years under a cruel dictatorship. They were forming a community, these women, and it would be a hard one to shatter if these shaky starts crystallized into something more.

The Nazis realized that, too. By Friday, the Gestapo had become desperate. Someone, somewhere, came up with the plan to scare the women with arrests.

Ten of the wives were plucked at random after nearly being run over. Word among her contacts was that they would only be taken to do a work detail for the day, but the women on the street who had watched with wide-eyed horror wouldn't know that.

And she saw the moment where they could have broken. She'd turned, walked away, sure that she would be proven right. The Nazis knew how to win.

Then a cry broke through, a wail. An indictment. "Murderers."

Annelise stopped, positive she had misheard.

But the word only gained in strength until it became a howl filling the narrow street, filling the chests of the Nazis.

The women hadn't shattered.

Annelise remembered Eitan back in that lake on that one perfect summer day asking her why she wanted to participate in acts of resistance even when they were dangerous.

I want to believe people are better than what Hitler thinks we are.

For the first time in five years, while watching the women of Rose Street stand their ground, Annelise actually let herself believe that once more.

Chapter 47

CHRISTINA

March 7, 1943

Lisbeth and Christina listened to Annelise's story about her journey from Bonn to London to Berlin. Neither of them moved an inch. In fact, they were barely breathing, both of them enthralled.

It took two hours to catch up to where they were now, and when she was done, Annelise sat back in her chair and downed the tea that had long gone cold.

Then she stared at the portrait window, at the sky that was in the earliest stages of dawn, and she stood.

"I must go," she said, her gaze lingering on Christina. Wistful? Fond? Christina found that she could no longer read Annelise's expressions. Maybe it was foolish to think she'd ever been able to.

"What shall we do about Eitan?" Lisbeth asked.

Whatever emotion had come into her face while looking at Christina disappeared, and she brushed her hands against her skirt, all business again. "Like I said, I'm fairly certain the RSHA won't allow the men who were deported to walk free like the rest from Rose Street. So we'll have to move fast. The good news is that I've been working on a plan to get him out of the country for about a year now. I've just been waiting for the pieces to fall into place." She shot Lisbeth a sad smile. "The bad news is that you may not get to say goodbye before we get him out of the city. I had originally planned on getting you both out, but with these new circumstances . . ."

Lisbeth shook her head, though. "I only want to know he's safe."

"It won't be easy," Annelise said. "And it's certainly not a sure thing. But it will be better than being sent to a labor camp."

"Thank you," Lisbeth whispered, urgent and sincere. Something flickered behind Annelise's eyes, but she just nodded.

Christina chewed on her lip, looking between the two women. And she made a decision.

Before Annelise could leave, Christina dashed to the bookshelf. The Poe volume that Christina had held a week ago was still there, the photo peeking out at the edges.

"He loved you, Annelise," Christina said, thrusting the book into Annelise's hands. "Always."

When Annelise finally tore her eyes off *Annabel Lee*, it was Lisbeth she looked at. "I'm sorry."

"We love each other but it was never that kind of love," Lisbeth reassured her.

"It was so long ago," Annelise said as if she hadn't heard Lisbeth.

Christina knew she wasn't only talking about the years that had passed. It felt like they had all been through a dozen lifetimes since 1938. And Christina could guess enough about Annelise's work that it was clear why she had lost that innate innocence, that hopefulness that had so defined her back in Bonn.

"Thank you for this," Annelise said, returning the book to Christina. "That was a kindness."

Christina took the book and wondered if this was really how they were going to leave each other. At least Annelise had saved her instead of letting her rot in a cell. Christina should probably be thankful she'd forgiven her at least that much.

But as she watched Annelise take her leave, she suddenly couldn't let well enough alone.

"I'll be back," she told Lisbeth, who grinned at her in approval.

She caught Annelise right before she stepped out onto the street.

It was just barely light enough to make out the contours of Annelise's face, but most of her was caught in the shadows.

There were a million things to say, starting and ending with *I'm sorry.* But Annelise hadn't wanted her apology back in thirty-eight, and Christina doubted she wanted it now.

"I'm proud of you," Christina said instead. "You are the very best of us."

Annelise's mouth did something strange. "It has never felt that way. It has only felt like I'm doing what needs to be done. What should be done."

Christina smiled, her heart swelling. "And that's the reason it's true."

"And what about you?" Annelise said. "What was the past week if not doing what needed to be done?"

"It's not the same," Christina protested. She was far from the very best of anything.

"And *that's* the reason it's true," Annelise said softly.

Before Christina could argue further, Annelise was through the door, out on the street. She paused once more at her automobile and lifted a hand in farewell.

When Christina walked back into the apartment, it was directly into Lisbeth's arms. They were careful with Christina's hand, but they ended up entangled on the bed, their mouths desperate.

Christina didn't remember falling asleep, but when she woke to the midday light, it was to Lisbeth watching her, affection written into every line of her face.

Her back was against the wall, and in her lap she cradled the Wilde that held her parents' photo.

To live is the rarest thing in the world. Most people exist, that is all.

After the events of the day before, Christina could finally admit why she'd nearly wept when she'd first read those words. She had not been living—perhaps had *never* been living. She'd only been existing, serving out a punishment from day to day that was far harsher than the crime deserved.

Why don't you hate me? Christina had asked Lisbeth so many times. But all that had been doing was revealing how much she couldn't tolerate herself. Maybe everything that had happened with Eitan and Annelise had amplified that feeling, but it had started long before Kristallnacht.

Now she understood that it had been cruel to ask Lisbeth to hate her, because she had been asking Lisbeth to hate herself.

One day you'll stop asking me that.

Christina reached out slowly and tugged Lisbeth until the book tumbled onto the bed beside them and Lisbeth was spread out on top of Christina.

"How do you feel?" Lisbeth asked. "No goodbye speeches, no deadlines, no sword to throw yourself on. How do you feel?"

"I feel good," Christina admitted, simply. It felt like five years' worth of weight had been lifted off her shoulders.

"And what do you want?" Lisbeth asked, dropping her forehead so that it almost touched Christina's, their lips a whisper apart.

Christina finally knew the answer to that. "I want to *live*."

June 1946

Brooklyn was beautiful, a little chaotic, and different than everything she'd been expecting.

She'd spent the morning in Manhattan at a diner, staring across the booth at Lucy, who was as glamorous and wonderful surrounded by turquoise and laminate as she had been cast in the soft relief of a sunset outside their shared cottage.

"I'll miss the women and children at the refugee camps, but I'm excited about the work I'll be doing here," Lucy said, slathering a piece of sourdough with butter. She'd only been stateside for a few days—same as Emmy—and they were both politely ignoring the other's gluttony over the abundance of food here.

Lucy had secured a position at the YIVO headquarters in New York, a job that required her to leave Offenbach sooner than planned. But Lucy would be able to work in YIVO's vast library, with access to hundreds of thousands of Yiddish books and texts. She had confessed that on the first day she might completely lose her head, and dance through the stacks, singing folk songs in the nearly exterminated tongue.

Emmy didn't think anyone would blame her.

"You should move here, too." Lucy pouted, and then when Emmy blushed and looked away, she sighed dramatically. "Bring the major, if you have to."

But Lucy was simply teasing. She had cheered and gloated when Emmy had returned from Berlin with what apparently—and mortifyingly—had been a *glow* that had made what she and the major had gotten up to obvious. Lucy was probably the most pleased about the turn of events out of the three of them.

After breakfast, they lingered on the sidewalk, not wanting to say goodbye. Like with the major, the relationship seemed far deeper than what should have come from a few months sharing a cottage.

"I suppose I can take a train," Lucy said, as she hugged Emmy tight. "But you better as well. Your children must call me Auntie Lucy, that is nonnegotiable."

Emmy laughed. "Let's not get ahead of ourselves."

"Why ever not? It's fun," Lucy said, pulling back, but still holding on to Emmy's arms. "We shall see each other, yes?"

"Yes," Emmy said, nodding fiercely. "It's a promise."

"And we'll always have Offenbach," Lucy said in a decent impression of Bogie that had Emmy giggling away the sadness that had settled into her at the thought of going months without seeing Lucy again.

"I think this is the beginning of a beautiful friendship," Emmy said, half playful, half serious. She squeezed Lucy's hands and the woman blinked too quickly to be doing anything other than holding back a rush of emotions.

They separated, but before she got too far, Emmy glanced over her shoulder to find Lucy watching her.

"Here's looking at you, kid," Lucy called out, and Emmy grinned. And in that moment, she knew if she ever had children, they would be calling Lucy auntie in no time.

It was still too early to drop in on a stranger, so Emmy wandered through the streets of Brooklyn killing time and seeing the sights.

She stopped at a tea shop near Eitan's apartment, and when she stepped back out onto the street, she bumped into a heavily pregnant woman. It was surprising enough, that she ended up dropping her bag, the Rilke spilling onto the sidewalk.

"Oh, I'm so sorry." The pregnant woman tried to bend over, but Emmy laughed and scooped the little book up quicker than the woman could figure out a way to lower herself much beyond the beginnings of a squat.

"I think it's me who should be apologizing," Emmy said, with an easy smile. The woman had a vivacious energy about her, the shape of her face combined with her red hair giving Emmy the sense of a fox.

The woman's eyes dropped to where Emmy was clutching the Rilke. "Oh! Did you get that from the Library of Nazi Banned Books?"

"No, it's from Germany," Emmy said, and then the question really sunk in. "What is the Library of—"

"Nazi Banned Books? Just what it says on the tin. It's over there," the woman said, throwing her thumb over her shoulder to a block-long, imposing building. "If you ever want to drop in, tell them Viv sent you, all right?"

And then she was gone in a whoosh of silk and a cloud of perfume.

Emmy almost headed for the library right then and there, but it was now an acceptable time of day to visit Eitan and she found herself eager to finally complete her mission. She made her way through the streets until she found the right address—a stocky brick building that looked fairly new and well-kept.

Eitan answered his door after one knock.

He was one of the most beautiful men she'd ever seen—like a romantic painting come to life. Dark tousled curls tumbled into whiskey-golden eyes. He had a slim build, and was too thin, on top of that. He also looked older than he probably was from years of living in constant fear for his life. But Emmy understood why Annelise had tumbled into love with him.

"I have your book," she blurted out and then winced. She'd had a whole introduction planned, but he'd stunned her with his appearance. Emmy tried not to picture the way Major Arnold's eyes would crinkle in amusement if she related this undignified greeting.

But Eitan only seemed confused for a moment. His eyes dropped to the Rilke she held out and he sucked in an overwhelmed breath.

"Annelise," he whispered, and she wasn't even sure he realized he'd said it out loud.

She kept silent, waiting in his doorway as he flipped to the title page.

He pressed a hand to his mouth, staring at the words she'd long since memorized.

"I'm being terribly rude, I apologize," Eitan finally said in English, though his words were saturated with his German accent. "Please come in. Can I offer you tea?"

She accepted, and then belatedly introduced herself. When he disappeared into the galley kitchen, she surveyed the place.

The apartment was small, but furnished with a classically comfortable sensibility. A desk had been pushed beneath a window that looked out onto a busy street, with shops and restaurants and people buzzing by. One wall was taken up completely by a large, sturdy bookshelf, and Emmy couldn't help but cross over to it.

A man who had his books taken away from him had made sure they would have a place of honor in his home.

The idea moved her even more when she thought of that first day at the Offenbach Depot, the endless expanse of boxes.

Eitan had chosen a wide variety of books to fill the shelves, from poetry to war strategy to Jane Austen. They were sorted alphabetically, and on a whim she checked to see if he'd purchased a new version of the Rilke.

"I couldn't replace it," he said from behind her.

She whirled and flushed at being caught snooping. Although, was it snooping if the books were out here in the open?

"Now I don't need to," he said softly and gestured toward the couch.

Emmy went to take her seat, but her eyes snagged on a photograph that stood framed on his desk.

Without conscious thought, she crossed over to it, unable to look away.

The edges were battered, and the ink had faded. It was old, it had survived a war.

A girl of about eighteen stared back at Emmy, her eyes laughing though her face was serious. She wore a short plaid skirt and leather sandals and a blouse that Emmy imagined had been brightly colored. On her chest was a pin. While Emmy had never seen an edelweiss flower before, she had a guess that's what it was.

My dearest Annelise, my brave Edelweiss Pirate.

"When did she die?" Emmy asked, because she couldn't keep the question back any longer. Lisbeth and Christina had told her so little, saying it wasn't their story to give.

"February 1945," Eitan said, his voice broken. Guilt swamped her for asking, but there was actually a soft, loving smile on Eitan's face when she turned around. "She almost saw the world she fought so hard to save."

"She must have known that we were going to win by then," Emmy said, though of course it was a small consolation.

"Yes, it was only a matter of time at that point."

"Were you able to see her again?" Emmy asked.

"No," Eitan said, breaking Emmy's heart. "Her British contact got me out of the country right after the Rosenstrasse protest. I had been marked as deported, which helped. But there was no time to say goodbye. Or to say thank you."

She knew, Emmy thought but didn't say because it sounded presumptuous.

"The two of us were a moment in time," Eitan continued. "She will always be my pirate and I her poet. But, to be honest, I'm not sure we would have been able to find our way back to who those people were if we'd both made it through the war."

The twinge of disappointment Emmy felt was silly and foolish. People weren't fairy tales, and it was better they weren't. She remembered her conversation with Major Arnold on the way to Bonn—that Eitan and Annelise put real faces to the victims of the war. But that wasn't true. She hadn't been seeing them as fully complicated, nuanced people, instead, only as two vessels to hold her romanticism. Love didn't conquer all, and expecting it to was unfair.

When she let go of the idea of Annelise and Eitan, she saw instead the real story—of two people whose lives were irrevocably changed in different and profound ways by a world that was cruel and unjust.

The fact that they had been in love was so much smaller than the rest of what their lives meant. Annelise and her courage, her conviction, her audacity, her moral fortitude. Eitan and his.

"Can you tell me about her?" Emmy asked, wanting to know even more. And Eitan obliged.

Once he started talking, he seemed not to want to stop. They settled in and even when he made her lunch, she trailed him into the kitchen. He didn't just tell her about Annelise, but of living in Bonn and then Berlin and finally Brooklyn. He was engaged to be married, and wanted to have children. He worked down at the docks, but at night he wrote poetry and he hoped to be published someday.

"Do you know of the edelweiss flower?" Eitan asked as the evening settled around them.

Emmy shook her head.

"It looks quite delicate, quite pretty," he said. "But it grows high up in the Alps, and thus is actually a hardy, determined thing. Once upon a time, only the bravest souls would climb up the mountains to retrieve a flower for their beloved." He smiled over at the picture of Annelise. "In Bavaria, they became a symbol for strength, adventure, tenacity, sacrifice, and courage."

Emmy smiled, her bruised heart soothed. "It sounds like it fit Annelise perfectly, then."

By the time the sun set, Emmy realized she should move on. She had a train to catch in the morning, back to Washington. There was plenty of work to do at the Library of Congress with the thousands of books that she'd sent back from Germany.

She might even start hunting for an apartment big enough to fit two. Major Arnold had made plenty of noise about a position available at the Smithsonian, one he was seriously considering taking. He was still in Germany, but the cleanup couldn't last forever.

Emmy thanked Eitan profusely for sharing his story with her, for helping her better understand the war from yet another perspective, and then she turned to leave.

"Wait," he said, and when she shifted back to look at him, he was holding out the Rilke.

"You brought it this far," he said, an impish smile making him seem so much younger than his years. She saw in that moment the boy Annelise had loved. He tilted his head toward the bookshelf. "Finish the job?"

Emmy's mouth wobbled with silly emotion, but she sniffed and took the thin volume of poetry. She could still feel the shape of it pressed against her chest, her heart.

There were so many books that would never find their way home after the war. They were stuck in boxes in that depot, and when the depot shut down they would, at best, be shipped off to Jewish communities around the world. While that might be a noble fate, they should have been with their owners. They should have been passed down to children, to be kept and cherished and loved.

There were so many that would be cast adrift.

But this one, this one had found its way home.

For the rest of her life, Emmy would be grateful for the small role she'd played in that.

Her fingers lingered for one last moment on the spine as she slid it into its rightful place.

We need, in love, to practice only this: letting each other go.

Emmy pulled her hand back and smiled.

ACKNOWLEDGMENTS

My sincere gratitude goes to every person who has helped bring this story to life.

That always seems to start with my agent, Abby Saul, who listens to my spark of an idea and goes, *Yes, awesome, let's do it!* Thank you endlessly for being the best cheerleader, first reader, mojo queen, advocate, and partner in crime a girl could ask for!

To my editor, Tessa Woodward, who makes me a better, more thoughtful writer every time we talk. Thank you for seeing the heart of my stories and making sure they're the best version of themselves. It's such a privilege to get to work with you.

To Julie Paulauski and Amelia Wood, two incredibly talented women who are instrumental in shining a light on stories when there are so many out there for readers to choose from.

To the rest of the village it took to get this one out, from designers to production editors to the library team, thank you so much. This book couldn't possibly be in better hands.

To my family and friends, without whom I would not be here. Your support means the world to me.

To my readers, who seem to always have the most beautiful, open minds and loving hearts. Thank you for trusting me with so much of your time. I never take that for granted.

To the random Tumblr user who reblogged a post about the Edelweiss Pirates onto my feed years and years ago, thank you for introducing me to this group that I could never get out of my mind. And thank you to K. R. Gaddy for writing *Flowers in the Gutter*, an indepth look at the real young people who deserve to be acknowledged by history.

Thank you to Nathan Stoltzfus for doing such incredible work with *Resistance of the Heart* and telling the story of the too-often-overlooked Rosenstrasse protest. And thank you to Anders Rydell for writing *The Book Thieves* and sparking not one but two separate story ideas for me.

Lastly, thank you to the brave men and women who inspired this story, who fought for justice in an unjust world, who shepherded books back to their rightful owners, and who stood toe-to-toe with Nazis and said no. I'll hold your memory in my heart for the rest of my life.

AUTHOR'S NOTE

The late Elie Wiesel, a Holocaust survivor and Nobel laureate, once said, "There may be times when we are powerless to prevent injustice, but there must never be a time when we fail to protest." This might as well be the thesis of this book, and I hope I did the concept some justice.

First and foremost—because it's always what I want to know when I'm reading historical fiction—all of my main characters are my own creations. They're inspired by real-life people, though not modeled on anyone in particular. But the world they're placed in, the events that go on around them, and the political and social landscape of the day are all as true to life as I could make them.

I stumbled on the story of the Edelweiss Pirates before I even started writing historical fiction. The fact that they risked their lives to protest a system that ultimately would have benefited them always struck me as compelling. One of the most important lessons from Germany's slide into fascism was best described in a quotation by Pastor Martin Niemöller, which begins, "First they came for the socialists, and I did not speak out—because I was not a socialist." The Edelweiss Pirates lived their lives in defiance of that mentality. They spoke up when they saw injustice, even though it made their lives difficult. While Annelise and her cohorts are my own creations, you can read about the real-life young people in the wonderful *Flowers in the Gutter* by K. R. Gaddy.

One of the historical liberties I took was with the term *Edelweiss Pirates*, which was an umbrella name for small, local chapters. There was a good chance Annelise's group, based outside Cologne, would have called themselves the Navajos. Although I wanted to use the broader term for a variety of reasons, it was important to me to include a conversation about that between Emmy and Major Arnold. And to note it here as a reminder that people in history are flawed and complex and can rarely be flattened out simply into a hero or a monster.

The minute I read about the only protest in Germany against the mass deportation of its Jewish citizens, I knew it would fit perfectly with the themes of this novel. The historical record, however, is a bit murky here. The theory is that both the Nazis and then the postwar German government wanted to obfuscate the details as much as possible. The former wanted to downplay the event to avoid sparking countrywide chaos, and the latter wanted to maintain the myth that protesting against the Nazis was impossible. In the face of this, I turned to primary sources—such as Goebbels's extensive diary—along with *Resistance of the Heart* by Nathan Stoltzfus. Stoltzfus's nonfiction account is incredibly researched—and old enough that he interviewed the women who were actually on the street. Where there were conflicting historical accounts, such as the number of protesters, I went with Stoltzfus's deep dive. Still, any mistakes are my own.

In terms of the known facts, the protest really *was* as cinematic as I portrayed it. The Nazis did bring out machine guns to scare the women, and then fired into the air over their heads, sending them scattering into doorways and alleys. On March 1, the RAF helped the Luftwaffe celebrate its birthday by bombing Berlin. Some of the women stayed to pray, though many were forced to flee to safety. As the week went on, the Nazis grew increasingly desperate to end the standoff. On Friday, the Nazis, in a scare-tactic move, drove a truck into the crowd and arrested ten women at random. They were sent to work detail for only a day, but the women on the street didn't know this.

On Saturday, March 6, exactly one week after the roundup, Goebbels, as Gauleiter of Berlin, ordered the men to be released. Before that happened, twenty-five of the childless detainees at the community center were put on a train to Auschwitz. The records are clear even if the reasoning is not. The men were separated from the rest of the deportees when they got to Poland, held in a different location, and then sent back to Berlin to be "freed." Everyone, including the Nazis, was so surprised by this development that they ended up giving the detainees the wrong clothes and returning them to Berlin without even a guard. Because the men had seen Auschwitz, the SS trumped up espionage charges against them and sentenced them to hard labor at camps closer to Berlin.

That is where I took the biggest liberty in the 1943 story line: it is extremely unlikely an Annelise-type character could have swooped in and saved Eitan from a hard labor detail. He had already been through so much, though, that I wanted to get him out of Germany.

In real life, fifteen of those twenty-five deported men survived the war, so it *is* believable that Eitan made it through, either way.

There are some reports that indicate the intermarried Jews who were freed after the protest were then rounded up the next day. That was not the case. Although Goebbels, in his diary, suggests that he would attempt to try again with the intermarried Jewish men in a few weeks after the fervor had died down, there's no evidence of that happening.

Instead, the freed detainees were told to stop wearing their stars and were deemed a privileged class of Jews in Berlin. A few days after Goebbels made his decision, Hitler acknowledged that it had been a prudent move in terms of the psychological effects and home-front morale.

There was also one more important moment of the protest that I dramatized: the release of the detainees. Given all the bureaucracy of the Third Reich, the release was more of a trickle than some grand moment. You can find release slips from as late as Monday, even though the decision was made that Saturday. But I wanted to reward both the women and the readers with a more satisfying scene.

When setting up the 1943 story line, I knew I wanted Christina to be a part of the Nazi machine—as a double agent. But I couldn't stand the idea of her working for the Gestapo, or even some other semieffective entity under Hitler. That's when I discovered the Abwehr. The information-gathering arm of the Wehrmacht really was run by a man—Admiral Canaris—who hated Hitler. He surrounded himself with loyalists and worked closely with British spies to undermine Germany's war efforts where he could. He's not a hero—for example, he gave the Gestapo a list of sixty thousand Polish Jews who should be rounded up and killed—but he did run a pretty leaky ship. The Abwehr was eventually dissolved after one too many of its traitorous plots came to light, such as the nearly successful July 20 plan to assassinate Hitler.

So, of course, there *is* a story line included that doesn't revolve around protesting fascism. The Offenbach Depot was the last piece of the plot to slide into place for me. I had always heard about the art restitution efforts, but I hadn't realized the same work had been put into finding the rightful owners of books. In *The Book Thieves*, by Andes Rydell, the author himself actually shepherded a personal copy of a book back to the daughter of a man who'd died in the Holocaust. When the daughter saw her father's handwriting once again, she broke down in tears. This idea moved and intrigued me.

While there are plenty of accounts and pictures of the depot, there are still a few details that remain blurred. For example, it is unclear what books were shipped back to the Library of Congress—there aren't any comprehensive records to be found. However, in the 1990s, Congress launched a broad investigation into the postwar restitution efforts conducted by the United States. The report can be found online, and it's worth looking at. But as a result, the Library of Congress officially designated a special collection for the books they *could* identify as having come from Offenbach.

As a flawed human being myself, I'm sure I've made a mistake or two throughout, but I hope you're able to grant me some grace in that regard. In the end, I've tried to portray everything accurately to the best of my ability while also telling an engaging and important story. Thank you for giving me the opportunity to shine a spotlight on these moments in history.

ABOUT THE AUTHOR

Brianna Labuskes is a *Wall Street Journal* and *Washington Post* best-selling author of historical fiction and psychological thrillers. Her books have been translated into more than a dozen languages. She grew up in Pennsylvania and will always call it home, but now lives in Asheville, North Carolina, with her puppy, Jinx.